THE ACID HOUSE

Irvine Welsh lives in Edinburgh. *Trainspotting*, his first book, was published in 1993, and reached the last ten for the Booker Prize. *The Acid House* was published in 1994, to critical acclaim. His new novel, *Marabou Stork Nightmares* is published by Jonathan Cape.

BY IRVINE WELSH

Trainspotting
The Acid House
Marabou Stork Nightmares

'Another season in hell with Irvine Welsh, and God it's invigorating. These 21 stories and one novella... return to the world of Edinburgh junkies, drunks and low-lifes that got the treatment in last year's excellent, in-your-face novel, *Trainspotting*. The main narrative voice is again Welsh's brand of Edinburgh street vernacular, with its "oafays", "boatils", "radges" and "swedgin", and again the most appalling violence and squalor is set off by vicious humour and a fierce sense of outrage. Aside from the vigour of the language, what is immediately striking is Welsh's narrative skill... Just when you think you worked out not just what's going on, but what sort of story you're dealing with, Welsh pulls off a fine narrative trick. All the clues were staring you in the face, but odds on you walked straight past them... The collection as a whole is sick, horrific, occasionally moving and very funny... Good, exhilarating, unpleasant fun, and it will be very interesting to see where this extraordinary young writer goes from here'

New Statesman & Society

'Irvine Welsh has been compared with James Kelman, and rightly so, because his novel and many of his stories refer, like Kelman's, to a sort of monomaniacal interior monologue in which despair and black humour complement each other, and because, like the Glaswegian writer, he is fascinated by the many layers of meaning in speech and the difficulty of communication... Welsh's ear is tuned to a phenomenally fine degree. Not only does he render speech rhythms accurately and sensually but he is sensitive to nuances of class and character among all his variegated characters, rendering the minute distinctions of vocabulary and emphasis in different kinds of profane speech to which most of us would probably be tone-deaf'

Independent on Sunday

'Welsh's new short-story collection, *The Acid House*, reminded me, among other things, that what we often put down to brilliance in the work of some writers is, in fact, nothing more than the pleasant shock of our own recognition. It's only when a book forgoes that easy option, choosing instead to stake out a territory that most of its readers will find alien and unwelcoming, that it really puts itself to the test: and this is where Welsh emerges triumphant. These uniformly bleak, comfortless stories are told with such vigour and alertness, such scathing, unmerciful humour, such compassion and such reserves of linguistic and structural invention, that nobody could come away from them without feeling thoroughly exhilarated'

Jonathan Coe, *Sunday Times*

'*The Acid House*... demonstrates that there is much more to Irvine Welsh than the semi-autobiographical voice of an ethnographer. It shows him pushing the limits of his versatility, experimenting with form, style and structure, with typographic innovation, surrealism and fantasy, and always finding something new to say . His brittle wit and unerring eye for the humour that can be drawn from absurd conjunctions of situation and character leaves you feeling utterly exhilarated'

Independent

Irvine Welsh

THE ACID HOUSE

VINTAGE

Published by Vintage 1995

19 20

Copyright © Irvine Welsh 1994

The right of Irvine Welsh to be identified as the author
of this work has been asserted by him in accordance
with the Copyright, Designs and Patents Act, 1988

First published in Great Britain by
Jonathan Cape Ltd, 1994

Vintage
Random House, 20 Vauxhall Bridge Road, London SW1V 2SA

Random House Australia (Pty) Limited
16 Dalmore Drive, Scoresby, Victoria 3179

Random House New Zealand Limited
18 Poland Road, Glenfield,
Auckland 10, New Zealand

Random House South Africa (Pty) Limited
PO Box 2263, Rosebank 2121, South Africa

Random House UK Limited Reg. No. 954009

A CIP Catalogue record for this book
is available from the British Library

ISBN 0 09 927716 6

Printed and bound in Australia by
Griffin Press

For my parents, Pete and Jean Welsh,
for all their love and support.

ACKNOWLEDGMENTS

Some stories in this collection have appeared in the following magazines and anthologies: 'Disnae Matter' in *Rebel Inc*, 'Where the Debris Meets the Sea' in *Pig Squealing, New Writing Scotland No. 10*, 'Sport For All' in *The Ghost of Liberace, New Writing Scotland No. 11*. 'The Sexual Disaster Quartet' appeared in *Folk*, published by Clocktower Press.

Thank you to the editors: Janice Galloway, A. L. Kennedy, Duncan McLean, Hamish Whyte and Kevin Williamson.

Thanks also to the following whose inspiration, ideas, encouragement, and cruel slaggings have influenced this collection:

Lesley Bryce, Colin Campbell, Jim Carrol, Max Davis, Debbie Donovan, Gary Dunn, Jimmy Easton, James Ferguson, Tam Ferguson, Adeline Finlay, Minna Fry, Janet Hay, Davie Inglis, Mark Kennedy, Stan Kieltyka, Miles Leitch, John McCartney, Helen McCartney, Willie McDermott, Kenny McMillan, James McMillan, Sandy Macnair, Andrew Miller, Robin Robertson, Stuart Russell, Rosie Savin, Colin Shearer, John Shearer, Bobby Shipton, George Shipton, Susan Smith, Angela Sullivan, Dave Todd and Kevin Williamson (again).

Special thanks to that soul-brother of the new salons of psychic insurrection, Paul Reekie, for permission to use his poem.

Extra-special thanks to Anne, for the lot.

Rave on.

When Caesar's mushroom is in season
It is the reversal of the mushroom season
As Caesar's mushroom comes in March
The mushroom season is in September
Six months earlier
One half year
Equinoctal
Autumnal to vernal

Do you hope for more
Than a better balance
Between fear and desire
It'll only be the straying
That finds the path direct
Neither in the woods nor in the field
No robes, like Caesar's, trimmed with purple
Rather an entire street trimmed with purple
And every door in it
Wrapped in a different sort of christmas paper

The September mushrooms of midnight
Show the rhythms of vision
Can't move for tripping over them
Wipe your tapes
Wipe your tapes with lightning.

PAUL REEKIE
'When Caesar's Mushroom is in Season . . .'

CONTENTS

THE SHOOTER

— Lovely casserole, Marge, I remarked in between frantic mouthfuls. It really was good.

— Glad ya like it, she replied, her face screwing up in an indulgent smile behind her glasses. Marge was a good-looking woman, no doubt about it.

I was enjoying myself, but Lisa was pushing the food around her plate, her bottom lip curling outwards and downwards.

— Doncha like it, Lisa? Marge quizzed.

The child said nothing, merely shook her head, her expression unaltered.

Gary's eyes burned in his face. Little Lisa was spot-on keeping her gaze firmly on the plate.

— Oi! You'll bleedin well eat that, my gel! he snapped ferociously. Lisa buckled as if his words had a physical impact.

— Leave er, Gary. If she don wan it, she don need ta eat it, Marge reasoned. Gary's gaze left the child. Seizing the opportunity, Lisa sprang from the table and left the room.

— Where do you think . . . Gary began.

— Oh leave er be, Marge snorted.

Gary looked at her and gestured manically with his fork. — I says one fing, you say another. No wonder I don't get no fuckin respect in my own bleedin house!

Marge shrugged sheepishly. Gary had a temper and he'd been really uptight since he got out. He turned to me, pleading for understanding. — You see how it is, Jock? Every fucking time! Treated like I'm bleedin invisible! My own fucking house. My

1

own bleedin kid! My own bleedin missus for Christ sakes, he moaned, pointing derisively at Marge.

— Take it easy, Gal, I said, — Marge's done us proud wi this spread. Great bit of scran, Marge. It isnae Lisa's fault that she doesnae like it, ye know how weans are. Different taste buds fae us n aw that. Marge smiled approvingly; Gary just shrugged and scowled into space. We ate the rest of the meal, punctuating our scoffing with stiff ritualised conversations; the Arsenal's chances for next season's championship were discussed, the merits of the new Co-op store in Dalston indoor centre were compared to that of the existing Sainsbury's over the road, the likely parentage and sexual orientation of the new manager who'd taken over Murphy's was ascertained, and the pros and cons of re-opening London Fields local railway station, shut down years ago due to fire damage, was passionlessly debated.

Eventually Gary sat back and belched, then stretched and stood up. — Nice bit of tucker, gel, he said appeasingly. Then he turned to me: — You fit?

— Aye, I replied, rising.

Gary answered the query on Marge's quizzical face. — Me n Jock ere, we got a bit of business to talk about, ain't we.

Marge's face set into a tense snarl. — You ain't thievin again are ya?

— I told ya I wasn't, didn't I? Gary aggressively replied. Her twisted mouth and narrowed eyes met his stare. — You promised me! YOU FUCKING PROMISED! All those fucking things you said . . .

— I ain't thieving! Jock! he appealed. Marge fixed her large pleading eyes on me. Was she begging me to tell her the truth or to tell her what she wanted to hear? Gary's promises. The number of times made, the number of times broken. Irrespective of what I said to her at that point, she'd be let down again: by Gary, or by some other guy. For some people there's no escaping certain types of disappointment.

— Naw, this is legit. Straight up, I smiled.

My bullshit was authentic enough to give Gary confidence.

Taking on an expression of injured innocence he said: — There. You got it straight from the horse's maff, gel.

Gary went upstairs to take a slash. Marge shook her head and dropped her voice. — He worries me, Jock. He's been so uptight lately.

— He worries aboot you n the wean, Marge. That's Gal; he's a worrier. It's in his nature.

We're all fuckin worriers.

— You ready or wot? Gary poked his head round the door.

We departed for the Tanners. I made for the back room, and Gary followed me with two pints of best. He set them down slowly on the polished table, with great concentration. He looked at the pints and said softly, shaking his head: — The problem ain't Whitworth.

— He's a fuckin problem tae me. Two fuckin grands' worth of a problem.

— You ain't gettin my drift, Jock. Ain't him that's the problem, innit. It's you, his extended digit rigidly pointed at me, — and me, he said, drumming his finger heavily on his chest. — The fucking donkeys here. We can forget that dough, Jock.

— Like fuck . . .

— Whitworth's gonna bullshit us, stonewall us, ignore us, until we just shut up abaht it, like two good little boys, he smiled grimly, his voice carrying a cold, implacable resonance. — He don't take us seriously, Jock.

— So what're ye saying, Gal?

— Either we forget it, or we make him take us seriously.

I let his words play around inside my head, checking and double-checking their implication, an implication in reality I had instantly recognised.

— So what dae we dae?

Gary took in a deep breath. It was strange that he was now so calm and reasoned, compared to his uptight state over the meal. — We teach the slag to take us seriously. Teach him a fucking lesson. Teach him a little bit of respect, innit.

How he proposed we did that, Gary made crystal clear. We

would get tooled up and take a drive to Whitworth's flat in Haggerston. Then we would knock seven types of shite out of him on his doorstep and issue a deadline for the repayment of the money owed to us.

I pondered this strategy. Certainly, there was no chance of resolving this matter legally. Moral and emotional pressure had failed to prove fruitful, and, Gary was right, had actually compromised our credibility. It was our money, and Whitworth had been given every opportunity to repay us. But I was scared. We were about to open an ugly Pandora's box and I felt that events were spinning out of my control. I had visions of the Scrubs, or worse, concrete slippers and a dip in the Thames, or some variation on the cliché, amounting in reality to much the same thing. Whitworth himself would be no problem, he was all flash; mouthy, but not a man of violence. The issue was: how well was he connected? We'd soon find out. I had to go along with this. Either way I couldn't win. If I didn't go ahead I'd lose credibility with Gary, and I needed him more than he needed me. More importantly, someone would have my money and I'd be left skint and consumed with self-hatred for having capitulated so tamely.

— Let's sort the cunt out, I said.

— That's my man, Gary slapped my back. — Alway's knew you had the bottle, Jock. All you fucking Jocks, all fucking crazy! We'll show that cunt Whitworth just who he's fucking abaht wiff here.

— When? I asked, feeling a bit nauseous with excitement and anxiety.

Gary shrugged and raised an eyebrow. — Ain't no time like the present.

— You mean right now? I gasped. It was broad daylight.

— Tonight. I'll call for you at eight with a motor.

— Eight, I agreed weakly. I had been feeling big vibes of anxiety about Gary's unstable behaviour lately. — Listen Gal, there isnae anything other than money between you and Tony Whitworth, is there?

4

— The money's enough in my circumstances, Jock. More than enough, innit, he said, throwing back his pint and rising. — I'm orf home. You should go too. You don't wanna be knocking back too much of the Jonathan Ross, he pointed at my glass. — We got a job to do.

I watched him lumber away purposefully, pausing only to wave at old Gerry O'Hagan at the bar.

I left shortly after, taking Gal's advice about the sauce consumption. I went up to the sports store in Dalston and purchased a baseball bat. I thought about buying a ski mask, but that would be too obvious, so I went to the Army and Navy and got a balaclava. I sat in my gaff, unable for a while to look at the purchases. Then I picked up the bat and began swinging it through the air. I pulled the mattress off my bed and stuck it against the wall. I thrashed at it with the bat, checking swing, stance and balance. The anxiety flowed from me as I swiped, lunged and snarled like a maniac.

It was not long in returning. It had gone eight and I thought that Gary may have had a bout of sanity and called the whole thing off, perhaps after Marge tippled that something was up and got on his case. At 8.11 on the digital clock radio I heard the car horn blast truculently outside. I didn't even go to the window. I just picked up the balaclava and the bat and went downstairs. My grip on the weapon now felt weak and insipid.

I climbed into the passenger seat. — I see you're prepared, Gary smiled. Even after he'd spoken, his face remained frozen in that strange smile, like a bizarre Halloween mask.

— What've you got? I feared that he'd produce a knife.

My heart stopped when, from under the seat, he pulled out a sawn-off shotgun.

— No way, man. No fuckin way. I moved to get out of the car. His hand fell on my arm.

— Relax! Ain't fucking loaded, is it? You know me, Jock, for fuck sakes. Shooters ain't my fucking scene, never have been. Credit me wiff a little bit bleedin sense, innit.

— You're telling me that gun is empty?

— Course it's bleedin empty, innit. You think I'm fucking daft? Do it this way, we don't need no violence. No aggravation, nobody gets hurt. A geezer inside told me; people change when you point a gun at them. The way I see it is: we want our money. We ain't bothered about hurting the cunt; we just want the dough. If you get carried away wiff that bat, you might make im into a bleedin cabbage. Then we got no money and a berth in the bleedin Scrubs. We terrorise him, we show him this – he waved the shooter, which now seemed like a pathetic toy, — and he's shiting pound notes at us.

I had to concede that it sounded so much simpler Gary's way. Scaring Whitworth was preferable to doing him over. Smash the cunt up and he'd possibly get a team together for revenge. If you scared the shit out of him with a shooter, the chances were that he'd know not to fuck with you. We knew the gun wasn't loaded, Whitworth didn't. Who would take the risk?

Whitworth's flat was on the ground floor of a 1960s systems-built maisonette block in a small council estate off the Queensbridge Road. It was dark, though not pitch black, as we parked the car a few yards from his front door. I debated whether or not to put on the balaclava, then decided against it. Gary had no mask, and besides, we wanted Tony Whitworth to see who was pointing the gun. Instead I concealed the bat under my long coat as we stepped out the car.

— Ring the fucking bell, Gary urged.

I pressed the buzzer.

A hall light clicked on, shining through the gap at the top of the door. Gary stuck his hand inside his coat. The door opened and a boy of about eight years old, wearing an Arsenal tracksuit, stood warily before us.

— Tony in? Gary asked.

I hadn't bargained for this. I'd made Whitworth into a cartoon figure, a mouthy ponce-spiv stereotype, in order to justify what we were going to do to him. I'd never imagined him as a real person, with kids, people who depended on him, probably even loved him. I tried to make a signal to Gary that this was not the time or place, but the young boy had vanished back into the house and was almost simultaneously replaced in the doorway by Whitworth. He wore a white t-shirt and jeans, and a beaming smile across his face.

— The lads, he grinned expansively. — Glad to see ya! I've got somefink for ya, if . . . he stopped in mid-sentence as his eyes grew bigger and the colour drained from him completely. The side of his face seemed to crinkle up as if he was having some kind of stroke.

Gary had whipped out the shooter and was pointing it straight at him.

— Oh no, please to god, I've got what you want, Gal, that's what I was trying to say . . . Jock . . .

— Gal, I started, but he ignored me.

— We got what you want cunt! he snapped at Whitworth, as he squeezed the trigger.

There was a shuddering bang and Whitworth seemed to vanish into the house. For an instant, it was like some kind of theatrical illusion, as if he was never there. In that split-second I thought I'd been the victim of an orchestrated wind-up between Gal and Tony Whitworth. I even started laughing. Then I looked into the lobby. Tony Whitworth's convulsing body lay there. What was once his face was now a broken, crushed mass of blood and grey matter.

I remember nothing after that until I was in the car and we were driving along the Balls Pond Road. Then I remember getting out, into another motor and heading back towards Stoke Newington. Gary started laughing and ranting like he was on speed. — Did you see the cunt's fucking head?

I felt like I was on heroin.

— Did ya? he asked, then he grabbed my wrist. — Jock, I'm really fucking sorry, mate, sorry to have got you involved. I couldn't have done it on my own though. I had to do it Jock, I had to waste the cunt. When I was in the Scrubs, you know, I heard all abaht him. He was round ours all the time, hanging around Marge, flashing his fucking wad abaht. Marge broke

7

down, Jock, told me the whole fucking story. Course I don't blame her, Jock, it ain't that, it was my fault getting banged up. I should've been around; any woman skint with her old man banged up is gonna be tempted by some flash git with dough fussing over er. The cunt beasted little Lisa though, Jock. Made her go down on him, you know what I'm saying here, Jock? Yeah? You'd've done the same, Jock, don't fucking tell me otherwise cause you're a liar; if it was your bleedin kid, you'd've done the same. You n me, we're the same, Jock, we look after each other, we look after our own. I'll make the money up to you one day, Jock, I bleedin well swear I will, believe you me, mate, I'll sort it all out. Couldn't have done nuffink else, Jock, it just festered away inside of me. I tried to ignore it. That's why I wanted to work with Whitworth, suss out the slag's MO, see if I could find a way to get him back. I thought abaht hurting one of his kids, like an eye for an eye an all that bleeding cobblers. I couldn't have done anything like that though, Jock, not to a little kiddie, that would make me no better than that fucking beast, that fucking nonce slag . . .

— Yeah . . .

— Sorry to drag you into this mess, Jock, but as soon as you got word of this fucking scam with Whitworth, you wouldn't fucking leave it. Had to be involved, you did. Gis a stake, Gal, you kept saying; mates n all that. You was like my bleedin shadow, you was. I tried to send out the fucking vibes, but no, you didn't pick them up. Had to cut you in for a piece of the action, didn't I? That was how you needed to have it, Jock; mates, partners.

We went back to my place. My lonely flat, even lonelier with two people in it. I sat on the couch, Gary sat in the chair opposite. I put the radio on. Despite the fact that she'd taken her stuff and gone months ago, there was still traces of her here; a glove, a scarf, a poster she'd bought stuck up on the wall, these Russian dolls we'd got from Covent Garden. The presence of such articles always loomed large in times of stress. Now they were overpowering. Gary and I sat drinking neat vodka and waiting for the bulletins.

After a bit Gary got up to take a piss. When he returned, he came back with the gun. He then sat back down in the chair opposite me. He ran his fingers along the narrow barrel. When he spoke his voice seemed strange; far away and disembodied.

— Did ya see his face, Jock?

— It wisnae fuckin funny, Gal, ya fuckin stupid cunt! I hissed, anger finally spilling through my sick fear.

— Yeah, but his face, Jock. That fucking smarmy nonce face. It's true, Jock, people change when you pull a gun on them.

He's looking right at me. Now he's pointing the shooter at me.

— Gal . . . dinnae fuck about man . . . dinnae . . .

I can't breathe, I feel my bones shaking; from the soles of my feet upwards, shaking my whole body in a jarring, sickening rhythm.

— Yeah, he says, — people change when you pull a gun on them.

The weapon is still pointed at me. He reloaded it when he took that slash. I know it.

— I heard that you were seeing quite a bit of my missus when I was inside, mate, he says softly, caressingly.

I try to say something, try to reason, try to plead, but my voice is dry in my throat as his finger tenses on the trigger.

EUROTRASH

I was anti-everything and everyone. I didn't want people around me. This aversion was not some big crippling anxiety; merely a mature recognition of my own psychological vulnerability and my lack of suitability as a companion. Thoughts jostled for space in my crowded brain as I struggled to give them some order which might serve to motivate my listless life.

For others Amsterdam was a place of magic. A bright summer; young people enjoying the attractions of a city that epitomised personal freedom. For me it was but a dull, blurred series of shadows. I was repelled by the harsh sunlight, seldom venturing out until it got dark. During the day I watched English and Dutch language programmes on the television and smoked a lot of marijuana. Rab was a less than enthusiastic host. Without any sense of his own ridiculousness he informed me that here in Amsterdam he was known as 'Robbie'.

Rab/Robbie's revulsion for me seemed to blaze behind his face, sucking the oxygen from the air in the small front room on which I had made up a couch-bed. I'd note his cheek muscles twitch in repressed anger as he'd come in, dirty, grimy and tired from a hard, physical job, to find me mellow in front of the box, the ubiquitous spliff in my hand.

I was a burden. I had been here for only a fortnight and clean for three weeks. My physical symptoms had abated. If you can stay clean for a month you've got a chance. However, I felt it was time I looked for a place of my own. My friendship with Rab (now, of course, re-invented as Robbie) could not survive the one-sided, exploitative basis I had re-modelled it on. The worse thing was: I didn't really care.

One evening, about a fortnight into my stay, it seemed he'd had enough. — When ye gaunny start lookin for a job, man? he asked, with obviously forced nonchalance.

— I am, mate. I hud a wee shuftie aroond yesterday, trying tae check a few things out, y'know? The lie of the land, I said with contrived sincerity. We went on like this; forced civility, with a subtext of mutual antagonism.

I took tram number 17 from Rab/Robbie's depressing little scheme in the western sector into the city centre. Nothing happens in places like the one we stayed in, Slotter Vaart they call it; breeze-block and concrete everywhere; one bar, one supermarket, one Chinese restaurant. It could've been anywhere. You need a city centre to give you a sense of place. I could've been back in Wester Hailes, or on Kingsmead, back in one of those places I came here to get away from. Only I hadn't got away. One dustbin for the poor outside of *action strasser* is much the same as any other, regardless of the city it serves.

In my frame of mind, I hated being approached by people. Amsterdam is the wrong place to be in such circumstances. No sooner had I alighted in The Damrak than I was hassled. I'd made the mistake of looking around to get my bearings. — French? American? English? an Arabic-looking guy asked.

— Fuck off, I hissed.

Even as I walked away from him into the English bookshop I could hear his voice reeling of a list of drugs. — Hashish, heroin, cocaine, ecstasy . . .

During what was meant to be a relaxing browse, I found myself staging an internal debate as to whether or not I would shoplift a book; deciding against it, I left before the urge became unbearable. Feeling pleased with myself, I crossed over Dam Square into the red-light district. A cool twilight had descended on the city. I strolled, enjoying the fall of darkness. On a side-street off a canal, near where the whores sit in the windows, a man approached me at a threatening pace. I decided quickly that

I would put my hands around his neck and choke him to death if he attempted to make any contact with me at all. I focused on his Adam's apple with murderous intent, my face twisting into a sneer as his cold, insect eyes slowly filled with apprehension. — Time . . . do you have the time? he asked fearfully.

I curtly nodded negative, striding satisfyingly past him as he arched his body to avoid being brushed onto the pavement. In Warmoesstraat it was not so easy. A group of youths were fighting a series of running battles; Ajax and Salzburg fans. The UEFA Cup. Yes. I could not handle the movement and the screaming. It was the noise and motion I was averse to more than the threat of violence. I took the line of least resistance, and slipped down a side-street into a brown bar.

It was a quiet, tranquil haven. Apart from a dark-skinned man with yellow teeth (I had never seen teeth so yellow), who was wired up to the pinball machine, the only other occupants of the place were the barman and a woman who sat on a stool at the bar. They were sharing a bottle of tequila and their laughter and intimate behaviour indicated that their relationship went beyond that of publican-customer.

The barman was setting the woman up with tequila shots. They were a little drunk, displaying a saccharine flirtatiousness. It took the man a while to register my presence at the bar. Indeed, the woman had to draw his attention to me. His response was to give her an embarrassed shrug, though it was obvious that he couldn't care less about me. Indeed, I sensed that I was an inconvenience.

In certain states of mind I would have been offended by this negligence and would definitely have spoken up. In other states of mind I would have done a lot more. At this point in time, however, I was happy to be ignored; it confirmed that I was as effectively invisible as I intended to be. I didn't care.

I ordered a Heineken. The woman seemed intent on drawing me into their conversation. I was just as intent on avoiding contact. I had nothing to say to these people.

— So where do you come from with an accent like that? she

laughed, her X-ray gaze sweeping over me. When her eyes met mine I saw a type of person who, despite their apparent camaraderie, has an instinctive drive towards manipulative schemes. Perhaps I was looking at my reflection.

I smiled. — Scotland.

— Yeah? Where about? Glasgow? Edinburgh?

— All over really, I replied, bland and blasé. Did it really matter which indistinct shite-arsed towns and schemes I was dragged through, growing up in that dull and dire little country?

She laughed, however, and looked thoughtful, as if I'd said something really profound. — All over, she mused. — Just like me. All over. She introduced herself as Chrissie. Her boyfriend, or he who, given his indulgence of her, intended to be her boyfriend, was called Richard.

From behind the bar, Richard stole injured glances at me, before I turned to face him, having clocked this in a bar mirror. He responded with a ducking motion of his head, followed by a 'Hi' in a dislocated hiss, and a furtive grope of a ratty beard which grew out of a pock-marked face but merely seemed to accentuate rather than conceal the lunar landscape it sprang from.

Chrissie talked in a rambling, expansive way, making observations about the world and citing mundane examples from her own experience to back them up.

It's a habit of mine to look at people's bare arms. Chrissie's were covered in healed track marks; the kind where ugly scar tissues is always left. Even more evident were the slash marks; judging by depth and position, the self-hating, response-to-frustration type rather than the serious suicide-bid variety. Her face was open and animated but her eyes had that watery, diminished aspect common to the traumatised. I read her as a grubby map of all the places you didn't want to go to: addiction, mental breakdown, drug psychosis, sexual exploitation. In Chrissie I saw someone who'd felt bad about herself and the world and had tried to shoot and fuck herself into better times without realising that she was only compounding the problem. I was no stranger to at least some of the places Chrissie had been. She looked as if she was very ill-equipped for these visits, however, and that she tended to stick around a bit too long.

At the moment her problems seemed to be drink and Richard. My first thought was that she was welcome to both. I found Chrissie pretty repulsive. Her body was layered with hard fat around her gut, thighs and hips. I saw a beaten woman whose only resistance to the attentions of middle-age was to wear clothes too youthful, tight and revealing for her meaty figure.

Her doughy face twisted flirtatiously at me. I was vaguely nauseated at this woman; gone to seed, yet unselfconsciously attempting to display a sexual magnetism she no longer possessed, and seemingly unaware of the grotesque vaudevillian caricature which had supplanted it.

It was then, paradoxically, that a horrible impulse struck me, which appeared to have its origins in an unspecific area behind my genitals: this person who repulsed me, this woman, would become my lover.

Why should this be? Perhaps it was my natural perversity; perhaps Chrissie was that strange arena where repulsion and attraction meet. Maybe I admired her stubborn refusal to acknowledge the remorseless shrinking of her possibilities. She acted as if new, exciting, enriching experiences were just around the corner, in spite of all the evidence to the contrary. I felt a gratuitous urge, as I often do with such people, to shake her and scream the truth in her face: *You're a useless, ugly piece of meat. Your life has been desperate and abominable so far, and it's only going to get worse. Stop fucking kidding yourself.*

A conflicting mass of emotions, I was actively despising someone while simultaneously planning their seduction. It was only later that I acknowledged, with some horror and shame, that these feelings didn't really conflict at all. At that stage, though, I was unsure as to whether Chrissie was flirting with me or merely trying to tease the seedy Richard. Perhaps she wasn't sure herself.

— We're going to the beach tomorrow. You must come, she said.

— That would be great, I smiled lavishly, as the colour drained from Richard's face.

— I may have to work . . . he stammered nervously.

— Well, if you won't drive us, we'll just go alone! she simpered in a little-girl manner, a tactic commonly used by whores, which she almost certainly once was, when she still had the looks to make it pay.

I was definitely pushing at an open door.

We drank and talked until the increasingly nervous Richard shut the bar and then we went to a cafe for some blow. The date was formalised; tomorrow I was forsaking my nocturnal life for a day of seaside frolics with Chrissie and Richard.

Richard was very uptight the following day when he drove us down to the beach. I derived pleasure from watching his knuckles go white on the steering wheel as Chrissie, arched around from the front passenger sat, indulged in some frivolous and mildly flirtatious banter with me. Every bad joke or dull anecdote which spilled lazily from my lips was greeted with frenetic peals of laughter from Chrissie, as Richard suffered in tense silence. I could feel his hatred for me growing in increments, constricting him, impairing his breathing, muddying his thought processes. I felt like a nasty child jacking up the volume on the handset of the television control for the purpose of annoying an adult.

He inadvertently gained some measure of revenge, sticking on a Carpenters tape. I writhed in discomfort as he and Chrissie sung along. — Such a terrible loss, Karen Carpenter, she said solemnly. Richard nodded in sombre agreement. — Sad, isn't it, Euan? Chrissie asked, wanting to include me in their strange little festival of grief for this dead pop star.

I smiled in a good-natured, carefree way. — I couldn't give a toss. There's people all over the world who haven't got enough to eat. Why should I give a fuck about some over-privileged fucked-up Yank who's too screwed up to lift a forkful of scran into her gub?

There was a stunned silence. Eventually Chrissie wailed, — You've a very nasty, cynical mind, Euan! Richard wholeheartedly agreed, unable to conceal his glee that I'd upset her. He even started singing along to 'Top of the World'. After this, he and Chrissie began conversing in Dutch and laughing.

I was unperturbed at this temporary exclusion. In fact I was enjoying their reaction. Richard simply did not understand the type of person Chrissie was. I sensed that she was attracted to ugliness and cynicism because she saw herself as an agent of change. I was a challenge to her. Richard's servile indulgence would amuse her from time to time; it was, however, just a holiday retreat, not a permanent home, ultimately bland and boring. In trying to be what he thought she wanted, he had given her nothing to change; denied her the satisfaction of making a real impact in their relationship. In the meantime, she would string this fool along, as he indulged her boundless vanity.

We lay on the beach. We threw a ball at each other. It was like a caricature of what people should do at the seaside. I grew uncomfortable with the scene and the heat and lay down in the shade. Richard ran around in his cut-offs; tanned and athletic, despite a slightly distended stomach. Chrissie looked embarrassingly flabby.

When she went to get ice-cream, leaving Richard and I alone for the first time, I felt a little bit nervous.

— She's great, isn't she, he enthused.

I reluctantly smiled.

— Chrissie has come through a lot.

— Yes, I acknowledged. That I had already deduced.

— I feel differently about her than I've done about anyone else. I've known her a long time. Sometimes I think she needs to be protected from herself.

— That's a wee bit too conceptual for me, Richard.

— You know what I mean. You keep your arms covered up.

I felt my bottom lip curl in knee-jerk petulance. It was the childlike, dishonest response of someone who isn't really hurt but is pretending to be so in order to justify future aggression towards, or elicit retraction from, the other party. It was second nature to me. I was pleased that he felt he had my measure; with a delusion of power over me he'd get cocky and therefore careless. I'd pick my moment and tear out his heart. It was hardly a difficult target, lying right there on the sleeve of his blouse. This whole thing was as much about me and Richard as it was about me and Chrissie; in a sense she was only the battleground on which our duel was being fought. Our natural antipathy on first meeting had incubated in the hothouse of our continuing contact. In an astonishingly short time it had blossomed into fully-fledged hatred.

Richard was unrepentant about his indiscreet comment. Far from it, he followed up his attack, attempting to construct in me an appropriate figure for his hatred. — We Dutch, we went to South Africa. You British oppressed us. You put us into concentration camps. It was you people who invented the concentration camp, not the Nazis. You taught them that, like you taught them genocide. You were far more effective at that with the Maoris in New Zealand than Hitler was with the Jews. I'm not condoning what the Boers are doing in South Africa. No way. Never. But you British put the hatred in their hearts, made them harsh. Oppression breeds oppression, not resolution.

I felt a surge of anger rise in me. I was almost tempted to go into a spiel about how I was Scottish, not British, and that the Scots were the last oppressed colony of the British Empire. I don't really believe it, though; the Scots oppress themselves by their obsession with the English which breeds the negatives of hatred, fear, servility, contempt and dependency. Besides, I would not be drawn into an argument with this moronic queen.

— I don't profess to know a great deal about politics, Richard. I do find your analysis a tad subjective, however. I stood up, smiling at Chrissie who had returned with cartons of Häagen-Dazs topped with *slagroom*.

— You know what you are, Euan? Do you? she teased. Chris-

17

sie had obviously been exploring some theme while she was getting the ices. Now she'd inflict her observations on us. I shrugged. — Look at him, Mister Cool. Been there, done it all. You're just like Richard and me. Bumming around. Where was it you said you wanted to head for later on?

— Ibiza, I told her, or Rimini.

— For the rave scene, the ecstasy, she prompted.

— It's a good scene to get into, I nodded. — Safer than junk.

— Well that's as maybe, she said petulantly. — You're just Eurotrash, Euan. We all are. This is where all the scum gets washed up. The Port of Amsterdam. A dustbin for the Eurotrash.

— I smiled and opened another Heineken from Richard's cold basket. — I'll drink to that. To Eurotrash! I toasted.

Chrissie enthusiastically bashed my bottle with hers. Richard reluctantly joined in.

While Richard was obviously Dutch, I found Chrissie's accent hard to place. She occasionally had a Liverpool affectation to what generally seemed to be a hybrid of middle-class English and French, although I was sure it was all a pose. But there was no way I was going to ask her where she was from just so that she could say: all over.

When we got back to the 'Dam that night, I could see that Richard feared the worst. At the bar he tried to ply us with drink in what was obviously a desperate attempt to render what was about to happen null and void. His face was set into a beaten expression. I was going home with Chrissie; it couldn't have been more obvious had she taken out an advertisement in the newspaper.

— I'm shattered, she yawned. — The sea air. Will you see me home, Euan?

— Why don't you wait until I finish my shift? Richard desperately pleaded.

— Oh Richard, I'm completely exhausted. Don't worry about me. Euan doesn't mind taking me to the station, do you?

— Where do you stay? Richard interjected, addressing me, trying to gain some control over events.

I flipped up my palm in a halting gesture, and turned back to Chrissie. — The very least I could do after yourself and Richard giving me such a good time today. Besides, I really need to get my head down too, I continued, in a low, oily voice, allowing a dripping, languid smile to mould my face.

Chrissie pecked Richard on the cheek. — Phone you tomorrow baby, she said, scrutinising him in the manner of an indulgent mother with a sulking toddler.

— Goodnight, Richard, I smiled as we made to leave. I held the door open for Chrissie and as she exited I looked back at the tortured fool behind the bar, winked and raised my eyebrows: — Sweet dreams.

We walked through the red-light district, by the Voorburg and Achterburg canals, enjoying the air and the bustle. — Richard is incredibly possessive. It's such a drag, Chrissie mused.

— No doubt his heart's in the right place, I said.

We walked in silence towards Centraal Station where Chrissie would pick up the tram to where she stayed, just past the Ajax Stadium. I decided that the time was ripe to declare my intentions. I turned to her and said. — Chrissie, I'd like to spend the night with you.

She turned to me with her eyes half shut and her jaw jutting out. — I thought you might, she smugly replied. There was an incredible arrogance about her.

A dealer, positioned on a bridge over the Achterburg canal, caught us in his gaze. Displaying a keen sense of timing and market awareness he hissed, — Ecstasy for the sex. Chrissie raised an eyebrow and made to stall, but I steered her on. People say that Es are good for shagging, but I find that I only want to dance and hug on them. Besides, it had been so long that my gonads felt like space hoppers. The last thing I needed was an aphrodisiac. I didn't fancy Chrissie. I needed a fuck; it was as simple as that. Junk tends to impose a sexual moratorium and the post-smack sexual awakening nags at you uncompromisingly; an itch that just has to be scratched. I was sick of sitting wanking in Rab/Robbie's front room, the stale musty smell of my spunk mixing with the hashish fumes.

Chrissie shared an apartment with a tense, pretty girl called Margriet who bit her nails, chewed her lower lip and spoke in fast Dutch and slow English. We all talked for a bit, then Chrissie and I went through to the bed in her pastel-coloured room.

I began kissing and touching her, with Richard never far from my thoughts. I didn't want foreplay, I didn't want to *make love*, not to this woman. I wanted to fuck her. Now. The only reason I was feeling her up was for Richard; thinking that if I took my time and made a good job of this, it would give me a greater hold over her and therefore the opportunity to cause him much more discomfort.

— Fuck me . . . she murmured. I pulled up the duvet and winced involuntarily as I caught a glimpse of her vagina. It looked ugly; red and scarred. She was slightly embarrassed and sheepishly explained: — A girlfriend and I were playing some games . . . with beer bottles. It was just one of those things that got a bit out of hand. I'm so sore down there . . . she rubbed her crotch, — do it in my bottom, Euan, I like it that way. I've got the jelly here. She stretched over to the bedside locker, and fumbled in a drawer, pulling a jar of KY out. She began greasing my erect cock. — You don't mind putting it in my bum, do you? Let's love like animals, Euan . . . that's what we are, the Eurotrash, remember? She spun round and started to apply the jelly to her arse, beginning with the cleft between her buttocks, then working it right into her arsehole. When she'd finished I put my finger in to check for shite. Anal I don't mind, but I can't handle shite. It was clean though, and certainly prettier than her cunt. It would be a better fuck than that floppy, scarred mess. Dyke games. Fuck that. With Margriet? Surely not! Putting aesthetics aside, I had castration anxiety, visualising her fanny still being full of broken glass. I'd settle for her arse.

She'd obviously done this before, many times, there was so much give as I entered her arsehole. I grabbed her heavy buttocks in both hands as her repulsive body arched out in front of me. Thinking of Richard, I whispered at her, — I think you need to be protected from yourself. I thrust urgently and got a shock as I caught a glimpse of my face in a wall mirror, twisted, sneering, ugly. Rubbing her injured cunt ferociously, Chrissie came, her fat folds wobbling from side to side as I shunted my load into her rectum.

After the sex, I felt really revolted by her. It was an effort just to lie beside her. Nausea almost overwhelmed me. I tried to turn away from her at one point, but she wrapped her large flabby arms around me and pulled me to her breast. I lay there sweating coldly, full of tense self-loathing, crushed against her tits, which were surprisingly small for her build.

Over the weeks Chrissie and I continued to fuck, always in the same way. Richard's bitterness towards me increased in direct correlation to these sexual activities, for although I had agreed with Chrissie not to disclose our relationship to him, it was more or less an open secret. In any other circumstances I would have demanded clarification of the role of this sweetie-wife in our scene. However, I was already planning to extract myself from my relationship with Chrissie. To do this, I reasoned, it would be better if I kept Chrissie and Richard close. The strange thing about them was that they seemed to have no wider network of close friends; only casual acquaintances like Cyrus, the guy who played pinball in Richard's bar. With this in mind, the last thing I wanted to do was to alienate them from each other. If that happened, I'd never be shot of Chrissie without causing the unstable bitch a great deal of pain. Whatever her faults, she didn't need any more of that.

I didn't deceive Chrissie; this isn't merely a retrospective attempt at self-justification for what was to happen. I can say this with confidence as I clearly recall a conversation that we had in a coffee shop in Utrechtesstraat. Chrissie was being very presumptuous and starting to make plans about me moving in with her. This was glaringly inappropriate. I said overtly what I had been telling her covertly with my behaviour towards her, had she cared to take note of it.

— Don't expect anything from me, Chrissie. I can't give. It's nothing to do with you. It's me. I can't get involved. I can never be what you want me to be. I can be your friend. We can fuck. But don't ask me to give. I can't.

— Somebody must have hurt you really badly, she said shaking her head as she blew hashish smoke across the table. She was trying to convert her obvious hurt into feelings of pity for me, and she was failing miserably.

I remember that conversation in the coffee shop because it had the opposite effect to the one I'd wanted. She became even more intense towards me; I was now more of a challenge.

So that was the truth, but perhaps not the whole truth. I couldn't give *with Chrissie*. You can never put feelings where they're not. But things were changing for me. I was feeling physically and mentally stronger, more prepared to open myself up, ready to cast aside this impregnable cloak of bitterness. I just needed the right person to do it with.

I landed a job as a reception-clerk-cum-porter-cum-dogsbody in a small hotel in The Damrak. The hours were long and unsocial and I would sit watching television or reading at the reception, gently ssshhing the young drunk and stoned guests who flopped in at all hours. During the day I started to attend Dutch language classes.

To the relief of Rab/Robbie, I moved out of his place to a room in a beautiful apartment in a particularly narrow canal house in the Jordaan. The house was new; it had been totally rebuilt due to subsidence of the previous building into the weak, sandy Amsterdam soil, but it was built in the same traditional style of its neighbours. It was surprisingly affordable.

After I moved out, Rab/Robbie seemed more like his old self. He was more friendly and sociable towards me, he wanted me to go out drinking and smoking with him; to meet all the friends he'd vigilantly kept away from me, lest they might be corrupted by this junky. They were typical sixties time-warp Amsterdam types, who smoked a lot of hash and were shit-scared of what they called 'hard drugs'. Although I didn't have much time for them, it was good to get back onto an even footing with Rab/Robbie. One Saturday afternoon we were stoned in the Floyd cafe and we felt comfortable enough to put our cards on the table.

— It's good to see you settled, man, he said. — You were in a bad way when you came here.

— It was really good of you to put us up, Rab . . . Robbie, but you weren't the friendliest of hosts, it has to be said. You had some coupon on ye when you walked in at night.

He smiled. — I take your point, man. I suppose I made ye even more uptight than ye were. It just freaked me a bit, y'know? Workin like fuck aw day and ye come in and there's this wasted cunt whae's trying tae git oaf smack . . . ah mean I was thinkin, likes, what have I taken oan here, man?

— Aye, I suppose I did impose myself, and I was a bit of a leech.

— Naw, you wirnae really that bad, man, he conceded, all mellow. — Ah was far too uptight, likes. It's just, you know, man, I'm the sort of punter who needs my own personal space, y'know?

— I can understand that, man. I said, then, swallowing a lump of spacecake, smirked. — I dig the cosmic vibes you're sending out here, man.

Rab/Robbie smiled and toked hard on a spliff. The pollem was very mellow. — You know, man, ye really caught me out acting the arsehole. All that Robbie shit. Call me what you always called me, back in Scotland. Back up Tollcross. Rab. That's who ah am. That's who ah'll always be. Rab Doran. Tollcross Rebels. T.C.R. Some fuckin times back there, eh man?

They were pretty desperate times really, but home always looks better when you're away from it, and even more so through a haze of hash. I colluded in his fantasies and we reminisced over more joints before hitting some bars and getting rat-arsed on alcohol.

Despite the rediscovery of our friendship, I spent very little time with Rab, due mainly to the shifts I was working. During the day, if I wasn't taking my language classes, I'd be swotting up, or getting my head down before my shift at the hotel. One of the people who lived in the flat was a woman named Valerie. She helped me with my Dutch, which was coming along in leaps and bounds. My phrasebook French, Spanish and German were also improving rapidly due to the number of tourists I was coming into contact with in the hotel. Valerie became a good friend to me; more importantly, she had a friend called Anna, with whom I fell in love.

It was a beautiful time for me. My cynicism evaporated and life started to seem like an adventure of limitless possibilities. Needless to say, I stopped seeing Chrissie and Richard and seldom went near the red-light district. They seemed a remnant of a seedier, more sordid time that I felt I had left behind. I didn't want or need to smear that gel on my cock and bury it in Chrissie's flabby arse anymore. I had a beautiful young girlfriend to make love to and that was what I did most of the day before staggering onto my late shift, strung out on sex.

Life was nothing short of idyllic for the rest of that summer. This state of affairs changed one day; a warm, clear day when Anna and I found ourselves on Dam Square. I tensed as I saw Chrissie coming towards us. She was wearing dark glasses and looked even more bloated than ever. She was cloyingly pleasant and insisted we went to Richard's bar in Warmoesstraat for a drink. Though edgy, I felt that a greater scene would have been caused by cold-shouldering her.

Richard was delighted I had a girlfriend that wasn't Chrissie. I had never seen him so open towards me. I felt a vague shame about my torturing of him. He talked of his home town of Utrecht.

— Who famous comes from Utrecht? I gently chided him.

— Oh, lots of people.

— Aye? Name one?

— Let me see, eh, Gerald Vanenberg.

— The PSV guy?

— Yes.

Chrissie looked at us in a hostile manner. — Who the fuck is Gerald Vanenburg? she snapped, then turned to Anna and looked at her with raised eyebrows as if Richard and I had said something ridiculous.

— A famous international footballer, Richard bleated. Trying to reduce the tension he added. — He used to go out with my sister.

— I bet you wish he used to go out with you, Chrissie said bitterly. There was an embarrassed silence before Richard set us up with more tequila slammers.

Chrissie had been making a fuss of Anna. She was stroking her bare arms, telling her that she was so slim and beautiful. Anna was probably embarrassed but was handling it well. I resented that fat dyke touching up my girlfriend. She became more hostile towards me as the drinks flowed, asking me how I was getting on, what I was up to. A challenging tone had entered her voice.

— Only we don't see him so much these days, do we, Richard?

— Leave it, Chrissie . . . Richard said uneasily.

Chrissie stroked Anna's peach cheek. Anna smiled back awkwardly.

— Does he fuck you like he fucks me? In your pretty little bottom? she asked.

I felt as if the flesh had been stripped from my bones. Anna's face contorted in discomfort, as she turned towards me.

— I think we'd better go, I said.

Chrissie threw a glass of beer over me and began verbally abusing me. Richard held her from behind the bar, otherwise she'd have struck me. — TAKE YOUR FUCKING LITTLE SLUT AND GO! A REAL WOMAN'S TOO MUCH FOR YOU, YOU FUCKING JUNKY VERMIN! HAVE YOU SHOWN HER YOUR ARMS YET?

— Chrissie . . . I said weakly.

— FUCK OFF! JUST FUCK OFF! BANG YOUR SILLY

LITTLE GIRL YOU FUCKING PAEDOPHILE! I'M A REAL WOMAN, A REAL FUCKING WOMAN . . .

I ushered Anna out of the bar. Cyrus flashed his yellow teeth at me and shrugged his broad shoulders. I looked back to see Richard comforting Chrissie. — I'm a real woman, not a silly little girl.

— You're a beautiful woman, Chrissie. The most beautiful, I heard Richard say soothingly.

In a sense, it was a blessing. Anna and I went for a drink and I told her the whole story of Chrissie and Richard, leaving nothing out. I told her how fucked up and bitter I was, and how, while I'd promised her nothing, I'd treated Chrissie fairly shabbily. Anna understood, and we put the episode behind us. As a result of that conversation I felt even better and more uninhibited, my last little problem in Amsterdam seemingly resolved.

It was strange, but as Chrissie was such a fuck-up, I half thought of her a few days later when they said that the body of a woman had been fished out of Oosterdok, by Centraal Station. I quickly forgot about it, however. I was enjoying life, or trying to, although circumstances were working against us. Anna had just started college, studying fashion design, and with my shifts at the hotel we were like ships in the night, so I was thinking of chucking it and getting another job. I'd saved up quite a healthy wad of guilders.

I was pondering this one afternoon, when I heard someone banging at the door. It was Richard, and as I opened up he spat in my face. I was too shocked to be angry. — Fucking murderer! he sneered.

— What . . . I knew, but couldn't comprehend. A thousand impulses flowed through my body, fusing me into immobility.

— Chrissie's dead.

— Oosterdok . . . it was Chrissie . . .

— Yes, it was Chrissie. I suppose you'll be happy now.

— NAW MAN . . . NAW! I protested.

— Liar! Fucking hypocrite! You treated her like shit. You and others like you. You were no good for her. Used her like an old rag then discarded her. Took advantage of her weakness, of her need to give. People like you always do.

— Naw! It wasn't like that, I pleaded, knowing full well it was exactly like that.

He stood and looked at me for a while. It was like he was looking beyond me, seeing something that wasn't apparent from my vantage point. I broke a silence which probably lasted only seconds, but seemed like minutes. — I want to go to the funeral, Richard.

— He smiled cruelly at me. — In Jersey? You won't go there.

— The Channel Islands . . . I said, hesitantly. I didn't know Chrissie was from there. — I will go, I told him. I was determined to go. I felt culpable enough. I had to go.

Richard examined me contemptuously, then started talking in a low, terse voice. — St Helier, Jersey. The home of Robert Le Marchand, Chrissie's father. It's next Tuesday. Her sister was here, making arrangements to take the body back.

— I want to go. Are you?

He scoffed at me. — No. She's dead. I wanted to help her when she was alive. He turned and walked away. I watched his back recede into nothingness, then went into the flat, shaking uncontrollably.

I had to get to St Helier by Tuesday. I'd find details of the Le Marchands' whereabouts when I got there. Anna wanted to come. I said I'd be a poor travelling companion, but she insisted. Accompanied by her, and a sense of guilt which seemed to seep into the body of the rented car, I drove along the highways of Europe, through Holland, Belgium and France to the small port of St Malo. I started thinking, about Chrissie, yes, but about other things, which I would generally never concern myself with. I started to think about the politics of European integration, whether it was a good or bad thing. I tried to marry up the politicians' vision with the paradox I saw in the miles of these ugly highways of Europe; absurd incompatibilities with an inexorable shared destiny. The politicians' vision seemed just another money-making scam or another crass power-trip. We ate up these dull roads before reaching St Malo. After checking into a cheap hotel Anna and I got roaring drunk. The next morning we boarded the ferry to Jersey.

We arrived Monday afternoon and found another hotel. There were no funeral notices in the *Jersey Evening Post*. I got a phonebook and looked up Le Marchand. There were six, but only one R. A man's voice came down the receiver.

— Hello.

— Hello. Could I speak to Mister Robert Le Marchand?

— Speaking.

— I'm really sorry to bother you at this time. We're friends of Chrissie's, over from Holland for the funeral. We understand that it's tomorrow. Would it be alright if we attended?

— From Holland? he repeated wearily.

— Yes. We're at Gardener's Hotel.

— Well, you have come a long way, he stated. His posh, bland, English accent grated. — The funeral's at ten. St Thomas's chapel, just around the corner from your hotel as a matter of fact.

— Thanks, I said, as the line clicked dead. *As a matter of fact* . . . It seemed as if everything was simply a matter of fact to Mr Le Marchand.

I felt totally drained. No doubt the man's coldness and hostility were due to assumptions made about Chrissie's friends in Amsterdam and the nature of her death; her body was full of barbituates when it was fished out of the dock, bloated further by the water.

At the funeral, I introduced myself to her mother and father. Her mother was a small, wizened woman, diminished even further by this tragedy into a brittle near-nothingness. Her father looked like a man who had a great deal of guilt to shed. I could detect his sense of failure and horror and it made me feel less guilty about my small, but decisive role in Chrissie's demise.

— I won't be a hypocrite, he said. — We didn't always like each other, but Christopher was my son, and I loved him.

I felt a lump in my chest. There was a buzzing in my ears and the air seemed to grow thin. I could not pick out any sound. I managed to nod, and excused myself, moving away from the cluster of mourners gathered around the graveside.

I stood shaking in confusion, past events cascading through my mind. Anna put her arm tightly around me, and the congregation must have thought I was grief-stricken. A woman approached us. She was a younger, slimmer, prettier version of Chrissie . . . Chris . . .

— You know, don't you?

I stood gaping into space.

— Please don't say anything to Mum and Dad. Didn't Richard tell you?

I nodded blankly.

— It would kill Mum and Dad. They don't know about his change . . . I took the body home. I had them cut his hair and dress him in a suit. I bribed them to say nothing . . . it would only cause hurt. He wasn't a woman. He was my brother, you see? He was a man. That's how he was born, that's how he was buried. Anything else would only cause hurt to the people who are left to pick up the pieces. Don't you see that? she pleaded. — Chris was confused. A mess. A mess in here, she pointed to her head. — God I tried, we all tried. Mum and Dad could handle the drugs, even the homosexuality. It was all experiments with Christopher. Trying to find himself . . . you know how they are. She looked at me with an embarrassed contempt, — I mean that sort of person. She started to sob.

She was consumed with grief and anger. In such circumstances she needed the benefit of the doubt, though what were they covering up? What was the problem? What was wrong with reality? As an ex-junky I knew the answer to that. Often plenty was wrong with reality. Whose reality was it, anyway?

— It's okay, I said. She nodded appreciatively before joining the rest of her family. We didn't stick around. There was a ferry to catch.

When we got back to Amsterdam, I sought out Richard. He

was apologetic at having dropped me in it. — I misjudged you. Chris was confused. It was little to do with you. It was nasty to let you go without knowing the truth.

— Naw, I deserved it. Shite of the year, that was me, I said sadly.

Over some beers he told me Chrissie's story. The breakdowns, the decision to radically re-order her life and gender; spending a substantial inheritance on the treatment. She started off on a treatment of female hormones, both oestrogen and progesterone. These developed her breasts, softened her skin and reduced her bodily hair. Her muscular strength was diminished and the distribution of her subcutaneous fat was altered in a female direction. She had electrolysis to remove facial hair. This was followed by throat surgery on her voicebox, which resulted in the removal of the Adam's apple and a softening of the voice, when complemented by a course of speech therapy.

She went around like this for three years, before the most radical surgery, which was undertaken in four stages. These were penectomy, castration, plastic reconstruction and vaginoplasty, the formation of an artificial vagina, constructed by creating a cavity between the prostrate and the rectum. The vagina was formed from skin grafts from the thigh and lined with penile, and/or scrotal skin, which, Richard explained, made orgasmic sensation possible. The shape of the vagina was maintained by her wearing a mould for several weeks after the operation.

In Chrissie's case, the operations caused her great distress, and she therefore relied heavily on painkilling drugs which, given her history, was probably not the best thing. That, Richard reckoned, was the real key to her demise. He saw her walking out of his bar towards Dam Square. She bought some barbs, took them, was seen out of her box in a couple of bars before she wandered along by the canal. It could have been suicide or an accident, or perhaps that grey area in between.

Christopher and Richard had been lovers. He spoke affectionately of Christopher, glad now to be able to refer to him as Chris. He talked of all his obsessions, ambitions and dreams; all *their* obsessions, ambitions and dreams. They often got close to finding their niche; in Paris, Laguna Beach, Ibiza and Hamburg; they got close, but never quite close enough. Not Eurotrash, just people trying to get by.

STOKE NEWINGTON BLUES

I took my last shot in the toilet on the ferry, then made my way
to the deck. It was amazing; spray in my face as squawking gulls
chased the boat; a prolonged rush surging through my body. All
hands on deck. I grip the rail and vomit acrid bile into the
North Sea. A woman gives me a concerned glance. I respond
with a smile of acknowledgement. — Struggling to find my sea
legs, I shout, before retiring to the lounge to order a black coffee
which I've no intention of drinking.

The crossing is okay. I'm mellow. I sit in silence, no doubt
a blank corpse to all the other passengers, but engaged in a
meaningful inner dialogue with myself. I replay recent history,
casting myself in a virtuous role, justifying the minor atrocities
I've inflicted on others as offering them important insight and
knowledge.

I start to hurt on the boat train: Harwich — Colchester —
Marks Tey — Kelvedon — Chelmsford — Shenfield THIS
TRAIN SHOULD NOT STOP AT FUCKIN SHEN-
FIELD — Romford EVERY INCH OF TRACK I WILL
THIS TRAIN ON (What about Manningtree, where the fuck's
Manningtree got to in all this?) TO LONDON Liverpool
Street. The tube goes everywhere except Hackney. Too marshy.
I alight at Bethnal Green and jump on the 253 to Lower Clap-
ton Road. I shuffle down Homerton Road and into the Kings-
mead Estate. I hope that Donovan is still squatting on the second
floor. I hope that he isn't grudging about the Stockwell inci-
dent, water under the bridge by now, surely. I push past some

harsh-faced domestic-pet-killing children who are aerosoling stylishly illegible slogans on the wall. So passé, so ghetto.

— Watch it! Fucking junky!

Should I fuck these children before, or after I kill them?

I do nothing of the kind. It's yon time.

Don's still there. That fortified door. Now I only have to worry about whether or not he's in, and if he is, whether or not he'll let me in. I rap heavily.

— Who is it? Angie's voice. Don and Ange. I'm not surprised; I always thought they'd end up getting it on.

— Open up, Ange, for fuck's sake. It's me, Euan.

A series of locks click open and Ange looks at me, her sharp features more prominent than ever, defined and sculpted by skag. She bades me enter and secures the door.

— Don aroond?

— Nah, gone out, ain't he.

— Any skag?

Her mouth turns downwards and her dark eyes hold me like those of a cat that's cornered a mouse. She contemplates a lie then, noting my desperation, decides against it.

— How was the 'Dam? She's toying with me, the fuckin cow.

— Ah need a shot, Ange.

She produces some gear and helps me cook up and take a shot. A rush shoots through me, followed by a rising tide of nausea. All hands on deck. I throw up on a *Daily Mirror*. Paul Gascoigne is on the front, winking and giving the thumbs up in traction and plaster cast. This paper is eight months old.

Ange prepares a shot for herself, using my works. I'm not too happy about this but I can't really say much. I look at her cold, fish eyes, cut into that crystalline flesh. You could lacerate yourself badly on her nose, cheekbones and jawline.

She sits beside me, but looks straight ahead instead of turning to face me. She starts to talk incessantly about her life in a slow, even monotone. I feel like a junky priest. She tells me that she was raped by a squad of guys and has felt so bad about it she's had

33

a habit since then. I get a feeling of déjà vu here. I'm sure she's told me this before.

— It hurts, Euan. It fucking hurts inside. The gear's the only thing that takes the pain away. There's nuffink I can do about it. I'm dead inside. You won't be able to understand. No man can understand. They killed a part of me, Euan. The best part. Wot you see here's a fucking ghost. It don't matter much wot happens to a fucking ghost. She taps up a wire, jabs home and convulses appreciatively as the gear pumps into her circuit.

At least the rush shuts her up. There was something unsettling about her talking in that disembodied way. I look at the *Mirror*. Several flies are feasting on Gazza.

— The rapist punters. Get a squad the gither, get the cunts, I venture.

She turns towards me, shakes her head slowly, then turns back. — No, it don't work like that. Nobody is more connected than these guys. They're still doing it to women. One of them pulls at a club, brings the woman back. The rest are waiting and they just use her like a fucking hanky for as long as they want.

I suppose to get close to understanding how it feels you have to think of about a dozen guys giving it Clapham Junction up your arsehole.

— That's the last, she murmurs in wistful content. — I hope Don brings some back.

— You n me both, doll, you n me both.

It could have been hours or minutes, but Donovan did show.

— What the fuck are you doing here man? He set his hands on his hips and thrust out his neck at me.

— Good tae see you n aw, mate.

It looked as if Don's skin tone had been diluted by the smack. Michael Jackson probably paid millions to get the same effect Don has from junk. He was like a Jubilee that the ice had been sucked out of. Come to think of it, Ange had been more pink in the past. It seemed that if you took enough junk you would lose all racial characteristics completely. Junk really did make every other feature of a person irrelevant.

— You holdin? His accent changed from a high-pitched effeminate North London whine to a rich, heavy Jamaican dread.

— Like fuck. Ah'm here tae score.

Don turned to Ange. You could tell he hadn't scored and was about to hit the roof at her for giving the last to me. Just as he started to speak, there was a bang at the door and although it held firm, after another couple of thrashes the frame split from the wall and the whole thing tumbled inwards. Two guys stood in the doorway with sledgehammers. They looked so mental I was almost relieved when a group of pigs stormed in and swarmed all over us. I watched the expression of disappointment on the face of one seasoned DS fucker. He knew that had we been holding it would have been a race to the lavvy to flush the gear away, but none of us had moved. Nobody was holding. They ritually turned the place over. One cop picked up my works and looked sneeringly at me. I raised my eyebrows and smiled lazily at him. — Let's get this rubbish down the fucking station, he shouted. We were bundled out of the flat, down the stairs and into a meatwagon. There was a loud crash as a bottle hit the top of the van. It stopped and a couple of cops got out, but couldn't be bothered giving chase to the kids who probably threw it from the balcony. They crushed us between their bulk, muttering the occasionally dark threat.

I looked at Don sat opposite. The car whizzed past the Lower Clapton Road cop shop, then past Dalston station. We were going to Stoke Newington. A name station. The name on my mind and almost certainly on Don's was Earl Barratt.

At the station they asked me to turn out my pockets. I did, but dropped a set of keys on the floor. I bent to pick them up and my scarf trailed on the ground. A cop stood on it, just pinning me there helpless, bent double, unable to lift my head up.

— Get up! another one snapped.

— You're standing on my scarf.

— Get your fucking sick junky arse up ere!

— I cannae fuckin move, yir standin oan ma scarf!

— I'll give you fucking scarves, you Jock cunt. He booted or punched me in the side and I toppled over onto the floor, collapsing like a deckchair. It was more from the shock rather than the force of the blow.

— Get up! Get fucking up!

I staggered to my feet, blood soaring to my head, and was pushed into an interview room. My brain felt hazy as they barked some questions at me. I manage to mumble some weak replies before they threw me in the drunk tank. It was a large white-tiled room with perimeter benches and an assortment of foam and vinyl mattresses on the floor. The place was full of piss-heads, petty criminals and cannabis dealers. I recognised a couple of black guys from the Line, at Sandringham Road. I tried not to make eye contact. The dealers up there hate smack-heads. They get hassled by the racists pigs for skag when all they deal in is blow.

Fortunately their attention is diverted from me as two heavily-built white guys, one with a strong Irish accent, begin boot-ing fuck out of a one-eared transvestite. When they feel they've done enough they start pissing on his prostrate figure.

I seem to be there for an age; getting sicker and sicker and more and more desperate. Then Don gets flung in, sick and hurting. The polis who bundles him into the tank can see that the one-eared boy on the deck has been well fucked over, but he just shakes his head contemptuously and bolts the door. Don sits beside me on the bench, his face in his hands. At first I notice blood on his hands, but then I see that it is coming from his nose and mouth which are quite badly swollen. He'd obviously slipped on something and fallen down a flight of stairs. This tended to happen in Stokie police station to black punters. Like Earl Barratt. Don is shivering. I decide to speak.

— Tell ye, man, ah'm a wee bitty disappointed wi the crimi-nal justice system of this country, at least as locally administered here in Stokie.

He turned towards me, showing the full extent of his kicking. It was quite healthy. — I ain't coming out of here man, he trembled, his eyes wide with fear. He was serious. — You heard about Barratt. This place is known for it. I'm the wrong fucking colour, especially for a guy with a habit. I ain't comin out alive.

I was about to try and calm him, but it seemed that he wasn't far off the mark. Three black guys came over to us. They'd been watching and listening.

— Hey brother, you hang around with this trash, you get what comes around to you, one guy scoffed. We were on a kicking. The guys started on about skag and dealers, working themselves up to unleash their fury on us. The kicking the whites had given the one-eared transvestite had obviously whetted their appetite.

It was cops to the rescue. As they grabbed us and crudely pushed us along, I thought about the frying pan and the fire. We were taken back into separate interview rooms. There were no chairs in the room so I sat on a table. I was made to wait for a long time.

I sprang up as two pigs came in and joined me. They brought in some chairs. A silver-haired but still fresh-faced pig told me to sit down. — Who gave you the stuff? C'mon, Jock. Euan, isn't it? You ain't a dealer. Who's knocking this gear out? he asked, his eyes filled with lazy tired compassion. He looked like a sound guy.

THEY'VE GOT FUCK ALL ON ME.

Another cop, stocky, bull-like and dark-haired with a kind of pudding-basin haircut snapped, — His fucking nigger friend. Old jungle-juice boy through there, innit, Jock? Well, you had better speak up, my son, cause we got the world's first black canary chirping away twenty to the dozen next door, and you would not, believe me, not like the song he is singing.

They kept this up for a while, but they couldn't get to the place in my head I'd crawled into.

Then one of them pulled out a bag of white powder. It looked good gear.

— Little kiddies over in the school been using this gear. Who's been giving it to em, Euan? Silver Dream boy asks.

THEY'VE GOT FUCK ALL ON ME.

— Ah jist use now and again. Ah've no goat enough for masel, nivir mind any cunt else.

—I can see we'll have to get a fucking interpreter in ere. Any cunt on duty tonight speak Jock? the black-haired cunt asks. Silver Dream Machine ignores him. He carries on. — That's the thing about you fucking scumbags. You all fucking use, don't you? Nobody sells it. It just grows on fucking trees, dunnit?

— Naw, fields, I said, regretting it instantly.

— What did you fucking say? he rose, knuckles white on the table.

— Poppy fields. Opium. Grows in fields, I mumbled.

His hand goes around my neck and he squeezes. He keeps squeezing. It's like I'm watching some other cunt being choked to death. Both my hands grab his arm, but I can't break his grip. Silver does. — Leave it, George. That's enough. Get your breath back, son. My head pounds remorselessly and I feel as if my lungs will never fill up to full capacity again.

— We know the score, son; we've prepared a statement for you to sign. Now I don't want you signing something you're not happy about. Take your time. Look at it. Read it. Digest it. As I said, take your time. Anything you want to change, we can change, he cooed soothingly.

The dark guy dropped the hostility from his tone. — Give us the wog, son, and you can walk right out of here with this. The best pharmaceutical gear, eh Fred? He waved the skag tantalisingly in front of me.

— So they tell me, George. C'mon, Euan, make it easy on yourself. You seem a decent enough sort, underneath it all. You're in way over your head here, sunshine.

— Jocks, Englishmen, don't matter none, does it? We're all white men. Do time for some bleeding Congo? Wise up, Jock. One more fucking shit-skin gets banged up, wot's he to you, eh? Ain't exactly a shortage of em, is there?

The Met. The cunts with the white shirts. They did over Drew, down from Monktonhall to Orgreave for the '84 strike.

Now they wanted Donovan. Wrong skin colour. They're fitting up the daft cunt as Mister Big. This statement reads like Agatha Christie. Don and I have crossed swords but he's alright. In fact he's more of a brother than I've ever had. But what was he saying about me? Solidarity, or was he talking me down the river? This fucking statement reads like Agatha Christie. What about Ange? She's probably blabbed to every cunt to save her skin. I'm starting to hurt, really bad. If I sign up, get the skag, I can fix myself up. Tell the story of how they got the confession to the papers. THEY'VE GOT FUCK ALL ON ME. Hurt. Poison Don. TOUGH IT OOT hurt skag GIVE ME THE FUCKIN PEN they'll pit Don away, pit him away fir fuck all Agatha fuckin Christie GIVE ME THE FUCKIN PEN.

— Give me the pen.

— Knew you'd see sense, Jock.

I stuck the packet of powder, my thirty pieces of silver, in my tail. They ripped up the charge sheet.

I was free to go. When I got to the reception, Ange was sitting there. I knew that she'd sold out as well. She looked at me bitterly.

— Right, you two, a desk cop said. — On your way, and keep out of trouble. The two cops who'd interrogated me were standing behind him. I was glad to leave. Ange was so eager she walked into the plate-glass door just as the cop told us to watch out for it. There was a sickening smack as the glass and her head connected. She seemed to reel back on the balls of her feet, vibrating, like a cartoon character. I laughed through nerves, joining the guffaws of the cops.

— Stupid fucking slag, the dark cop sneered.

Ange was in some distress when I got her out into the air. Tears were streaming down her face. An egg was forming on her forehead. — You fucking grassed him up, didn't ya? DIDN'T YA? Her eyeliner was running. She looked like Alice Cooper.

It was a lame performance though. — You didnae, then?

Her silence spoke volumes, then she wearily conceded.

— Yeah, well, had to for the time being, didn't we? Mean to say, I just had to get out. I had it really bad in there.

— Ken what ye mean, I agreed. — We'll git it sorted oot later. See a lawyer. Tell the cunt we made the statements under duress. Don'll walk oot laughin. Even git compensation. Aye, git sorted, then clean up, straighten oot n see a lawyer. A spell in remand'll dae Don good in the long run. Git him cleaned up. He'll fucking thank us fir it!

I knew, even as I spoke, that it was all pie in the sky. I'd vanish; leave Don to whatever fate befell him. It just made me feel better to go through this scenario.

— Yeah, get him cleaned up, Ange agreed.

Outside the station there was a group of demonstrators. It seemed like they had been on an all-night vigil. They were protesting about the treatment of young blacks by the local Old Bill, and particularly about Earl Barratt, a guy who went into the Stokie nick one night and came back out stiffed in a placky bag. Slippy fuckers, those stairs.

I recognised a guy from the black press, *The Voice*, and made up to him. — Listen, mate, they've got a black guy in there. They've really done him over. They forced us tae sign statements.

— What's his name? the guy asked, a posh English-African voice.

— Donovan Prescott.

— The guy from the Kingsmead? The smack head?

I stood looking at him as his face hardened.

— He didn't do nothing wrong, Ange pleaded.

I pointed at him, projecting my anger at myself out towards him. — Fuckin publish and be damned, ya cunt! Doesnae matter what he is, he's goat as much right as any other fucker!

— What's your name, mon, a sidekick asked.

— What's that tae dae wi anything?

— Come down the office. Get your picture taken, the African guy smiled. He knew there was no way. I'd say nothing to nae cunt; the polis would make it open season on me.

— Dae what yis fuckin like, I said, turning away.

A large woman came up to me and started shouting: — They holdin good Christian boys in there. Leroy Ducane and Orit Campbell. Boys that never done no wrong. That's the boys we're talking about here, not some dirty drug devil.

A tall rasta with John Lennon specs waved a placard threateningly in my face. It read:

ANDS OFF DE BLACK YUTE

I turned to Ange and slid, trembling, away from the scene, a few jeers and threats ringing in my ears. I thought we were being followed for a bit. We walked off in silence and didn't speak until Dalston Kingsland Station. Paranoia City.

— Where you off ta? Ange asked.

— Ah'm gittin the overland, the North London line tae this mate Albie's in Kentish Town. Ah'm gaunny git sorted wi this pig gear, then it's down to the Bush. Civilised there, ye ken? I've fuckin had it wi Hackney, it's worse than back up the road. Too fuckin parochial. Too many self-righteous nosey cunts. Isolated, that's its problem. Nae tube. No enough social contact wi the rest ay the Smoke. A fuckin urban backwater.

I was ranting. Sick and ranting.

— I gotta come with ya. The flat's fucked. It'll be torched by now. The pigs wouldn't bother to secure the door.

I didn't want Ange in tow; she had the bad luck virus really bad. Bad luck is usually transmitted by close proximity to habitual sufferers. There was little I could do or say, however, as the train pulled up and we boarded it, sitting opposite each other in crushed, sick silence.

As the train started I stole a glance at her. I hope she didn't expect me to sleep with her. I'm not into sex right now. Maybe Albie would, if she wanted it. It was a disturbing thought, but only because all thought on matters external to me was disturbing. I'd soon be free from it all though; free from its niggling persistence, I thought, fingering the packet in my trouser pocket.

VAT '96

Fiona had been hassling Valerie to get us to come for a meal at her and Keith's for an indecently long period of time. We'd let things slide, the way people do, but eventually we got embarrassed making excuses and it seemed less hassle to actually set a date and go round to their place one evening.

We found Fiona in high spirits. She'd gained a promotion in her job which was in corporate insurance, selling policies to big businesses. Selling policies at that level was ninety percent public relations, which, in turn, as any candid PR person will tell you, is ninety-five percent hospitality and five percent information. The problem with Fiona was, like many career-minded people, she couldn't switch off her occupational role and could therefore be a crushing bore.

— Come in! Wonderful to see you! Gosh! Gorgeous outfit, Val! Where did you get it? Crawford, you're putting on the beef. It suits you though. Has he been doing weights, Val? *Have* you been doing weights, Crawford? You're looking great, both of you! I'm going to get some drinks. Vodka and tonic for you, Val, sit down, sit down, I want to hear all your adventures, everything, gosh, have I got some things to tell you . . . I suppose you want a Jack Daniels, Crawford?

— Eh, a can of beer would do fine.

— Oh, beer. Oh. Sorry. Gosh. We're all out of beer. Oh God. Crawford and his beer!

After making a fuss, she ticked me off for the cardinal sin of asking for a beer. I settled for a Jack Daniels, which Fiona had got in *especially* for me.

— Oh Val, gosh, I must tell you about this amazing guy I met . . . Fiona began, before noticing our surprise and discomfort.

We didn't really have to say: Where's Keith? as our eyes must have done the talking for us.

— Gosh, I don't quite know how to put this. Some rather bad news on the Keithy-weithy-woo's front, I'm afraid. She crossed the spacious room and lifted the cover from a glass tank which stood against the wall. She clicked on a light at the side of the tank and said, — Wakey, wakey, Valerie and Crawford are here!

At first I thought it was a fish tank, that Keith had just shot the craw, and that Fiona, devastated, had transferred her emotional energy onto pets in the form of some tropical fish. With the benefit of retrospect, it was always an unlikely notion.

Then I noted that the tank had a head inside it. A human head, disembodied, decapitated. Moreover, the head seemed alive. I moved closer. The eyes in the head were moving. The hair was spread around it, Medusa-like, made weightless by the watery, yellow fluid it was immersed in. Various pipes, tubes and wires were going into the head, mainly at the neck, but also at other points. Under the tank was a control console, with various dials, switches and lights.

— Keith . . . I stammered.

The head winked at me.

— Don't expect much in the way of conversation, Fiona said. She looked down at the tank, — Poor darling. He can't speak. No lungs, you see. She kissed the tank, then fussed at the smudge of lipstick she'd left.

— What happened to him? Valerie took one step forward and two steps back.

— This machine keeps him alive. Wonderful, isn't it? It cost us four hundred and thirty-two thousand pounds. She mouthed the figure with a slow, conspirital deliberation and feigned shock. — I know, I know, she continued, — you're wondering how we can afford it.

— Actually, I said icily, — we were wondering what happened to Keith.

— Oh gosh yes, so sorry! It must be a hell of a shock to you. Keith was tearing down the M25 towards Guildford when the Porsche left the road. Tyre blow-out. Apparently, the car bounced across a couple of lanes, over the crush-barrier and straight into the on-coming traffic. So there's a head-on with this huge artic; the Porsche was a complete write-off, as you'd expect. Keith was almost finished; well in a sense he was. Poor Keithy-weithy-woo's. She looked down at the tank, appearing slightly strained and sad for the first time.

— The health-care company man said to me: In a sense, your husband is dead. His body has been smashed to pieces. Most of his major organs are useless. However, his head and brain are still intact. We have a new machine which has been developed in Germany and pioneered in the States. We'd like your consent to give Keith treatment. It's very costly, but we can do a deal on the life insurance because he's technically dead. It's a difficult question, the health-care man said, and we'll leave the ethics of it to the philosophers. After all, that's why we pay our taxes to have them sit and deliberate in their ivory towers. That was what he said. I rather liked that. Anyway, he told me that their legal people still had a few i's to dot and t's to cross, but they were confident of, as he put it, getting a result. Do we have your consent, he asked me. Well, gosh, what could I say?

I looked at Val, then down at Keith. There wasn't much to say. Perhaps some day, with the advances in medical science, they'd find a body with a useless damaged head and be able to do a transplant. There's no shortage of them; I was thinking of various politicians. I assumed that finding a healthy body to attach the head to was the reason for this sordid and bizarre exercise. I didn't really want to know.

We sat down to the meal. Fiona might have said the evening was a success, like a work-based task or a project which had to be completed. There were one or two minor blunders, like when I refused a glass of wine.

— I'm driving, Fiona. I'd better screw the nut . . . I looked at what was left of Keith in the tank and mouthed an apology. His eyes flickered.

While Fiona was darting around, in and out of the kitchen, Valerie bade her to sit down and relax. She almost told her she was running around like a headless chicken, but managed to change it to blue-arsed fly.

However, the evening was not too excruciating and the meal was edible. We made small talk for the rest of the night. As we got ready to go I meekly and self-consciously gave Keith the thumbs up sign. He winked again.

Valerie whispered to Fiona in the hallway, — One thing you didn't tell us, who's this super new man?

— Oh gosh . . . it's so strange how things work out. He's the chap from the health-care company who suggested the treatment for Keith. Gosh, Val, he's such a ram. The other day he just grabbed me, threw me down on the couch and had me right there and then . . . She put her hand to her mouth and looked at me. — Oh gosh! I'm not embarrassing you, Crawford, am I?

— Yes, I lied, unconvincingly.

— Good! she said cheerfully, then swept us back into the room. — One last thing I need your advice on: do you think that Keithy-kins would look better on the other side of the room, next to the CD unit?

Val gazed nervously at me.

— Yes, I began, noting that the couch was presently positioned directly opposite Keith's tank, — I think he definitely would.

A SOFT TOUCH

It wis good fir a while wi Katriona, but she did wrong by me. And that's no jist something ye can forget; no jist like that. She came in the other day, intae the pub, while ah was oan the bandit likes. It was the first time ah'd seen her in yonks.

— Still playing the bandit, John, she sais, in that radge, nasal sortay voice she's goat.

Ah wis gaunny say something like, naw, ah'm fuckin well swimming at the Commie Pool, but ah jist goes: — Aye, looks like it.

— No goat the money to get ays a drink, John? she asked ays. Katriona looked bloated: mair bloated than ever. Maybe she wis pregnant again. She liked being up the stick, liked the fuss people made. Bairns she had nae time fir but she liked being up the stick. Thing wis, every time she wis, people made less ay a thing about it than they did the time before. It goat boring; besides, people kent what she wis like.

— You in the family wey again, ah asked, concentrating oan getting a nudge oan the bandit. A set ay grapes. That'll dae me.

Gamble.

Collect.

Hit collect.

Tokens. Eywis fuckin tokens. Ah thought Colin sais tae ays that the new machine peyed cash.

— Is it that obvious, Johnny? she goes, lifting up her checked blouse and pulling her leggings ower a mound ay gut. Ah thought ay her tits and arse then. Ah didnae look at them likes, didnae stare or nowt like that; ah jist thought ay them. Katriona had a great pair ay tits and a nice big arse. That's what ah like in a bird. Tits and arse.

— Ah'm oan the table, ah sais, moving past her, ower tae the pool. The boy fae Crawford's bakeries had beat Bri Ramage. Must be a no bad player. Ah goat the baws oot and racked up. The boy fae Crawford's seemed awright.

— How's Chantel? Katriona goes.

— Awright, ah sais. She should go doon tae ma Ma's and see the bairn. No that she'd be welcome thair mind you. It's her bairn though, and that must count fir something. Mind you, ah should go n aw. It's ma bairn n aw, but ah love that bairn. Everybody kens that. A mother though, a mother that abandons her bairn, that's no bothered aboot her bairn; that's no a mother, no a real mother. No tae me. That's a fucking slag, a slut, that's what that is. A common person as ma Ma says.

Ah wonder whae's bairn she's cairrying now. Probably Larry's. Ah hope so. It would serve the cunts right; the baith ay them. It's the bairn ah feels sorry for but. She'll leave that bairn like she left Chantel; like she left the two other bairns she's hud. Two other bairns ah nivir even kent aboot until ah saw them at oor weddin reception.

Aye, ma Ma wis right aboot her. She's common, Ma said. And no jist because she wis a Doyle. It wis her drinking; no like a lassie, Ma thought. Mind you, ah liked that. At first ah liked it, until ah got peyed oaf and the hirey's wir short. That wis me toiling. Then the bairn came. That wis when her drinking goat tae be a total pain; a total fuckin pain in the erse.

She eywis laughed at ays behind ma back. Ah'd catch sight ay her twisted smile when she thought ah wisnae looking. This wis usually when she wis wi her sisters. The three ay them would laugh when ah played the bandit or the pool. Ah'd feel them looking at me. After a while, they stopped kidding that they wirnae daein it.

Ah nivir coped well wi the bairn; ah mean as a really wee bairn like. It seemed to take everything over; aw that noise fae that wee size. So ah suppose ah went oot a lot eftir the bairn came. Maybe a bit ay it wis my fault; ah'm no saying otherwise. There wis things gaun oan wi her though. Like the time ah gied her that money.

She wis skint so ah gies her twenty notes and sais: You go oot doll, enjoy yirself. Go oot wi yir mates. Ah mind that night fine well because she goes n gits made up like a tart. Make-up, tons ay it, and that dress she wore. Ah asked her where she wis gaun dressed like that. She just stood thair, smiling at me. Where, ah sais. You wanted ays tae go out, so ah'm fuckin well gaun oot, she telt ays. Where but? ah asked. Ah mean, ah wis entitled tae ken. She just ignored ays but, ignored ays and left, laughing in ma face like a fuckin hyena.

When she came back she wis covered in love bites. Ah checked her purse when she wis oan the toilet daein a long, drunken pish. Forty quid she had in it. Ah gave her twenty quid and she came back wi forty fuckin bar in her purse. Ah wis fuckin demented. Ah goes, whit's this, eh? She just laughed at ays. Ah wanted tae check her fanny; tae see if ah could tell that she'd been shagged. She started screaming and saying that if ah touched her, her brothers would be roond. They're radge, the Doyles, every fucker in the scheme kens that. Ah'm radge, if the truth be telt, ever getting involved wi a Doyle. Yir a soft touch son, ma Ma once said. These people, they see that in ye. They ken yir a worker, they ken yir easy meat fir thum.

Funny thing was, a Doyle can dae what they like, but ah thought that if ah goat in wi the Doyles then ah could dae what ah liked. And ah could fir a bit. Nae cunt messed wi ays, ah wis well in. Then the tapping started; the bumming ay fags, drinks, cash. Then they had ays, or that cunt Alec Doyle, he had ays looking eftir stuff fir um. Drugs. No hash or nowt like that; wir talking aboot smack here.

Ah could've gone doon. Done time; fuckin years ah could have done. Fuckin years for the Doyles and thir hoor ay a sister. Anywey, ah never messed wi the Doyles. Never ever. So ah didnae touch Katriona that night and we slept in different rooms; me oan the couch, likes.

It wis jist eftir that ah started knocking aroond wi Larry upstairs. His wife had just left um and he wis lonely. For me it wis, likesay, insurance: Larry wis a nutter, one ay the few guys living in the scheme even the Doyles gied a bit ay respect tae.

Ah wis working oan the Employment Training. Painting. Ah wis daein the painting in the Sheltered Hooses fir the auld folks, like. Ah wis oot maist ay the time. Thing is when ah came back in ah'd either find Larry in oor place or her up at his. Half-fuckin-bevvied aw the time; the baith ay thum. Ah kent he wis shagging her. Then she started tae stey up thair some nights. Then she jist moved upstairs wi him aw the gither; leaving me doonstairs wi the bairn. That meant ah hud tae pack in the painting; fir the bairn's sake, like, ken?

When ah took the bairn doon tae ma Ma's or tae the shops in the go-cart, ah'd sometimes see the two ay thum at the windae. They'd be laughing at ays. One day ah gits back tae the hoose and it's been broken intae; the telly and video are away. Ah kent whae had taken thum, but thir wis nothing ah could dae. No against Larry and the Doyles.

Their noise kept me and the bairn awake. Her ain bairn. The noise ay them shagging, arguing, partying.

Then one time thir wis a knock at the door. It wis Larry. He jist pushed past ays intae the flat, blethering away in that excited, quick wey he goes on. Alright mate, he sais. Listen, ah need a wee favour. Fuckin electric cunts have only gone and cut ays off, eh.

He goes ower tae ma front windae and opens it and pulls in this plug that's swingin doon fae his front room above. He takes it and plugs it intae one ay ma sockets. That's me sorted oot, he smiles at ays. Eh, ah goes. He tells ays that he's got an extension cable wi a block upstairs but he jist needs access tae a power point. Ah tell him that he's ootay order, it's ma electric he's using and ah goes ower tae switch it oaf. He goes: See if you ivir touch that fuckin plug or that switch, you're fuckin deid, Johnny! Ah'm fuckin telling ye! He means it n aw.

Larry then starts telling ays that he still regards me and him as mates, in spite ay everything. He sais tae ays that we'll go halfers oan the bills, which ah knew then wouldnae happen. Ah sais that his bills would be higher than mine because ah've no got anything left in the hoose that uses electricity. Ah wis thinking aboot ma video and telly which ah kent he had up the stair. He goes: What's that supposed tae mean then, Johnny? Ah just goes: Nowt. He says: It better fuckin no mean nowt. Ah sais nowt eftir that because Larry's crazy; a total radge.

Then his face changed and he sortay broke intae this smile. He nodded up at the ceiling: No bad ride, eh John? Sorry tae huv tae move in thair, mate. One ay these things though, eh? Ah jist nodded. Gies a barry gam though, he sais. I felt like shite. Ma electricity. Ma woman.

Ever fucked it up the erse? he asked. Ah jist shrugged. He crosses one ay his airms ower the other one. Ah've started giein it the message that wey, he said, jist cause ah dinnae want it up the stick. Bairn daft, that cunt. Once ye git a cunt up the stick, they think thuv goat thir hand in yir poakit fir the rest ay yir puff. Yir dough's no yir ain. Isnae ma fuckin scene, ah kin tell ye. Ah'll keep ma money. Tell ye one thing, Johnny, he laughed, ah hope you've no goat AIDS or nowt like that, cause if ye huv ye'd've gied it tae me by now. Ah never use a rubber when ah shaft her up the stairs thair. No way. Ah'd rather have a fuckin wank man.

Naw, ah've no goat nowt like that, ah telt him, wishing for the first time in ma life that ah did.

Just as well, ya dirty wee cunt, Larry laughed.

Then he stretched intae the playpen and patted Chantel on the heid. Ah started tae feel sick. If he tried tae touch that bairn again, ah'd've stabbed the cunt; disnae matter whae he is. Ah jist wouldnae care. It's awright, he goes, ah'm no gaunny take yir bairn away. She wants it mind, and ah suppose that a bairn belongs wi its Ma. Thing is, John, like ah sais, ah'm no intae huving a bairn aroond the house. So yuv goat me to thank fir still huvin the bairn, think aboot it like that. He went aw upset and angry and pointed tae hisel. Think aboot it that wey before ye start making accusations aboot other people. Then he goes cheery again; this cunt can jist change like that, and sais: See that draw for the quarter-finals? The winners ay St Johnstone v. Kilmarnock. At Easter Road, likes, he smiles at ays, then twists his face aroond the room. Fuckin pit this, he sais, before turning tae go. Just as he's at the front door he stops and turns tae me. One other thing, John, if ye want a poke at it again, he points at the ceiling, jist gies a shout. A tenner tae you. Gen up, likes.

Ah mind ay aw that, cause just after it ah took the bairn tae ma Ma's. That wis that; Ma goat ontae the Social Work; goat things sorted oot. They went and saw her; she didnae want tae ken. Ah goat a kicking fir that, fae Alec and Mikey Doyle. Ah goat another yin, a bad yin, fae Larry and Mikey Doyle when ma electric wis cut oaf. They grabbed ays in the stair and dragged ays through the back. They goat ays doon and started kicking ays. Ah wis worried cause ah hud a bit ay money ah'd won fae the bandit. Ah wis shitein it in case they'd go through ma poakits. Fifteen quid ah hud taken the bandit fir. They just booted intae ays but. Booted ays and she wis screamin: KICK THE CUNT! KILL THE CUNT! OOR FUCKIN ELECTRIC! IT WIS OOR FUCKIN ELECTRICITY! HE'S GOAT MA FUCKIN BAIRN! HIS FUCKIN AULD HOOR AY A MOTHER'S GOAT MA FUCKIN BAIRN! GO BACK TAE YIR FUCKIN MA! LICK YIR MA'S FUCKIN PISS-FLAPS YA CUNT!

Thank fuck they left ays withoot checking ma poakits. Ah thoat; well, that's seekened they cunts' pusses anywey, as ah staggered tae ma Ma's tae git cleaned up. Ma nose wis broken and ah hud two cracked ribs. Ah hud tae go tae the A and E at the Infirmary. Ma sais that ah should nivir huv goat involved wi Katriona Doyle. That's easy tae say now but, ah telt her, but see if ah hudnae, jist sayin like, jist supposin ah hudnae; we would nivir huv hud Chantel, like. Yuv goat tae think aboot it that wey. Aye, right enough, ma Ma said, she's a wee princess.

The thing wis thit some cunt in the stair hud called the polis. Ah wis thinking that it could mean criminal injuries compensation money fir me. Ah gied them a false description ay two guys thit looked nowt like Larry n Mikey. But then the polis talked like they thought ah wis the criminal, that ah wis the cunt in the wrong. Me, wi a face like a piece ay bad fruit, two cracked ribs and a broken nose.

Her and Larry moved away fae upstairs eftir that and ah just thought: good riddance tae bad rubbish. Ah think the council evicted them fir arrears; rehoosed them in another scheme. The bairn wis better oaf at ma Ma's and ah goat a job, a proper job, no just oan some training scheme. It wis in a supermarket; stackin shelves and checking stock levels, that kind ay thing. No a bad wee number: bags ay overtime. The money wisnae brilliant but it kept ays oot ay the pub, ken wi the long hours, like.

Things are gaun awright. Ah've been shaggin one or two burds lately. There's this lassie fae the supermarket, she's mairried, but she's no wi the guy. She's awright, a clean lassie, like. Then there's the wee burds fae roond the scheme, some ay them are jist at the school. A couple ay thum come up at dinnertime if ah'm oan backshift. Once ye git tae ken one, yir well in. They aw come roond; just fir somewhere tae muck aboot cause thirs nowt fir thum tae dae. Ye might git a feel or a gam. Like ah sais, one or two, especially that wee Wendy, thir game fir a poke. Nae wey dae ah want tae git involved again aw heavy like but.

As fir her, well, this is the first ah've seen ay her fir ages.

— How's Larry? ah ask, gaun doon tae connect wi a partially covered stripe. One guy's squinting his eye and saying that's no oan. The Crawford's bakery boy goes: — Hi you! Admiral Fuckin Nelson thair! Let the boy play his ain game. Nae coaching fae the touchline!

— Oh him, she goes as the cue clips the stripe and heads towards the boatum cushion. — He's gaun back inside. Ah'm back at ma Ma's.

Ah jist looked at her.

— He found oot that ah wis pregnant and he jist fucked off, she sais. — He's been steying wi some fucking slut, she goes. Ah felt like saying, ah fuckin well ken that, ah'm staring her in the fuckin face.

But ah says nowt.

Then her voice goes aw that high, funny way, like it eywis goes when she wants something. — Why don't we go oot fir a drink the night, Johnny? Up the toon likes? We wir good, Johnny, good the gither you n me. Everybody said, mind? Mind we used tae go tae the Bull and Bush up Lothian Road, Johnny?

— Ah suppose so, ah sais. Thing wis, ah supposed ah still loved her; ah suppose ah never really stoaped. Ah liked gaun up the Bull and Bush. Ah wis always a bit lucky oan the bandit up there. It's probably a new one now though; but still.

THE LAST RESORT
ON THE ADRIATIC

I never supposed for the love of me that it would all be so vivid;
it makes what I plan to do feel just right. I mean, I almost expect
to see Joan on the boat, to just sort of run into her on deck, in
the dining-room, or the bar, or even the casino. When I get to
thinking about her in that way, my heart races and I feel giddy
and generally have to retire to the cabin. When I turn the key I
even think that I might find her there, perhaps in bed, reading.
It's ridiculous I know, the whole thing, just blessed ridiculous.

I've been on this liner now for two weeks; two lonely weeks.
The sight of people having fun can be so hurtful, so offensive,
when you feel like I do. All I do is wander around the ship; as if
I'm looking for something. That and the weights, of course.
Surely I don't expect to see Joan here; surely not? I can't settle. I
can't lie on the deck with Harold Robbins or Dick Francis or
Desmond Bagley. I can't sit at the bar and get drunk. I can't
engage in any of these trivial conversations which take place
concerning the weather or the itinerary. I've walked out of two
movies in the cinema. *Dead Again*, with that British chap playing the American detective. Terrible film. There was another
one with that American fellow, the white-haired chap who used
to be funny but isn't anymore. Perhaps that's just me: a lot of
thing aren't funny anymore.

I go to my cabin and prepare my sports bag for another
excursion to the gym. The only blessed place I've any interest in
going to.

— You must be the fittest man on this ship, the instructor says to me. I just smile. I don't want to make conversation with this fellow. Funny fellow, if you know what I mean. Nothing against them myself, live and let live and all that, but I don't want to talk to anyone right now, let alone some blessed nancy boy.

— Never out of this place, he persists, giving a quick nod to a fat, puffing red-faced man on an exercise bike, — are you Mister Banks?

— Excellent facilities, I reply curtly, surveying the free weights and picking up two hand dumb-bells.

Thankfully the instructor chappie has noticed an overweight lady in a scarlet leotard attempting to do sit-ups. — No no no Mrs Coxton! Not like that! You're putting too much of a strain on your back. Sit further up and bend those knees. Forty-five degrees. Lovely. And one . . . and two . . .

I take a couple of weights from the dumb-bell and surreptitiously stick them into my sports bag. I go through the motions, but I don't need exercise. I'm fit enough. Joan always said that I had a good body; wiry, she used to say. That's what a lifetime in the building trade, combined with sober habits does for you. I have to concede that there is a bit of a paunch, as I've let myself go since Joan. Seemed no point. I drink more now than I've ever done, since the retirement. Well, I was never one for the golf.

Back in my cabin I lie down and drift off into that realm between thought and sleep, thinking of Joan. She was such a wonderful and decent woman, all you could hope for in a wife and mother.

Why Joan? Why, my darling, why? These could have been the best years of our life. Paul's at university, Sally's living in the nurses' home. They finally left the nest, Joan. We would have had it all to ourselves. The way they coped though, Joan, they were a credit to you, both of them. A credit to us. Me? Well I died with you, Joanie. I'm just a blessed ghost.

I'm not asleep. I'm awake and talking to myself and crying. Ten years after Joan.

At dinner I'm alone at the table with Marianne Howells. The Kennedys, Nick and Patsy, a very nice outgoing young couple, have not shown up for the meal. It's a deliberate ploy. Patsy Kennedy has a conspiratorial eye. Marianne and I are alone for the first time on the cruise. Marianne: unmarried, here to get away from her own bereavement, the recent death of her widowed mother.

— So I'm to have you all to myself, Jim, she said, in a manner far too jocular and self-deprecating to be flirtatious. There is no doubt, though, that Marianne is a fine-looking woman. Someone ought to have married a woman like that. A waste. No, that's a dreadful way to think. Old chauvinistic Jim Banks at it again. Perhaps that's the way Marianne wanted it, perhaps she got the best from life that way. Perhaps if Joanie and I hadn't . . . No. The seafood, the seafood.

— Yes, I smile, — this seafood salad is excellent. Still, if you can't get good seafood at sea, where can you get it, eh?

Marianne grins and we small-talk for a bit. Then she says, — It's a tragedy about Yugoslavia.

I'm wondering whether she means because we can't land there because of the troubles, or because of the misery the troubles have inflicted on people. I decide to plump for the compassionate interpretation. Marianne seems a caring sort. — Yes, terrible suffering. Dubrovnik was one of the highlights of the trip when I was here with Joan.

— Oh yes, your wife . . . what happened to her, if you don't mind me asking?

— Eh, an accident. If it's all the same to you, I'd rather not talk about it, I said, shoving a forkful of that lettuce into my mouth. I'm sure it's a garnish rather than there to be eaten, something to do with where it's positioned on the plate. I was never one for etiquette. Joanie, you'd have kept me right.

— I'm really sorry, Jim, she says.

I smile. The accident. On this boat, on this cruise. An accident? No.

She'd been down for a while. Depressed. The change in life,

or who can say what? I don't know why. That's the most horrible thing about it, I don't know why. I thought that the cruise would do her the world of good. It even seemed to, for a while. Just as we got towards the end of the Adriatic, on the way back into the Med, she took the pills and just slipped off the side of the boat into the night. Into the sea. I woke up alone; I've been alone ever since. It was my fault, Joan, the whole blessed thing. If I'd tried to understand how you felt. If I hadn't booked this bloody cruise. That's stupid old bloody idiot Jim Banks. Take the easy way out. I should have sat you down and talked, talked, and talked again. We could have sorted it all out, Joan.

I feel a hand on mine. Marianne's. There's tears in my eyes, like I'm some damned funny fella.

— I've upset you, Jim. I'm really so sorry.

— No, not at all, I smile.

— I really understand, you know I do. Mother . . . she was so difficult, she says. Now she's starting the waterworks. What a blessed pair we are. — I did all I could. I had my chances to make a different life for myself. I didn't really know what I wanted. A woman always has to choose, Jim, choose between marriage and children and a career. Always at some point. I don't know. Mother was always there, always needing. She won by default. The career girl became the old maid, you see.

She seemed so hurt and upset. My hand stiffened on hers. The way she looks at the floor and her head suddenly rises as her eyes meet mine: it reminds me of Joan.

— Don't sell yourself short, I tell her. — You're an exceptionally brave lady and a very beautiful one.

She smiles, more composed now, — You're a real gent, Jim Banks, and you say the nicest things.

All I can do is smile back.

I was enjoying being with Marianne. It had been a long time since I'd been like this with a woman. Since I'd had that intimacy. We talked all night. No subjects were taboo and I was able to talk about Joan without seeming maudlin and bringing the company down, as would have happened had the Kennedys been present. People don't want to listen to all that on holiday. However, Marianne, with her bereavement, could relate to it.

I talked and I talked, nonsense mostly, but to me beautiful, painful memories. I'd never talked like this to anyone before.
— I remember on the boat with Joanie. I got into a terrible situation. There were some Dutch folk, lovely people, at the table next to us. We shared a table with a rather stand-offish French chap and a lovely Italian girl. Real film-star looks. Strangely, the French chap wasn't interested. I think he may have been, well, that way, if you know what I mean. Anyway, this was a proper old League of Nations. The thing was that we had this elderly couple from Worcester who did not like Germans one bit, thinking back to the war years and all that stuff. Well, I feel that those things are best left in the past. So old Jim Banks here decided to play the peacemaker . . .

God, how I rabbitted on. My inhibitions seemed to dissolve with every sip of the wine, and we were soon on the second bottle, Marianne nodding conspiratorially at me as I ordered it. After the meal we proceeded to the bar where we had a few more drinks.

— I've really enjoyed myself tonight, Jim. I just wanted to tell you that, she said, smiling.

— It's been one of the best nights I've had . . . in years, I told her. I was almost going to say, since Joanie. It has though. This wonderful lady has made me feel blessed human again. She really is a fine person.

She held my hand as we sat looking into each other's eyes for a few seconds.

I cleared my throat with a sip of scotch. — One of the great things about getting older, Marianne, is that the impending presence of the grim reaper concentrates the mind somewhat. I'm very attracted to you Marianne, and please don't be offended by this, but I'd like to spend the night with you.

— I'm not offended, Jim. I think that would be marvellous, she glowed.

This made me a little coy. — Might be somewhat less than marvellous. I'm a little bit out of practice for this sort of thing.

— They say it's a little like swimming or riding a bike, she simpered, a little drunk.

Well, if that was the case, Old Jim Banks was about to get back in the saddle after a gap of ten years. We went to her room.

Despite the alcohol, I had no problem in getting an erection. Marianne pulled off her dress to expose a body that would have done justice to some women many decades, never mind years, younger. We embraced for a little while, before slipping under the duvet and making love, first slowly and tenderly, then with increasing passion. I was lost in it. Her nails scored the flesh on my back and I was screaming, — By God Joanie, by God . . .

She froze like a stiff corpse underneath me, and punched the mattress in frustration as tears bubbled up from her eyes. I moved off her. — I'm sorry, I half moaned, half sobbed.

She sat up and shrugged, staring into space. She spoke in a dulled, metallic tone, but without bitterness, as if conducting a cool and dispassionate epitaph. — I find a man I care about and when he makes love to me he's imagining I'm somebody else.

— It wasn't like that, Marianne . . .

She started sobbing; I put my arm around her. Well, Jim Banks, I thought, you've got yourself into another right blessed muddle-up here, haven't you?

— I'm sorry, she said.

I started to pull my clothes on. — I'd better go, I said. I walked towards the door, then turned back. — You're a wonderful woman, Marianne. I hope you find someone who can give you what you deserve. Old Banksie here, I pointed sadly at myself, — I'm just kidding myself. I'm a one-woman man. I exited, leaving her with her tears. I now had my business to attend to. There was to be no reprieve after all. I knew it was for the best; I knew it now more than ever. The kids, Paul and Sally, were strong enough. They'd understand.

Back at my cabin I left Marianne a note. I'd left letters for the kids in the ship's mail with a videotaped recording, explaining what I intended to do. The note to Marianne didn't say much. I just told her that I was here for a specific purpose; I was sorry we'd got so involved. I had to fulfil my destiny, that was how I saw it.

According to the maps I consulted we were in the Adriatic now, no doubt about it. I tied the length of cord through the holes in the middle of the weights, and slung it over my shoulder. It was difficult to get the stretchy tracksuit bottoms over the weights and the rest of my clothes on. I fought into my waterproofs, barely able to walk by the time I left my cabin.

I slipped along the empty deck, struggling to remain erect. The sea was calm and the night balmy. A couple of lovers enjoying the moonlight looked suspiciously at me as I shuffled past them to my spot on the starboard side. Ten years, almost to the day, Joan, when you slipped out and away from me, away from the pain and hurt. I lift one leg, with an almighty effort, over the barrier. I'll just get my blessed breath back, take one last long look at the purple sky, then allow my weight to shift and I'll spill from this rail into the Adriatic.

SEXUAL DISASTER QUARTET

A GOOD SON

He was a good son, and like all good sons, he really loved his mother. In fact, he completely worshipped the woman.

Yet he couldn't make love to her; not with his father sitting there, watching them.

He got out of bed and threw a dressing-gown around his self-conscious nakedness. As he passed his father on his way out of the room, he heard the old man say: Aye Oedipus, yir a complex fucker right enough.

SEXUAL DISASTER QUARTET

THE CRUEL BASTARD AND THE SELFISH FUCKER
GET IT ON

She was a cruel bastard; he was a selfish fucker. They literally bumped into each other one night in a Grassmarket pub. They were vaguely acquainted from somewhere neither could remember. Or at least that was what they told themselves and each other.

She was highly insulting, but he didn't mind as he was indifferent to everything except the eighty shilling he was tipping down his throat. They decided to go back to her place for a shag. He didn't have a place of his own; as his parents did everything for him, he saw little point in getting one.

Sitting up in bed, she watched him undressing. Her face hardened in a contemptuous scowl as he removed his purple boxer-shorts. — Who dae ye expect tae satisfy wi that? she asked.

— Masel, he said, getting into bed beside her.

After the event, she bitterly disparaged his performance with a vitriol which would have torn the fragile sexual ego of most men to shreds. He scarcely heard a word she said. His final thoughts as he drifted into a drunken sleep were concerned with breakfast. He hoped she had plenty of provisions in and that she made a good fry-up.

Within a few weeks they were living together. People say it seems to be working out.

LOTS OF LAUGHTER AND SEX

You said, when we embarked on this great adventure together, that lots of laughter was essential in a relationship.

I agreed.

You also made the point that a great deal of sex was of equal importance.

Again, I agreed. Wholeheartedly.

In fact I remember your exact words: laughter and sex are the barometers of a relationship. This was the statement you made, if I remember correctly.

Don't get me wrong. I couldn't agree more. But no at the same time, ya fuckin cow.

ROBERT K. LAIRD: A SEXUAL HISTORY

Rab's nivir hud a ride in ehs puff; perr wee cunt. Disnae seem too bothered, mind you.

SNUFF

The television screen flickered luminously in the darkness as the credits at the end of the movie came up. Not long to go now, Ian Smith noted, as he reached across to his dog-eared copy of *Halliwell's Film Guide*. With a yellow fluorescent pen, he highlighted the boldly-typed entry: *Goodfellas*. In small capital letters he wrote in the margin:

8. BRILLIANT, ANOTHER MESMERISING PERFORMANCE
FROM DE NIRO. SCORSESE THE UNDISPUTED MASTER OF
HIS GENRE.

He then removed the video cassette and inserted another, *Mad Max Beyond Thunderdome*. Fast-forwarding it past the trailers, he scrutinised the grimly serious face of the Radio One disc jockey who described the certification of the film. Finding the appropriate entry in this most up-to-date but already well-worn copy of *Halliwell's*, Smith was tempted to highlight it now, prior to viewing the film. He resisted this impulse, reasoning that you had to actually watch the movie first. There were so many things that could happen to stop you. You could be disturbed by the phone or a knock at the door. The video could malfunction and chew up the tape. You could be struck down by a massive cardiac arrest. Such happenings were, he considered, equally unlikely for him, nonetheless he held to his superstition.

They called him the Video Kid in the office where he worked, but only behind his back. He had no real friends and had the sort of personality which defied familiarity. It was not that he was unpleasant or aggressive, far from it. Ian Smith, the

Video Kid, was just extremely self-contained. Although he had worked with the Council's Planning Department for four years, most of his colleagues knew little about him. He did not social-ise with them, and the extent of his self-disclosure was extremely limited. As Smith was not interested in his workma-tes, they reciprocated, not being concerned enough about this unobtrusive person to detect a hint of enigma in his silence.

Every evening, Smith rented between two and four video-tapes at the shop he passed on the way home from work. The actual number rented depended on what was on television, and as a subscriber to satellite he had a lot of options. Additionally, he enjoyed membership of several specialist video clubs, which catered for old, rare, foreign, arthouse and pornographic films which were unobtainable from the shops but listed in *Halliwell's*. His dinner-break was usually spent making up a schedule of forthcoming viewings, which, once compiled, was never devi-ated from.

While Ian Smith occasionally watched a few soaps and a bit of football on Sky Sport, this was usually just filling in time if there was nothing satisfactory on offer on Sky's Movie Channel, in the video shop, or arriving through the post. He always kept the most recent *Halliwell's Film Guide*, religiously crossing off every film he had seen with a yellow highlighter pen, also giving it his own rating on an advancing scale of 0–10. Additionally, he kept a notebook to list any offerings too new to find their way into the 'bible'. Every time a new edition of *Halliwell's* came out, Smith would have to transfer the highlighted ticks across to the new text and throw the old one away. He often felt compelled to spend his lunch hours on this mundane undertaking. There were now very few films left unhighlighted.

As a broader concept, beyond the daily routine of work, viewing and sleep; time became insignificant for Smith. The weeks and months which flew by could not be delineated by changes or events in his life. He had almost complete control over the narrow process he imposed upon his existence.

Sometimes, however, Smith would become disengaged from

the film and he would be forced to contemplate this life of his. This happened during *Mad Max Beyond Thunderdome*. The film was a disappointment. The first two Max efforts were a couple of low-budget cult classics. The sequel was an attempt to give Max the Hollywood treatment. It struggled to hold Smith's attention, the span of which always decreased as the night wore on. But it had to be watched; it was another mark-off in his book and there were not many left now. Tonight he was tired. Though anything but a reflective person, when Smith was tired, thoughts he normally repressed could spill into the realm of conscious cerebral activity.

His wife had left him almost a year ago. Smith sat in his armchair, trying to allow himself to feel the loss, the pain, yet somehow he couldn't. He could feel nothing, only a vague uncomfortable guilt at having no feelings. He thought of her face, of having sex with her, and he aroused himself and managed to come through minimal masturbation, but he could feel nothing else beyond the resultant reduction in tension. His wife seemed not to exist beyond a transient image in his mind, indistinguishable from the ones he relieved himself to in the more pornographic films he rented. He had never achieved climax as easily when he had actually been with her.

Ian Smith forced his attention back to the film. Something in his mind always seemed to shut down a line of thought before it could cause him discomfort; a form of psychic quality control.

Smith did not like to talk about his hobby at work; after all, he did not really like to talk. One day in the office, however, Mike Flynn caught him compulsively highlighting his *Halliwell's*, and made a comment which Smith didn't quite catch, but he did pick up the derisive laughter from his colleagues. Stirred, he found himself, somewhat to his surprise, rabbitting uncharacteristically, almost uncontrollably, about his passion and the extent of it.

— You must like videos, Yvonne Lumsden said, raising her eyebrows suggestively.

— Always liked films, Smith shrugged.

— Tell me, Ian, Mike asked him, — what will you do when you've seen all the films listed? What happens after you've marked off the lot?

These words hit Smith hard in the chest. He couldn't think straight. His heart pounded.

What happens after you've marked off the lot?

Julie had left him because she found him boring. She went to hitchhike around Europe with a promiscuous friend whom Smith mildly resented as a contributory factor in the break-up of his marriage. The only consolation was Julie's praise for his sexual prowess. While he had always found it difficult to come with someone, she had climax after climax, often in spite of herself. Afterwards, Julie would feel inadequate, worrying at her inability to give her husband that ultimate pleasure. Insecurity defeated rationality and forced her to look inwards; she did not consider the simple truth that the man she had married was an aberration in terms of male sexuality. — Wasn't it good for you? she'd ask him.

— Great, Smith would reply, trying, and invariably failing, to project passion through his indifference. Then he'd say: — Well, it's time for lights out.

Julie hated the words 'lights out' more than any other ones which came from his lips. They made her almost physically sick. Smith would click off the bedside lamp and fall into an instant deep sleep. She would wonder why she stuck with him. The answer lay within her throbbing sex and her exhausted body; he was hung like a horse and he could fuck all night.

That wasn't enough though. One day Julie casually walked into the sitting-room where Smith was preparing to view a video, and said: — Ian, I'm leaving you. We're incompatible. I don't mean sexually, the problem isn't in bed. In fact you've given me more orgasms than any of the other . . . I mean what I'm trying to say is, you're good in bed, but useless everywhere else. There's no excitement in our lives, we never talk . . . I mean . . . oh, what's the use? I mean to say, you couldn't change, even if you wanted to.

Smith calmly replied: — Are you sure you've thought this one out? It's a big step to take.

All the while, the prospect of being able to install that satellite dish his wife had resisted gnawed excitingly at the back of his mind.

He waited until a decent period had passed, then, convinced that she was not returning, had the dish fitted.

Smith's social life had not exactly been hectic prior to Julie's departure and the purchase of the satellite dish. After these events, however, the minimal and token social ties he had with the outside world were severed. Apart from going to work he became a recluse. He stopped visiting his parents on Sundays. They were relieved, weary at attempting to force conversation, jumpy in the embarrassed silences to which Smith seemed oblivious. His infrequent visits to the local pub also ceased. His brother Pete and his best friend Dave Carter (or at any rate the best man at his wedding) didn't really notice his absence. One local said: — Never see what's his name in here these days.

— Aye, said Dave. — Don't know what he's up to.

— Pimping, protection racketeering, contract killings, probably, Pete laughed sardonically.

In the tenement block where Smith lived, the Marshal children would be screaming, fraying their distraught and isolated mother's nerves further. Peter and Melody Syme would be screwing with all the passion of a couple just back from honeymoon. Old Mrs McArthur would be making tea or fussing over her orange and white cat. Jimmy Quinn next door would have some mates round and they would be smoking hash. Ian Smith would be watching videos.

At work, one particular newspaper story was bothering people. A six-year-old girl named Amanda Heatley had been snatched from the pavement into a car a few yards from her school.

— What sort of animal does that? Mike Flynn asked, in a state of indignant rage. — If ah could git ma hands oan the bastard . . . he let his voice tail off menacingly.

— He obviously needs help, Yvonne Lumsden said.

— Ah'd gie um help. A bullet through his skull.

They argued from their polarised positions, one focusing on the fate of the kidnapped girl, the other on the motivations of the kidnapper. At an impasse, they turned to an uncomfortable looking Smith in appeal.

— What do you think, Ian? Yvonne asked.

— Dunno. Just hope they find the kid unharmed.

Yvonne thought that Ian Smith's tone indicated that he didn't hold out much hope of that.

It was shortly after this discussion that Smith decided to ask Yvonne out. She said no. He was neither surprised nor disappointed. In fact, he only asked her out because he felt that it was something he should do, rather than something he wanted to. An invitation to a cousin's wedding had come through the post. Smith felt that he should attend with a partner. As usual, he went home to a weekend of videos. He resolved that he would decline the invitation, and cite illness as an excuse. There was a bug doing the rounds.

That Saturday evening, his brother Pete came up to see him. Smith heard the bell but chose to ignore it. He could not be bothered freezing the action on *Point Break* as it was at a key scene where undercover FBI agent Keanu Reeves was about to be befriended by surfer Patrick Swayze and they were going to join forces against some formidable-looking adversaries. The next evening, the bell went again. Smith ignored it, immersed as he was in *Blue Velvet*.

A note dropped through the door, which was not discovered by Smith until Monday morning, when he was ready to leave for work. It told him that his mother had had a stroke and was seriously ill. He phoned Pete up.

— How's Mum? he asked, guilty at not being able to instil more concern into his tone.

— She died last night, Pete's flat, hollow voice told him.

— Aw . . . right . . . Smith said, then put down the phone. He didn't know what else to say.

In the year since he got satellite television, Ian Smith had gained three stones in weight, just by sitting in the armchair and munching biscuits, chocolate bars, ice-creams, fish suppers, pizzas, Chinese takeaways, and convenience snacks from the microwave. He had even started to take the odd day off work on the sick so that he could watch videos in the morning and afternoon. However, on the morning he learned of his mother's death, he went into work.

There was a soft ache in his chest at the funeral; a contrast to the shell-shocked grief of his brother and the disbelieving hysteria displayed by his older sister. Smith's pain was at its most acute when he thought of the love she'd given him as a child. However, images from films kept interspersing with those memories, anaesthetising the pain. Try as he might, Smith was unable to sustain these reflections to an extent that their poignancy might hurt him. As soon as the opportunity presented itself, he sloped off from the funeral and headed home via two video rental shops, his chest pounding and mouth salivating in anticipation of being able to tick off another couple of entries from *Halliwell's*. He was getting closer.

Over the days that followed, he took advantage of his bereavement by using the special leave to watch more videos. He hardly slept, staying up all night and most of the day. On occasion, he took amphetamine, scored from his neighbour Jimmy Quinn, in order to keep him awake. His mind was not at its customary ease, however; images of Julie seemed to be sandwiched between his every conscious thought. He never thought of his mother; it was as if she had never existed. Eventually he came to inhabit a zone which embraced conscious thought, dreams and the passive viewing of the television screen, but where the boundaries between these states could not be easily discerned.

It became too much, even for Ian Smith. Barring work, his only forays outside his flat had been quick visits to the video shops and the supermarket. One evening he switched off the video and went for a walk by the Water of Leith, unsettled and unable to concentrate on his evening's viewing. A row of cherry blossoms by the landscaped bank of the stagnant river gave off a pleasing aroma. Smith strolled along as the twilight began to give way to darkness. His steps disturbed a group of youths in hooded tops who dropped their voices and sneaked furtive then brazenly threatening looks at him. Smith, blind to them in his thoughts, strode on. He passed the wheezing alcoholics on the benches, whose dislocated growls snapped at demons remembered or imagined; the empty cans of superlager; the broken glass; the used condoms and the dog shite. A hundred yards away an old stone bridge arched darkly across the still, rancid waters.

Someone stood on the bridge. Smith increased his stride, observing her figure as it came into focus. Approaching her, he stood for a moment watching her smoke a cigarette. Her sallow face buckled inwards as she inhaled powerfully. It gave him the strange impression that the tobacco was the consumer and she was the depreciating product: with every puff she was being used up. On reflection, he considered, that impression was spot on.

— Ye lookin fir a date? she asked him, without any charm in her voice.

— Eh, aye, ah suppose, Smith shrugged. He really didn't know.

Her eyes travelled down his body and she quickly coughed out a short list of terms and conditions. Smith nodded in the same vague acquiescence. They walked silently back to his flat, taking a narrow road bounded by disused warehouses on one side and a large stone wall on the other. A car trundled slowly over the cobblestones, pulling up at the solitary figure of another woman, who, after a short conversation, disappeared into it.

At Smith's flat they went straight to the bedroom and undressed. The stale stench of her breath did not stop him from kissing her. She never brushed her teeth because she hated men kissing her. They could do anything except that. Kissing was the only thing which prevented her from forgetting what she was

doing, which made her confront its hideous reality. Smith, however, had no intention of kissing her.

He mounted her thin body, at first uncomfortable on her
jagged bonyness. Her expression was frozen; her eyes clouded by
opiates or apathy. Smith saw his own countenance reflected in
hers. He forced himself through her dryness in short jabs, the
both of them gritting their teeth in pain and concentrating until
her juices began to flow. Smith found a rhythm and pumped
mechanically, all the time wondering why he was doing this.
She moved with him, bored and grudging. The minutes passed;
Smith implacably maintained his activity. After a certain length
of time had elapsed, Smith knew he would never come. His
penis seemed to grow harder but at the same time experience
a growing numbness. Expressions of shock, then denial, then
disbelief came over the woman as a demanding ache in her body
forced her reluctant mind into step with it, joining it in the
chase for the climax.

After she came, fighting to maintain her silence, he stopped,
still hard and erect. He withdrew, and made his way to his jacket
pocket where he extracted some notes and paid her. She felt
confused, and vulnerable; a failure in the only thing she had ever
been able to do successfully. She got dressed and left full of
shame, unable to make eye contact.

— Cheers then, Smith said, as she exited into the stair.

— Prick. Fuckin prick, she hissed back at him.

As far as he was concerned there was nothing more to say.

A few days after this incident, a far more significant event
took place. Smith came into the office whistling. This constituted an extrovert performance by his normal standards of
behaviour and was picked up on by his workmates.

— You're looking pleased with yourself, Ian, Mike Flynn
observed.

— Just bought a new video camera, Smith stated, then added,
with unbecoming smugness, — state of the art.

— Christ, there'll be nae stopping ye now, Ian eh? Holly-

wood here we come! Tell you what, we'll get Yvonne here to
star in a porno movie. You direct, I'll produce.

Yvonne Lumsden looked bitterly at them. She had recently
rejected clumsy, drunken advances from Mike on a night out,
and was concerned that they might be colluding against her,
nasty in rejection, reverting to adolescence, like some men
tended to do.

Mike turned to Smith and said: — No, we'd better keep
Yvonne out of it. We want it to be a box-office success, after all.
She threw a pencil eraser at him, which bounced off his forehead, causing him more alarm than he let on. Alistair, the thin,
anaemic supervisor looked over with a tetchy expression
designed to register his disapproval of this horseplay. He liked
things to be what he constantly referred to as 'ordered'.

— Alistair can be the leading man, Mike whispered, but
Smith's expression had returned to its normal state: a study in
detachment.

That evening Smith took the bus home as it was raining
heavily. Scanning the evening paper he noted that eighteen-
year-old Paul McCallum was in the Royal Infirmary intensive-
care unit, fighting for his life after being the victim of an apparently motiveless attack in the city centre yesterday evening. I
hope the boy makes it, Smith thought. He reflected that human
life has to be sacred, it has to be the most important thing in the
world. There was still no news of Amanda Heatley, the kidnapped child. Smith went to his flat, tried out the camera, then
watched another video.

The video is hard to get into. Smith's mind wanders. He tries
to make himself feel hurt, forces himself to think about Julie.
Did he love her? He thinks so. He can't be sure, because whenever that rising feeling in his chest starts, something seems to just
shut it off.

The next day Smith notes that there is nothing about the guy
Paul McCallum in the paper. He doesn't know whether this is
good or bad. What is no news? He opens *Halliwell's* and trembles
with excitement. The book has been completed. Every film

listed has been viewed and reviewed. The words that Mike Flynn had spoken at the office came back to haunt him: *What do you do when you've marked off the lot?* The highlighter pen cruises over the title: *Three Men and a Little Lady.* He briefly thinks of Amanda Heatley. One man and a little lady. Real life was often less sentimental than Hollywood. Then something hits Smith. He realises that out of all the entries, this one, the last one, is the only one he has ever ranked zero. He writes in the margin:

0. SICKENING YANK SCHMALTZ, A SEQUEL EVEN MORE NAUSEATING THAN THE ORIGINAL.

Then he wonders: surely there must have been a worse film than that. He checks the entry on the Marty Robbins produced, directed, written, starred-in and soundtracked effort *El Paso,* but no, that got one point. He checks out some of the British films, because if the British know how to do one thing, it is how to make terrible films, but even *Sammy and Rosie Get Laid* scored two points. It's time, he decides. He stands up and puts another videotape in the machine. He stares at the screen.

The video Smith is watching shows a man climbing a set of stepladders with diligence, but at the same time looking straight into the camera. His eyes are full of fear, staring out at Smith. Smith feels and mirrors his fear and gazes straight back at the screen. Still staring out, the man reaches for a rope tied like a noose, which is secured to decorative but sturdy, parallel pine beams which run across the ceiling. He puts the noose round his neck, tightens it and kicks away the stepladders. Smith feels himself being pulled into the air and experiences a disorientation as the room swings and jerks and he feels a weight crashing around his neck, choking him. He spins around in the air and catches a glimpse of the figure on the screen; kicking, swinging, dying. Smith tries to scream CUT! but he cannot make a sound. He thinks that human life is important, always sacred. He thinks this, but his arms cannot reach up to the beams to take his weight nor can they free the tightening band from around his neck. He asphyxiates; his head hangs to one side and piss streams down the inside of his leg.

The camera is positioned above the TV screen; its cold, mechanical eye dispassionately observing everything. The apparatus is set up on RECORD. It keeps running as the body hangs limp, turning gently towards a complete stillness. Then the tape runs out without saying THE END, but that is what it is.

A BLOCKAGE IN THE SYSTEM

Knoxie wis hoverin in the doorway; ehs face set in that kind ay expression thit cries out fir our attention, whin eh kens thit every cunt'll ignore um until eh speaks. Then will git some bullshit about how eh'd telt Manderson tae stick ehs fuckin joab up ehs erse whin the truth is thit the cunt's shat ehs fuckin keks again.

— That cunt Manderson, eh wheezed.

— Trouble at mill? ah asked, no lookin up fae ma cairds. This wis a shite hand. Ah turned tae gie ma foreman ma undivided attention, as a conscientious employee. A null n void declaration by Knoxie here wid suit ays doon tae a fuckin tee, the shite ah'm hudin.

— Wuv goat tae jildy. Thir's fuckin chaos doon at the flats.

— Hud oan the now, Lozy sais nervously. Obviously this wide-o's goat the maist tae lose.

Pickin up ehs anxiety, Calum flings ehs hand in. Ah follay suit.

— Duty calls, Calum laughs.

— Fuck sakes, ah'm oan a fuckin straight run here, ya cunts! Lozy whinges.

— Tough titty then, cuntybaws. Yir peyed good money by the council, that's the fuckin poll-tax peyer tae you, tae dae a joab ay work, no tae sit oan yir erse playing fuckin cairds aw day, Calum smirked.

— That's right, Knoxie said. — It's a pure bastard ay a joab n aw, boys. Thir's a blockage doon at Anstruther Court again. An auld boy oan the first flair goes through tae ehs lavvy fir a wash n shave. Aw they cunts oan the flairs above uv been shitein oot thir weekend curry n lager this mornin; one ay they near simultaneous flushin joabs. Aw the shite faws doon, n remember wir talking twinty storeys it Anstruther Court, hits the fuckin blockage n comes back up it the first available space. Yis ken whair that wis.

Wi collectively screwed up oor eyes and sucked in smoky air through puckered lips.

— Aw the shite came ootay the auld boy's pan wi such force thit it hit the fuckin roof. We've goatay sort this oot.

Lozy wisnae too chuffed. — Sounds like it's the drains ootside the flats tae me. Mair like a joab fir the Region, no us.

— Dinnae gies that shite! Call yirsels tradesmen? Tell ye one thing, if we dinnae fuckin shape up, will aw be doon the fuckin road. Ye ken how much money the DLO's losin?

— Ah bit that's no the point, Knoxie. We're oan the council now, no workin fir a private contractor. Thir's a nae redundancy policy.

— Wir under fuckin compulsory competitive tendrin. If we cannae git oor act the gither wir fucked. Simple as that. That's the governmint, that's the fuckin law. It disnae matter a fuck whit some fuckin toss in the Labour Party thit gits ehsel voted oantay the council sais. Wi dinnae dae the business, wi dinnae win contracts. Wi dinnae win contracts, thir's nae Direct Labour Organisation. Endy fuckin story.

— Naw it's no endy story, Lozy continued, — because the union boy wis sayin . . .

— That's jist some cunt thit gits made rep because nae other fucker wants the job. These cunts talk through thir fuckin erses. C'moan! Lit's move it.

Ah jist shrugged, — Well, as one anarchist plumber sais tae the other: smash the cistern.

We jumped intae the van. Knoxie's been deid nippy since eh came back fae that Supervision Part Two course up the City Chambers. They seemed tae fuck the cunt's heid up thair. Eftir Part One, eh wis aw sweetness n light tae us. Wisnae Knoxie.

Made us right fuckin suspicious. Ah goat a deek ay the notes they gave the cunt. Went oan aboot the motivation ay staff in an action-centred leadership framework. Sais thit it's no the supervisor's joab tae dae the work, it's the supervisor's joab tae make sure thit the work gits done. It sais thit the supervisor gits the joab done by meetin the individual and group needs ay the team. So we pilled Knoxie up aboot this. Calum sais thit eh needed tae score some Es fir this rave eh wis gaun tae; Lozy sais thit eh needed tae spend some time in a massage parlour. As a group wi needed an all-day bevvy session in the *Blue Blazer*. Could Knoxie arrange aw that? The cunt wisnae chuffed. Eh sais that wisnae whit it wis aboot n thit wi shouldnae be lookin it ehs notes unless wid been oan the course.

Anywey, it didnae last. It wis soon back tae the same auld Knoxie. So we wir quite lookin forward tae gittin the cunt oot the road fir a couple ay days, whin they pit um oantay Part Two. Ah dinnae ken whit they did tae the fucker this time bit; whitivir it wis it made um even mair ay a Nazi. Now the the radge jist willnae listen tae reason. N Lozy's right. The blockage is bound tae be in the fuckin drain. We've no goat the tools tae go doon thair, even it if wis oor joab.

Doon at the flats it's really fuckin boggin. Thir's a polisman standin aroond like a spare prick. This housin officer boy n this social worker lassie uv goat the perr auld cunt oan the couch wi some forms, tryin tae git um sorted oot. The environmental health boys ur doon here n aw. Thir wis nae wey ah wis gaun intae that bathroom.

Calum goes tae ays, — Wir talkin aboot an ootside joab here. Defo.

Knoxie overheard n goat aw fuckin stroppy. — Eh? eh goes.

— Likesay, jist sayin thit the blockage'll be doon in the drains, ken, no the stink pipe. Probably the bend, likes.

— That would seem logical, ah sais in ma Spock-oot-ay-*Star Trek* voice.

— Nae cunt kens that fir sure until we gie it a go, Knoxie contended.

Ah wisnae fir gaun intae that bog tae check it oot. — Ye ken whit happens, Knoxie. Burds pit thir fanny pads doon the pan, they aw clog up at the bend, ken?

— It's these cunts thit flush they fuckin disposable nappies away, that's the cunts thit git oan ma fuckin tits, Lozy shook ehs heid. — That's whit does the real fuckin damage, no the jam-rags.

— Ah'm no arguin wi yous cunts. Git they fuckin rods oot the van n doon that fuckin pan.

— Thir's nae point, ah goes. — Fill in an MRN 2 n lit they drainage cunts fae the Region sort it oot. Thill huv tae in the long run, wir jist wastin oor time here.

— Dinnae you tell me ma fuckin joab, son! Right! Knoxie isnae pleased. The cunt's bein too nippy here. Eh's no backin doon. Well, ah'm no either.

— Waste ay fuckin time, ah repeated.

— Aw aye, n whit else wid ye be daein? Sittin in the fuckin howf playin cairds!

— That's no the fuckin point, Lozy sais, — it's no oor fuckin joab. MRN 2 up tae the Region. That's whit's needed.

This social worker lassie turns roond n gies us a stroppy look. Ah jist smiles bit she looked away aw fuckin nippy likes. Disnae cost nowt tae be social. A social worker thit cannae be fuckin social; that's nae good tae nae cunt, thon. Like a lifeguard thit cannae fuckin swim. Shouldnae be daein that kinday joab.

— Yous cunts, jist fuck off. Ah'll dae it masel. Gaun, jist fuck off, Knoxie sais.

We jist looked it each other. Every cunt wis scoobied, so we jist turned n went doon the stair. We jist thought: if that's whit the cunt wants . . .

— Dis that mean wuv goat oor cairds? Calum asked.

Lozy jist fuckin laughed in the cunt's face, — The only cairds ye git at the DLO come in packs ay fifty-two. We're jist obeyin orders n ye eywis follay the last yin. Go, the cunt sais, so wir gaun. Eh shrugged.

— Whin ye think ay it though, ah sais, — Knoxie didnae

learn much fae that fuckin course. They sais thit it's the supervisor's joab tae make sure thit the work gits done, no tae dae it ehsel. There's the cunt up thair graftin oan ehs puff while we're aw oot here.

— Fancy a pint? Lozy asks. — Whitsons?

Calum raises a hopeful eyebrow.

— Why no, ah goes, — if yir gaunny git hung fir stealin a sheep ye might as well shag it n aw.

We walked across the forecourt. Thir wis a pungent, shitey smell and Lozy's face crinkled up aw that satisfied wey n eh nods doon tae a river ay stagnant water thit wis bubblin tae the surface fae around the rim ay a rusty iron drain-cover.

Calum turned back taewards the flats and raised baith airms in the air. Eh gave a double V-sign. — Game set and match, ya masonic bastard.

Lozy goes: — The union boy'll chew ehs fuckin nuts oaf if eh tries tae take this yin tae a disciplinary.

— Widnae git that far, ah sais, — we gave oor professional opinion. Whit's it the gadge thit took us fir the ONC at Telford College sais? The maist important skill in any trade is accurate problem diagnosis. Ah goat a fuckin distinction, ah pointed at masel.

Lozy raised ehs eyebrows, the cheeky cunt.

— Eh did, Calum backs ays up.

— Aye, n that cunt Knoxie chose tae disregard oor professional advice.

— Waste ay council resources, Lozy agreed. — Manderson'll nivir back that cunt up.

We swagger through the centre towards the pub. That pint's gaunny taste sweet, right enough.

WAYNE FOSTER

Two Sparryheids sit at a table in a public house talking shite about the football. The Sparryheids are almost indistinguishable from each other with their soft brown feathery heads, open, tense, belligerent beaks and slimy liquorice eyes. The only thing that sets them apart is that one Sparryheid has a trail of black gunge weeping from the corner of his left eye, the result perhaps of some injury or infection.

— Some trouble the day at the match, eh?

— Aye, casual infiltrators. Shouldnae huv been thair, no at that end.

— Ah heard it wisnae casuals, but. Ah heard it wis a couple ay boys thit wir in each other's company, arguing about Wayne Foster. One cunt goes: Git that fuckin English cunt oaf the park. The other boy sais: Gie the cunt a chance. So the first boy sais something back and one things leads tae another, one boy panels the other. Next thing ye ken, yuv goat a big fuckin swedge oan yir hands.

— Naw, says one Sparryheid, with an unconvinced shake of his beak, — it'll be they fuckin casuals. No interested in the fitba, these cunts.

— Naw naw. This wis aboot Wayne Foster. That's what ah heard.

— Casuals, the unconvinced Sparryheid shakes his beak again. A few brown feathers float to the lino floor, — that's who it'd be. Fuckin troublemakers.

— Naw, explains his friend, now slightly exasperated, — no this the day. Ah agree wi ye aboot the casuals, but wir talkin

82

aboot *this the day*. This wis two boys thit kent each other. They started swedgin, then every other cunt jumps in. Frustration, ken. Frustration wi the way things are gaun. Ken?

— Awright, mibbe, n wir jist sayin mibbe, it wis they boys n Foster, Wayne Foster – who's awright by the way; at least ye always git one hundred and ten percent fae Foster – mibbe it wis Foster this time thit started it, but it's usually they casuals . . . that's aw ah'm sayin.

— Aye, bit no this time. This the day wis definitely this Foster thing. Ah heard two boys spraffin aboot it.

— Admittedly Foster husnae goat that much skill. Fast as fuck though, man.

— Foster . . .

— Another thing aboot Foster, wi goat that cunt for fuck all. Derek fuckin Ferguson; three quarters ay a million fir that! A fuckin prima donna!

— Naw, that's a fitba player, man.

— Foster. That's the boy. See if they aw hud Foster's commitment . . .

— Awright, awright. If ye could combine Foster's commitment wi Ferguson's class . . .

— Aye, nods the other Sparryheid, — ah'll gie ye that.

— Foster's commitment n speed wi Ferguson's class n vision.

— Foster.

— Right. Foster, ya cunt.

— Aye. Wayne Foster. Right enough, the Sparryheid considers, before turning to his mate: — Another pint?

— Aye.

One Sparryheid goes up to the bar but the barman refuses him service as he, the barman, has sectarian leanings which make him averse to Sparryheided cunts. Additionally this barman has enjoyed the benefits of a classical education which makes him feel superior to most people, particularly Sparryheids, who he hates to wait on. There is another reason. *She* is in the bar. Worse still: *She* is in the bar with *Her*. The Sparryheid's keen vision is focused on these two women, who sit in the corner of the bar, deep in conversation. If *She* went home with a Sparryheid it would be the end for the Classical Scholar; as for *Her*, well she could do what she wanted.

— Bit how no? asks the Sparryheid at the bar, how's it wir no gittin served? His beak is open at ninety degrees and his huge black eyes radiate anxiety.

The barman is no ornothologist. The classics are his field, but even he can sense the Sparryheid's discomfort. However, he shakes his head slowly, refusing to make eye contact with the Sparryheid. Instead, he makes a grim, intense ritual of washing a glass.

The Sparryheid at the bar goes back over to the table. — Wir no gettin served! he announces to his friend.

— Eh! Whit for no?

The Sparryheids move over to the other end of the bar to make an appeal to Ernie, the other duty barman. The Classical Scholar was head duty barman, and even if Ernie had the power to overide his decision, he would be reluctant to do so as he also enjoyed seeing Sparryheids distressed. — It's no up tae me, boys, he shrugged at the bemused beaks and went back to his conversation with two guys at the bar.

The Classical Scholar looks over at the two women in the corner. In particular he looks at *She*; even more particularly he is unable to take his eyes off her glossy lips. He recalls that blow-job at New Year; that had been something else. There was always a tension in his mind and body; this was part and parcel of being a classical scholar in a world where the classics were undervalued. His depth and breadth of knowledge went unrecognised. He was forced to pull pints for Sparryheids. This caused depression, anxiety, tension. That blow-job at New Year; that had sucked all the tension out of his tightly-strung body, taken all the poisonous thoughts out of his head. He'd lain there for a bit, on the bed outside the coats; just lain there in a daze. When he recovered she'd left the room. He went through to find her but when he approached her she was cold and off-hand.

— Please keep away from me, she had said to him. — I'm not

interested in you. This is New Year. I'm a bit pissed. Understand, that was a one-off, okay?

All he could do was respond with a bemused nod, stagger through to the kitchen and get drunk.

Now *She* was in the bar with *Her*, a woman he'd gone home with previously; a woman he'd fucked. He didn't like *Her*, but the thought that he'd been with both of them made him feel good. Two women under thirty in the bar and he'd shagged both of them. Well, shagged one and got a blow-job from the other one. A technicality, surely. He replayed it: two women under thirty in the bar and he'd come with his prick inside a different orifice with each one. That sounded even better. But it didn't feel better for long because *She* was looking over at him and laughing; they both were. *She* held her hands up at the level of her chest, protruding index fingers a few inches apart. The other woman, *Her*, nodded negatively as they stole another glance at the Classical Scholar, then *She* put her fingers closer together until there was hardly any space between them and *Her* head bobbed approvingly, before they both collapsed into heaps of laughter.

The Classical Scholar was far too sensitive a man to be treated in this manner. He went into the small room at the back of the bar and picked up an old hard yellow piece of soap from the dirty sink. He chewed a chunk off the cake and after wincing at the sickening taste, swallowed hard. It burned all the way down to his stomach in a slow, poisonous trail. He slammed a fist into his palm, curled his toes and began humming a soft mantra: — Slags slags slags slags slags . . .

Getting control of himself, he emerged to find one of the Sparryheids standing before him at the bar.

— How's it wir no gittin served, mate? Whit huv wi done? Wir no steamin or nowt like that. Jist in fir a quiet drink, ken. Jist spraffin aboot the match, ken? Wayne Foster n that.

The best thing to do was not to even talk to Sparryheids. It was important to remember the golden rules of barwork as they related to Sparryheids.

1. **ACT DECISIVELY.**
2. **REMAIN IMPLACABLY IN CONTROL OF THAT INITIAL DECISION, IRRESPECTIVE OF WHETHER THAT DECISION IS JUST OR NOT.**
3. **NEVER ATTEMPT TO EXPLAIN TO THE SPARRYHEID THE REASON(S) FOR YOUR DECISION. BY JUSTIFYING OR RATIONALISING YOU MERELY COMPROMISE YOUR AUTHORITY.**

Those were the rules of the game. Always.

He shook his head negatively at the Sparryheids. They uttered some curses and left.

A few minutes later *She* stood up. Ernie, positioned at the other end of the bar moved over to serve her, but went back to chatting to a couple of customers as he realised she was heading for the Classical Scholar.

— Craig, she said to him, — I liked the way you handed those weird beaky guys with the feathered faces. They were giving us the creeps. When do you finish tonight?

— Eh, half an hour.

— Good, I want you to come back with me and my friend Rosalyn. You know Rosalyn don't you . . . ha ha ha of course you do.

— Okay.

— Understand, Craig, we won't fuck you, you'll get nothing off us. You're quite a sexy man but you take yourself far too seriously. We want to show you something about yourself. Right? She smiled and moved back over to where her friend was sitting.

The Classical Scholar wondered what they wanted him for. He would go, though. It could be enlightening. It didn't matter whether you were a Sparryheid, or even a Classical Scholar; there were always lessons to be learned in life.

WHERE THE DEBRIS MEETS
THE SEA

The house in Santa Monica sat tastefully back from Palisades Beach Road, the town's bustling ocean boulevard. This was the top end of the town, its opulence serving as the height to aspire to for the yuppie dwellers of the condominiums further down the Pacific coast. It was a two-floored Spanish-style dwelling, partly obscured from the road by a huge stone wall and a range of indigenous American and imported trees. A few yards inside the wall, an electrified security fence ran around the perimeter of the property. Inside the gate at the entrance to the grounds, a portable cabin was discreetly tucked, and outside it sat a burly guard with mirror-lens shades.

Wealth was certainly the overall impression given by the property. Unlike nearby Beverly Hills, however, the concept of wealth here seemed more utilitarian, rather than concerned with status. The impression was that wealth was here to be consumed, rather than flaunted ostentatiously for the purpose of inducing respect, awe or envy.

The pool at the back of the house had been drained; this was not a home that was occupied all the year round. Inside, the house was expensively furnished, yet in a stark, practical style.

Four women relaxed in a large room which led, through patio doors, to the dry pool. They were at ease, lounging around silently. The only sounds came from the television, which one of them was watching, and the soft hissing of the air-conditioning which pumped cool, dry air into the house.

A pile of glossy magazines lay on a large black coffee table. They bore such titles as *Wide-o, Scheme Scene* and *Bevvy*

Merchants. Madonna flicked idly through the magazine called *Radge*, coming to an abrupt halt as her eyes feasted on the pallid figure of Deek Prentice, resplendent in a purple, aqua and black shell-suit.

'Phoah! Ah'd shag the erse oafay that anywey,' she lustily exclaimed, breaking the silence, and thrusting the picture under Kylie Minogue's nose.

Kylie inspected the image clinically, 'Hmm . . . ah dunno . . . No bad erse oan it like, bit ah'm no really intae flat-toaps. Still, ah widnae kick it oot ay bed, likesay, ken?'

'Whae's that?' Victoria Principal asked, filing her nails as she reclined on the couch.

'Deek Prentice fi Gilmerton. Used tae be in the casuals, bit eh's no intae that anymair,' Madonna said, popping a piece of chewing-gum into her mouth.

Victoria was enthusiastic. 'Total fuckin ride. Ah bet eh's hung like a hoarse. Like that photae ah goat ay Tam McKenzie, ken fi the Young Leith Team, original seventies line-up. Fuckin welt oan it, man, ah'm telling ye. Phoah, ya cunt ye! Even through the shell-suit, ye kin see ehs tackle bulgin oot. Ah thoat, fuck me, ah'd gie ma eye teeth tae get ma gums aroond that.'

'Ye'd probably huv tae, if ehzis big is ye say!' smirked Kylie. They all laughed loudly, except Kim Basinger, who sat curled up in a chair watching the television.

'Wishful thinkin gits ye naewhaire,' she mused. Kim was studying the sensual image of Dode Chalmers; bold shaved head, Castlemaine XXXX t-shirt and Levis. Although Rocky, his faithful American pit-bull terrier was not visible on the screen, Kim noted that his leather and chain leash was bound around Dode's strong, tattooed arm. The eroticism of the image was intense. She wished that she'd videotaped this programme.

The camera swung over to Rocky, whom Dode described to the interviewer as: 'My one faithful friend in life. We have an uncanny telepathy which goes beyond the archetypal man-beast relationship . . . in a real sense Rocky is an extension of myself.'

Kim found this a bit pretentious. Certainly, there was little doubt that Rocky was an integral part of the Dode Chalmers legend. They went everywhere together. Kim cynically wondered, however, just how much of this was a dubious gimmick, manufactured, perhaps, by public relations people.

'Fuck . . .' gasped Kylie, open mouthed, '. . . what ah'd gie tae be in that dug's position now. Wearin a collar, chained tae Dode's airm. That wid dae me fine.'

'Some fuckin chance,' Kim laughed, more derisively than she'd intended.

Madonna looked across at her. 'Awright then, smart cunt. Dinnae you be sae fuckin smug,' she said challengingly.

'Aye Kim, dinnae tell ays ye widnae git intae his keks if ye hud the chance,' Victoria sneered.

'That's whit ah sais, bit. Ah'm no gaunny git the chance, so whit good's it talkin aboot it, likesay? Ah'm here in Southern California n Dode's ower in fuckin Leith.'

They fell into a silence, and watched Dode being interviewed on *The Jimmy McGilvary Show.* Kim thought that McGilvary was a pain in the arse, who seemed to feel that he was as big a star as his guests. He was asking Dode about his love-life.

'In all honesty, I don't have time for heavy relationships at the moment. Right now I'm only interested in all the overtime I can get. After all, one has to remember that trades fortnight isn't that far away,' Dode explained, slightly flushed, his thin mouth almost curling in a smile.

'Ah'd cowp it,' Kylie licked her bottom lip.

'In a fuckin minute,' Victoria nodded severely, eyes widened.

Madonna was more interested in Deek Prentice. She turned her attention back to the article and continued reading. She was hoping to read something about Deek's split from the casuals. The full story had not come out about that one, and it would be interesting to hear Deek's side of things.

there is hope for us all yet, as Deek is keeping an open mind on romance since his much publicised split with sexy cinema usherette,

Sandra Riley. It's obviously an issue where Deek is keen to set the record straight.

'I suppose, in a way, we loved each other too much. There's certainly no hard feelings or bitterness on either side. In fact, I was talking to Sandra on the phone only the other night, so we're still the best of friends. Our respective careers made it difficult to see as much of each other as we would have liked. Obviously cinema isn't a nine-to-five thing, and furniture removals can take me all over the country, with overnight stays. We got used to not being together, and sort of drifted apart. Unfortunately, it's the nature of the business we're in. Relationships are difficult to sustain.'

Deek's social life is another area where he feels that he has had more than his share of unwelcome publicity. While he makes no secret of an enjoyment of the high life, he feels that 'certain parties' have somewhat exaggerated things.

'So I enjoy the odd game of pool with Dode Chalmers and Cha Telfer. All I can say is: guilty as charged. Yes, I'm in the habit of visiting places like the Spey Lounge, Swanneys and the Clan Tavern; and I enjoy a few pints of lager. However, the public only see the glamorous side. It's not as if I'm swilling away every night. Most evenings I'm home, watching Coronation Street and EastEnders. Just to illustrate how the press get hold of nonsense, a report appeared in a Sunday newspaper, which shall be nameless, stating that I was involved in an altercation at a stag night in Fox's Bar. It's not a boozer I use, and in any case I was working overtime that night! If I was in the pub as often as certain gossip columnists claim, I'd hardly be able to hold down my driving job with Northern Removals. With three million people unemployed, I've certainly no intention of resting on my laurels.'

Deek's boss, the experienced supervisor Rab Logan, agrees. Rab probably knows Deek better than anyone in the business, and Deek unreservedly credits the dour Leither with saving his career. Rab told us: 'Deek came to us with a reputation for being, should we say, somewhat difficult. He's very much an individual, rather than a team man, and tended to go off to the pub whenever it took his fancy. Obviously, with a flit to complete, this lack of application caused some bad feeling with the rest of the team. We crossed swords for the first and last time, and since then, Deek's been a joy to work with. I can't speak highly enough of him.'

Deek is only too willing to acknowledge his debt to the removal Svengali.

'I owe it all to Rab. He took me aside and told me that I had what it took to make it in the removals game. The choice was mine. At the time I was arrogant, and nobody could tell me anything. However, I remember that exceptionally grim and lonely journey home on the number six bus that day Rab told me a few home truths. He has a habit of stating the transparently obvious, when you're so close to it, you can't see the woods for the trees. After a dressing-down from Rab Logan, one tends to shape up. The lesson I learned from Rab that day was an important one. In a sense, the removal business is like any other. The bottom line is, you're only as good as your last flit.'

What Deek eventually wants however, is the opportunity to

'Thir's nought tae stoap us gaun tae Leith, fir a hoaliday n that,' Victoria suggested, tearing Madonna's attention from the magazine.

'Hoaliday . . . hoaliday . . .' Madonna sang.

'Aye! We could go tae the *Clan*,' Kylie enthused. 'Imagine the cock in thair. Comin oot the fuckin waws.' She screwed up her eyes, puckered her lips and blew hard, shaking her head from side to side.

'Ye'd nivir git served in thair,' Kim sniffed.

'Ken your problem, Kim? Ye nivir think fuckin positively enough. We've goat the poppy. Dinnae you sit thair n tell ays ye've no goat the hireys,' Madonna remonstrated.

'Ah nivir sais that. It's no jist aboot poppy . . .'

'Well then. We could go tae Leith. Huv a fuckin barry time.

Hoaliday ay a lifetime,' Madonna told her, then continued her singing. 'It wid be, it wid be so nice, hoaliday . . .'

Victoria and Kylie nodded enthusiastically in agreement. Kim looked unconvinced.

'You cunts crack ays up.' She shook her head. 'No fuckin real.'

'Whit's wrong wi your fuckin pus, ya stroppy cunt?' Madonna mouthed belligerently, sitting up in the chair. 'Ye git oan ma fuckin tits, Kim, so ye do.'

'We'll nivir go tae fuckin Leith!' Kim said, in a tone of scornful dismissal. 'Yous ur fuckin dreamin.'

'We might go one time!' said Kylie, with just a hint of desperation in her voice. The others nodded in agreement.

But in their heart of hearts, they knew that Kim was right.

GRANNY'S OLD JUNK

The warden, Mrs French I think they call her, is looking me up and down. It's fairly obvious that she doesn't like what she sees; her gaze has a steely ice to it; it's definitely a negative evaluation I'm getting here.

— So, she says, hands on hips, eyes flitting suspiciously in that glistening yellow-brown foundation mask topped by a brittle head of brown hair, — you're Mrs Abercrombie's grandson?

— Aye, I acknowledge. I shouldn't resent Mrs French. She's only doing her job. Were she less than vigilant in keeping her eye on the auld doll, complaints from the family would ensue. I also have to acknowledge that I am less than presentable; lank, greasy black hair, a scrawny growth sprouting from a deathly white face broken up by a few red and yellow spots. My overcoat has seen better days and I can't remember when I changed into these jeans, sweatshirt, t-shirt, trainers, socks and boxershorts.

— Well, I suppose you'd better come in, Mrs French said, reluctantly shifting her sizeable bulk. I squeezed past, still brushing against her. Mrs French was like an oil tanker, it took a while for her to actually change direction. — She's on the second floor. You don't come to see her very often, do you? she said with an accusatory pout.

No. This is the first time I've been to see the auld doll since she moved into this Sheltered Housing scheme. That must be over five years ago now. Very few families are close nowadays. People move around, live in different parts of the country, lead different lives. It's pointless lamenting something as inevitable as

93

the decline of the extended family network; in a way it's a good thing because it gives people like Mrs French jobs.

— Ah don't stay local, I mumble, making my way down the corridor, feeling a twinge of self-hate for justifying myself to the warden.

The corridors have a rank, fetid smell of pish and stale bodies. Most people here seem in such an advanced state of infirmity it merely confirms my intuitive feeling that such places are just ante-chambers to death. It follows from this that my actions won't alter the auld doll's quality of life: she'll scarcely notice that the money's gone. Some of it would probably be mine anyway, when she finally snuffs it; so what the fuck's the point of waiting until it's no good to me? The auld doll could hang on for donkey's years as a cabbage. It would be utterly perverse, self-defeating nonsense not to rip her off now, to allow oneself to be constrained by some stupid, irrelevant set of taboos which pass as morality. I need what's in her tin.

It's been in the family for so long: Gran's shortbread tin. Just sitting there under her bed, crammed full of bundles of notes. I remember, as a sprog, her opening it up on our birthdays and peeling off a few notes from what seemed to be a fortune, the absence of which made no impact on the wad.

Her life savings. Savings for what? Savings for us, that's what, the daft auld cunt: too feeble, too inadequate to enjoy or even use her wealth. Well I shall just have my share now, Granny, thank you very much.

I rap on the door. Abercrombie, with a red tartan background. My back chills and my joints feel stiff and aching. I haven't got long.

She opens the door. She looks so small, like a wizened puppet, like Zelda out of *Terrahawks*.

— Gran, I smile.

— Graham! she says, her face expanding warmly. — God, ah cannae believe it! Come in! Come in!

She sits me down, babbling excitedly, hobbling back and

forth from her small adjoining kitchen as she slowly and cumbersomely prepares tea.

— Ah keep askin yir mother how ye nivir come tae see me. Ye always used tae come oan Saturday for yir dinner, mind? For yir mince, remember, Graham? she says.

— Aye, the mince, Gran.

— At the auld place, mind? she said wistfully.

— Ah remember it well, Gran, I nodded. It was a vermin-infested hovel unfit for human habitation. I hated that grotty tenement: those stairs, the top floor surprise surfuckingprise, with the backs of my legs already fucked from the sickening ritual of walking up and down Leith Walk and Junction Street; her standing oblivious to our pain and discomfort as she prattled on a load of irrelevant, mundane shite with every other auld hound that crossed our path; big brother Alan taking his exasperation out on me by punching me or booting me or twisting my airm when she wisnae looking, and if she was she didnae bother. Mickey Weir gets more protection from Syme at Ibrox than I ever did from that auld cunt. Then, after all that, the fuckin stairs. God, I detested those fuckin stairs!

She comes in and looks at me sadly, and shakes her head with her chin on her chest. — Your mother was saying that yuv been gettin intae trouble. Wi these drugs n things. Ah sais, no oor Graham, surely no.

— People exaggerate, Gran, I said as a spasm of pain shot through my bones, and a delirious shivering tremor triggered off an excretion of stale perspiration from my pores. Fuck fuck fuck.

She re-emerges from the kitchen, popping out like a crumpled jack-in-the box. — Ah thoat so. Ah sais tae oor Joyce: No oor Graham, he's goat mair sense thin that.

— Ma goes oan a bit. Ah enjoy masel, Gran, ah'm no sayin otherwise, bit ah dinnae touch drugs, eh. Ye dinnae need drugs tae enjoy yirself.

— That's whit ah sais tae yir mother. The laddie's an Abercrombie, ah telt her, works hard and plays hard.

My name was Millar, not Abercrombie, that's the auld lady's side. This auld hound seemed to believe that being referred to as an Abercrombie is the highest possible accolade one can aspire to; though perhaps, if you want to demonstrate expertise in alcoholism and theft, this may very well be the case.

— Aye, some crowd the Abercrombies, eh Gran?

— That's right, son. Ma Eddie — yir grandfaither — he wis the same. Worked hard n played hard, n a finer man nivir walked the earth. He nivir kept us short, she smiled proudly.

Short.

I have my works in my inside pocket. Needle, spoon, cotton balls, lighter. All I need is a few grains of smack, then just add water and it's all better. My passport's in that tin.

— Whair's the lavvy, Gran?

Despite the small size of the flat, she insisted on escorting me to the bog, as if I'd get lost on the way. She fussed, clucked and farted as if we were preparing to go on safari. I tried a quick slash, but couldn't pee, so I stealthily tiptoed into the bedroom.

I lifted up the bedclothes that hung to the floor. The large old shortbread tin with the view of Holyrood Palace sat in full magnificent view under the bed. It was ridiculous, an act of absolute criminal stupidity to have that just lying around in this day and age. I was more convinced than ever that I had to rip her off. If I didn't somebody else would. Surely she'd want me to have the money, rather than some stranger? If I didn't take the cash, I'd be worried sick about it. Anyway, I was planning to get clean soon; maybe get a job or go to college or something. The auld hound would get it back right enough. No problem.

Prising open the lid of the fucker was proving extremely difficult. My hands were trembling and I couldn't get any purchase on it. I was starting to make headway when I heard her voice behind me.

— So! That's whit this is aw aboot! She was standing right over me. I thought I'd have heard the clumsy auld boot sneaking up on me, but she was like a fuckin ghost. — Yir mother wis right. Yir a thief! Feeding yir habit, yir drugs habit, is that it?

— Naw Gran, it's jist . . .

— Dinnae lie, son. Dinnae lie. A thief, a thief thit steals fae his ain is bad, but a liar's even worse. Ye dinnae ken whair ye stand wi a liar. Get away fae that bloody tin! she snapped so suddenly that I was taken aback, but I sat where I was.

— I need something, right?

— Yill find nae money in thair, she said, but I could tell by the anxiety in her voice that she was lying. I prised, and it transpired that she wasn't. On top of a pile of old photos lay some whitish-brown powder in a plastic bag. I'd never seen so much gear.

— What the fuckin hell's this . . .

— Git away fae thair! Git away! Fuckin thief! Her bony, spindly leg lashed out and caught me in the side of the face. It didn't hurt but it shocked me. Her swearing shocked me even more.

— Ya fuckin auld . . . I sprang to my feet, holding the bag in the air, beyond her outstretched hands. — Better call the warden, Gran. She'll be interested in this.

She pouted bitterly and sat down on the bed. — You got works? she asked.

— Aye, I said.

— Cook up a shot then, make yourself useful.

I started to do as she said. — How Gran? How? I asked, relieved and bemused.

— Eddie, the Merchant Navy. He came back wi a habit. We had contacts. The docks. The money wis good, son. Thing is, ah kept feedin it, now ah huv tae sell tae the young ones tae keep gaun. The money aw goes upfront. She shook her head, looking hard at me. — Thir's a couple ay young yins ah git tae run messages fir me, but that fat nosey yin doonstairs, the warden, she's gittin suspicious.

I took up her cue. Talk about falling on your feet. — Gran, maybe we kin work the gither on this.

The animal hostility on her small, pinched face dissolved into a scheming grin. — Yir an Abercrombie right enough, she told me.

— Aye, right enough, I acknowledged with a queasy defeatism.

THE HOUSE OF JOHN DEAF

John Deaf's hoose wis weird. Ah mean, thir wis eywis some scruffy hooses in the scheme, bit nowt like John Deaf's. Fir a start, John Deaf's hoose hud fuck all in it; nae furniture or nowt like that. Nowt oan the flair, no even any lino. Jist they cauld black tiles thit ivray hoose hud, fir the underflair heatin thit nae cunt could afford tae switch oan.

Aw thit wis in John Deaf's hoose wis one chair thit ehs Grandfaither sat oan, ben the livin-room. Thir wis a boax wi a telly oan toap ay it. The auld cunt jist used tae sit thair watchin the telly aw day n night. Thir wis eywis loads ay boatils n cans it ehs feet. The auld radge must've slept in that chair, cause thir wis jist one mattress in the hoose, n that wis in John Deaf's room. Thir wis nae beds or nowt like that.

The only thing thit wis in the hoose wis the white mice. Loads ay thum, crawlin aboot ivraywhair. John Deaf really liked white mice. Eh boat thum ootay Dofo's Pet Shoap, took thum back tae the hoose n jist lit thum go. Eh wis it Dofo's ivray Setirday. Whin they tippled tae what the cunt wis aboot, they knocked um back. Aw he'd dae though, wis jist gie one ay us the money tae go in n git um the mice.

So the mice ran aroond free. They jist multiplied, scurryin aroond the place, aw ower they black tiles. Sometimes eh'd hurt thum. Some ay thum goat crushed tae death, n thir wis one thit eh hud kicked thit hud baith ay its back legs broken. It used tae drag itsel acroass the flair wi its front legs. Wi used tae git a fuckin laugh at it. That yin though, that wis John Deaf's favourite. Ye could stomp any ay the wee cunts, bit eh widnae lit ye touch that yin.

Wi didnae call John Deaf John Deaf cause the cunt wis deef n dumb. Eh wis, bit that wisnae the main reason. It wis cause thir wis a John Hyslop n a Johnny Paterson n soas no tae git thum mixed up. That wis the main reason. Aw John Deaf could say wis ehs name, n thit eh wis deef. Whin eh moved intae the scheme, intae Rab's block, ye'd go up n say tae um: Whit's yir name, mate? n eh'd say: John. Then ye'd say somethin else bit eh'd jist touch ehs ear n go: Deaf.

So John Deaf it wis.

Ivray cunt kent um is John Deaf. The guy thit took us fir the fitba it Sporting Pilton used tae say: Ah want John Deaf tae play oot wide oan the wing. Ah want yis tae feed John Deaf. Remember, feed John Deaf, eh'd say tae us. Naebody could run like John Deaf. Eh wis really strong n aw. Eh'd go fuckin radge if some cunt did a sneaky tackle fae behind oan um, bit that wis the only wey ye could stoap John Deaf. The cunt's strength n speed wirnae real, believe you me.

John Deaf nivir went tae school. They didnae ken eh existed. Course, John Deaf wid huv went tae one ay they special schools, fir the deef, likesay that big posh yin it Haymarket, bit eh didnae go tae any school at aw. Ivray time one ay us wis skivin, we'd meet up wi John Deaf, sure as fuck.

Wi aw used tae hing aroond in John Deaf's hoose. It wis really mingin likesay, bit that nivir bothered ye sae much in they days. It wis like oor base, oor HQ. Ehs auld grandfaither nivir hassled naebday, jist sat thair watchin the telly n drinkin ehs cans ay beer. He wis deef n aw.

Once whin wi wir in John Deaf's hoose, jist fartin aboot likes; wi couldnae find John Deaf or ma sister. Wi went up the stairs n heard noises comin fae the the big press whair the water tank wis. Whin wi opened the door wi saw that cunt John fuckin Deaf n ma sister. Thir fuckin neckin n John Deaf's goat ehs willy oot n eh's goat ehs hand up hur skirt.

Now she gits called a slag n that makes me look a right fuckin cunt, nae two weys aboot it. So ah pills hur away n pushes hur doon the stairs, tellin hur tae git tae fuck. She wis shitin ursel n so she fuckin shoulduv been, cause there wis me thinkin: see if the auld man kent aboot it . . . Bit anywey ah punches John Deaf in the mooth n wi starts swedgin which wis a bad fuckin move oan ma part because ay John Deaf's strength, n eh gits oan toap ay ays n ehs knockin fuck oot ay ays, batterin ma heid oaf they black tiles. Ah suppose it wis then thit ah tippled tae how auld John Deaf wis. It wisnae sae much the size ay ehs willy, because it wis still oot, wi this cunt oan toap ay ays, or the baws wi hairs oan thum. It wis mair the bumfluff oan ehs face, n ehs strength. In spite ay ehs wee height, it came tae ays thit John Deaf wisnae the same age as the rest ay us. Eh wis mibbe sixteen; mibbe even mair. Whin ah realised this, that's whin ah really shat ma keks. Ah'm greetin ma eyes oot, ah wis only aboot eleven likes, n ivray cunt's sayin: Eh's hud enough. Leave um.

Bit John Deaf's deef, right?

Anywey, it wis some fuckin doin ah goat. It only stoaped whin some cunt drags John Deaf oafay ays tae git um tae go doonstairs. Ah think it wis Cammy, bit ah'm no really sure. Anywey, whaeivir it wis, eh starts pillin John Deaf doon the stair. John Deaf didnae resist, ah suppose eh could tell fae the boy's face thit somethin wis wrong.

Ah staggers tae ma feet, ma sister tryin tae help ays up. Ah pushes hur ootay the road. Dirty cow deserved tae be shopped tae the auld man. Ah wis thinkin, mibbe ah will, mibbe ah willnae, cause ah thoat thit ma Ma n Dad wid'uv went radge.

Whin ah gits doonstairs, thir aw crowded aroond the grand-faither's chair. Thir's a big pool ay pish under it. The auld gadge's heid's twisted tae the side, ehs eyes ur shut, bit ehs mooth's open. White mice ur walkin aroond the edge ay the puddle ay pish. One wis in it, the cunt wi the broken back legs, draggin ehsel through it. Making sure thit John Deaf wisnae noticin, ah brought ma heel doon hard oan the wee cunt. Ah kent John Deaf liked that moose, n that wid help tae pey the cunt back fir the doin eh'd gied ays. Whin ah looked doon, the moose wis still alive, bit sortay split open. Its spilled guts wir trailin in the pish; bit it wis still dragging its boady forward.

Ah didnae ken whithir or no the auld cunt in the chair wis deid, bit eh wisnae far oaf it. Ah wis really sair, especially ma heid, bit ah wis happy, because ah kent thit they'd take John Deaf away cause ay the auld cunt bein deid, or half-deid.

They did n aw. John Deaf nivir came back tae the scheme. Thir wis loads ay stories gaun aboot: like the auld gadge wisnae really John Deaf's grandfaither n they baith slept oan that one mattress, if ye git ma meanin. Ah widnae pit it past thum, that's aw ah'm sayin oan the subject. It's jist talk bit, n the only two people thit really ken whit went oan in that hoose cannae tell any cunt aboot it.

Ah nivir sais nowt tae ma Ma n faither aboot ma sister n John Deaf. She kent tae watch ur mooth aroond ays bit, n no gie ays any lip. They soon worked oot thit somethin wis wrong though, n whin they asked ur aboot it, she started greetin. Thing wis, ah wis the cunt thit goat the fuckin blame! Me! The auld man sais thit ah wis a blackmailer, n ah blackmailer wis the lowest ay the low, specially wi faimly n that. Eh telt ays this story aboot how this poof eh kent in the army wis blackmailed n the perr wee cunt kilt ehsel. So ah gits leathered n she gits aw this sympathy oafay thum. Fuckin ootay order man, ah'm tellin ye.

Ah wis gled whin they took that John Deaf away. Ah hated the radge. Ah've nivir been the same since that doin eh gied ays, ah kin tell ye.

ACROSS THE HALL

15/2 COLLINGWOOD	15/8 GILLESPIE

<table>
<tr><td>

it's not being kept in the picture
that i resent the most. he sees me
as a glorified typist; never tells
me anything. not that i want to be
a secretary forever, but i saw this
as a stepping stone to something a
little more interesting. i'm
planning to go to college and take
the institute of marketing
diploma exams, that's if i get day
release; which is a big if, working
for him. and that's if i even get the
chance to ask him for day release
in the first place. he's so sexist and
patronising as well, if you know
what i mean. not like you mister
gillespie . . . sorry frank, of
course. am i embarrassing you
frank? you see it's not that i'm a
big feminist or anything like that,
well i am, but i don't believe in
that brand of feminism that says
it's only men that are power-
crazed warmongers, i mean look

</td><td>

that's important to me. it's him
getting it, after all the experience
in the firm i've gained over the
years. and let's be upfront about
it, it's not only me that's saying it,
most of my colleagues feel the
same; he simply isn't up to the
job. it's not the money i'm
worried about, it's just that good
numbers like that are hard to
come by nowadays. mind you,
i'm not really that upset about it. a
fair day's work for a fair day's pay:
that's my philosophy; and with
the sweeties they pay at that
bloody place, it means that they
get the bare minimum out of old
frank gillespie here. i wouldn't
give you the bare minimum
though stephanie, but then
you're special. i don't mean to be
crude stephanie, i'm not a coarse
person, but when my passions are
aroused i say what i feel. i want

</td></tr>
</table>

at thatcher in the falklands, it's just that i don't want you to think i'm on some big dykey castrating men trip here because it's not that at all. i really know how to please a man frank, and how to get a man to please me so why don't you show me what you've got frank, why don't you give it to me baby, why don't you frank? i bet it's a big one, yes! you can always tell in a man, it's something about the way he carries himself . . . yes it is big, and it feels good in my hand, throbbing away like that, but it would feel even better inside me . . . frank . . . now frank . . . OHHH YESSS! that feels so wonderful, magnificent, you really . . . let's keep doing it like this . . . getting there already . . . this is so . . . OH . . . OH . . . OH . . . OH . . .

you to know that i'm a sensitive guy and i don't go in for all that caveman stuff, i see a woman as a person first and foremost. if i'm attracted to someone i'll just come right out and say it. i may not put a lot into my work these days, but when it comes to relationships, especially the physical side of things, i've never been found wanting. i know you want it stephanie. is this what you want? i think you want it really badly. what about it then? is this enough for you? I could tell that you wanted it, right from the very start, as much as i did . . . god, your skin's so smooth . . . you're so beautiful . . . i want to fuck you, stephanie . . . let's just do it baby . . . OHHH it feels so wonderful, oh god this is beautiful, OH SHIT . . . i'm FUCKING BEAUTIFUL . . . OH . . . OH . . . OH . . . OH . . .

Stephanie lay on the bed naked, enjoying the sense of brief contentment. It was fleeting; she knew her heart would hollow and she'd soon feel tense and debased again, her self-esteem starting to crumble at the edges like a faulty dam. She unplugged the vibrator, which was wet with her come, then pulled herself off the bed and went through to the bathroom.

Frank looked at the deflating plastic doll, its latex vagina filled with his semen. It seemed to be dissolving simultaneously with his erection. His genitals looked like an ugly, embarrassing growth; alien, external to his self. The doll now just looked like what it was: a sheet of plastic spilling from a grotesque mannequin head.

Later that evening, Stephanie passed Frank in the hallway. She was going out to see an arthouse movie and she was going alone. He was returning from the Chinese takeaway with some food. They blushed in mutual recognition, then he smiled meekly at her, and she timidly returned the compliment. He cleared his throat to speak. — It's raining outside, he lisped self-consciously.

— Is it? Stephanie replied shakily.

— Quite heavy, Frank mumbled.

They stood facing each other for an excruciating few seconds, both lost for words. Then they smiled in tense synchronicity before Frank retreated to his room and Stephanie marched down the hall. Out of sight of each other, both stiffened as if trying to stop the spasm, that pulse of pain, self-loathing and embarrassment.

LISA'S MUM
MEETS THE QUEEN MUM

I was so excited when we met the Queen Mum; oh, it was marvellous. It was a shame about my little girl Lisa's presentation to her. That bit went horribly wrong. It was my little girl Lisa, her fault. Didn't understand, you see. I've always told Lisa to tell the truth: truth at all times, madam, I tell her. Well, you never really know what to tell them these days, do you?

The Queen Mum was coming to Ilford to open Lisa's new infant school. The local MP was going to be there too. We was ever so thrilled when Lisa was picked to present the Queen Mum with the bouquet of flowers. I had Lisa practising her curtseying all the time. Anybody who came in I'd say: show Mummy your curtsey, Lisa, the one you're going to do for the Queen's mummy . . .

Cause she really is lovely, the Queen Mum, ain't she? Really, really, really, really, lovely. We was ever so excited. My mum was going back to the time when she met the Queen Mum at the Festival of Britain. She's really lovely, marvellous for her age; the Queen Mum that is, not my mum. Mind you, my mum's a treasure, I don't know what I would've done without her, after Derek left me. Yeah, I wouldn't swap my mum for all the Queen Mums in the world, really.

Anyway, Mrs Kent, that's Lisa's headmistress, said to me that Lisa would be lovely presenting the Queen Mum with the bouquet. My friend Angela went a bit funny with me, because her little girl, Sinead, wasn't picked. I suppose that I'd have been the same if it had been the other way around and Sinead had got picked instead of Lisa. It was the Queen Mum after all. It don't happen every day, does it?

Well she looked really lovely, the Queen Mum, really really lovely; a lovely hat she had on. I was ever so proud of Lisa, I just wanted to tell the whole world; that's my little gel Lisa! Lisa West, Golfe Road Infants, Ilford actually . . .

So Lisa hands over the bouquet, but she didn't curtsey nice, not nice n proper like we'd practised. The Queen Mum takes the bouquet and bends down to give Lisa a little kiss but Lisa turns away with her little face all screwed up and runs over to me.

That old lady's got bad breath and smells of wee, Lisa said to me. This was in front of all the other mums and Mrs Kent and Mrs Fry n all. Mrs Fry was ever so upset.

You're a naughty little girl, Lisa! Mummy's ever so cross, I told her.

I'm sure I saw my friend Angela sniggering out of the side her mouth, the rotten cow.

Well, she was smiling on the other side of her face when Mrs Kent took *me* over to the Queen Mum and introduced me as Lisa's mum! The Queen Mum was lovely. Nice to meet you again, Mister Chamberlain, she said to me. Poor thing must get a bit confused, all these people she meets. They work ever so hard, you've got to give them that. Not like some I could mention, Derek, Lisa's dad, being a case in point. Not that I'm going into that little story just now, thank you very much.

Another thing was that Lisa had managed to get a stain down the front of her dress. I hoped the Queen Mum didn't notice. Just wait till I get you home, madam, I thought. Ooh, I was ever so cross. Really, really cross.

THE TWO PHILOSOPHERS

It was damn hot for Glasgow, Lou Ornstein thought, as he pulled his sweating body into the Byres Road hostelry. Gus McGlone was already at the bar, chatting to a young woman.

— Gus, how goes it? Ornstein asked, slapping his friend on the shoulder.

— Ah Lou. Very well indeed. And yourself?

— Great, Ornstein said, noting that McGlone's attention was still very much centred on the young woman.

The woman whispered something to McGlone, then flashed Ornstein a searing smile which was all teeth and eyes. It cut through him. — Professor Ornstein, she began in the Scotch tearoom accent he found so attractive, — at the risk of sounding sycophantic I just wanted to say that your paper on the rational construction of magic was just superb.

— Why thank you. I shall accept that as a scholarly, rather than sycophantic view, Ornstein smiled. He thought that was quite a self-conscious response, but hell, he was an academic.

— I find your central hypothesis interesting . . . the young woman continued, as Ornstein felt a small pellet of resentment crystallise in his breast. This day was about drinking beer, not conducting an involuntary seminar with one of Gus's naive students. Oblivious to his growing unease, the woman continued, — . . . tell me, if you don't mind, how do you distinguish between what you call 'unknown science' and what we generally refer to as magic?

I do goddamn mind, thought Ornstein. Pretty young women were all the same; completely goddamned self-obsessed. He had

had to earn the right to be self-obsessed, to slog his guts out in libraries for years and brown-nose the right people, generally assholes who you wouldn't piss upon if they were on fire. Along comes some some nineteen-year-old undergrad destined for at best a lower second honours, who thinks that her opinion counts, that she's important, just because she has a sweet face and a god-given ass. The horrible thing, the worst goddamn thing about it, thought Ornstein, was that she was absolutely right.

— He can't, McGlone smugly remarked.

This intervention by his old adversary was enough to set Ornstein off. Accepting his pint of eighty shilling, he began, — Don't listen to this old Popperian cynic. These guys are just anti-social science, which means anti-science, and each generation of them get increasingly goddamn juvenile in their analysis. My contention is a fairly standard materialist proposition: so-called unexplained phenomena are merely scientific blind-spots. We have to accept the inherently logical concept of further knowledge outside of the human range of what we consciously, and even sub-consciously know. Human history illustrates this; our forefathers would have described the sun, or the internal combustion engine as magic, when they are nothing of the kind. Magic, like ghosts and all that stuff, it's just hocus-pocus bullshit for the ignorant, while unknown science is a phenomena that we may or may not be able to observe but cannot yet explain. That does not mean that it is inexplicable; merely that it cannot be explained with due reference to our current body of knowledge. That body of knowledge is constantly expanding; some day we will be able to explain unknown science.

— Don't get him started, Fiona, McGlone smiled, — he'll go on all night.

— Not if you don't beat me to it. Indoctrinating your students with Popperian orthodoxies.

— Indoctrination's what the other side do, Lou. We educate, McGlone smiled. The two philosophers laughed at that one, an old quip from their student days. Fiona, the young student, excused herself. She had a lecture to attend.

The two philosophers watched her leave the pub.

— One of my brightest undergrads, McGlone smirked.

— Terrific ass, Ornstein nodded.

They adjourned to a conspiratorial corner of the pub. Lou took a mouthful of beer. — It's great to see you again, Gus. But listen buddy, we gotta enter into a pact. As much as I enjoy coming through to Glasgow to see you, I get a little pissed at us going through the same argument. No matter how much we say we ain't gonna do it, we always go back to the Popper–Kuhn debate.

McGlone gave a sombre nod. — It's a pain in the arse. It's made our careers, but it seems to overshadow our friendship. You were just in the door and we were at it again. It's always the same. We talk about Mary, Philippa, the kids, then we go back to work, slag off a few people. As the bevvy takes effect, it's back to Popper–Kuhn. Problem is, Lou, we're philosophers. Debate and argument are as natural to us as breathing is to others.

This was indeed the case. They had argued with each other over the years; in bars, at conferences and in print in philosophical journals. They had started off as undergraduate students of philosophy at Cambridge University, developing a bond of friendship, based on drinking and womanising; the former usually conducted with more success than the latter.

Both men swam against the ideological tide of their country's culture. The Scot Gus McGlone was a supporter of the Conservative Party. He regarded himself as a classical liberal, a descendant of Hume and Ferguson, though he found the classical economists, even Adam Smith, and his latter disciples with philosophical bents like Hayek and Friedman, a little bland. His real hero was Karl Popper, whom he had studied under as a post-graduate student in London. As a follower of Popper's, he was antagonistic to what he saw as the deterministic theories of

Marxism and Freudianism and what he considered to be the attendant dogma of their disciples.

The American Lou Ornstein, a Chicago-born Jew, was a convinced rationalist, who believed in Marxist dialectical materialism. His interest was science and scientific ideas. He was greatly influenced by the philosopher Thomas Kuhn's concept that the rightness of pure science does not necessarily prevail. If ideas went against the current paradigm, they would be rejected by vested interests. Such ideas, while perhaps scientific 'truths', rarely become recognised as such until the pressure for change becomes unbearable. This, Ornstein felt, was in tune with his political belief in the need for revolutionary social change.

Ornstein and McGlone had had parallel careers, working together in London and then in Edinburgh and Glasgow respectively. McGlone had advanced to a professorial chair about eight months before Ornstein. This irked the American, who considered his friend's elevation had been the result of the political fashionability of his ideas under the Thatcher paradigm. Ornstein contented himself with noting he had a greater publication track record.

The natural political antagonism of the two men was centred around a famous debate between Kuhn and Popper. Popper, who had established himself as a great philosopher by attacking the approaches of the intellectual nineteenth-century giants Sigmund Freud and Karl Marx, and what he saw as the partisanship associated with their ideologies, was less than temperate when he himself had his views of scientific progression attacked by Thomas Kuhn, in his seminal work, *The Structure of Scientific Revolutions.*

Yet one thing was agreed on by both Ornstein and McGlone: the argument, which was their bread and butter, always spilled over from the professional into the personal. They tried all sorts of ways to break this pattern, but nothing could prevent this energy-sapping subject from re-emerging. On a couple of occasions, the friends, exasperated and drunk, had almost come to blows.

— I wish we could find some way to keep it to the journals and conferences and out of our shitfaced sessions, Lou mused.

— Yeah, but how? We've tried everything. I've tried using your arguments, you've tried using mine; we've agreed to say nothing but it inevitably resurfaces. What can we do?

— I think I know a way out of this cul-de-sac, Gus, Lou gave a coy look.

— What are you suggesting?

— Independent arbitration.

— Come on, Lou. No philosopher, no member of our peers could satisfy us as to their independence of mind. They would have formed a prior view on the issue.

— I'm not suggesting a peer. I'm suggesting we find someone in the street, or better still, a pub, and advance our propositions, and let them decide which is the superior argument.

— Ridiculous!

— Hold on, Gus, hear me out. I'm not suggesting for one minute that we let go of our academic standpoints on the basis of one informed opinion. That would be ludicrous.

— What are you suggesting?

— I'm suggesting that we have to split the professional from the personal. Let's remove the argument from our social context by letting another party judge the relative merits of our propositions from that social, pub point of view. It will prove nothing academically, but at least it will let us see whose argument is the most user-friendly for the average man in the street.

— Mmmm . . . I suppose that way we can accept that our various arguments have strengths and weaknesses with the lay person . . .

— Exactly. What we are doing is subjecting those ideas to the real world where they are not discussed, the world of our drinking. What we are agreeing to is giving the victor's ideas sovereignty in the pub context.

— This is nonsense, Lou, but it's interesting nonsense and good sport. I accept your challenge, not because it will validate anything, but because it will hold the loser to shutting up about the scientific logic debate.

They shook hands firmly. Ornstein then took McGlone onto the underground at Hillhead station. — Too many student and intelligentsia types around here, Gus. The last thing I wanna do is get into some discussion with some squeaky undergrad fuck. We need a better laboratory for this little experiment.

Gus McGlone was somewhat uneasy when they alighted at Govan. Despite the Glasgow wide-boy persona he cultivated, he was in fact from Newton Mearns and had led quite a closeted life. It was easy to con the impressionable bourgeois who filled the University staff-rooms that he was the genuine article. In somewhere like Govan, it was another matter.

Lou strode purposefully down the street. There was a feel to the place, a mixture of the traditional and the new, and the huge gap sites reminded him of the Jewish-Irish neighbourhood he'd grown up in on Chicago's North Side. Gus McGlone sauntered behind him, trying to affect a casualness he didn't feel. Ornstein stopped an old woman in the street.

— Pardon me, ma'am, can you tell us where the nearest pub is?

The small woman dropped her shopping bag, turned around and pointed across the road. — Yir right here, son.

— Brechin's Bar! Excellent, Lou enthused.

— It's Breekins Bar, not Bretchins, Gus corrected Lou.

— As in Brechin City, right? Brechin City two, Forfar one, yeah?

— Yeah.

— So the guys that drink in here must root for Brechin City.

— I think not, Gus said, as two men in blue scarves exited from the bar. There was a big game on today at Ibrox; Rangers versus Celtic. Even McGlone, who had little interest in football, knew that.

They went in. The formica-topped island bar was busy, with some groups of men watching TV, others playing dominoes. There were only two women in the place. One was a barmaid of indeterminate middle age, the other a slavering old drunkard. A group of young men in blue scarves were singing a song about something that their father wore, which Lou couldn't quite make out. — Is that a Scottish football song? he asked Gus.

— Something like that, Gus remarked uneasily as he procured two pints. They found a seat beside two old guys who were playing dominoes.

— Awright boeys? one of the old men smiled.

— Yeah, sure thing, buddy, Ornstein nodded.

— You're no fae roond here, the old guy laughed, and they struck up a conversation.

One of the old domino players was particularly talkative, and seemed to have a view on everything. The two philosophers gave each other a sly nod: this was their man. They started to spell out their respective arguments.

The two old guys considered the points. — It's like the boey here sais, one opined, — thir's mair tae this world thin we know about.

— S'only names bit, the other one said. — Magic, science, whit the fuck's the difference? S'only names we gie thum!

The debate raged on, and became increasingly passionate as more drink was consumed. The two philosophers felt a little drunk, and grew very antagonistic towards each other. They had scarcely realised that the argument had attracted several spectators, young men decked in blue, red and white, who had surrounded their table.

However, the atmosphere began to get tense as the younger men got more drunk and charged up with the prospect of the football match. One bloated youth in a blue football strip intervened in the discussion. He carried a distinct air of menace which unnerved the philosophers. — See yous cunts? Yous come doon here fill ah aw yir shite, treat ma da's auld mate, auld Tommy thair, like a fuckin monkey.

— The boey's awright, the boey's awright, auld Tommy

said, but he was speaking to himself, in a soft drunken mantra.

— It wasn't like that, McGlone said shakily.

— You! Shut it! The fat youth sneered. — Yous come doon here wi yir silly wee arguments, n yis still canny agree. Thir's only wahn way tae settle this argument: yous two in a squerr go ootside.

— Ridiculous, McGlone said, worried at the changing vibes.

Ornstein shrugged. He realised that part of him had wanted to punch McGlone's smug face for ages. There had been a girl, at Magdalen College. McGlone had known how he felt about her but he still . . . goddamn his ass . . .

The fat youth took Ornstein's shrug as a signal of acquiescence. — Squerr goes it is then!

— But . . . McGlone was pulled to his feet. He and Ornstein were taken to an empty carpark at the back of a shopping centre. The youths in blue formed a ring around the two philosophers.

McGlone was about to speak, to appeal for rational and civilised behaviour, but to his shock saw the Professor of Metaphysics from the University of Edinburgh bearing down on him. Ornstein struck the first blow, a solid jab to McGlone's chin. — Come on, asshole! he snarled, taking up a boxing stance.

McGlone felt a surge of rage and swung at his friend, and soon the two philosophers were tearing into each other, urged on by the swelling ranks of the Ibrox enclosure mob.

Ornstein gained the upper hand quickly. The telling blow was a powerful punch to the classical liberal's stomach, causing him to double over. Ornstein then hit the Glasgow professor on the side of the jaw. Gus McGlone staggered back from the blow, losing his footing. His head hit the paving-stones with a hollow crack so jarring you felt that outright death would be preferable to the messy range of possibilities which lay just to this side of it. The Chicago materialist, urged on by the crowd, put the boot into the prostrate classical liberal.

Lou Ornstein stood back and examined the gasping, bloodied

figure of McGlone. Far from feeling shame, Ornstein had never felt better. He was basking so thoroughly in his triumph, it took him a while to recognise the dispersal of the crowd and the appearance of a police van. As Gus McGlone rose unsteadily to his feet and tried to get his bearings, he was unceremoniously bundled into a meatwagon.

The two philosophers were locked up in separate cells.

The duty sergeant was going through his routine of asking each brawling set of prisoners who the Billy and who the Tim was. If the handshake is right he will let the Billy go and slap the Tim around a bit. That way everybody's happy. The Billy gets to feel superior and delude himself that being a non-churchgoing 'protestant' is somehow important; the Tim gets to feel persecuted and indulge his paranoia about masonic conspiracies; the sergeant gets to slap the Tim around.

— Whit fit ye kick wi, mate? Duty Sergeant Fotheringham asked McGlone.

— I don't kick with any. I am Professor Angus McGlone, John Pulanzo Professor of Moral Philosophy at the University of Glasgow.

Fotheringham shook his head. Another bampot turfed out the nuthouse under this community care bullshit. — Aye, of course ye are son, he said encouragingly, — n ye know who ah am?

— No . . . McGlone said unsteadily.

— Ah'm David Attenborough. N ah'm used tae dealin wi fuckin animals. Animals like you that terrorise the public . . .

— You stupid bloody fool. You don't know who I am! I could get you into serious trouble. I sit on several government committees and I number . . . McGlone never got to finish the sentence. He was silenced by another digging blow to his stomach and taken to the cells where he was detained before being charged with breach of the peace.

Lou Ornstein, who was on his best behaviour with the police, and whose story was believed due to his accent, emerged from the station without being charged. He made his way to the underground. He had never known that he could fight, and had learned something about himself.

A small youth came up to him. — Ah saw you fightin this eftirnin, big man. Ye were magic, so ye wir.

— No, Ornstein replied, — I was unknown science.

DISNAE MATTER

Ah wis it that Disneyland in Florida, ken. Took hur n the bairn. Wi me gittin peyed oaf fi Ferranti's, ah thoat it's either dae somethin wi the dough or pish it doon the bog it the Willie Muir. Ah saw whit happened tae a loat ay other cunts; livin like kings fir a while: taxis ivraywhair, chinkies ivray night, cairry-oots, ye ken the score. N whit dae they huv tae show fir it? Scottish Fuckin Fitba Association, that's what, ya cunt.

Now ah wisnae that keen oan Disneyland, bit ah thoat: fir the bairn's sake, ken? Wish ah hudnae bothered. It wis shite. Big fuckin queues tae git oan aw the rides. That's awright if ye like that sortay thing, but it's no ma fuckin scene. The beer ower thair's pish n aw. They go oan aboot aw thir beer, thir Budweiser n aw that; its like drinkin fuckin cauld water. One thing ah did like aboot the States though is the scran. Loadsay it, beyond yir wildest dreams, n the service n aw. Ah mind in one place ah sais tae hur: Fill yir fuckin boots while ye kin, hen, cause whin wi git back hame will be livin oafay McCain's oven chips till fuck knows when.

Anywey, it this fuckin Disneyland shite, this daft cunt in a bear suit jumps oot in front ay us, ken? Wavin ehs airms aboot n that. The bairn starts fuckin screamin, gied ur a real fright, ken? So ah fuckin panels the cunt, punches the fuckin wide-o in the mooth, or whair ah thought ehs mooth wis, under that suit, ken? Too fuckin right! Disneyland or nae fuckin Disneyland, disnae gie the cunt the excuse tae jump oot in front ay the bairn, ken.

Thing is, these polis cunts, fuckin guns n aw ya cunt, nae

fuckin joke, ah'm tellin ye, they sais tae ays: Whit's the fucking score here, mate, bit likesay American, ken? So ah goes, noddin ower tae this bear cunt: Cunt jumped oot in front ay the bairn. Well ootay fuckin order. The polis cunt jist says somethin aboot the boy mibbe bein a bit too keen it ehs joab, ken. The other yin sais somethin like: Mibbe the wee lassie's frightened ay bears, ken?

So then this radge in a yellay jaykit comes along. Ah tipples right away thit eh's that bear cunt's gaffer, likesay. Eh apologises tae ays, then turns tae the bear cunt n sais: Wir gaunny huv tae lit ye go mate. They wir jist gaunny, likes, gie the boy ehs fucking cairds like that. This is nae good tae us, eh tells the boy. This perr cunt in the bear suit, eh's goat the head oaf now, likes; the cunt's nearly greetin, gaun oan aboot needin the joab tae pey ehs wey through college. So ah gits a hud ay this radge in the yellay jaykit n sais: Hi mate, yir ootay order here. Thir's nae need tae gie the boy ehs cairds. It's aw sorted oot.

Mean tae say, ah banged the cunt awright, bit ah didnae want the boy tae lose ehs joab, ken. Ah ken whit it's fuckin like. It's aw a great laugh whin they chuck that redundancy poppy it ye, bit that disnae last firivir, ken. Aw they doss cunts thit blow the dough oan nowt. Thuv goat mates they nivir kent they hud — till the fuckin hireys run oot. Anywey, this supervisor radge goes: S'up tae you mate. You're happy, cunt keeps ehs joab. Then eh turns tae the boy n sais: Yir fuckin lucky, ah'm tellin ye. If it wisnae fir the boy here, ken, ye'd be pickin up yir cairds, but this is aw American, likesay, ye ken how aw they doss cunts talk, oan the telly n that.

The cunt ah gubbed, this bear cunt goes: Really sorry, mate, ma fault, ken. So ah jist sais: Sound by me. The polis n the supervisor boy fucked off n the bear cunt turns n sais: Thanks a lot, buddy. Have a nice day. Ah thoat fir a minute, ah'll fucking gie ye nice day, ya cunt, jumpin oot in front ay the fuckin bairn. Bit ah jist left it, ken, nae hassle tae nae cunt. Boy's entitled tae keep ehs joab; that wis ma good deed fir the day. Ah jist goes: Aye, you n aw, mate.

THE GRANTON STAR CAUSE

It hit Boab Coyle hard, right in the centre of his chest. He stood at the bar, open-mouthed, as his mate Kev Hyslop explained the position to him.

— Sorry, Boab, but we aw agree. We cannae guarantee ye a game. Wuv goat Tambo n wee Grant now. This team's gaun places.

— Gaun places!? Gaun places!? Churches League Division Three! It's a kick aboot, ya pretentious cunt. A fuckin kick aboot!

Kev did not like Boab's stroppy response. Surely the Granton Star cause was bigger than any one individual's ego. After all, in an open vote, he had been the one entrusted with the captain's armband for the season. The Star were challenging for promotion to Division Two of the Edinburgh Churches League. Additionally, they were only three games away from a cup-final appearance at City Park – with nets – in the Tom Logan Memorial Trophy. The stakes were high, and Kev wanted to be the man who skippered the Star to cup glory in their own backyard. He knew, though, that part of his responsibilities involved making unpopular decisions. Friendships had to be put on the back burner.

— Yir bound tae be disappointed mate . . .

— Disappointed!? Too fuckin right ah'm disappointed. Which cunt washes the strips nearly every week? Eh? Boab pleaded, pointing to himself.

— C'moan Boab, huv another pint . . .

— Stick yir fuckin pint up yir erse! Some mates yous, eh?

Well fuck yis! Boab stormed out of the pub as Kev turned to the rest of the boys and shrugged.

Before returning home, Boab went for a few unenjoyable pints of lager on his own in two other pubs. He brimmed with resentment when he thought of Tambo, who had had his eye on Boab's number 10 jersey ever since the posing cunt had got involved with the Star at the start of the season. Orange-juice drinking bastard. It had been a mistake to fill the side with wankers like that. It was, after all, just a kick about; a laugh with the mates. *Fresh orange n lemonade. Fresh orange n lemonade.* Tambo's nasal tones grated mercilessly in his head.

In the pubs Boab visited, he failed to recognise anybody. This was unusual. Additionally, auld drunkards who normally plagued him, looking for company, or to cadge a pint, avoided him like he was a leper.

Boab's mother was hoovering when her son returned home. As soon as she heard him at the door, however, she switched the machine off. Doreen Coyle looked conspiratorially at her husband, Boab senior, who shifted his considerable bulk in his chair and cast the *Evening News* onto the coffee table.

— Ah want a wee word, son, Boab senior said.

— Eh? Boab was somewhat alarmed by the challenging and confrontational tone of his father's voice.

But before Boab senior could speak, Doreen started to rant nervously.

— S'no likesay wir tryin tae git rid ay ye, son. S'no likesay that at aw.

Boab stood there, a sense of foreboding cutting through his bemusement.

— That's enough, Doreen, Boab's father said, with a hint of irritation. — Thing is, son, it's time ye wir ootay this hoose. Yir twenty-three now, which is far too auld fir a laddie tae be steyin wi his ma n faither. A mean, ah wis away tae sea wi the Merchant Navy at seventeen. It's jist no natural, son, d'ye understand?

Boab said nothing. He couldn't think straight. His father continued.

— Dinnae want yir mates tae think thit yir some kinday queer felly, now dae ye? Anywey, yir ma n me's no gittin any younger. Wir ent'rin a funny phase in oor lives, son. Some might say . . . Boab Coyle looked at his wife, — . . . a dangerous phase. Yir ma n me son, we need time tae sort oot oor lives. Tae git it the gither, if ye ken whit ah mean. You've goat a lassie, wee Evelyn. You ken the score! Boab senior winked at his son, examing his face for a sign of understanding. Although none was apparent, he carried on. — Yir problem is, son, yir huvin yir cake n eatin it. N whae suffers? Ah'll tell ye whae. Muggins here, Boab senior pointed to himself. — Yir ma n me. Now ah ken it's no that easy tae find somewhair tae stey these days, especially whin yuv hud everybody else, like muggins here, runnin aroond eftir ye. Bit we'll no say nowt aboot that. Thing is, me n yir ma, wir prepared tae gie ye two weeks' grace. Jist as long as ye make sure that yir ootay here within a fortnight.

Somewhat stunned, Boab could only say, — Aye . . . right . . .

— Dinnae think thit wir tryin tae git rid ay ye, son. It's jist thit yir faither n me think thit it wid be mutually advantageous, tae baith parties, likesay, if ye found yir ain place.

— That's it, Doe, Boab's faither sang triumphantly. — Mutually advantageous tae baith parties. Ah like that. Any brains you n oor Cathy've got, son, they definitely come fae yir ma thair, nivir mind muggins here.

Boab looked at his parents. They seemed somehow different. He had always regarded his auld man as a fat, wheezing, chronic asthmatic, and his auld girl as a blobby woman in a tracksuit. Physically they looked the same, but he could, for the first time, detect an unsettling edge of sexuality about them which he'd previously been oblivious to. He saw them for what they were: sleazy, lecherous bastards. He now realised that the look they gave him when he took Evelyn upstairs for sex, was not of embarrassment or resentment, but one of anticipation. Far from concerning themselves with what he was doing, it gave them the chance to do their own thing.

Evelyn. Once he talked to her things would be better. Ev always understood. Ideas of formal engagement and marriage, so long pooh-poohed by Boab, now fluttered through his mind. He'd been daft not to see the possibilities in it before. Their own place. He could watch videos all evening. A ride every night. He'd get another club; fuck the Star! Evelyn could wash the strips. Suddenly buoyant again, he went out, down to the call-box at the shops. He already felt like an intruder in his parents' home.

Evelyn picked up the phone. Boab's spirits rose further at the prospect of company. The prospect of understanding. The prospect of sex.

— Ev? Boab. Awright?

— Aye.

— Fancy comin ower?

— . . .

— Eh? Ev? Fancy comin ower, likesay?

— Naw.

— How no? Something wasn't right. A shuddering anxiety shot through Boab.

— Jist dinnae.

— But how no? Ah've hud a bad day, Ev. Ah need tae talk tae ye.

— Aye. Well, talk tae yir mates well.

— Dinnae be like that, Ev! Ah sais ah've hud a hard day! Whit is it? Whit's wrong?

— You n me. That's whit's wrong.

— Eh?

— Wir finished. Finito. Kaput. Endy story. Goodnight Vienna.

— Whit've ah done, Ev? Whit've ah done? Boab could not believe his ears.

— You ken.

— Ev . . .

— It's no whit yuv done, it's whit yuv no done!

— But Ev . . .

— Me n you Boab. Ah want a guy whae kin dae things fir ays. Somebody whae kin really make love tae a woman. No some fat bastard whae sits oan ehs erse talkin aboot fitba n drinkin pints ay lager wi his mates. A real man, Boab. A sexy man. Ah'm twinty Boab. Twinty years auld. Ah'm no gaun tae tie masel doon tae a slob!

— Whit's goat intae you? Eh? Evelyn? Yuv nivir complained before. You n me. Ye wir jist a daft wee lassie before ye met me. Nivir knew whit a ride wis, fir fuck sake . . .

— Aye! Well that's aw changed! Cos ah've met somebody, Boab Coyle! Mair ay a fuckin man thin you'll ivir be!

— . . . Eh? . . . Eh? . . . WHAE? . . . WHAE IS THE CUUUHHNNT!

— That's fir me tae ken n you tae find oot!

— Ev . . . how could ye dae this tae ays . . . you n me, Ev . . . it wis eywis you n me . . . engagement n that . . .

— Sorry, Boab. Bit ah've been wi you since ah wis sixteen. Ah might huv kent nowt aboot love then, bit ah sure as fuck ken a bit mair now!

— YA FAAHKIN SLAG! . . . YA HORRIBLE FUCKIN HING-OOT! . . .

Evelyn slammed the receiver down.

— Ev . . . Ev . . . Ah love ye . . . Boab spoke those words for the first time, down a dead telephone line.

— SLAAHT! FAAHKIN SLAAAHHT! He smashed the receiver around in the box. His segged brogues booted out two glass panels and he tried to wrench the phone from its mounting.

Boab was unaware that a police squad-car had pulled up outside the phone-box.

Down at the local police station, the arresting officer, PC Brian Cochrane, was typing up Boab's statement when Duty Sergeant Morrison appeared. Boab sat in depressed silence at the foot of the desk while Cochrane typed with two fingers.

— Evening, sarge, PC Cochrane said.

The sergeant mumbled something which may or may not have been 'Brian', not pausing to look around. He put a sausage roll into the microwave. When he opened the cupboard above the oven, Morrison was angered to note that there was no tomato sauce. He despised snacks without ketchup. Upset, he turned to PC Cochrane.

— Thir's nae fuckin ketchup, Brian. Whae's turn wis it tae git the provisions?

— Eh . . . sorry sarge . . . slipped up, the constable said, embarrassed. — Eh . . . busy night, sarge, likes.

Morrison shook his head sadly and let out a long exhalation of breath.

— So what've we goat the night, Brian?

— Well, there's the rapist, the guy who stabbed the boy at the shopping centre and this comedian here, he pointed at Boab.

— Right . . . ah've already been doon n hud a word wi the rapist. Seems a nice enough young felly. Telt ays the daft wee hoor wis askin fir it. S'the wey ay the world, Brian. The guy who knifed the boy . . . well, silly bugger, but boys will be boys. What aboot this tube-stake?

— Caught him smashin up a phone-box.

Sergeant Morrison clenched his teeth shut. Trying to contain a surge of anger which threatened to overwhelm him, he spoke slowly and deliberately: — Get this cowboy doon tae the cells. Ah want a wee word wi this cunt.

Somebody else wanting a wee word. Boab was beginning to feel that these 'wee words' were never to his advantage.

Sergeant Morrison was a British Telecom shareholder. If one thing made him more angry than snacks without tomato ketchup, it was seeing the capital assets of BT, which made up part of his investment, depreciated by wanton vandalism.

Down in the cells, Morrison pummelled Boab's stomach, ribs and testicles. As Boab lay lying groaning on the cold, tiled floor, the sergeant smiled down at him.

— Ye ken, it jist goes tae show ye the effectiveness ay they privatisation policies. Ah would nivir huv reacted like that if ye hud smashed up a phone-box when they were nationalised. Ah know it's jist the same really; vandalism meant increased taxes for me then, while now it means lower dividends. Thing is, ah feel like ah've goat mair ay a stake now, son. So ah don't want any lumpen-proletarian malcontents threatening ma investment.

Boab lay moaning miserably, ravaged by sickening aches and oppressed by mental torment and anguish.

Sergeant Morrison prided himself on being a fair man. Like the rest of the punters detained in the cells, Boab was given his cup of stewed tea and jam roll for breakfast. He couldn't touch it. They had put butter and jam on together. He couldn't touch the piece but was charged with breach of the peace, as well as criminal damage.

Although it was 6.15 a.m. when he was released, he felt too fragile to go home. Instead, he decided to go straight to his work after stopping off at a cafe for a scrambled-egg roll and a cup of coffee. He found a likely place and ordered up.

After his nourishment, Boab went to settle the bill.

— One pound, sixty-five pence. The cafe owner was a large, fat, greasy man, badly pock-marked.

— Eh? Bit steep, Boab counted out his money. He hadn't really thought about how much money he had, even though the police had taken it all from him, with his keys and shoelaces, and he'd had to sign for them in the morning.

He had one pound, thirty-eight pence. He counted out the money. The cafe proprietor looked at Boab's unshaven, bleary appearance. He was trying to run a respectable establishment, not a haven for dossers. He came from behind the counter and jostled Boab out of the door.

— Fuckin wise cunt . . . wide-o . . . ye kin see the prices . . . ah'll fuckin steep ye, ya cunt . . .

Out in the cold, blue morning street, the fat man punched Boab on the jaw. More through fatigue and disorientation than the power of the blow, Boab fell backwards, cracking his head off the pavement.

He lay there for a while, and began weeping, cursing God, Kev, Tambo, Evelyn, his parents, the police and the cafe owner.

Despite being physically and mentally shattered, Boab put in a lot of graft that morning, to try and forget his worries and make the day pass quickly. Normally, he did very little lifting, reasoning that as he was the driver, it wasn't really his job. Today, however, he had his sleeves rolled up. The first flit his crew worked on saw them take the possessions of some rich bastards from a big posh house in Cramond to a big posh house in the Grange. The other boys in the team, Benny, Drew and Zippo, were far less talkative than usual. Normally Boab would have been suspicious of the silence. Now, feeling dreadful, he welcomed the respite it offered.

They got back to the Canonmills depot at 12.30 for dinner. Boab was surprised to be summoned into the office of Mike Rafferty, the gaffer.

— Sit doon, Boab. I'll come straight to the point, mate, Rafferty said, doing anything but. — Standards, he said enigmatically, and pointed to the Hauliers and Removals Association plaque on the wall, bearing a logo which decorated each one of his fleet of lorries. — Counts for nothing now. It's all about price these days, Boab. And all these cowboys, who have fewer overheads and lower costs, they're trimming us, Boab.

— Whit ur ye tryin tae say?

— We've goat tae cut costs, Boab. Where can ah cut costs? This place? He looked out of the glass and wooden box of an office and across the floor of the warehouse. — We're tied doon tae a five-year lease here. No. It has to be capital and labour costs. It's aw doon tae market positioning, Boab. We have to find our niche in the market. That niche is as a quality firm specialising in local moves for the As, Bs and Cs.

— So ah'm sacked? Boab asked, with an air of resignation.

Rafferty looked Boab in the eye. He had recently been on a training course entitled: 'Positively Managing The Redundancy Scenario.'

— Your post is being made redundant, Boab. It's important

to remember that it's not the person we make redundant, it's the post. We've overstretched ourselves, Boab. Got geared up for continental removals. Tried, and I have to say failed, to compete with the big boys. Got a wee bit too carried away by 1992, the single market and all that. I'm going to have to let the big lorry go. We also need to lose a driver's job. This isnae easy, Boab, but it has tae be last one in, first one out. Now ah'll put it around in the trade that I know of a reliable driver who's looking for something, and obviously, ah'll give you an excellent reference.

— Obviously, said Boab, with sarcastic bitterness.

Boab left at lunchtime and went for a pint and a toastie down the local pub. He didn't bother to go back. As he sat and drank alone, a stranger approached him, sitting down next to him, even though plenty free seats were available. The man looked in his fifties, not particularly tall, yet with a definite presence. His white hair and white beard reminded Boab of a folk singer, the guy from the Corries, or maybe the boy in the Dubliners.

— Yuv fucked this one up, ya daft cunt, the man said to him, raising a pint of eighty shilling to his lips.

— Eh? What? Boab was suprised again.

— You. Boab Coyle. Nae hoose, nae joab, nae burd, nae mates, polis record, sair face, aw in the space ay a few ooirs. Nice one, he winked and toasted Boab with his pint. This angered, but intrigued Boab.

— How the fuck dae you ken? Whae the fuckin hell ur you?

The man shook his head, — It's ma fuckin business tae ken. Ah'm God.

— Way tae fuck ya auld radge! Boab laughed loudly, throwing his head back.

— Fuckin hell. Another wise cunt, said the man tiredly. He then trudged out a spiel with the bored, urbane air of someone who had been through all this more times than they cared to remember.

— Robert Anthony Coyle, born on Friday the 23rd of July, 1968, to Robert McNamara Coyle and Doreen Sharp. Younger brother of Cathleen Siobhain Shaw, who is married to James

Allan Shaw. They live at 21 Parkglen Cresent in Gilmerton and they have a child, also called James. You have a sickle-shaped birthmark on your inner thigh. You attended Granton Primary School and Ainslie Park Secondary, where you obtained two SCE O Grades, in Woodwork and Technical Drawing. Until recently, you worked in furniture removals, lived at hame, hud a bird called Evelyn, whom you couldn't sexually satisfy, and played football for Granton Star, like you made love, employing little effort and even less skill.

Boab sat totally deflated. There seemed to be an almost translucent aura around this man. He spoke with certainty and conviction. Boab almost believed him. He didn't know what to believe anymore.

— If you're God, what ur ye daein wastin yir time oan me?

— Good question, Boab. Good question.

— Ah mean, thir's bairns starvin, likesay, oan telly n that. If ye wir that good, ye could sort aw that oot, instead ay sitting here bevvyin wi the likes ay me.

God looked Boab in the eye. He seemed upset.

— Jist hud oan a minute, pal. Lit's git one thing straight. Every fuckin time ah come doon here, some wide-o pills ays up aboot what ah should n shouldnae be fuckin daein. Either that or ah huv tae enter intae some philosophical fuckin discourse wi some wee undergraduate twat aboot the nature ay masel, the extent ay ma omnipotence n aw that shite. Ah'm gittin a wee bit fed up wi aw this self-justification; it's no for yous cunts tae criticise me. Ah made yous cunts in ma ain image. Yous git oan wi it; yous fuckin well sort it oot. That cunt Nietzsche wis wide ay the mark whin he sais ah wis deid. Ah'm no deid; ah jist dinnae gie a fuck. It's no fir me tae sort every cunt's problems oot. Nae other cunt gies a fuck so how should ah? Eh?

Boab found God's whingeing pathetic. — You fuckin toss. If ah hud your powers . . .

— If you hud ma powers ye'd dae what ye dae right now: sweet fuck all. You've goat the power tae cut doon oan the pints ay lager, aye?

— Aye, bit . . .

— Nae buts aboot it. You've goat the power tae git fit and make a mair positive contribution tae the Granton Star cause. You hud the power tae pey mair attention tae that wee burd ay yours. She wis tidy. Ye could've done a loat better there, Boab.

— Mibbe ah could, mibbe ah couldnae. Whit's it tae you?

— Ye hud the power tae git oot fae under yir ma n dad's feet, so's they could huv a decent cowp in peace. Bit naw. No selfish cunt Coyle. Jist sits thair watchin *Coronation Street* n *Brookside* while they perr cunts ur gaun up the waws wi frustration.

— S 'nane ay your business.

— Everything's ma business. Ye hud the power tae fight back against the fat cunt fi the cafe. Ye jist lit the cunt panel ye, fir a few fuckin pence. That wis ootay order, bit ye lit the cunt git away wi it.

— Ah wis in a state ay shock . . .

— And that cunt Rafferty. Ye didnae even tell the cunt tae stick his fuckin joab up his erse.

— So what! So fuckin what!

— So ye hud they powers, ye jist couldnae be bothered usin thum. That's why ah'm interested in ye Boab. You're jist like me. A lazy, apathetic, slovenly cunt. Now ah hate bein like this, n bein immortal, ah cannae punish masel. Ah kin punish you though, mate. That's whit ah intend tae dae.

— But ah could . . .

— Shut it cunt! Ah've fuckin hud it up tae ma eyebaws wi aw this repentence shite. Vengeance is mine, n ah intend tae take it, oan ma ain lazy n selfish nature, through the species ah created, through thir representative. That's you.

God stood up. Although he was almost shaking with anger, Boab saw that this was not easy for him. He could still be talked out of doing whatever he was going to do. — Ye look jist like ah always imagined . . . Boab said sycophantically.

— That's cause ye've nae imagination, ya daft cunt. Ye see ays n hear ays as ye imagine ays. Now you're fuckin claimed, radge.

— Bit ah'm no the worst . . . Boab pleaded. — . . . Whit

aboot the murderers, the serial killers, dictators, torturers, politicians . . . the cunt's thit shut factories doon tae preserve thir profit levels . . . aw they greedy rich bastards . . . what aboot thaim? Eh?

— Might git round tae they cunts, might no. That's ma fuckin business. You've hud it cunt! Yir a piece ay slime, Coyle. An insect. That's it! An insect . . . God said, inspired. — . . . ah'm gaunny make ye look like the dirty, lazy pest thit ye are!

God looked Boab in the eye again. A force of invisible energy seemed to leave his body and travel a few feet across the table, penetrating Boab through to his bones. The force pinned him back in his chair, but it was over in a second, and all Boab was left with was a racing heartbeat and a sweating brow, genitals and armpits. The whole performance seemed to take it out of God. He stood up shakily in his chair and looked at Boab. — Ah'm away tae ma fuckin kip, he wheezed, turning and leaving the pub.

Boab sat there, mind racing, feverishly trying to rationalise what had happened to him. Kevin came into the pub for a quick pint a few minutes after this. He noted Boab, but was reluctant to approach him, after Boab's outburst in the pub the day before.

When Kevin eventually did come over, Boab told him that he had just met God, who was going to turn him into an insect.

— You dinnae half talk some shite, Boab, he told his distraught friend, before leaving him.

That evening, Kevin was at home alone, eating a fish supper. His girlfriend was on a night out with some friends. A large bluebottle landed on the edge of his plate. It just sat there, looking at him. Something told him not to swat it.

The bluebottle then flew into a blob of tomato sauce on the edge of the plate, and soared up to the wall before Kev could react. To his astonishment, it began to trace out KEV against the white woodchip paper. It had to make a second journey to the sauce to finish what it had started. Kev shuddered. This was crazy, but there it was; his name, spelt by an insect . . .

— Boab? Is that really you? Fuckin hell! Eh, buzz twice fir aye, once fir naw.

Two buzzes.

— Did eh, what's his name, did God dae this?

Two buzzes.

— Whit the fuck ur ye gaunny dae?

Frantic buzzing.

— Sorry Boab . . . kin ah git ye anything? Scran, likesay?

They shared the fish supper. Kev had the lion's share, Boab sat near the edge of the plate licking at a little bit of fish, grease and sauce.

Boab stayed with Kev Hyslop for a few days. He was encouraged to lie low, in case Julie, Kev's girlfriend, discovered him. Kev threw the fly-spray away. He bought a pot of ink and some notepaper. He'd pour some ink into a saucer, and let Boab trace out some laborious messages on the paper. One, particuarly, was written in anxiety: CUNT OF A SPIDER IN BATHROOM. Kev flushed the spider down the toilet. Whenever he came in from work, Kev was concerned that something might have happened to Boab. He could not relax until he heard that familiar buzz.

From his location behind the bedroom curtains, Boab plotted revenge. He'd all but absolved Kev for dropping him from the Star, on account of his kindness. However, he was determined to get back at his parents, Evelyn, Rafferty, and the others.

It wasn't all bad being a bluebottle. The power of flight was something he'd have hated to have missed; there had been few greater pleasures than soaring around outside. He also gained a taste for excrement, its rich, sour moistness tantalising his long insect tongue. The other bluebottles who crowded onto the hot shite were not so bad. Boab was attracted to some of them. He learned to appreciate the beauty of the insect body; the sexy, huge, brown eyes, the glistening external skeleton, the appealing mosaic of blue and green, the rough, coarse hairs and the shimmering wings which refracted the sun's golden light.

One day, he flew over by Evelyn's, and caught sight of her

leaving the house. He followed her, to her new boyfriend's place. The guy was Tambo, who'd displaced Boab in the Granton Star line-up. He found himself buzzing involuntarily. After watching them fuck like rabbits in every conceivable position, he flew down into the cat's litter tray, checking first that the creature was asleep in its basket.

He munched at a skittery turd not properly buried in the gravel. He then flew into the kitchen, and puked the shite into a curry that Tambo had made. He made several journeys.

The next day Tambo and Evelyn were violently ill with food-poisoning. Observing them feverish and sick gave Boab a sense of power. This encouraged him to fly over to his old workplace. When he got there, he lifted some smaller granules of blue rat-poison from a matchbox on the floor, and inserted them into Rafferty's cheese salad sandwich.

Rafferty was very sick the next day, having to go to casualty and get his stomach pumped. The doctor reckoned he'd been given rat-poison. In addition to feeling terrible physically, Rafferty was also devastated with paranoia. Like most bosses, who are regarded with at best contempt and at worst hated by all their subordinates, except the most cringing sycophants, he imagined himself to be popular and respected. He wondered: Who could have done this to me?

Boab's next journey was to his parents' home. This was one journey he wished he hadn't made. He took up a position high on the wall, and tears condensed in his massive brown eyes as he surveyed the scene below him.

His father was clad in a black nylon body-stocking with a hole at the crotch. His arms were outstretched with his hands on the mantelpiece and his legs spread. Boab senior's flab rippled in his clinging costume. Boab's mother was naked, apart from a belt which was fastened so tightly around her body it cut sharply into her wobbling flesh, making her look like a pillow tied in the middle with a piece of string. Attached to the belt was a massive latex dildo, most of which was in Boab senior's anus. Most, but still not enough for Boab senior.

— Keep pushin Doe . . . keep pushin . . . ah kin take mair . . . ah *need* mair . . .

— Wir nearly at the hilt already . . . yir an awfay man, Boab Coyle . . . Doreen grunted and sweated, pushing further, smearing more KY jelly around Boab senior's flabby arse and onto the still-visible part of the shaft.

— The questionin, Doe . . . gies the questionin . . .

— Tell ays whae it is! Tell ays ya fuckin philandering bastard! Doreen screeched, as Boab the bluebottle shuddered on the wall.

— Ah'll nivir talk . . . Boab senior's wheezing tones concerned Doreen.

— Ye awright, Boab? Mind yir asthma n that . . .

— Aye . . . aye . . . keep up the questionin, Doreen . . . the crocodile clips, GIT THE CROC CLIPS DOE! Boab senior filled his cheeks with air.

Doreen took the first clip from the mantlepiece and attached it to one of Boab senior's nipples. She did the same with the other one. The third clip was a larger one, and she snapped it harshly onto his wizened scrotum. Turned on by his screams, she pushed the dildo in further.

— Tell ays, Boab! WHAE HUV YE BEEN SEEIN?

—AAAGGHHH . . .' Boab senior screamed, then whispered, — . . . Dolly Parton.

— Whae? Ah cannae hear ye, Doreen said, menacingly.

— DOLLY PARTON!

— That fuckin slut . . . ah knew it . . . whae else?:

— Anna Ford . . . n that Madonna . . . bit jist the once . . .

— SCUMBAG! BASTARD! YA DIRTY FUCKIN PRICK! . . . Ye ken whit this means!

— No the shite, Doe . . . ah cannae eat yir shite . . .

— Ah'm gaunny shite in your mooth, Boab Coyle! It's whit wi baith want! Dinnae deny it!

— Naw! Don't shite in ma mooth . . . don't . . . shite in ma mooth . . . shite in ma mooth . . . SHITE IN MA MOOTH!

Boab saw it all now. While he was mechanically relieving

himself upstairs by skillessly poking Evelyn in the missionary position, his parents were trying to cram the three-piece suite up each other's arses. The very thought of them have a sexuality had repulsed him; now it shamed him in a different way. There was one aspect, however, where it was like father, like son. He knew he could not trust himself to see his mother's shite. It would be too arousing, that succulent, hot sour faeces, all going into his father's mouth. Boab felt his first conscious twinges of an Oedipus complex, at twenty-three years old, and in a metamorphosised state.

Boab sprang from the wall and swarmed around them, flying in and out of their ears.

— Shite . . . that fuckin fly . . . Doreen said. Just then, the phone went. — Ah'll huv tae git it! Boab. Stey thair. It'll be oor Cathy. She'll jist pester us aw night if ah dinnae answer now. Don't go away. She undid the belt, leaving the dildo in Boab's senior's arse. He was at peace, his muscles stretched, but holding the latex rod comfortably and securely. He felt filled, complete, and alive.

Boab junior was exhausted after his efforts and retreated back to the wall. Doreen grabbed the telephone receiver.

— Hiya Cathy. How are you doin, love? . . . Good . . . Dad's fine. How's the wee felly? . . . Aw, the wee lamb! N Jimmy . . . Good. Listen love, wir jist sitting doon tae oor tea. Ah'll phone ye back in aboot half an hour, n will huv a proper blether . . . Right love . . . Bye the now.

Doreen's reactions were quicker than the weary Boab's. She picked up the *Evening News* as she put down the phone and sprang over to the wall. Boab didn't see the threat until the rolled newspaper was hurtling towards him. He took off, but the paper caught him and knocked him back against the wall at great speed. He felt excruciating pain as parts of his external skeletal structure cracked open.

— Got ye, ya swine, Doreen hissed.

Boab tried to regain the power of flight, but it was useless. He dropped onto the carpet, falling down the gap between the wall and the sideboard. His mother crouched down onto her knees, but she couldn't see Boab in the shadows.

— Tae hell wi it, the hoover'll git it later. That fly wis a bigger pest thin young Boab, she smiled, clipping on the belt and pushing the dildo further into Boab senior's arse.

That night, the Coyles were awakened by the sound of groaning. They went tentatively down the stairs and found their son lying battered and bloodied, under the sideboard in the front room, suffering from terrible injuries.

An ambulance was called for, but Boab junior had slipped away. The cause of death was due to massive internal injuries, similar to the type someone would sustain in a bad car crash. All his ribs were broken, as were both his legs and his right arm. His skull had fractured. There was no trail of blood and it was inconceivable that Boab could have crawled home from an accident or a severe kicking in that condition. Everyone was perplexed.

Everyone except Kev, who began drinking heavily. Due to this problem, Kev became estranged from Julie, his girlfriend. He has fallen behind on the mortgage payments on his flat. There are to be further redundancies at the north Edinburgh electronics factory where he works. Worst of all for Kev, he is going through a lean spell in front of goal. He tries to console himself by remembering that all strikers have such barren periods, but he knows that he has lost a yard in pace. His position as captain, and even his place in the Star line-up, can no longer be considered unassailable. Star are not going to be promoted this year due to a bad slump in form and Muirhouse Albion almost contemptuously dismissed them at the quarter-final stage of the Tom Logan Memorial Trophy.

SNOWMAN BUILDING PARTS FOR RICO THE SQUIRREL

The silver squirrel undulated across the yard and scuttled up the bark of the large Californian Redwood tree which overhung the rickety wooden fence. A tearful little boy in sneakers, t-shirt, jeans and baseball-cap watched, helpless in torment as the animal moved away from him.

— We love you Rico! the boy shouted. — Don't go Rico! he screamed in anguish.

The squirrel scrambled deftly up the tree. At the sound of the boy's despairing voice he stopped and looked back. His sad brown eyes glistened as he said, — Sorry Babby, I have to go. Some day you'll understand.

The small creature turned and launched itself along a branch, catching onto another, disappearing into the dense foliage of the woods behind the border of the flimsy fence.

— Mommy! young Bobby Cartwright shouted back towards the house. — It's Rico! He's going, Mommy! Tell him to stay!

Sarah Cartwright appeared on the porch and felt her chest tighten at the sight of her disconsolate son. Tears welled up in her eyes as she strode forward and held the boy to her. In a breathless, sugary voice she said wistfully, — But Rico has to go, honey. Rico's a very special little squirrel. We knew that when he came to us. We knew that Rico would have to go, for it's Rico's mission to spread love all over the world.

— But that means Rico doesn't love us, Mom! If he loved us he'd stay! Bobby screamed, inconsolable.

— Listen Babby, there are other people that need Rico too.

He has to go to them, to help them, to give them the love they need, to make them realise just how much they need each other.

Bobby was not convinced. — Rico doesn't love us, he whimpered.

— No Babby, that's nat it at all, sugar-pie, Sarah Cartwright simpered, — the greatest gift that Rico ever gave to us was making us remember just how much we loved each other. Remember when Daddy got paid off from the plant? We lost our home? Then your little sister, our little Beverley, was run over, killed by that drunk Sheriff? Remember how we all fought and yelled at each other all the time? Sarah Cartwright explained, tears rolling down her cheeks. Her face slowly broke into a smile, like the sun rising triumphantly over dirty grey clouds. — Then Rico came. We thought we'd lost each other, but with Rico's love, we came to realise that the greatest gift we had was our love for each other . . .

— I hate Rico! Bobby snarled, pulling away from his mother and running into the house. He mounted the stairs two at a time.

— Babby, come back . . .

— Rico left us! Bobby shouted miserably, slamming his bedroom door.

— *Switch that fuckin telly oaf! Ah've telt yis before! Oot n play! Maggie Robertson snapped at her children, Sean and Sinead. — Watchin fuckin telly aw day! Daft wee cunts! she half-laughed, half-sneered as Tony Anderson's hand slipped under her t-shirt and bra and roughly grappled her breast.*

Young Sean switched off the television and looked up at her, a briefly uncomprehending but fearful expression frozen onto his face. Then it relaxed again into dead apathy. Sinead just played with her broken doll.

— *Ah said oot! Maggie screamed. — AH'M NO TALKIN TAE MASEL, SEAN, YA DAFT WEE CUNT!*

The children had become inured to her normal level of scream-

ing. It was only this hacking, throttled noise that drew a response from them.

— Gies a bit ay peace yous two, c'moan, Tony pleaded, rummaging in his chinos' pocket for change. All he could feel was his erection though. — C'MOAN! he shouted in angry exasperation. The children departed.

— C'moan doll, get thum oaf, Tony said with urgency but no passion.

— N yir tellin ays ye wirnae wi hur last night?

Tony shook his head in a gesture which was intended to convey exasperation but only came across as belligerent recalcitrance. — Ah fuckin telt ye! Fir the last fuckin time: ah wis doon the snooker wi Rab n Gibbo!

Maggie held his gaze for a second. — See if you're fuckin lyin . . .

— Ud nivir fuckin lie tae you, doll, you kin read ays like a book, Tony said, sticking his hands up her skirt and sliding down her panties. They were stained with discharge from the combination of a severe UTI and a non-specific sexual disease, but he scarcely noticed. — Ye ken whit's oan ma mind now, eh? Extra fuckin sensory perception n that. A right fuckin Paul Daniels you, eh . . . he gasped, undoing his trousers, allowing his constrained gut and erection to fly freely into space.

Bob Cartwright tapped gingerly on the bedroom door. He felt a sadness lie heavily around his heart as he saw his son Bobby junior lying face down on the bed. He pushed onto a corner of it and said softly, — Hi sport, room for another? Bobby junior grudgingly shuffled along. — Hey pitcher, still sore about Rico? Huh?

— Rico hates us!

Bob senior was somewhat taken aback by his son's vehemence, in spite of the warning from his wife, Sarah. He sat back and thought for a while. He'd kept a brave face on, but if the truth be known, he'd sure miss that little guy too. After taking a sad few moments to consider the depths of his own pain, Bob senior began, — Well, you know, Babby, sometimes it maybe seems like that, but Babby, let me tell you, folks, well, they got a habit of doing all sorts of things for all sorts of reasons, some of which we don't rightly know about.

— If Rico really loved us, he'd have stayed!

— Let me tell you a story, Babby. When I was a kid, prabably nat more then your age, maybe just a lill bit older, there was one guy who was my hero. Thet was Al 'Big Al' Kennedy.

Bobby's face lit up. — The Angels! he screamed.

— Yeah sport, that's it. Al Kennedy, the best goddamn pitcher I've ever seen. Phoo-ee! I remember that World Series when we were up against the Kansas Royals. It was Big Al who came through for us. Those Royals hitters fell one by one. STRIKE ONE!

— STRIKE TWO! Bobby squealed gleefully, mimicking his father.

— STRIKE THREE! Bob senior roared.

— STRIKE FOUR! Bobby yelped, as father and son gave each other the high five.

— I'll give you strike four! C'mon sport, lets give it the seventh-inning stretch!

They sang in a lusty chorus:

> Take me up the ball game
> Take me up to the crowd
> Buy me some peanuts and crackerjacks
> I don't care if I ever get back
> and it's root root root for the Angels
> if they don't win it's a shame
> cause it's one, two, three strikes you're out
> at the old ball game!

Bob senior felt gooey inside. That one always got the kid going. — Thing was, son, he said, his face focusing into grim seriousness, — Big Al went away. Signed up for the Cardinals. I said, if Big Al loved us, he wouldn't have gone. God, I hated Al

140

Kennedy, and every time I saw him on TV, playing for the Cardinals I used to put this curse on him: Die, Big Al, I'd say, die, you lousy punk! My pop would say: Hey son, take it easy. There was once I got real mad, started screamin at the box about how much I hated Big Al, but the old man just said: Son, that hate's a funny old word, one you wanna be a little careful bout usin.

— A few days later my dad brought me some newspaper cuttins. I got em here. Always kept these cuttins, Bob senior said, putting them down in front of his son. — Don rightly expect you to read all these now, sport, but lemme tell you, they told me a story, a very special story, Babby, one which I've never forgotten. It was about a school-bus crash in St Louis, Mo. One little fella, why, I guess he drew the short straw in the whole goddamn affair. This little tyke was seriously ill, in a coma. Turned out thet this kid rooted for the Cardinals and his hero was none other than Big Al Kennedy. Anyway, when Big Al heard about this kid, he cut short a hunting trip in Nebraska and travelled back down to St Louis to be by the kid's side. Big Al said to this kid: Listen champ, when you get outta here, I'm gonna show you howta pitch, ya know? Bob senior explained. — Then something incredible happened, Bob senior said softly and dramatically.

Bobby's eyes opened wide in anticipation. — Waht Ded? Waht?

— Well, son, Bob senior continued, swallowing hard, his Adam's apple bobbing, — that little kid opened his eyes. And something else happened. Guess what?

— I dunno, Ded, Bobby junior replied.

— Well, I guess I kinda opened my eyes as well. You know what I mean, Babby?

— I guess . . . the young boy said quizzically.

— What I guess I'm tryin to say, son, is just cause Rico had to go don't mean that he ain't thinkin of us, that he don't love us; it's just that maybe there's somebody that needs him a whole laht more then we do just now.

Bobby junior thought about this for a bit. — Will we ever see Rico again, Pop?

— Who knows, son, perhaps we will, Bob senior said wistfully, as he felt a hand touch his shoulder softly and he looked around and met the open, watery eyes of his wife.

— You know Babby, Sarah Cartwright spoke with wavering emotion, — everytime you see somebody with the light of love in their eyes, you'll see Rico, cause there's one thing you can be sure of, honey, if there's love in people's eyes, it was Rico that put it there!

Sarah looked at her husband who smiled broadly and put his arm around her waist.

He'd been at her now for five minutes and his attention was starting to wander. Bri and Ralphie would be down the Anchor now, their names up for the pool. It was prize money night. As he thrusted, he saw the balls shooting from the tip of the cue, ricocheting off the cushion and rattling softly into the pockets. He had to dump his load into her soon.

Tony poked away as hard as he could and he felt himself so close, but yet so far from that relief. He reached across the coffee table which was adjacent to the couch and picked up the burning cigarette. He arched his neck back and took a long puff and thought of images of Madonna on the singles collection video.

It's no even thit Madonna's a bigger fuckin shag thin a loat ay the fanny roond here, bit whit she dis is dress up. Burds roond here ey dress the fuckin same; each day ivray fuckin day. How ur ye supposed tae cowp somethin thit looks the same ivray fuckin day? That's whit fanny like Madonna understand, yuv goat tae dress up fuckin different, pit oan a bit ay a fuckin show . . .

They were together, Madonna and Anthony Anderson, joined in a mutual coupling of shimmering, sensual, passionate lovemaking. Not a million miles away, Maggie Robertson was giving her man, Keanu Reeves, the most exciting time that Hollywood star ever had. He was about to come, and although a long, long way from climax herself, she was pleased, she was delighted, that she had been able to please her man so . . . that was satisfaction enough because that fat hoor could never have turned him on like this . . .

Then Keanu/Tony saw the face pressed against the window-pane, staring in, watching them, watching him; his stiff jaw, his dead eyes. As his penis grew limp, those eyes filled with passion, for the first time. — SEAN, GIT AWAY FAE THAT FUCKIN WINDAE, YA DURTY WEE CUNT! YOU'RE FUCKIN DEID BY THE WAY! GUARAN-TEED! THAT'S FUCKIN GUARANTEED, SEAN, YA DURTY WEE CUNT! Tony ranted as his limp dick spilled out of Madonna/Maggie.

Springing up, and pulling on his jeans, Tony stormed into the stair and headed into the back green in violent pursuit of the children.

— This is terrible, Mr C. switched off the television. They shouldn't have this on before nine o'clock. C'mon, sport, he looked at Bobby, — time for bed.

— Aw pop, do I have to?

Yep, you do, sport, Bob senior shrugged, — we could all use some shut-eye!

— But I wanna watch *The Skatch Femilee Rabirtsin.*

— Listen Babby, Sarah began, *The Skatch Femilee Rabirtsin* is a horrible programme and your father and I agree that it's not good for you . . .

— Gee Mom, I like *The Skatch Femilee Rabirtsin* . . .

They were diverted from their discussion by a scraping sound which came from the window. They looked out and saw a squirrel on the ledge.

— Rico! they shouted in concert. Sarah opened the window and the animal scampered in and ran up Bobby junior's arm, perching on his shoulder. The young boy stroked his friend's warm fur lightly.

— Rico, you came behk! I noo you'd come behk!

— Hey buddy, Rico laughed, lifting up his paw and giving Bobby junior the high five.

— Rico . . . Sarah simpered, as Bobby senior felt a spasm of emotion rise in his chest.

— I thought to myself, the squirrel said, — there's a lot of good work needs doin, so I'd better get me some help.

He turned his head to the window. The Cartwrights looked outside and could see hundreds, or perhaps even thousands of squirrels, their eyes glowing with love, and ready to spread that love across a cold world.

— I wonder if one of those squirrels will go and help the little Skatch boy n girl on the television, Bobby junior thought out loud.

— I'm sure one of them will, Babby, Sarah simpered.

— Don't hold your fuckin breath on that one honey, Rico the squirrel muttered, but the family failed to hear him, as they were so consumed with joy.

SPORT FOR ALL

See that big skinny gadge wi
the tartan skerf? Big Adam's
aypil hingin ower the toap ay
it? Ah'm jist gaunny huv a wee
word wi the cunt.

Whit d'yis mean leave um?
Ah'm jist spraffin wi the boy,
aboot the game n that, likesay.

                    Hi mate, been tae the rugby?
                    Murrayfield, aye? Scotlin win,
                    aye?

                    Fuckin sound.

Hear that Skanko? Scotlin
fuckin won.

                    Whae wis it thi wir playin,
                    mate?
                    Fiji. FIJI? Who the fuck's
                    that?!

FIJI? Some fuckin islands ya
doss cunt.

Aye?

Aye, well we're jist some
fuckin islands tae these cunts,
think aboot it that wey.

It's right enough though, eh
mate?

Still, wir aw fuckin Scotsmin
the gither, eh mate?

No thit ah ken much aboot
rugby masel. S'a fuckin poof's
game if ye ask me. Dinnae ken
how any cunt kin watch that
fuckin shite. It's true though,
it's aw fuckin queers thit play
that game.

Yir no a poof ur ye, mate?

Whit d'ye mean leave um? Jist
askin the boy if eh's a poof or
no. Simple fuckin question.
Mibbe the cunt is, mibbe eh
isnae.

Whair's it ye come fae, mate?

Marchmont!

Hi Skanko, the boy's fi
Marchmont.

Big hooses up thair mate. Bet
you've goat plenty fuckin
poppy.

Naw? Bit ye stey in a big
hoose bit.

No that fuckin big!

No that fuckin big, eh sais!

You stey in a fuckin castle!

D'ye hear the cunt? No that
fuckin big.

Whit's it ye dae, mate, ye
wurkin?

Aye, fuckin right ya cunt!

Aye . . . bit whit dis that make
ye? Whit's it make ye whin yir
finished?

A fuckin Accountint!

Hear that Skanko! SKANKO!
C'mere the now. C'MERE
THE NOW, YA CUNT!

This cunt's fuckin tellin ays
eh's an Accountint.

Eh? What the fuck you sayin?

147

Aye, right.

Well, a trainee Accountint.

Trainee Accountint,
Accountint, same fuckin
thing; tons ay fuckin hireys.

Naw.

Naw, the boy isnae a poof.

Ah jist thoat that, mate, ken wi
you bein intae the rugby n
that.

Ye goat a burd, mate?

Eh?

Thoat ye sais ye wirnae a poof.
Ivir hud a ride?

Whit d'ye mean leave the
cunt? Jist askin a simple
question.

Ivir hud a ride, mate?

Either ye huv or ye huvnae.
Jist a fuckin question. Ye
dinnae huv tae git a beamer.

That's awright then.

Jist a question, see.

Jist wi you bein intae rugby, ken.

That's ma burd ower thair.

HI KIRSTY! AWRIGHT DOLL! Be ower in a minute. Jist huvin a wee blether wi ma mate here, likesay.

No bad, eh? Tidy, eh?

Eh! You fancy ma burd, ya dirty cunt?

Eh! You tryin tae say ma burd's a fuckin hound? You tryin tae git fuckin wide?

Naw?

Jist is well fir you, ya cunt.

So ye like rugby, eh? Fitba's ma game. Ah nivir go bit. Barred fae the fuckin groond. Anywey, fitba's fuckin borin shite n aw. Dinnae huv tae go tae the game. Maist ay the action takes place before n eftir the game. Heard ay the Hibs Boys? The CCS? Aye?

Take the swedgin ootay fitba, it's fuckin deid.

Goan gies a song, mate. One ay they poof songs ye sing in the rugby clubs before yis aw shag each other.

Jist a wee fuckin song then, cunt!

Jist askin the boy tae gies a fuckin song. Nae hassle likes.

Gies a song, mate. C'Moan!

EH! SHUT UP WI THAT SHITE! Flower ay fuckin Scotlin. Shite! Ah hate that fuckin song: Oh flow-ir-ay-Scot-lin . . . fuckin pish. Gies a real song. Sing Distant Drums.

Whit dae ye mean leave um? Ah'm jist askin the cunt tae sing. Distant Drums.

Eh?

Ye dinnae ken Distant fuckin Drums? No? Listen tae me, mate, ah'll fuckin sing it.

I HEAR THE SOUND
DUH-DUH-DUH-DUH
DUH-DUH-DUH-DUH
OF DIS-TINT DRUMS

DUH-DUH-DUH-DUH-
DUH-DUH-DUH-DUH

SING YA CUNT!

I hear the sound of distant
drums. It's easy. You're the
cunt wi degrees n that. Ye kin
understand that. I-HEAR-
THE-SOUND-OF-
DISTANT-DRUMS.

That's better, hi, hi, hi.

Skanko! Kirsty! Hear the cunt!
Distant fuckin Drums!

Barry. Right. Mine's a boatil
ay Becks mate. The mate n
aw. The burds ur oan
Diamond Whites. That's
Leanne, Skanko thair's burd
ken?

Cheers, mate.

See Skanko, the cunt's
awright. Sound fuckin mate
ay mines, by the way.

Whit did ye say yir name wis,
mate?

Alistair, right

That's fi Alistair.

Cheers, mate

S'at you away now, mate? Aye?
See ye then.

Distant Drums, eh mate!

What a fuckin nondy cunt!
Hud the daft cunt singin that
auld song.

Distant fuckin Drums, ya
cunt.

Becks then Skanko. Jist cause
ay the the boy gittin yin,
disnae mean tae say you
dinnae need tae. Short airms
n deep poakits this cunt, eh
Leanne?

Cheers! Tae rugby cunts;
fuckin poofs bit here's tae
thum!

THE ACID HOUSE

Something strange was happening over Pilton. Probably not just Pilton, Coco Bryce considered, but as he was in Pilton, the here and now was all that concerned him. He gazed up at the dark sky. It seemed to be breaking up. Part of it had been viciously slashed open, and Coco was disconcerted by what appeared to be ready to spill from its wound. Shards of bright neon-like light luminated in the parting. Coco could make out the ebbs and flows of currents within a translucent pool which seemed to be accumulating behind the darkened membrane of the sky, as if in readiness to burst through the gap, or at least rip the wounded cloud-cover further. However, the light emanating from the wound seemed to have a narrow and self-contained range; it didn't light up the planet below.

Then the rain came: at first a few warning spits, followed by a hollow explosion of thunder in the sky. Coco saw a flash of lightning where his glowing vision had been and although unnerved in a different way, he breathed a sigh of relief that his strange sighting had been superceded by more earthly phenomena. *Ah wis crazy tae drop that second tab ay acid. The visuals ur something else.*

His body, if left to its own devices would tend towards rubber, but Coco had enough resources of the will and enough experience of the drug to remember that fear and panic fed off themselves. The golden rule of 'stay cool' had been mouthed by wasters down the decades for good reason. He took stock of his situation: Coco Bryce, tripping alone in the park at roughly three o'clock in the morning, lightning flashing from a foreboding sky above him.

The possibilities were: at the very least he'd be soaked to the skin, at worst he'd be struck by lightning. He was the only tall thing around for a few hundred yards, standing right in the middle of the park. — Fuck sakes, he said, pulling the lapels of his jacket together. He hunched up and stole quickly down the path that split the massive canine toilet which was West Pilton Park.

Then Coco Bryce let out a small whisper, not a scream, just a murmur, through a soft gasp. He felt his bones vibrate as heat surged through his body and the contents of his stomach fell to displace those of his bowels. Coco had been struck by something from the sky. Had his last vision before he let go of consciousness not been one of the concrete path rising to meet him, he might have thought: lightning.

Who   What   Where   How   WHAT AM I?

Coco Bryce. Brycey fae Pilton. Brycey: one ay the Hibs Boys. Coco Fuckin Bryce, ya radge, he tried to shout, but he had no voice with which to make himself heard. He seemed to be blowing limply in a wind, but he could feel no currents of air nor hear their whistle. The nearest he could approximate to any sensation was that of being a blanket or a banner, floating in a breeze, yet he had still no sense of dimension or shape. Nothing conveyed to his cauterised senses any notion of his extent; it seemed as if he both encompassed the universe and was the size of a pin-head.

After a while he began to see, or sense, textures around him. There were images alright, but there was no sense of where they were coming from, or how they were being processed, no real sense of him having a body, limbs, a head, or eyes. Nonetheless these images were clearly perceived; a blue-black backdrop, illuminated by flickering, sparkling shapeless objects of varying mass, as unidentifiable as he was himself.

Am ah deid? Is this fuckin deid? COCO FUCKIN BRYCE!

The black was becoming more blue; the atmosphere he was moving around in was definitely getting thicker, offering more resistance to his sense of momentum.

Coco Bryce

It was stopping his movement. It was like a jelly, and he realised that he was going to set in it. A brief panic gripped him. It seemed important to keep moving. There was a sense of a journey needing to be completed. He willed himself on and could make out, in the distance, an incandescent centre. He felt a strong sense of elation, and using his willpower, travelled towards this light.

This fuckin gear isnae real. Eftir ah come doon, that's it, that's me fuckin well finished!

* * *

Rory Weston's hands shook as he put the receiver down. He could hear the screams and shouts coming from the other room. For a moment, no more than a few seconds, Rory wished he wasn't occupying this particular space and time. How had all this happened? He began to trace the sequence of events that led to this, only to be disrupted by another violent shriek from through the wall. — Hang on, Jen, they're on their way, he shouted, running through towards the source of the agonised cacophony.

Rory moved over to the swollen, distressed figure of his girl-friend, Jenny Moore, and crushed her hand in his. The Parker Knoll settee was soaked with her waters.

Outside, the thunder roared on, drowning out Jenny's screams for the neighbours.

Jenny Moore, through her pain, was also thinking about the cumulation of circumstances which led her to be in this condition in this Morningside flat. Her friend Emma, also pregnant, though a month less advanced than Jenny, had caught sight of their waddling figures reflected in a shop window in Princes Street. — God sakes, Jen, look at us! You know, I sometimes wish, looking back to that cold winter's evening, that I'd given Iain that blow-job instead, she exclaimed.

They had laughed at this; laughed loudly. Well, Jenny wasn't laughing now.

I'm being torn apart and this bastard sits over me with that stupid fucking expression on his face.

What did it take out of them physically? It was just another fuck for those bastards. We had it all to do, but there they all were telling us how to do it, controlling us — gynaecologists, fathers to be, all men; together in a sickly pragmatic conspiracy . . . the scumbags have already disengaged emotionally from you; you're just the receptacle to carry the precious fruit of their sweaty bollocks into the world, through your fucking blood . . . But you're being hysterical darling . . . it's all those hormones, all over the place, just listen to us, we know best . . .

The bell went. The ambulance had arrived.

Thank god they're here, the men. More bloody men. Ambulance-MEN. Where the fucking hell were the ambulanceWOMEN?

— Easy Jen, there we go . . . Rory said with what was meant to be encouragement.

There WE go? she thought, as another wave of pain, worse this time than anything she had known, tore through her. This time the thunder and lightning of the freakiest freak storm to hit Scotland simply couldn't compete. She was almost blacking out with the pain as they got her on the stretcher, down the stairs and into the van. No sooner did they start up than they realised they wouldn't make the hospital.

— Stop the van! shouted one of the ambulancemen. — It's happening now!

They stopped the van by the side of the deserted Meadows. Only the flashing bolts of lightning; strange, persistently luminous and following awkward, uncharacteristic trajectories, lit up the starkly darkened sky. One of these bolts struck the ambulance parked in that deserted road as Jenny Moore was trying to push the offspring of her and her partner Rory Weston out into the world.

* * *

AW THIS IS NOWT TAE FUCKIN DAE WI ME

COCO

COCO BRYCE

BRYCEY

COLIN STUART BRYCE

```
        C              T      BR Y C  E     Y
        O              R                    A
        L          A                        F
        I          U                        U
        N     S T                           C
                                            K
                                            I
                                            N

                                            R
                                            A
                                            D
                                            G
How long dae ah go oan fir                  E
```

I N   STUUUUUAAAAAAAARRRTTTT T T T   B R
COLINSTUARTBRYCE

Colin Stuart Bryce, or Coco Bryce, the Pilton casual, as he perceived himself to be, although he could not be too sure anymore, floated in the heightless void of gel, toward its white luminous centre. He became aware of something racing toward

```
+-----------------+
| Hi-bees here    |
| Hi-bees there   |
| Hi-bees every   |
+-----------------+
```

him at great speed, approaching from that far-off central point he had sensed. While the now thick and solidifying gel had begun to constrain the life-force that was Coco Bryce, this other energy source negotiated it with the ease of light travelling through air. He could not see this, only gain a notion of it through some strange, indefinable conglomeration of the senses.

> fuckin where
> na na na na na
> na na na na

It seemed to sense him too, for it slowed down as it approached him, and after hesitating, shot past him at speed and was gone, vanishing into the indistinct environment around him. However, Coco had a

> we scored one
> we scored two
> we scored seven
> more than you

chance to sense what it was, and it was like nothing he'd witnessed before, an elongated blue, glass-like, cylindrical-shaped force, yet in a bizarre way it felt human; just as he, Coco Bryce, still considered himself to be human.

> Dad's comin back tae us, Colin.
> He's better now son. He's
> changed, Colin. We'll soon be the
> gither again son. Yill see a big
> difference, you mark ma words.
> Dinnae be frightened son, yir Ma
> widnae lit um hurt us again. Ah
> widnae lit um back in the hoose
> unless he'd changed, son . . .

He felt elated as the light grew closer, more powerful, beckoning him. He felt that if he could get to it, everything would be all right. Hopeful, he willed himself on through the rapidly thickening gel. Propulsion, achievable purely through the exercise of will, was becoming increasingly difficult. No idea of where he was, of his shape, size, or his senses in the discrete

> There is one nasty,
> malignant little
> creature in this
> class, an odious
> young fool of a
> boy who spreads

categories of sight, touch, taste, smell, hearing, these seeming obsolete, yet him somehow able to experience the exploding kaleidoscope of colours beyond the gel that engulfed him; to feel the movement and the resistance to that movement.

> his poisonous
> influence to
> other, keener
> pupils. I am
> referring, of
> course, to

It was growing darker. As soon as that awareness hit him, he noted it was pitch black. Coco felt fear.

Colin Bryce, the most common and disgusting little man I've ever had the displeasure of teaching in one of my classes. Step forward, Colin Bryce! What have you to say for yourself?

He had slowed down completely now, grinding to a halt. His will no longer served as a driving mechanism. The light was closer though. The Light.

It was upon him, around him, in him. LIGHT LIGHT LIGHT LIGHT LIGHT LIGHT LIGHT LIGHT LIGHT LIGHT LIGHT LIGHT LIGHT LIGHT

YILL DAE IS YIR FUCKIN WELL TELT, COLIN, YUH WEE CUNT! AH SAIS TWINTY FUCKIN REGAL! NOW! MOVE IT!

LIGHT LIGHT LIGHT LIGHT LIGHT LIGHT LIGHT LIGHT LIGHT LIGHT LIGHT LIGHT LIGHT LIGHT

Yir a tidy cunt, mate. Coco, is it no? Welcome tae the family. Fuckin main man!

LIGHT LIGHT LIGHT LIGHT LIGHT LIGHT LIGHT LIGHT LIGHT LIGHT

Kirsty, ah really like ye, ken? Ah mean, ah'm no much good it talkin like this, bit ye ken whit ah mean, likesay you n me, ken?

LIGHT LIGHT LIGHT LIGHT LIGHT LIGHT LIGHT LIGHT LIGHT LIGHT LIGHT LIGHT

Ye shag that burd Coco? Fill hoose? Tony's been up it likes. C'moan Coco, dinnae git stroppy. Only sayin likes! Hey boys, Coco's in luurrve! Hi! hi! hi!

LIGHT LIGHT LIGHT LIGHT LIGHT LIGHT LIGHT LIGHT LIGHT LIGHT LIGHT LIGHT LIGHT LIGHT LIGHT LIGHT LIGHT LIGHT LIGHT LIGHT

Too much fuckin ridin, too many fuckin collies n no enough fuckin swedgin. That's whit's wrong wi us these days.

LIGHT LIGHT

LIGHT LIGHT LIGHT LIGHT LIGHT LIGHT LIGHT
LIGHT LIGHT LIGHT LIGHT LIGHT LIGHT LIGHT

> You're on a slippery slope, Bryce. It's no
> game, son. I kid you not. The next time I get
> a hold of you, the key gets thrown away.
> You're vermin, son, pure vermin. You think
> you're a gangster, but you're just a silly
> wee laddie to me. I've seen them all come
> through here. Oh, they aw think they're so
> hard, so cool. They usually die in the gutter
> or the lodging house or rot their miserable
> lives away in a cell. You've blown it Bryce,
> totally blown it, you silly little toe-rag.
> The saddest thing is, you don't even realise
> it, do you?

LIGHT LIGHT LIGHT LIGHT LIGHT LIGHT LIGHT
LIGHT LIGHT LIGHT LIGHT LIGHT LIGHT LIGHT
LIGHT LIGHT LIGHT LIGHT LIGHT LIGHT LIGHT
LIGHT LIGHT LIGHT LIGHT LIGHT LIGHT LIGHT
LIGHT LIGHT LIGHT LIGHT LIGHT LIGHT LIGHT

> The thing is that ah'm a fuckin
> businessman. Right? The demolition
> business.

LIGHT LIGHT LIGHT LIGHT LIGHT LIGHT LIGHT
LIGHT LIGHT LIGHT LIGHT LIGHT LIGHT LIGHT
LIGHT LIGHT LIGHT LIGHT LIGHT LIGHT LIGHT
LIGHT LIGHT LIGHT LIGHT LIGHT LIGHT LIGHT
LIGHT LIGHT LIGHT LIGHT LIGHT LIGHT LIGHT
LIGHT LIGHT LIGHT LIGHT LIGHT LIGHT LIGHT
LIGHT LIGHT LIGHT LIGHT LIGHT LIGHT LIGHT
LIGHT LIGHT LIGHT LIGHT LIGHT LIGHT LIGHT
LIGHT LIGHT LIGHT LIGHT LIGHT LIGHT LIGHT
LIGHT LIGHT LIGHT LIGHT LIGHT LIGHT LIGHT
LIGHT LIGHT LIGHT LIGHT LIGHT LIGHT LIGHT
LIGHT LIGHT LIGHT LIGHT LIGHT LIGHT LIGHT
LIGHT LIGHT LIGHT LIGHT LIGHT LIGHT LIGHT
LIGHT LIGHT LIGHT DARKER DARKER DARKNESS

Heaven or hell, wherever this is, ah'm fuckin closin in! Thir's gaunny be some changes aroond here, ya cunts! Coco Bryce. Pilton. Distinguished honours at Millwall (pre-season friendly), Pittodrie, Ibrox and Anderlecht (UEFA Cup). Coco Bryce, a top boy. A cunt that messes is a cunt that dies. See if any cunt . . . if any cunt gits . . . if any cunt . . .

His thoughts trailed out insipidly. Coco was frightened. At first the fear was an insidious quease, then it became brutally stark and raw as he felt great forces on him, crushing and pulling at him. It felt as if he was in the grip of a vice while simultaneously another power tried to tear him from its grasp. These forces, though, enabled him to define his body for the first time since this strange journey had begun. He knew he was human, all too human, too vulnerable to the powers that crushed and wrenched at him. Coco prayed for a victor in the struggle between the two great and evenly matched forces. The torture lasted for a while, then he felt himself being torn from the void. He had only sensed THE LIGHT before, but now he could actually see it, burning through his closed eyelids, which he could not open. And then he realised there were voices:

— It's a beauty!

— A wee laddie for ye, hen, eh's a wee cracker n aw.

— Look, Jen, he's wonderful!

Coco could sense himself being held up; could sense his body, where his limbs were. He tried to shout: Coco Bryce! Hibs Boys! What's the fuckin score, ya cunts?

Nothing came from his lungs.

He felt a slap on his back and an explosion of air within him, as he let out a loud, wrenching scream.

* * *

Dr Callaghan looked down at the young man in the bed. He had been comatose, but now that he had emerged into consciousness, he was displaying some strange behavioural patterns. He couldn't speak, and writhed around in his bed, thrashing his arms and legs. Eventually he had to be constrained. He screamed and cried.

Cold.
Help.

— Waaahhh! screamed the youth. At the foot of his bed he had a nametag: COLIN BRYCE.

Hot.
Help.
— Waaahhh!

Hungry.
Help.
— Waaahhh!

Need hug.
Help.
— Waaahhh!

Want to pish, shite.
Help.
— Waahhh!

Dr Callaghan felt that, through his screaming, the youth was perhaps trying to communicate; though he couldn't be sure.

* * *

On the ward Jenny held her son. They would call him either Jack or Tom, as they had agreed, because, she considered with a sudden surge of cynicism, that's what people like them tended to do. They were located in an eighties English-speaking strata where culture and accent are homogenous and nationality is a largely irrelevant construct. Middle-class, professional, socially-aware, politically-correct people, she reflected scornfully, tended to use those old proletarian craftsperson names: ideal for the classless society. Her friend Emma had announced her intention to call her child Ben, if it was a boy, so the choice had been narrowed to one of two.

How's my little Jack, Rory said to himself, his index finger touching the baby's doughy hand.

Tom, Jenny thought, cradling her son.

What's the fuckin story here then, ya cunt?

* * *

Over the following few days the family of Colin Bryce became resigned to the fact that their son seemed to alternate between the vegetative and the rambling lunatic states after the accident. Friends testified that Coco had taken not one, but two tabs of acid, Supermarios to boot, and the press seized onto this. The youth in the hospital became a minor celebrity. The newspapers posed the same rhetorical question:

> DID COLIN BRYCE GET HIS BRAINS FRIED BY
> LIGHTNING OR LSD?
> COLIN BRYCE — A VICTIM OF A FREAK ACCIDENT OR YET
> ANOTHER OF OUR YOUNGSTERS DESTROYED BY
> THE DRUGS MENACE?

While the press seemed to know for sure, the doctors were baffled as to the nature of the young man's condition, let alone the possible causes of it. However, they could see signs of improvement. There was growing eye contact over the weeks, definite indications of intelligence. They encouraged friends and family to visit the youth, who it was felt would benefit from as much stimulation as possible.

* * *

The baby was called Tom.

Coco, ya radge cunts! Coco Bryce! Brycie! CCS! Hibs boys smash all fuckin opposition. Too true.

Becks then, cunt.

Jenny breastfed her baby.

Phoah, ya fucker! This'll fuckin dae me. Coco Bryce, who he? Ma name's Tam, eh Tom!

The child fed greedily, sucking hard on Jenny's nipple. Rory, who had taken some holiday time on top of his paternity leave, observed the scene with interest. — He seems to be enjoying himself. Look at him, it's almost obscene, Rory laughed, concealing the growing feeling of unease which swept over him. It was the way the baby looked at him sometimes. It actually seemed to focus on him and look, well, contemptuous and aggressive. That was ridiculous. A small baby. His baby.

He reasoned that this was an important issue to share with some of the other Persons Of The Male Gender at his men's group. It was, he reasoned, perhaps a natural reaction at the inevitable exclusion of the male partner from the woman–parent and child bonding process.

Phoah, ya cunt ye! Some fuckin jugs oan it!

Jenny felt something small and sharp pressing on her stomach. — Oh look, he's got a stiff little willy! she exclaimed, holding up the naked baby. — Who's a naughty little boy? she kissed his plump stomach and made quacking noises.

Lower, ya big fuckin pump-up-the-knickers! Git yir fuckin gums roond it!

— Yes, interesting . . . Rory said uneasily. The child's face; it looked like a leering, lecherous old man. He'd have to see about this terrible jealousy, talk it through with other men who were in touch with their feelings. The thought of having a genuine hang-up to share with the rest of the group thrilled him.

That night Rory and Jenny made love for the first time since she'd come home with the baby. They started gently, warily testing the tenderness of her sex, then became increasingly passionate. Rory, though, was distracted during his performance by sounds he thought he heard coming from the cot at the side of the bed. He looked around and shuddered, sure that he could see the outline of the baby, this baby only a couple of weeks old, standing up in the cot watching them!

Ya dirty cunts! Doggy style n aw! Phoah . . .

Rory stopped his strokes.

— What is it Rory? What the fuck is it? Jenny snapped, angry at the interruption as she was chasing her first post-birth climax.

They heard a soft thud from the cot.

— The baby . . . it was standing up, watching us, Rory said weakly.

— Don't be bloody stupid! Jenny hissed. — C'mon Rory, fuck me! Fuck me!

Rory, however, had gone limp, and he spilled out of her. — But . . . it was . . .

— Shut up for fuck's sake! She moved around, angrily pulling the duvet over them. — It's not an it, HE is a HIM. Your own bloody son! She turned away from him.

— Jen, he put his hand on her shoulder, but she shrugged it off, its limp creepiness sickening her.

After that, they decided it was time to put the baby in the room they'd made into a nursery. Jenny found the whole thing pathetic, but if Rory was put off that much, well, so be it.

The following night the baby lay silently awake in its new location. Rory had to concede that he was a good baby, he never seemed to cry. — You never seem to cry, do you, Tom? he asked wistfully as he stood over the child in the cot. Jenny, who'd had a panic attack in the night due to the child's silence, had sent Rory through to check on him.

Ah'm feart ay nae cunt. Whin ah goat cornered by they fuckin cunts at Cessnock whin wi pissed aw ower thum at Ibrox, ah jist goes: Come ahead then, ya fuckin weedjie cunts. Ah'm no exactly gaunny burst oot greetin cause some specky cunt's five minutes late wi ma feed now, um uh? Fuckin tube.

Could handle a fuckin Becks.

* * *

There was still no change in the condition of the youth in the hospital, although Dr Callaghan was now sure that he was using attention-seeking behaviour to meet his basic needs of food, changing and body-temperature regulation. Two of his friends, young men in hooded sweatshirts, came to see him. They were called Andy and Stevie.

— Fuckin shame, man, Andy gasped, — Coco's fucked. Jist lyin thair greetin like a bairn, eh.

Stevie shook his head sadly, — Tell ays that's fuckin Coco Bryce lyin thair, man.

A nurse approached them. She was a pleasant, open-faced, middle-aged woman. — Try to talk to him about some of the things you did together, things he'd be interested in.

Stevie stared at her with open-mouthed bemusement; Andy gave a snigger followed by a mocking shake of his head.

— You know, like discos and pop, that sort of thing, she cheerfully suggested. They looked at each other and shrugged.

Too warm.

— Waah!

— Right, Andy said. — Eh, ye missed yirsel the other day thair, Coco. The semi, ken? Wi wir waitin fir they Aberdeen cunts at Haymarket, eh. Booted fuck ootay the cunts, man, chased thum back doon tae the station, back ontae the train, doon the fuckin tracks, the loat! Polis jist fuckin standin thair n aw, didnae ken what tae fuckin dae, eh no. How good wis it Stevie?

— Fuckin barry, ya cunt. Couple ay boys goat lifted; Gary n Mitzy n that crew.

— Waah!

They looked at their screaming, unresponsive friend and fell into silence for a while. Then Stevie started: — N ye missed yirsel at Rezurrection n aw, Coco. That wis too mad. How radge wir they snowballs, Andy?

— Mental. Ah couldnae dance, bit this cunt wis up aw night.

Ah jist wanted tae spraff tae ivray cunt. Pure gouchin the whole night, man. Some fuckin good Es floatin aroond the now, Coco, ye want tae git it the gither man, n will git sorted and git some clubbin done . . .

— It's nae fuckin use, Stevie moaned, — eh cannae hear us.

— This is fuckin too radge, man, Andy conceded, — cannae handle aw this shite, eh.

Feed.

— Waah! WAAAHHHHH!

— That's no Coco Bryce, Stevie said, — no the Coco Bryce ah ken anywey.

They left as the nurse came in with Coco's food. All he would eat was cold, liquidised soup.

* * *

Rory reluctantly started back at work. He'd grown worried about Jenny, concerned about how she was coping with the baby. It was obvious to him that she was suffering from some form of post-natal depression. Two bottles of wine had been taken from the fridge. He'd said nothing to her, waiting for her to raise the matter. He'd have to keep his eye on her. The men at the group would support him; he'd have their admiration, not just for being in touch with his own feelings, but also for his unselfish responsiveness to his partner's needs. He remembered the mantra: awareness is seventy percent of the solution.

Jenny had a bad fright on Rory's first day back at work. The baby had been very sick in his cot. There was a strange smell coming from him. It was like . . . alcohol.

We do not carry hatchets, we do not carry chains, We only carry straws to suck our lemonade.

Oh, ya cunt ye . . . ma heid's fuckin nippin wi that vino. Cannae drink as much as ah used tae, no as a sprog . . .

The horrible truth dawned on Jenny: Rory was trying to poison their baby! She found the empty bottles of wine underneath the bed. That sick, warped, spineless fool . . . she would take the child to her mother's. Though perhaps it hadn't been Rory. A couple of workmen had been in, young lads, sanding and staining the woodwork: the doors and skirting boards. Surely they wouldn't have tried to give a new baby alcohol. They wouldn't be that irresponsible . . . she'd get onto the firm. Perhaps even contact the police. It could be Rory though. Whatever, Tom's safety was all that mattered. That inadequate fool could bleat piteously about his sick little problems to the inspid like-minds in his pathetic group. She was leaving.

— Who did it, Tom? Was it bad Daddy? Yes! I bet it was! Bad Daddy's tried to hurt little Tom. Well we're going away, Tom, we're going to my mummy's down in Cheadle.

Eh? What?

— That's near Manchester, isn't it Tom-Tom? It is! Yes, it is! And she'll be so pleased to see little Tom-Tom, won't she? Won't she?! Yes, she will! Will Will Will Will Will! She smothered the baby's doughy cheek with wet kisses.

Git tae fuck, ya daft cunt! Ah cannae go tae fuckin Manchester! Goat tae pit this fuckin sow in the picture. Ah'm no her fuckin bairn. The name's Coco Bryce.

— Look, eh Jenny . . .

She froze as she heard the voice coming from that small mouth which twisted unnaturally to form the words. It was an ugly, shrieking, cackling voice. Her baby, her little Tom; he looked like a malevolent dwarf.

Fuck sakes. Ah've done it now. Stey cool, Coco, dinnae freak this daft hoor oot.

— You spoke! Tom. You spoke . . . Jenny gasped in disbelief.

— Look, said the baby, standing up in his cot, as Jenny swayed unsteadily, — sit doon, eh sit down, he urged. Jenny obeyed in silent shock. — You'd better no say nowt tae nae cunt aboot this, right? the baby said, looking keenly and sharply at its mother for signs of understanding. Jenny just looked bemused. — Eh, I mean, Mother, they would not understand. They would take me away. I would be treated like a freak, cut up oan a laboratory table, tested by aw they specky cunts . . . eh, the people in white coats. Ah'm a sortay, eh, a sort of phenomenon, I've got eh, special intelligence n that. Right?

Coco Bryce was pleased with himself. He thought back to the videos of *Star Wars* he'd watched avidly as a kid. He had to act cosmic to keep this gig going. He was doing alright here. — They'd want tae take ays away . . .

— Never! I'd never let them take my Tom away! Jenny screamed, the prospect of losing her baby galvanising her into some sort of sense. — This is incredible! My little Tom! A special baby! But how, Tom? Why? Why you? Why us?

— Eh, jist the wey it goes. Nae cunt kens, ah mean, it's just the way I was born, Mother, my destiny n that.

— Oh, Tom! Jenny scooped up the baby in her arms.

— Eh right! the child said with embarrassment. — Eh listen, Ma, eh, Jenny, one or two wee things. That scran, eh, the food. It's no good. I want what grown-ups get. No aw that veggie stuff that yous eat. Meat, Jenny. A bit ay steak, ken?

— Well, Rory and I don't . . .

— Ah'm no giein a fuck aboot you n Rory . . . ah mean, eh, yous have no right to deny me my free choice.

This was true, Jenny conceded. — Yes, you're right, Tom. You're obviously intelligent enough to articulate your own needs. This is amazing! My baby! A genius! How do you know about things like steak though?

Oh, ya cunt. Dinnae fuck up here. This is a good fuckin doss yiv goat.

— Eh, I picked a lot of it up from the telly. I heard they two joiner boys that ye hud in daein yir woodwork bletherin. Ah picked up a lot fae them.

— That's very good, Tom, but you shouldn't talk like those workmen. Those men are, well, a little common, probably a bit sexist in their conversation. You should have more positive role models.

— Eh?

— Try to be like somebody else.

— Like Rory, the baby scoffed.

Jenny had to think about that, — Well, maybe not, but, oh . . . we'll see. God, he's going to be so shocked when he finds out.

— Dinnae tell um, it's oor secret, right.

— I have to tell Rory. He's my partner. He's your father! He has the right to know.

— Mother, eh Jenny, it's jist this ah git a vibe offay that radge. He's jealous ay me. He'd shop ays, git ays taken away.

Jenny had to concede that Rory had been unstable enough in his behaviour towards their child to suggest that he wasn't emotionally equipped to handle this shock. She would go along with this. It would be their secret. Tom would just be a normal little baby with others around, but when they were alone he'd be her special little man. With her guiding his development he would grow up non-sexist and sensitive, but strong and genuinely expressive, rather than an insipid clown who clings to a type of behaviour for limp ideological reasons. He'd be the perfect new man.

* * *

The youth they called Coco Bryce had learned to speak. At first it was thought that he was repeating words parrot fashion, but he then began to identify himself, other people and objects. He seemed particularly responsive to his mother and his girlfriend, who came to visit regularly. His father never visited.

His girlfriend Kirsty had cut her hair short at the sides. She had long wanted to do this, but Coco had discouraged her. Now he was in no position to. Kirsty chewed on her gum as she looked down at him in the bed. — Awright, Coco? she asked.

— Coco, he pointed at himself. — Caw-lin.

— Aye, Coco Bryce, she said, spitting out the words between chews.

His heid's finally fried. It's that acid, they Supermarios. Ah telt um, bit that's Coco, livin fir the weekends; raves, fitba. The week's jist something tae get through fir him, and he'd been daein too much fuckin

acid tae get through it. Well, ah'm no gaunny hing aboot waitin fir a
vegetable tae git it the gither.

— Skanko n Leanne's suppose tae be gittin engaged, she
said, — that's what ah heard anywey.

This statement, though it elicited no response from Coco,
sparked off an interesting line of thought for Kirsty. If he could
remember nothing, he might not remember the status of their
relationship. He might not remember what a pain in the arse he
could be when it came to talking about their future.

Toilet.

— Number twos! NUMBER TWOS! the youth screamed.

A nurse appeared with a bedpan.

After he had shat, Kirsty sat on the edge of her boyfriend's
bed and bent over him. — Skanko n Leanne. Engaged, she
repeated.

He pushed his mouth towards her breasts and began sucking
and biting at them through her t-shirt and bra. — Mmmmm . . .
mmmm . . .

— Get the fuck offay ays! she shouted, pushing him away. —
No here! No now!

The sharpness in her voice made him wail. — WAAHH!!

Kirsty shook her head scornfully, spat out her gum, and left.
If, though, as the doctors were suggesting, he was a blank piece
of paper, Kirsty had realised that she could colour him in as she
liked. She'd keep him away from his mates when he got out.
He'd be a different Coco. She'd change him.

* * *

All Jenny's material on post-natal care hadn't quite prepared her
for the type of relationship she and her baby were developing.

— Listen Jenny, ah want ye tae take ays tae the fitba oan
Setirday. Hibs–Herts at Easter Road. Right?

— Not until you stop talking like a workman and speak
properly, she said. The content of his conversation and the tone
of his voice concerned her.

171

— Yes, sorry. I thought I'd like to see some sport.

— Em, I don't know much about the football, Tom. I like to see you express yourself and develop interests, but football . . . it's one of those terribly macho things, and I don't think I want you getting into it . . .

— Aw aye, I mean, so I can grow up like that wanker! Eh, my father? C'mon Mum, wise up! He's a fuckin toss!

— Tom! That's enough! Jenny said, but she couldn't help smiling. The kid was definitely onto something here.

Jenny agreed to take the child onto the East Terracing at Easter Road. He made her stand over by a heavily policed barrier which divided the rival sets of fans. She noted that Tom seemed to spend more time watching the youths in the crowd than the football. They were moved away by startled police who remonstrated with Jenny on her irresponsible behaviour. She had to admit the grim truth; great freak of nature and genius he may be, but her baby was a yob.

Over the weeks, though, Coco Bryce grew happier in the new body. He would have it all. Let them think that the old body in the hospital was the real Coco Bryce. He was fine here; there were opportunities. At first he thought that he missed shagging and drinking, but he found that his sex drive was very low and that alcohol made his baby body too sick. Even his favourite food was no longer palatable; he now preferred lighter, runny, easily digested stuff. Most of all, he felt so tired all the time. All he wanted to do was sleep. When he was awake, he was learning so much. His new knowledge seemed to be forcing out much of his old memories.

* * *

An extensive programme of reminiscence and recall therapy had failed the youth in the hospital. Educational psychologists had decided that rather than try to get him to remember anything, he would learn everything from scratch. This programme paid instant dividends and the young man was soon allowed home. Visiting the surroundings he had seen in photographs gave him a sense of who he was, even if it was a learned rather than a recalled concept. To his mother's shock, he even wanted to visit his father in prison. Kirsty came round a lot. They were, after all, as good as engaged, she had told him. He couldn't remember, he remembered nothing. He had to learn how to make love all over again. Kirsty was pleased with him. He seemed eager to learn. Coco had never been one for foreplay before. Now, under her instruction, he discovered his tongue and fingers, becoming a skilful and responsive lover. They soon became formally engaged and moved into a flat together.

The papers took an occasional interest in Coco Bryce's recovery. The young man renounced drugs, so the Regional Council thought that it would be good publicity to offer him a job. They employed him as a messenger, though the youth, continuing and rapidly progressing with his studies, wanted to get into clerical work. His friends thought that Coco had gone a bit soft since the accident, but most put it down to his engagement. He had stopped running with the casuals. That was Kirsty's idea; it could get him into bother and they had their future to think of. Coco's ma thought this was great. Kirsty had been a good influence.

One evening, around eighteen months later, the young man known as Colin Bryce was travelling on a bus with his wife Kirsty. They had been visiting her mother and were now heading back to their flat in Dalry. A young woman and her chubby infant sat in front of them. The child had turned around and was facing Colin and Kirsty. It seemed fascinated by them both. Kirsty jokingly played with the toddler, pressing his nose.

— Tom, the baby's mother laughed, — stop disturbing people. Sit round straight.

— No, he's awright, Kirsty smiled. She looked at Coco, trying to gauge his reaction to the child. She wanted one. Soon.

The infant seemed mesmerised by Coco. His doughy hand reached out and played over the youth's face, tracing its contours. Kirsty stifled a laugh as her husband pulled his head back and looked self-conscious.

— Tom! The baby's mother laughed in mock exasperation, — You little pest. C'mon, it's our stop.

— KOKORBIGH! KOKORBIGH! the child squealed as she scooped him up and carried him away. He pointed back at the youth, tearfully wailing as they left the bus, — KOKORBIGH!

— That's not Kokirbigh, she explained, referring to the dream demon that persistently plagued her son Tom, — that's just a young man.

Kirsty talked about babies for the rest of the journey, engrossed in the subject, never noticing the fear and confusion on her husband's face.

174

A Smart Cunt

A NOVELLA

For Kevin Williamson,
rebel with several causes

CONTENTS

CONTENTS

1

PARK PATROL

I'd been living and working in the park for a month now, which was too radge. The digs were adequate and free. The wages were pretty shite but the poackle was good, if ye got a chance in the golf starter's box, which I generally did a couple of times a week. If I could get another month out of it before the cunts in the mobile tippled tae ma scam, I'd have a splendid bankroll the gither for London.

Inverleith was an okay park, dead central like. I couldn't have crashed in a park on the ootside of the city, that would've been a drag. I'd be better off at the auld man's place. The bothy I slept in was spacious and comfortable. It already had a Baby Belling, for my cooking, and an electric-bar fire, so all I needed to conceal was my mattress, which I crushed behind the boiler, the sleeping-bag and my black-and-white portable telly, which I could keep in the locker provided. I had a spare set of keys cut, so that after the mobile patrol picked up the set at the end of the shift, I could go for a pint then return and let myself in.

There were more than adequate toilet and shower facilities in the pavilion, which contained the footballers' changing-rooms as well as my bothy. So my outgoings were purely drink and drugs which, although substantial enough, with a bit of dealing, insurance and credit-card fraud, could be met fairly comfortably while allowing me to save. How good was that?

And yet it wisnae such a good life. There was the small problem of actually having to be on the job.

The great killer for the parkie (or Seasonal Park Officer as we were somewhat pompously entitled) was boredom. Humans

179

tend tae adjust tae their environment and subsequently, in the parks, you become so inactive that even thinking of doing anything feels threatening. This goes for the essential duties of the job, which only take up about half an hour of the eight-hour shift, as well as any extras. I'd rather sit all day reading biographies (I read nothing else) and occasionally have a wank than go and clean out the changing-room, which would be just as dirty within a few hours as the next set of footballers came in. Even the prospect of a short trip to the cupboard a few feet away to switch on the thermostat becomes fraught with tension and loathing. It seemed easier, when my mind was set in this way, to tell six filthy teams of footballers that the showers were broken, or playing up, than to just go over and switch the cunts on. It was also a way of testing out how the Park Patrol hierarchy reacted tae such occurrences. The lessons learned could always be used in the future.

The players, for their part, reacted fairly predictably:

— NAE FUCKIN SHOWERS! MOAN TAE FUCK! FIR FUCK SAKES!

— YE PEY YIR FUCKIN DOUGH FIR THE FACILITIES . . .

— WE SHOULD GIT A REFUND! YE NEED SHOWERS FIR FUCK'S SAKE!

I find myself surrounded by seventy-odd sweaty players and nippy, rid-faced officials. At that point, yes, I wished I'd got ma arse intae gear and turned the showers oan. My strategy on such occasions is tae come out fighting and act even more disgusted with the shower problem than they are. Steal those clothes of righteous indignation.

— Listen, mate, I said, shaking ma heid angrily, — ah fuckin telt the cunts the other week that the immersion was dodgy. Ah'm fuckin well fed up tellin thum. That fuckin immersion. Sometimes it works fine, other times ye git fuck all ootay it.

— Aye, it was working fine the other week whin that other boy wis oan . . .

— That's the fuckin thing; jist cause it works two or three

times oan the trot, they cunts think they dinnae huv tae bother gittin thir erses doon here tae huv a look at it! Ah telt the cunts fae the council tae send the engineer doon. Complete fuckin overhaul, that's what's needed. Ye need reliable showers in this type ay weather, ah telt the boy. Did they move thir fuckin erses?

— Aye, no these cunts, they widnae bother.

— Aye, bit the thing is, yous boys come doon here eftir the match wantin yir fuckin shower. It's no these cunts thit git the hassle; it's fuckin muggins here, I pouted tersely, thrashing my chest with my finger.

— Hud oan pal, said one of the skippers, — wir no sayin nowt against you.

— Aw naw, naw, naebody's blamin the boy, another player says to the skipper. They all nod in acquiescence, apart from a few cunts on the periphery, who moan away. Then one skipper stands up oan the bench and shouts: — Wi cannae git the showers tae work, lads. Ah know it's a pain, but that's it. The boy's done his best.

A series of loud hisses and curses fills the air.

— Well, that's the way it goes. It's no the boy's fault. He telt the council, another player says supportively.

They grumblingly get dressed; the daft cunts. That's their night fucked. They'll have tae go hame tae shower, rather than hitting the pub straight away to discuss the match and pontificate on the state of fitba, music, television, shagging and the embarrassment of mates in the modern world. The momentum for the night has been lost. The pub they go to, with its shitey beer garden, will experience lower than normal takings. Tough shit, in these recession-hit times. Girlfriends and wives will be met with sour expressions by partners who feel deprived of their night out with the boys. The men will sullenly head for the bathroom shower feeling despondent and cheated: a win which cannot be savoured, or a defeat which cannot be consoled and massaged by lager. Councillors and recreation officials will be harassed by the squeaky, rid-faced, menopausal, bloated, sexually inadequate turds who run the beautiful game at all levels in Scotland.

All this misery because the parkie can't be bothered clicking on a switch. That's real fuckin power for you. Take that, ya cunts! How crazy am I.

As the last of the players files out, I go intae the boiler-room at the back of my bothy and switch on the immersion. I'll need hot water for ma shower before I go oot the night. I do some push-ups and squat thrusts before settling down to another chapter in the book I'm reading: a biography of Peter Sutcliffe.

All I read are biographies; I don't know why, it's not as if I particularly enjoy them. I just cannae seem tae get intae anything else. Jim Morrison, Brian Wilson, Gerald Ford, Noele Gordon, Joyce Grenfell, Vera Lynn, Ernest Hemingway, Elvis Presley (two different ones), Dennis Nilsen, Charles Kray (Reg and Ron's brother), Kirk Douglas, Paul Hegarty, Lee Chapman and Barry McGuigan have all been consumed since I started working in the parks. I cannae really say I've enjoyed any of them, with the exception, perhaps, of Kirk Douglas.

Sometimes I wonder whether taking oan this job was a good career-move. I like it because I enjoy my own company and can get a bit ratty after too much social contact. I dislike it because I can't move around and I hate being stuck in the one place. I suppose I could learn to drive, then I could get a job which offered the two important features of solitude and mobility, but a car would tie me down, stop me from taking drugs. And that would never do.

Mr Garland, the parks boss, was a kindly man, liberal enough by parks standards. He understood the condition of the parkie. Garland had been through enough council disciplinaries to suss out the problem. — It's a boring job, he told me on my induction, — and the devil makes work and all that stuff. The thing is, Brian, that so few Park Officers show initiative. The slovenly Park Officer will do the bare minimum, then just slope off, while the more conscientious officer will always find work to do. Believe you me, we know who the bad apples are, and I can tell you this: their days are numbered. So if you make an impression, Brian, we could very well be in a position to offer you a permanent post with the Parks Department.

— Eh, right . . .

— Of course, you've not even started the job yet, he smiled, realising that he was leaping massively ahead of himself, — but while it might not be the most exciting job in the world, many officers make it worse than it need be. You see, Brian, his eyes went large and evangelistic, — there's always work to do in a park. The job needs walking, Brian. The children's swing park has to be kept free from broken glass. The teenagers who congregate behind the pavilion; I've found needles there, Brian, you know . . .

— Terrible, I shake my head.

— They have to be discouraged. There are forms we have to complete on damage and vandalism to Parks property. There is always rubbish to pick up, weeding around the bothy and of course the constant cleaning of changing-rooms. The enterprising Park Officer will always find something to do.

— I think it's better to do a good day's graft; makes the time pass quicker, I lied.

— Precisely. I admit that sometimes, especially if the weather is inclement, boredom can be a problem. Are you a reader, Brian?

— Yes. I'm a fairly avid reader.

— That's good, Brian. A reader is never bored. What sort of stuff do you read?

— Biographies mainly.

— Excellent. Some people stuff their heads with political and social theory: it can only cause resentment and discontent with one's lot, he mused. — Anyway, that's besides the point. I'll concede that this job could be better. The service has been run down. We can't even replace the old mobile vans and intercom equipment. Of course, I blame our political masters on the Recreation Committee. Grants for single-parent black lesbian collectives to put on experimental theatre projects; that sort of stuff they'll always find money for.

— I couldn't agree more, Mister Garland. It's criminal, that sort of misuse of the poll-tax payer's money.

I remember that thoughtful, acknowledging nod Garland gave me. It seemed to say: I see a model Park Officer in the making. What's the cunt like.

I took a quick shower before the mobile came. I was just in time; no sooner had I dried off and got dressed than I heard the Park Patrol van pulling up. The Park Patrol vans, the mobile, are the uniformed cunts. These fuckers are on the same grade as us, only mobile. Technically, they are supposed to check the smaller parks which are unstaffed by a Park Officer. Unofficially, it's a different matter. What they actually do is to police us; we who, I suppose by reverse definition, have to be called the stationary Park Officers. They make sure that we are on the job, at our official work-stations, and not in some pub. They caught one guy, Pete Walls, literally on the job last week at Gilmerton. He was shagging a schoolie in the bothy. They suspended him with pay, pending enquiry. The council really knows how to hurt you; giving you official licence to do what any parkie strives to do unofficially: not be there but get paid for it.

I empty some roaches out the ashtray into a bin-liner as mobile Park Officer Alec Boyle steps out of the car. Boyle has his cap pulled down over his mirror-lens shades. His shirt-sleeves are rolled up, he usually leans out the window of the car when it's at the lights, and he must spend a fortune on chewing-gum. All that's missing is the Brooklyn accent. What sort of shite is going through that cunt's heid is anybody's guess. A wee guy; a few inches too small and brain cells too few even for the polis. How fucked-up is he.

— What's this aboot the fuckehhnn showers? he asks.

— Dinnae mention these cunts tae me, Alec. Ah've been at the fuckers aw day. It's sortay like the pilot light keeps gaun oot, ken? Ah've goat it started now; but the water wisnae hoat enough for the fitba guys, ken? They wir daein thir nut.

— Ah ken that. Jist hud the fuckehhnn Shark oan the radio. Gaun fuckin radge.

The Shark. Divisional Park Superintendant Bert Rutherford. He's on today. That's aw we fuckin well need. — Well, we'll huv tae git the engineer doon.

— He's fuckehhnn been doon but, couldnae find nowt wrong.

—How's it this always hus tae happen when it's me oan shift? I moan in the self-pitying way guys on the job here always do. — Ah think ah'm fuckin jinxed.

Park Officer Boyle nods empathetically at me. Then a reptilian smile twists his features. — Your mate Pete Walls, he's some fuckenhhn cunt, is he no?

I wouldnae really class Wallsy as a mate, just an okay guy I've done a bit of work on the golf with, a bit of poacklin. I suppose that's as good a mate as you can get, on the parks like. That's where the real money's made in the parks; on the golf starter's box. Every cunt wants in on that action.

— Aye, Wallsy wis caught wi his pants doon ah heard, I nodded.

— Stoat the baw, Boyle's face crinkled as he idly polished his shades with a hanky. The daft cunt doesnae suss that he's smearing snotters over the lenses, then he tipples and stops, vaguely self-conscious for a moment.

I spare his embarrassment. — Ah heard that the lassie wis sixteen; it wis his girlfriend. Getting engaged n that like. She just came in wi some sannys and it got a bit oot ay hand.

— Ah heard aw that shite. Disnae matter a fuck. That cunt's oot the door. Fuckehhnn dismissal joab.

I wisnae so sure about that. — Naw, ah'll bet ye a fiver he gets oaf wi it.

I had a feeling about this. The council was a very asexual organisation. If things got a bit steamy they'd bottle out. This was a potential Pandora's box that they might not want to open. Cha McIntosh at the union would find an angle. I thought there

185

was a very good outside chance that Wallsy would get off scot-free. Well worth a fiver.

— Git away, Boyle sneers.

— Naw, come oan. Bet ye a blue one.

— Done, said Boyle. As I shook his greasy paw, he assumed a conspiratorial expression and whispered, although we were in an empty pavilion in the middle of a deserted park, — Watch the fuckehhnn Shark. He's got his beady eye oan ye. Thinks yir a wide-o. He goes tae me: How's that boy at Inverleith? Ah goes: Awright, good lad likes. He said: Seems a bit ay a smart cunt tae me.

I set my face in an expression of contrived sincerity. — Thanks, Alec. Appreciate ye giein ays the nod.

Bullshitting wee cunt. The Shark might be oan ma case, then again, he might no. I didn't fuckin care. These mobile cunts always played games to keep you para and set themselves up in a better light. They were just as bored by the job as us; they needed to generate intrigue to keep the interest levels up.

He departed, screeching his car tyres across the gravel outside the bothy. I went to the local pub and had a voddy and a game of pool with a guy with a nervous tick. After this, I went back, had a wank and read another chapter in Peter Sutcliffe's biography. Boyle came back to pick up his set of keys and my shift was over. I left the park, but doubled-back after Boyle departed, letting myself back intae the pavilion. Before I prepared to set off intae toon, I set up my telly and bed, in case I was too wrecked tae dae it the night. Then I realised that I was off for four days. In the parks you had five days on and two days off, the two days changing each week. My days were running intae each other, so I had a long weekend. This meant that someone else would be here the morn. I locked my stuff back up. It was unlikely that I'd crash here tonight. I usually crashed out in some cunt's gaff at the weekend, or at my auld man's.

I hit the toon feeling that alienated, traumatised way I generally did when I came off a shift, especially from the backshift, which finished at nine. There was that sense of having being shut out of things, that everybody had already started having serious fun. No doubt I had a bit of catching up to do. I went to see if I could get some speed from Veitchy.

2

AFTERNOON TELLY

My auld man sat drinking tea with Norma Culbertson from up the stairs. He puffed on a cigarette as I was making a sanny: a piece on Dundee steak.

— Thing is, Norma, it's always places like this they pick oan. As if the area hasnae goat enough bloody problems as it is.

— Couldnae agree mair, Jeff. It's a bloody disgrace. Let them build it in Barnton or somewhere like that. Supposed tae be a council for the ordinary working person, Norma shook her head bitterly. She looked quite sexy with her hair piled up and those large hooped earrings.

— What's this? I ask.

The auld man snorts. — Thir planning tae open a centre fir aw they junkies. Needle exchange n prescriptions n aw that. It's eywis the same; cater fir aw these bloody misfits, never mind the tenants that have been peyin their rent every single week regular as clockwork.

Norma Culbertson nods in agreement.

— Aye, it's a sick scene, right enough, Dad, I smile.

I note that they seem to be getting some kind of petition the gither; daft cunts. What are they like? I leave the kitchen and eavesdrop for a bit from behind the door.

— It's no that ah'm hard, Jeff, Norma says, — it's no that at aw. Ah ken these people have goat tae git help. It's jist thit ah've goat wee Karen n ah'm oan ma ain. The thought ay aw they needles lying aroond . . .

— Aye, Norma, it disnae bear thinkin aboot. Well, we will fight them on the beaches, as they say.

The pompous auld fuck.

— Ye ken though, Jeff, ah really admire ye, bringin up they two laddies oan yir ain. Couldnae huv been easy. Rare laddies thuv turned oot n aw.

— Ach, thir no bad. At least thuv goat mair sense thin tae git involved in any ay this drugs nonsense. Brian's the problem. Ye never ken whair he is, or whair he's gaun. Still, at least he's working now, just a temporary job in the parks like, but at least it's something. Mind you, ah dinnae think he kens what he wants tae dae wi his life, that one. Sometimes ah think he lives on another planet fae the rest ay us. Wait till ye hear the nerve ay this: hudnae seen or heard ay him for weeks, n he comes back wi this lassie. Takes her up the stairs. Then later, he's doonstairs wi her cooking up a big meal. Ah takes him aside and sais: Hi you, c'moan, this isnae a knockin shop ye ken. He gies ays some money for the food. Ah sais: That's no the point, Brian. Ye treat this place wi a bit ay respect. This is him that's supposed tae be heartbroken cause his girlfriend went away tae some college doon in London. Well, he's goat a funny wey ay showin it. Too smart for his ain good that yin. Now Derek, he's a different story . . .

So, it looks as if I'm getting on the auld man's tits. It's true that you never hear anything good about yourself if you listen in like that, but sometimes you're better knowing the way the wind's blowing.

I sit up in my room watching my telly; well, Derek's telly if we're being pedantic about it, which the wee cunt invariably is. I hear my auld boy shouting on me and go to the top of the stairs. — We're eh, jist gaun upstairs tae Norma's. A few things tae sort oot aboot the committee, he says, all furtive and uneasy.

Good show. I light a candle. Then I produce my works and start to cook up some smack. This gear looks okay, there's a bit of a glut on right now. God bless Raymie Airlie; God bless Johnny Swan. I'm no a smack-heid, no really, but a feast usually precedes a famine. Best take advantage.

I look for a belt, but I can only find a useless, elasticated snake-belt, so I fling it away and use the flex fae Derek's bedside lamp. I wrap it round my bicep and tap my wrist until a huge dark vein materialises. Then I stick the needle in, and draw back some blood before shooting for goal. Barry.

Fuck.

I can't fuckin breathe.

Fuck sake, how bad is this.

I stand up and make a move towards the lavvy, but I don't get that far. I manage to direct my puke onto an old NME. I lean against the wall for a bit and get my breath, then I open the windae, and fling the mess out intae the backsquare.

I lie on the bed. That's better. There's a nice-looking woman in the soap opera on the telly. Suddenly I see her as a wizened old witch, but she's no longer on the telly, she's in the room. Then things change and I'm with a guy called Stuart Meldrum who, when we were kids, slid off the roof of this factory in Leith. This was before we moved out here. It was a corrugated-iron roof, sloping steeply. Stu lost his footing, fell off and started sliding down it. Thing was, there was a row of double rivets sticking out and they sort of tore him apart.

Now I'm with him again, and his face is ripped open, with parts of him spilling out of his bloodied body. He's got a ball, a yellay ball under his arm. — Fancy a game ay shapes, Bri? he asks.

That seems awright tae me. Shapes. Against the factory wall. He moves up dead close to the wall and kicks the ball hard against it. It ricochets off at a tight angle and starts rolling away, this yellay ball. I start running eftir it, but it seems to be gathering speed. I'm trying to get a bend on but I can't seem to get any pace up. All I can see is this ball, bouncing down the road, like it's wind-assisted, like it's nearly a balloon, but at the same time everything else is still and quiet. My Ma stands in front of me in a floral dress, holding the ball. She looks young and beautiful, like she did when I last saw her, when I was still at the primary. I'm the same size as her, the same as I am now, but she takes my hand and leads me up this hilly street, full of suburban, posh hooses and I ask her, — Ma, why did you leave us?

— Because I made a mistake, son. You were a mistake. It was never meant to happen. You, your father, these places where we lived. I love you and Derek, but I needed my own life, son. You were never meant to happen. I never wanted to give birth to a Smart Cunt.

I see Alec Boyle and the Shark, dressed in white suits. They are nodding sagely. Then I realise that I'm staring at the screen and it's all okay, I'm back in the telly's soap opera, not my own.

I start to get really bad cramps after a bit, so I get under the duvet and try to sleep it off. When my old man comes in I tell him I think I've got a flu bug and spend three days in bed, before I'm due back on the park.

3

ASSOCIATES AS OPIATES

I'm never touching smack again. That's a loser's game. Every cunt I've met who said that they can control it is either dead, dying or leading a life no worth living. What a radge I've been. I'm still strung out here in the bothy. A waste ay a weekend. Naw, speed's ma drug, speed and ecky. Fuck smack.

It's going to be a boring backshift. Sutcliffe's book was okay. A good read. The truth is stranger than fiction. Sutcliffe was a very disturbed man. Sutcliffe was an arsehole. How tapped was that cunt. Some things you can never understand, some things don't lend themselves to reason, to rational analysis and explanation. I've started on Mother Teresa's biography, but I can't get into it. I don't really have that much time for her; she seems a bit fuckin loopy tae me. She claims God tells her tae dae the things she does; it's got fuck all tae dae wi her. This is precisely the same argument Sutcliffe uses. That's all jist pure shite; people should take on a bit mair personal responsibility.

This park is depressing. It's like a prison. No it's not. You can leave, go to the warm, inviting pub, but it will mean your cards if the mobile catches you. The parks are about appearance money; you get paid to be here. Not to do, but to be. I sit in a bothy; therefore I'm a bam.

There's a knock on the door. It can't be the patrol; they never knock. I open the bothy and there's Raymie Airlie. He looks at me with a grim smile scored onto his face. — The renegade robots are now long dead, the metal ones rusted, the human ones bled.

My sentiments entirely. Raymie is either a moron or a genius and it doesn't interest me enough to even try to work out which.

— Awright, Raymie? Moan in.

He strides into the bothy. Then he inspects the changing-rooms and showers with a thoroughness that would credit the most vigilant mobile Park Patrol Officer. He returns to the bothy and picks up the Mother Teresa book and arches his eyebrows, before throwing it back on the table.

— Got works? he asks.

— Aye . . . ah mean, naw. No oan ays, likes.

— Fancy a hit?

— Eh, no really, ah mean, ah'm likes workin, eh . . . aye, but just a bit, likes . . .

He cooked up some smack and I took a shot, using his works. I started thinking a lot about swimming, and fish. The extent of freedom they have; two thirds of the planet's surface n that.

The next think I knew, the Shark was standing over me. Raymie had gone.

— Keys, he snapped.

I looked at him through glazed eyes. I felt as if my body was a corridor and the Shark was at the door at the other end of that corridor. What the fuck did he mean? Keys?

Keys.

Keys.

Mother Teresa and the children of Calcutta. Feed the world.

Keys.

Keys open doors; keys lock doors.

Keys.

It sounds good. — Keys.

— Have ye goat thum then? The keys? he asks. — C'moan, son, it's knockin oaf time. You no goat a home tae go tae?

I started to take the keys out of my pocket, not my set, the set I had made, but their set. Have I no got a home to go to?

Mum, where are you?

— This is my home, I tell him.

— You're tapped pal. You been drinking? He moves closer to

see if he can smell anything on my breath. He seems puzzled, but stares deep into my eyes. — You're as high as a bloody kite, son. What are you on? You been on that whacky baccy? What are you on?

I am on planet Earth. We all are. All pathetic Earthling scum. Me, Shark, Mother Teresa, Sutcliffe . . . I hand him the keys.

— Jesus Christ! Ye cannae even speak, can you?

Jesus Christ. Another Earthling. This is planet Earth. The Shark and I; human lifeforms sharing the same planet in this universe. Both humans, members of the dominant species on planet Earth. Humans have set up structures, institutions to govern our lives here on this planet. Churches, nations, corporations, societies, and all that shite. One such structure is the council. Within its sphere, leisure and recreation, of which the Parks Service is part. The human known as the Shark (a humanoid referred to by the name of another species due to his perceived similarity in appearance and behaviour to this species, by members of his own) and myself are engaged in economic activity. We are paid, in our small way, to maintain the structure of human society. Our role is a small one, but an integral part of a mystic and wondrous whole.

— We have a role to play . . .

— Eh? What's that?

— A role to play in the maintenance of human society . . .

— You're tapped, son, fuckin tapped. What are ye oan?

The Shark. An ocean to swim in, a whole ocean. Two thirds of the planet's surface to roam around in. Moreover, he can swim at different levels, so the possibilities are almost endless. Infinite choices in the ocean and this thing has to come onto dry land; has to come onto this small patch of dry land I occupy. I cannot stand being in the vicinity of this creature.

I walk past him, out of this bothy, out of this park.

— Garland's gaunny hear aboot this! he shouts.

Well, neh-neh-neh-neh-neh, cuntybaws.

The thing about the Montparnasse Tower is that it's so tacky, really dirty and shoddy looking. It's a marvellous structure though, but it's in the wrong city, the wrong continent. It's a very new world structure, but because it's in Paris, nobody's impressed. The Louvre, the Opera, the Arc de Triomphe, the Eiffel Tower; people are impressed with all that shite, all those beautiful buildings. Nobody really gies a fuck aboot the Montparnasse Tower. Thing is, you get great views over Paris from the observation floor of the Montparnasse.

We're sitting, the two of us, at the restaurant on the top of the tower. It's an ugly, overpriced restaurant with garish fittings and a poor selection of food. But we're happy there, because it's just the two of us. We've had a little look around the internal observation floor, with its huge glass frames which are marked and grubby. Rubbish, old rotting foods and fag-ends have been dropped behind the radiators underneath the handrail which surrounds the observation floor. The most impressive things on this floor are the pictures of the Montparnasse Tower in various stages of construction, from foundations to completion. Even these fine pictures, though, have been faded by the sun. Soon you'll be able to see nothing in them.

However, I don't care about the dirt and grime, because we're together and it's beautiful. I can't think of the parks. The only reality is the texts and images. I tell her that I wrote a poem about her when I was on duty in the park. She asks me to recite it, but I can't remember it.

She stands up and tells me she wants to walk down. All those floors. She moves down the steps, out of the restaurant towards the fire escape. — C'mon, she says, moving into the darkness. I look into the darkness, but I can't see her, I can only hear her voice. — C'mon, she shouts.

— I can't, I shout.

— Don't be scared, she says.

But I am. I look back onto the observation floor and it's light. Out here is light and she's trying to lead me into the darkness. I know if I start after her now I'll never be able to catch up with her. It's not normal dark down there, it's not shades of dark; it's ugly, stark, pitch blackness. I turn around, back into the white and yellow light. As well as her voice down there, others are present. Voices which have nothing to do with her but everything to do with me. Voices I can't face; it's too mad.

I get into the lift. The door closes. I press for the ground; forty-two floors below.

It doesn't move. I try to open the door but it seems to be stuck. I feel uneasy. My feet are sticking to the floor; it's like there's bubble-gum on the floor of this lift. Sticky strands of pink gum cling to the soles of my boots. I look down at the lift floor; it starts swelling. It's like the floor covering is bubbling up. My feet sink into it, then my legs seem to go right through it. I fall through the lift floor, slowly, covered in a stretchy, transparent pink film which is all that stands between me and falling to my death in this dark lift-shaft.

It's not snapping though; it's still stretching. I look up and see myself descending slowly from a hole in the floor of the lift. Floor 41   40   39   38

Then I start to speed up as large white-painted letters indicating the marked floors whizz by: 37 36 35 34 33 32 31 30 29 28 27 26 25 24 23 22   21   20   (slowing down again, my bubble still holding, thank fuck.)

19 (Dangling stationary, my cord now just the width of a string, and so tensile.)

(Then more movement, more fast movement.) 18 17 16 15 14 13 12 11 10 9 8 7 6 5 4 3 OHH NOOOO!! 2 1 G B −1 −2 −3 −4 −5 −6 −7 −8 −9 WHAT THE FUCK IS THIS? −10 −11 −12 −13 −14 −15 −16 −17 −18 −19 −20 −21 −22 −23

I'm still sliding down trapped in this bubble-gum film. I'm now at minus −82 −83 −84 −85 −86   −87   −88   and at   −89 my feet gently touch solid ground. It seems as if I've landed in another lift, this one roofless. I put my hand above my head and the tensile gum-like strand snaps under my touch.

My body is covered in this pink film, covered from head to toe. It corrodes my clothes, just dissolves them, but it doesn't react to my skin. It settles on it, like a second layer, hard and protective. I must look like a mannequin. I'm naked but I don't feel vulnerable. I feel strong.

The lift indicator tells me that minus 89 is the bottom. More than two-thirds of this building lies underground. I must be miles, well yards or metres, underneath the earth's surface.

I step out of the lift-shaft. The lift door seems to have gone and I just alight at minus 89. I'm still inside some sort of structure, and although the walls seem to be moving and breathing, it still seems like the huge basement it should be. It's barren and appears deserted. Giant concrete pillars support this weird structure which is man-made and organic at the same time.

A small human-like figure with the head of a reptile shuffles along in a brown overcoat, wheezing, pushing what looks like a shopping trolley full of boxes.

— Excuse me, I shout, — where is this?

— The fuckehhnn boatum flair, this thing shouts, seeming in distress.

— What's through there? I pointed to a sign marked EXIT, a sign that the creature was heading towards.

— Complaints, he smiles at me, his lizard tongue lapping the side of his scaly face. — Some cunts've been fuckehhnn well pittin greenfly in ma central heating. Ah want that sorted oot right now. You doon here fir a woman?

— Eh, naw . . . ah mean, aye, I was thinking of her, where she was, how far up this building.

His cold eyes rest on me. — Ah'll fuck ye the now if ye want. Ah'll fuck ye fir nowt. Ye dinnae need women, he gasps, moving towards me. I back away . . .

BLEEEEEEGGGHHHH! — STUPID FUCKIN CUNT!

A horn sounds and a voice roars.

I'm on Ferry Road with the heavy traffic bound for Leith docks whizzing past me. A lorry pulls over and the driver leans out the cab and shakes his fist. — Daft fuckin cunt! Ah nearly fuckin kilt ye! He opens the cab, jumps down and comes towards me. — Ah will fuckin kill ye!

I run along. I don't mind being hit by his lorry, but I don't want to be hit by him. It's the indignity of it all. It's all too personal. There's nothing worse than a violent beating from an unremarkable person. Physical violence with someone is too much like shagging them. Too much id involved.

I feel terrible, but I can't go home. I can't go back to the park. I walk around for a bit, trying to get my head together. I end up at Veitchy's gaff in Stockbridge. Minus 89. Thank fuck I'm out of that place. But now I'm shaking, feeling sick. I can either tough it out or go back to level minus 89.

— Awright, cuntybaws?

— Ha ha ha, the man himself! Veitchy smiles and lets me in. — Ye look like yuv seen a ghost.

— Naw. Ah saw worse: Raymie, a Shark, a woman, a reptile. Nae ghosts, but.

— Ha, ha ha, yir some cunt, Brian, so ye are. Want a beer?

— Naw, any speed?

— Naw.

— Ah'll take a cup ay tea offay ye. Milk, nae sugar. Penman aroond?

That's obviously a sair yin for Veitchy. — Dinnae talk tae ays aboot that cunt. Thinks he kin jist leave shite here in ma gaff. Tellin ye, Bri, ah'll help a mate oot, but he's takin liberties. Liberties the cunt's takin, I kid you not.

I sit down on the sofa and watch the telly, leaving Veitchy slavering on about Penman. Fuck this life; give me another please.

Next day Ian Caldwell tells me that I was up at his flat in Inchmickery Court in Pilton. A tower block. I can't remember. I have to go back to Paris one day, back to the Montparnasse tower. With her. But she's gone. All the women in my life have gone. My own fuckin mother's gone.

The backshift was more eventful than I thought it would be.

4

CONSTRUCTIVE DISCIPLINE

Garland wore a sad expression; he was a man more disappointed and hurt than angry.

— The worse thing, Brian, he told me, is that I took you for an intelligent and decent young man. I thought that you would prove a diligent and conscientious Park Officer.

— Yeah, ah suppose ah messed things up a bit . . .

— Is it drugs, Brian? Is it? he pleaded.

— No, it's more a kind of depression, you know?

The Shark was in attendance. — Depression my arse! He was zonked out of his bloody brains!

— That's enough, Mister Rutherford! Garland snapped.
— Let Brian speak for himself.

— It's just that ah've been oan these anti-depressants. Sometimes ah go over the score, forget ah've taken the pills and take a double dosage, ken?

Garland looked thoughtful. — How can a young man who has everything to look forward to possibly be depressed?

How indeed. Working in a temporary job in the parks. Staying in a drab scheme wi his dad, who's just about to alienate every psycho that lives in it with an anti-drugs crusade. No seen his Ma since he was eight years old. Knocked back by his girlfriend. He's got the whole wide world in his hands . . . everybody, join in . . .

— It's exogenous depression, the doctors say. Chemical imbalance. Comes on without warning.

Garland shook his head sympathetically. — You didn't mention this at the interview, this condition.

— Ah know, ah apologise for that. Ah just felt that it would by prejudicial to my employment prospects with the District Council's Recreation Department, Park Patrol Division.

The Shark's bottom jaw twitched. The union boy nodded solemnly. The personnel guy remained impassive. Garland took a deep breath. — You've given us food for thought, Brian. Leaving the job, though, that is a serious breach of discipline. If you'd kindly leave us for a few minutes.

I went outside into the corridor. I stood around for a wee while before Garland summoned me back in.

— We're going to suspend you for the rest of the week, with pay, pending a decision.

— Thank you, I said, and I meant it.

I went drinking with my mate The PATH that night. I checked my account. Whatever happened regarding this disciplinary, I was off to London.

I got back to my auld man's, carrying the portable telly I kept at the park. Deek was crashed out in my bed. What the fuck was he daein in ma bed?

As I went to shake him, I saw him appear at the door. Either there were two Deeks or it wasn't him in ma bed. Both propositions seemed equally plausible in my current frame of mind.

— What's this? I asked the Deek at the door, pointing tae the possible Deek in the bed.

— It's Ronnie. He wis looking fir ye. He's really jellied. Ah took him up here soas the auld man widnae see um. Ye ken how he is about drugs n that.

— Aw right, thanks. That useless cunt Ronnie. Ah'll let the fucker sleep it oaf.

Ronnie lay there for hours. I couldn't move him. When I was ready to go to bed I pulled him onto the floor and threw a blanket over him.

The next morning I packed for London. As I got ready, Ronnie was coming to.

— Heavy day yesterday, Ron? I asked.
— Fucked, he said, pointing to his head.
I was looking forward to London.

5

SPEEDING

I've still got that out of it fae the night before feeling; or is it still the night before or what, but who cares cause Simmy's racked up the balls and ordered up one Guinness and one pint of bitter and auld Harry's saying: Fucking drunken Jock gits and Simmy's hugging the grumpy auld cunt then picking him up and sticking him on the bar and Vi's telling me that I was in some state last night, her sulky, mean doughy face propped up on her white flabby arms and I'm hating Simmy's automatic, arrogant, soap-dodging assumption that I want to play fuckin pool, as if it's just part of the natural order of things . . .

Oh ya cunt ye

Fuck . . . I thought it was all coming back up there; that curry. I don't know whether to spit, swallow or chew and Simmy's split the pack, he's looking at my flushed, sweaty, uncomfortable face and is explaining the concept of:

— Momentum. Momentum big man, that's what it's aw about. MO-MEN-TUM. Wuv goat tae ride that wave, go wi the flow, take it aw as far as it'll go. Momentum. When it's workin fur ye, ye jist cannae ignore it.

Simmy's been talking to Cliff in the flat. Cliff reads *The Independent*. They use words like that; usually in the sports pages.

I send a stripe down the table into the bottom left-hand pocket. A fine effort. The butt of Simmy's cue thumps the lino appreciatively. — Nice wahn, ma man, Simmy says.

— Momentum ma fuckin arse, it's this speed we've been snortin and dabbin at for days now n see when ah stoap this, whin ah finally settle doon and say: beddy boys, it'll be fir days, naw, make that fuckin weeks, naw months, fuckin months.

Simmy goes: — Tell ye whit though, ma man, you n me up fuckin west next week. Straight oan that 207 bus doon the Uxbridge Road. No gettin oaf at Ealing Broadway or stallin at the Bush. Up west. Clubs n wimmin. No compromise. No surrender.

He starts whistling 'Derry's Walls'.

The cunt's broken my concentration and I fuck up on an easy ball into the centre pocket. Too busy trying to get position on the yellow.

It's that cunt who's always shitein it tae go up west, it's him that gets us lumbered in Ealing or the Bush, mashed out of our fuckin brains. That's okay for him; he's a fat, ugly, weedjie, soapdodging orange–bigoted, hun bastard with a small cheesy cock and a face disfigured by Indian ink, scar tissue, burst blood vessels, and he's got that frizzy hair that a lot of huns seem to have which looks like it's been transplanted from somebody's pubes and he also has a gross arse which is prone to faecal leakage. All of which makes his chances of meeting a woman who doesnae look as if she could eat tomatays through a tennis racket highly improbable. How repulsive is he. The problem is, though, that the cunt's a hindrance tae me, in ma quest tae meet somebody reasonable, and he has the flat as boggin as he is with fish and chip wrappers and chinky cartons everywhere, plates piled up all ower the place, n as for his room, well, you'd have to get Rentokil in tae make that fuckin bed. Then there's that cunt Cliff, n his fuckin soacks, that lie in the lobby ootside his room, stinking the whole flat oot. Even they lassies that we've got tae ken fae ower the road, Nazneem, Paula and Angela, they'll no come over for a blow now, so how can I take anybody back there? It was me who got pally with them n all, going up to them wi ma classic chat up line: — I share the same birthday as Ian Curtis, Linda Ronstadt and Trevor Horn, you know Trevor Horn? 'Video Killed The Radio Star'? 'Living In The Plastic Age'? Big pop producer of the eighties, he wis. How could anybody fail with chat-up lines like that? But fail I did, thanks to ma association with that cunt. Now they don't want me coming over to their place because it encourages him to go over and make a nuisance of himself. But I have to go there to get out of our place because the smell of that cat's litter tray is overpowering, swimming with pish and shite. It's no the animal's fault, although the bastard sprays everywhere. Simmy should've hud it done; it rips the wallpaper n curtains n sofa tae bits but he just says that cats are hygienic creatures and they keep the mice doon . . . I'd have been better off at my auld boy's, better off with the fuckin parks who didn't even sack me, at least it was a job . . .

— C'moan big man, yir sleepin . . .

I down two balls. Tonight I'll go over and see Nazneem and tell her that I'm in love with her. No. That would be a lie. I only want to have sex with her. I've had enough of cynical games now that she's gone, gone, gone, gone, and never wrote although the last time I saw her she says hopefully we can carry on where we left off once she's got a few things sorted out and that was months ago now and she's here, here in London, and I suppose that's why I'm here; as if it was possible to casually bump into someone in London, shopping in London, like on Oxford Street, like you can on Prinny. Perhaps I could run into her at a club, the Ministry of Sound or something, but I never shop in London, in CENTRAL LONDON, I never go to clubs, just pubs or late-night drinking clubs full of alcoholics Simmy describes as the salt of the earth, but who are just beaten, broken people with nothing to say, no insights, nothing . . . I'm on the black, auld Harry sniggers maliciously and a Scots guy from Greenford says: — C'moan mate, sort out this orange bastard, and he and Simmy burst into the mundane, tedious double-act of football and religious rivalry that passes for high weedjie wit and we're all supposed to fall around pissing ourselves and be interested and only the black ball stands between me and the humiliation of this fat hun bastard.

He silently lets me pot it.

— Sorry, big man, ma gemme. Ye didnae nominate yir poakit. Auld Harry nods sagely. The ranks are closing even before I start to protest. Simmy's never out of Greenford's Red Lion, I hate it here. They all take the side of the house rules and the avuncular chatty Glaswegian. How sneaky is that cunt.

— Hard lines, big man, nae luck at aw, he smiles extending his hand and shaking mine theatrically.

— Moral victory, the other Scots guy says, — cheated by masonic refereein. That's huns fir ye.

— Right, I say, — ah'm off. I said I'd meet Cliff down the Lady Margaret. I can't conceal my annoyance. Fuck Cliff, it's Nazneem I want to see; this woman who shares the same birthday as Barbara Dickson, Meat Loaf and Alvin Stardust.

— They east-coast punters. A few days oan the bevvy n that's thum fucked. Nae stayin power, Simmy laughs. — See ye back at the flat, big man.

I leave him holding court with the prospective victims of lung cancer, cirrhosis of the liver, alcohol-induced asphyxiation through vomit inhalation, chip-pan fires and domestic stabbings who inhabit the Red Lion at Greenford, Middlesex.

I go back home and try and read for a bit, but my head is buzzing and I can't concentrate, even on Marilyn Monroe's story.

When I go to Nazneem's and put forward the proposition, I get knocked back. — I don't have sex with people like that, she says. — I like you as a friend, that's all. She laughs a little then passes over the joint. Nazneem's room is all fresh, pastel, planty and feminine. I feel like staying here forever.

I suck on the joint. — Okay then, what about swapping gaffs? Ah'll stay here and you can move intae ma room, over the road with Simmy and Cliff.

This second proposition has, if anything, even less appeal tae her than the first.

— No, I don't think that's on, she smiles. Then she looks penetratingly at me and says, — You're not happy in yourself, are you?

It hits me in the centre of my chest. I always thought I was. Maybe not though. — I don't know. Who is?

— I am, she said. — I like my friends, I like my job, like where I stay, like the people I live with.

— No, you need to be in love to be happy. Ah'm not in love, I tell her.

— I don't know if that's true, she says. Then: — You're a bit of a smart

NONONONONONONONONONONONONONOOOOOO

My brain involuntarily makes loud echoing, ringing noises in my ear, which drown out her words.

— Sorry, a bit of a what? I ask.

— A smart-alec. You think you know all the answers.

A smart-alec. A posh name for a smart cunt.

We spraff all afternoon and I go to the Ministry of Sound with her and some of her pals. It's a nice night, great vibes, great sounds, good ecky, nice people. We sit around and chill the next day. I pray for a bad road-traffic accident for Simmy. Later on that Sunday night I decide to face the music. I go across.

— Whair you been, big yin? Our company no good enough fir ye? Ye'll git nuthin sniffin aroond that wee wog tart, tell ye that fir nowt.

I got more from her in a few hours than I had from him in two months. Just when you think the gig's totally fucked, someone like Nazneem comes along and you think the world isn't so bad after all. As for Simmy, what was I doing breathing the same rancid air as that prick?

It was time I headed back up the road. On Monday I bought a one-way bus ticket to Edinburgh. On Tuesday I used it. It was near enough Christmas anyway. I'd probably be back after the New Year. Probably.

6

CHRISTMAS WITH BLIND CUNT

Our antipathy towards Blind Cunt had simmered away for as long as I could recall, but it fairly blazed once we broke that shared taboo of its acknowledgement. The taboo had been a fairly powerful one. After all, you are supposed to empathise with, and perhaps give greater social licence to, someone with such a terrible disability. Fate has been cruel to some people; you as a human being are expected to compensate. The arbitrary nature of this disability is striking; the attitude of there but for the grace of God go I prevails. Or should.

This attitude, though, is governed by self-righteousness and fear. Self-righteousness, as the sighted are able to appear superior and benevolent, or even worthier because they make a big thing out of treating people like Blind Cunt in exactly the same manner as they treat everybody else. Fear comes into this too: as well as the primitive fear that we will be struck down by an omnipotent force if we are not good, there's a more sophisticated one. It states that we are contributing towards defining what is acceptable behaviour towards individuals in such circumstances and if a similar fate befalls us, then we should expect to be treated decently.

However, being blind does not make you a good person. You can be just as much of a cunt as any sighted fucker. Sometimes even more of a cunt. Like Blind Cunt.

It was on the fourth pint in Sandy Bell's that the taboo was shattered. We were slagging people we disliked and Roxy eventually drew in a breath and glared at me over the silver frames of his glasses. — And ah'll tell ye one cunt who I fuckin cannot stand: that blind cunt that drinks in the Spider's. Tell ays he's no a fuckin pain!

I spluttered nervously into my beer. A chill briefly descended on me, only to be quickly supplanted by a glorious feeling of liberation. Blind Cunt. — That cunt gits oan ma fuckin tits, I agreed.

The following Thursday night me, Roxy and The PATH were up at Sidney's flat having a blow. It was a fucker of a night; icy roads, gale-force winds which had caused much damage, and occasional snowstorms. A night to stay in; but as it was a Friday, this was simply not possible. After we finished the blow, we braved the elements and struggled up Morrison Street to the pub.

— Fuckin Bertie Auld, The PATH said, as we staggered into the boozer, shaking and tramping the snow from our coats and boots.

— Fuckin brutal, man, Sidney agreed.

Big Ally Moncrief was at the bar, doing the *Evening News* crossword. I started moving towards him, but then I saw Blind Cunt's twisted face poking out from behind the big fucker. I stopped in my tracks as I heard Blind Cunt's high, jagged squeal:

— CORRECKSHIN! HEART OF MIDLOTHIAN FOOTBALL CLUB PLC, AS THEY ARE OFFICIALLY REFERRED TO IN THE REGISTER OF COMPANIES!

Bobby from behind the bar looked at Blind Cunt as if he wanted to burst his mouth. Big Moncrief smiled tolerantly, then noted us. — The boys! What yis fir?

So we were thus sucked into the company of Ally Moncrief and, as Blind Cunt had been enjoying the big bastard's sponsorship, that of the visually challenged vagina himself.

We had to put up with Blind Cunt's pedantic asides for most of the evening. It didn't bother Sidney or The PATH, they were both really stoned, but Roxy and I had worked up a fair steam of hate and loathing for the fucker in Sandy Bell's the other night, and he was quickly reactivating it.

The crunch came when The PATH, Roxy and Big Moncrief

were discussing some seventies revival programme that had recently been televised.

— The classic clip though, Roxy enthused, — was that Roxy Music one from the Whistle Test.

A few nods followed, but I thought: well, Roxy would say that, being a Roxy Music freak.

— CORRECKSHIN! Blind Cunt snaps. — THE OLD GREY WHISTLE TEST TO BE PRECISE, jabbing a pedantic finger in the air.

After this Roxy and I extracted ourselves from the company, making the excuse that we wanted to talk to Keith Falconer, who was sitting down the other end of the bar. We sat blethering to Keith for about an hour. When he made to leave, we talked to a couple of guys we didn't know, rather than go back up beside the others.

After a bit, The PATH waved his hand and shut his eyes as he and Sidney staggered past us, out into the snow. The last bell had gone. Later Big Moncrief, obviously drunk, slipped away, quiet and stoical, into the blizzard. Blind Cunt was left alone at the bar.

— That Blind Cunt, Roxy said, pointing down the bar at him, — ye check oot the size ay his wad there? Tell ays he wisnae fuckin flush.

— Naw.

He looked at me, treachery filling his eyes. — Something tae think aboot but.

We managed to get another beer out of them before we braved the storm. It was horrible, the snow driving into us at force, my face numb and throbbing, my head splitting in no time. It was impossible to see more than a few feet ahead. We could make out one slow, ambling figure holding onto the black railings, however.

— There's Blind Cunt! Roxy shouted.

At that point, a slate dislodged from a tenement roof, crashing down a few feet in front of us. — Fuck sake, Roxy gasped, — that could've taken our fuckin heids oaf! Then he grabbed a hold of me, his eyes charged up in realisation and anticipation. He picked up the slate and hurried down the road. Standing a few feet behind Blind Cunt, he hurled the slate like a frisbee. It flew past his ear, but in the racket the driving snow and gale-force winds made, Blind Cunt heard and, of course, saw, nothing.

— Ah'll gie the cunt CORRECKSHIN! Roxy snarled. He picked up another slate from the snow and ran up behind Blind Cunt. Two-handedly and with great force, he brought it crashing down over his head. Blind Cunt staggered forward and hit the deck. Roxy whipped the wallet out of his coat pocket. I kicked a pile of snow in his face, for no reason other than malice, and we departed in silent haste along the road, bouncing mirthfully up the subway to Fountainbridge as Roxy extracted the notes from Blind Cunt's wallet, throwing the empty purse over the graveyard wall. We got a number 1 bus which struggled up to Tollcross where we went into Tipplers for a late drink.

Blind Cunt did have a fair old wad. — Christmas shoapping dosh, ah bet, Roxy said gleefully. — Try telling ays that's no fuckin sound! Two hundred odd sobs!

— CORRECKSHIN! I snapped. — Two hundred and seventeen pounds and thirty-four pence to be exact.

Roxy was intae a fifty-fifty split, but I was happy with eighty bar, as he had taken all the risks, such as they were.

The next day we were back in the same pub for a lunchtime drink. We were soon joined by Big Moncrief. — Ye hear aboot last night?

— Naw, we said in chorus.

— Ye ken what's his name, the blind boy, likes? The boy we hud a drink up at the bar wi last night?

— Aye, Roxy said, with a fake concern.

— Died last night; brain haemorrhage. The poor bastard died in the snaw at Dalry Road. The council gritters found um last night.

— Fuckin hell! We wir jist wi the boy the other night! Roxy said.

I was too shocked to admire his front.

— Fuckin sin, Big Moncrief snarled, — a harmless cunt n aw. Ye ken what? Some rotten cunt dipped ehs poakits. The perr cunt's lyin in the snaw dyin. Did they phone an ambulance? Did they fuck! Some cunt jist goes, aye, aye, what's this then? Instead ay phonin an ambulance, the cunt's dipped ehs poakits, took ehs wallet. They found it empty in the graveyard.

— That's fuckin terrible, Roxy shook his head. — Ah hope they find the cunt that did it.

— See if ah goat ma fuckin hands oan thum . . . Moncrief growled.

— How bad is that? I said timidly, before changing the subject. — What's everybody fir?

Poor Blind Cunt. No a bad punter n aw. Wish I could mind ay his name but.

7

JELLIES AND COCK SUCKING

You could tell that the boy was suspect when he says, I've got to
see a man about a brown-paper package. You could tell that the
boy thought that I thought he was suspect. You could tell that
he enjoyed the fact that I thought he was suspect. The problem
was that I thought he was suspect not because, as he thought, I
saw him as some big sleazy dealer or all that shite; I thought that
he was suspect because I thought that he was a wanker.

Brown-paper package my Granny's sagging tits. What's he
like.

Ronnie might have thought that the guy was a wanker n aw
had he not, as the song goes, been so busy playing carousel. His
pupils were like pin-pricks despite the heavy, hooded eyelids
which hung loosely over them. The pint of poison which lay
untouched in front of him was losing its chill and fizz, leaving it
looking like the rancid pish it was. It would not be touched now.

I was continuing my successful boycott of Scottish and Newcastle Brewers products, swilling away at my Becks. This boycott, which I tried vainly to pursue over a number of years, was
now abetted by the stagnant mediocrity of the S&N products;
they had stood still in the face of competition.

I wearily raised my hand in acknowledgement as the wanker
departed; no doubt to procure the first ever quart of Edinburgh
hash which came in a brown-paper package. As he said, ——
Cheerio boys, Ronnie managed to do something marginal with
his eyes and lips.

—— Jellied, Ron? I asked.

In reply, Ronnie rested his head in his hand, elbow propped up on the table, and allowed his lips to faintly crease.

I looked again at the pint before him; the dealers had no real competition from the legal drug sector. I resented more than ever the fact that S&N had managed to fight off that take-over bid from the Australian punters. I remember it being described as a hostile bid. Hostile to who? No me anyway. Surely no other race in the world put up with such crap drugs.

I get Ronnie out into a taxi, mildly resentful that we have missed an hour's worth of the mis-named happy hour, which is neither: a bit like the fuckin moral majority. Its duration was a five-till-eight weekday slot at this pretentious dive where they sold toxic chemicals at prices which were merely exploitative rather than criminal. Looking at the punters fighting for the attention of the barstaff, happiness was the last emotion on display. It should be renamed the desperate hours.

Ronnie flopped back into the taxi, his face slamming hard off a side window. — Stockbridge, mate, I shout to the driver, reasoning that Ronnie was suffering from chemical imbalance and what he needed was some amphetamine to get him back into some kind of equilibrium.

When we get to Veitchy's place Denise and Penman are there. They're all quite high, through snorting coke. Ronnie can go and get fucked. No way would we consider wasting coke on him. He'd have to sleep his way through this gig. Veitchy helps me to put him on the couch, and he just crashes out unconscious. Denise puckers his lips, — My my my, Brian's brought us a trophy. Is that what Ronnie is, Brian, our ain wee trophy?

— Yeah, that's it, I say, catching Penman's eye. He chops out a line for me and I go down on it like it was a fanny that pished Becks. Suddenly, everything's better.

— What have we here? Denise has unzipped Ronnie's flies and taken his floppy dick out. It looks pretty repulsive, bouncing around on his thighs like a broken jack-in-the-box.

Veitchy laughs loudly, — Ha ha ha ha ha ha perr Ronnie ha ha ha ha, no real. Denise yir some cunt so ye are ha ha ha ha.

— Now that's a whopper, Denise pouts with a saucy wink, — but it'll be even bigger erect. Let's see if ah kin breathe some life intae poor old Ronnie.

He starts sucking on Ronnie's cock. Veitchy and I check Ron's face for signs of recognition, signs of enjoyment, but it seems dead to me. Veitchy then produces a magic marker and draws glasses and a Hitler moustache on Ronnie's coupon.

— Fuck sakes, I turn to Penman, — there's me lugged that cunt intae a taxi and brought him doon here tae look eftir him. Cannae leave the cunt in the pub like that, ah thought. Ah'll take him tae Veitchy's, he'll be awright thair.

— Yeah, typical ay they cunts, Penman snorts, then he picks a bogey out of his nose. He sees that there's a load of coke stuck to it, so he swallows it. — How ye livin they days anywey? he asks me.

— Shite, I tell him. — It's funny though man, but ah'm gaunny miss the parks this summer, ken? Shouldnae huv burned it doon. Gies me time tae write songs, for the band n that, ken?

A few of us had been thinking of starting a band. That was what I was into; being in a band.

— Well, ah'm pittin ma name doon fir the bins this summer. Intae that? The Cleansing Department, ken?

— Aye, mibbe, I said. It sounds a bit too much like work for me, too many people aroond. No enough time tae think, tae get in touch wi yirself, tae just enjoy the isolation. No like the parks.

Denise is having no luck with Ronnie's cock. It's still as jellied as the rest of him, but Veitchy's got the polaroid out and he's taking snaps of them.

— Ah wee bit ay love talk first, Denise, whisper some ay they sweet nothins intae the cunt's ear, Penman advises.

Denise puckers his lips and says, — Tsk, Penman, ye ken ah keep aw that talk jist for you. Ye think ah'm a slut or something?

Penman smiles, stands up and gestures me to the door. We go through to the bedroom. He stoops down at a chest of drawers;

producing a box which he unlocks. It contains a plastic bag full of pills.

— Eckys? I ask.

— Snowballs, he nods, smiling. — Many kin ye punt fir ays?

— Ah could dae forty nae danger. Thing is, ah've nae dough up front.

— Disnae matter, he says, counting them intae a smaller bag. — Gies it when ye git it. Ah only want ten quid fir one. They'll go fir fifteen easy, eighteen if ye hud them until the week before Rezurrection. Square ays eftir. Veitchy's nervous wi the number ah'm hudin here.

— One question, Penman. How's it ye always stash them at Veitchy's gaff?

— Veitchy's a fuckin radge; he's he only cunt that'll let ays. Ah'm no gaunny keep thum at ma ain place, um ah now?

It sounded logical enough.

A few minutes later, Denise's excited screams follow us into the bedroom. — BRI-IN! PEEHN-MIN!

I return into the front room to find Denise and Veitchy straddling the back of the couch, facing each other. They have their cocks out, both erect. Ronnie is still slumped unconscious, his head resting on the back of the sofa. Denise and Veitchy have their erections poking into his ears.

— The camera, Denise hisses, — take a picture!

— This'll be a fuckin classic ha ha ha, Veitchy babbles.

I pick up the camera and get into position. — Whair's the fuckin button? I ask.

— The toap, Denise squeals excitedly, — press the fuckin black button oan the toap! Mind yir fingers oan the lens, daft radge thit ye are!

I take a couple of shots which come out well. They really capture the personalities of the three punters involved. That's surely what portrait photography is all about.

We pass the snaps around and laugh for a bit, then Denise goes: — Ah need mair coke. Any mair fuckin coke?

Veitchy says, — Naw man, that's it finished, likes.

— Could dae wi a bit mair but, Veitchy, Penman says. Penman and I have taken half an ecky each, but mair coke would be sound.

— Suppose ah could nick doon tae Andy Lawton's in the motor, Veitchy agreed.

That sounded okay. We sorted Veitchy out with some cash and he left us in the flat.

After a while I was getting a bit bored watching the telly. — Any fuckin beer in this doss? I asked.

— Yuv jist taken half an ecky. Ye no gittin a rush oaf that ecky yit?

I was getting fuck all off the ecky. I pretended I was though; it's crucial tae think positive on such occasions. — Aye, it's sound, but it's a bit mellow likes. Stick oan some techno. Git this telly shite oaf; kills the art ay fuckin conversation.

We ploughed our way through Veitchy's record and tape collection. I'd never seen so much shite.

— This is fuckin rubbish. Cunt wants his fuckin jaw tanned fir huvin shite like this. Nae fuckin house stuff at aw man, Penman moaned.

— Some ay this isnae bad, Denise opined.

— Stuck in eighties disco shite that cunt, said Penman bitterly. — That cunt is a fuckin erse. He always hus been an erse, he always fuckin will be an erse.

— C'moan, Penman, I said, — Git oaf the cunt's case. It's his hoaspitality wir enjoyin here.

—Aye, Penman, yir such a fuckin bitch at times, Denise said, kissing his cheek softly, — bit yuv goat yir bad side n aw.

— Well ah'm gaunny git a beer, I said. As I spoke I started rushing. What a fuckin waste, rushing like this here when I could be at a club.

— Dinnae take alcohol wi yir ecky, Denise says. — Ye cannae drink if yuv taken ecstasy, he minces smartly, — cancels oot aw the effects.

— That's a myth, I say.

— Tsk, listen tae yirsel, Brian! Mind the time at The Pure ye sais tae ays: Yir mad tae drink, bevvy n ecky dinnae mix, yill bring yirsel doon, Denise remonstrates.

— Aye, bit that's whin yir tryin tae dance, but. Dehydration n that. If ye jist want tae gouch, it doesnae really matter. Besides, ah've been oan the Becks maist ay the day.

— Ah'm no touchin the bevvy again, no fir ages anywey. Ah'm no takin any ecky either until ah find oot the coke situation. Ye should pick jist one drug n stick tae it. That's the lesson ah've learned. Last week ah wis up the toon pished ootay ma heid. Ah'd hud eight Becks n six Diamond Whites. Some cunt went n gied ays a tab ay acid. Then this radge wis hasslin ays in The Pelican so ah jist turns roond n sais: Dinnae fuckin bother ays man, kick yir fuckin cunt in! Anyway ah goat pure para so ah ends up in the City Cafe. Ken that goth burd, quite a hard-faced lassie?

— Her that used tae hing aboot wi that Moira? I asked.

— Ah think so.

— Moira. You legged that, did ye no? Penman asked.

— Aye, in the lassies' bogs at the Ceilidh House, I told him.

— Anywey, Denise snapped curtly, irritated by our interruptions and digressions, — this burd wis really fag-hagging ays oot, man. Ah goes hame wi her, she says she's goat some blow. Then she starts askin ays aboot ma sexuality, ken, aw that how'd ye like tae come ower tae the other side, aw that vain crap that fag-hags come oot wi man, ken? Ah mean, as if ah've nivir fucked a lassie before! Stupid wee hoor!

— Ye gie hur the message? Penman asked.

— Hud oan, hud oan a minute, I cut in. I hated interrupting Denise in full flight, but something about this tale was disturbing me. I needed something clarified. — Lit's git this straight. Wir talkin aboot that lassie that hings aboot wi Moira n Tricia. Olly, or something doss like that, is it no?

— That's hur! Denise says.

— Hammer n sickle earrings? Oan some sortay Stalinist trip?

— That's the yin awright, Denise says. — So ah'm shagging her like, in the fanny n aw, he says, standing up and doing a theatrical pelvic thrust. — She kept they long black gloves oan, like a silly wee tart, n she's gaun: AW THIS IS GREAT . . . THIS IS MAGIC . . . FUCK ME HARDER n aw that. Then she comes n ah starts thinkin aboot Hutchie fae Chapps, this big fuckin piece ay meat ah've been cruisin fir yonks, n ah comes n aw. Then this daft hoor turns aroond n sais tae ays: Tell ays that wisnae somethin else, she goes, aw cocky like. Like she'd expected me tae throw away the tub ay KY n run doon tae St James's Centre fir a fuckin engagement ring! Well, ah hud tae pit hur in the picture; ah tells her it wisnae even as fuckin good as a bad wank, wi her ah hud tae use ma imagination mair, tae pretend ah wis shaggin something worthwhile. She goes aw fucked up and tells ays tae go. Ah jist sais: Dinnae you fuckin worry, hen, ah'm gaun.

This was a disturbing story. I remember being kb'd by that lassie. I think it was the City Cafe, but it might have been Wilkie House. I saw her a few times at 9Cs, even once at The Pure. As I smiled at Denise the phantom quiver of that woman's rejection slid through me, setting off that internal crumbling dam of self-esteem that our pals can seldom sense. However, I tempered that feeling with the thought of her humiliation at the hands of Denise. I felt a delicious vindication, followed by a vague sense of guilt. This is what being alive's all about, all those fucked-up feelings. You've got to have them; when you stop, watch out.

God, the telly was fuckin boring, and there were only two cans of McEwan's pish in the fridge. I couldn't bring myself to look at that shite. — Whair's fuckin Veitchy? I cursed, to nobody in particular. Chancellor Norman Lamont came on the telly.

— Ah'd like tae kill that cunt, if he wisnae already deid, Denise bitched.

I felt another ecky surge and got up and started dancing on the spot. I couldn't keep it going though; there was no fuckin stimulus. I fancied doing another one and heading up to the Citrus or 9Cs. — That cunt, I said, pointing at Ronnie, who was still slumbering with his flaccid prick hanging out off his keks like some dead surrealist snake, — what's he like: a fuckin liability. Cartin that fuck around, n he jist crashes oot aw ower the place!

In a surge of anger I pulled Ronnie off the couch onto the floor. He inspired a wave of disgust in me, his stupid glasses and moustache. — He's as well oan the flair, gie us a shot ay the couch. He's too fucked tae notice the difference.

The three of us sat on the couch, using Ronnie as a footstool. He was dead to the world. We were still bored, so I got up, brought some flour back from the kitchen and poured it over Ronnie. I gasped at a brief acid-style flashback of Blind Cunt lying in the snow.

— Hi, Penman guffaws, splitting his keks with laughter, — better mind perr Veitchy's cairpit.

— It's only flour, I said, but Denise had gone through to the kitchen and he returned with some eggs and started breaking them over Ronnie's prostrate body.

That was the cue for us to go mental, gripped by a collective hysteria. We went to the kitchen and saw what there was. We then systematically covered Ronnie with every sort of foodstuff, cleaning fluid and powder we could get our hands on.

When we were finished he was covered in a largely grey-white evil sludge, partly coloured in places by orange beans, yellow egg yolks and green washing-up liquid. Penman came back from the kitchen and emptied the contents of a bin-liner over him. I tipped a couple of full ashtrays across him. The sludge rolled off him and seeped into the ugly red carpet. Still Ronnie wouldn't wake up. Denise then shat on his face; a huge, steaming, wet turd. By this time I was fearing for my own health. I was convulsing, with a crippling pain in my side caused by too much laughter, and Penman had almost blacked out after a giggling fit.

We took more pictures. I'd made myself sick, easy considering the mess, and what I'd had to drink, and vomited over Ronnie's unrecognisable face and chest. He looked like a mound of bacterial sludge from a septic tank; a lump of toxic waste; a spillover from a council tip.

We laughed ourselves out and our adrenalin dipped simultaneously as we surveyed the mess.

— Fuck sakes, I said. — What are we like. How mad is this!

— Veitchy's gaunny be well pissed-off at us. His cairpit's fucked, Denise goes.

Penman looked a bit shat up. — Ronnie n aw. Ron's pretty radge. He hud a blade that time in the Burnt Post. Ye dinnae ken what any cunt whae's jellied'll go n dae whin thir cairryin a chib.

This was true. — Let's fuck off, I suggested. — Leave some money fir Veitchy n Ron. They can git cleaned up.

Nobody was putting up too many strong arguments for staying and facing the music. We took off and headed for Tollcross in a taxi. We got very drunk but were still thinking about chancing our arm and trying to get into the Citrus Club, when Veitchy walked into the pub. To our surprise, he took it okay, better than Ronnie apparently.

Veitchy looked really freaked, as in amazed, by the whole thing. — Ah've never seen anybody look like that in ma puff. It wis just fuckin crazy. Ah shat masel when ah came in and pit the light oan. Ah jist pit doon some auld newspapers, aw the wey tae the bathroom. It wis radge whin Ronnie woke up. He just shouted: THE FUCKIN BASTARDS! THE FUCKIN CUNTS! SOME WIDE–O FUCKIN DIES FIR THIS! Then he jist trails through tae the shower, n gits under it, fully-clathed likes, n hoses hisel doon. Then he walks oot soakin wet n goes: Ah'm away hame.

I looked at Denise n Penman. Sometimes mates are the last people ye kin trust.

— Ye git any coke, Denise asks Veitchy.

— Naw, jist these, he says holding out some capsules.

— Eckys? Penman asks. — No wantin eckys. Goat loads ay fuckin ecky ya daft fucker.

— Naw, it's ketamine. Special-Ks like. Ken?

— Ah'm no touchin thaim, Denise shudders.

Penman looks at me. — Ah'm game, he says.

— Might as well, I agree, — jist fir the crack like.

We each down one, except Denise, but within minutes he's begging Veitchy to sort him out as well. I start to feel heavy and tired. We're all talking shite.

The next thing I remember is dancing on my own in the Meadows at five o'clock on a Sunday morning.

8

PARANOIA

I'm thinking about my life and that is always a very, very stupid thing to do. The reason for this is that there are some things that don't bear thinking about, some things that if you try to think of them they'll just fuck you up even mair.

I hear my auld man shouting at me, — BRIAN! UP! C'MOAN! MOVE IT!

— Aye, jist comin. It's pointless arguing. I have to sign on today. Once the auld boy decides I should be up, then he won't stop.

I rise wearily. Derek's in his bed, stretching tae life.

— You no workin the day? I ask him.

— Naw. Day oaf.

Derek's doing well for himself. Planning to sit the Civil Service Executive Officer exam, or perhaps has already sat it. I don't know. The details of the working classes' trivial activities have never held much attraction for a man of leisure.

— Mind ay Ma, Deek? I can't believe I just asked him that.

— Aye, of course ah do.

— You wir jist six when she took off.

— Still mind ay her likes.

— Aw . . . ah mean it's jist been a long time since ye talked aboot it . . . ah suppose ah mean since we talked aboot it, I said.

— Thir isnae that much tae talk aboot, he snorted, — she went, we stayed.

I didn't like that c'est la vie attitude, and wondered if he was trying to conceal something, then I wondered what. I supposed it was just because Deek was a bit thick. He'd probably pass the Civil Service Executive Officer exam though.

Downstairs the auld man had made a plate of toast and some tea. — You were in some bloody state again last night, he says sourly.

Actually, I wasn't in some state. I was a wee bit pished. Roxy, Sidney and I had broken into a chip shop in Corstorphine and stolen a load of confectionery and tobacco. We'd managed to fence a bit to the Rox's brother-in-law, who has an ice-cream van. Then we'd got a bit drunk. I know I wasn't in some state, for if I had been in some state I wouldn't have come home.

— Jist a few pints, I mused.

— If ye want tae make yirsel useful, come roond the scheme wi me n Norma collecting some names for this petition.

Now why didn't I think of that. A sound idea. I'd only be fuckin crucified, that's all. It's bad enough him trying to get me killed with his stupid, pointless activities, he now wants me to pull the fuckin trigger masel.

— Ah'd love tae, Dad, mibbe some other time, yeah? It's just this signing-oan shite the day. Then ah've goat tae go round the Job Centre. How's the campaign going?

— We went tae see that bloody councillor. That's nivir a Labour man. Ah've voted Labour aw ma life, but nivir again, ah'm tellin ye.

I took a hike into the city. It's fuckin miles, but I grudge paying fares. I'm skint. That chippie job paid sweeties, metaphorically as well as literally. I go and sign on. Then I head up to Sidney's gaff for a blow. It's weird how I tend to hang around with different people when in different drug scenes:

Alcohol:	The PATH, Roxy, Sidney, Big Moncrief
Non-opiate illegal drugs: (speed, acid, ecky, etc.)	Veitchy, Denise, Penman

Opiates: Swanney, Raymie, Spud

But whatever scene, there's always Ronnie. That cunt is my
penance for being a . . . for some crime committed in a previous
life.

That afternoon, I meet Penman who's fucked from a scene he
was in over the weekend. His eyes are bleary and red. We do
acid. Monday afternoon and we do a microdot. It's strong stuff n
aw. — You know your problem man? he asks in a way which
disconcerts me.

— Eh, I say, — ah didnae ken ah hud one . . .

— Ye jist illustrated it fir ays, man. Ye jist provided ays wi, as
you might say, a graphic illustration ay what ah meant wi what
you sais thair, ken?

— What dae ye mean? I ask, a bit nippy.

— Dinnae git stroppy, mate. This is mates talkin. Ah'm only
sayin this cause me n you go back a long way. Right?

— Right, I agree, full of unease. I haven't been sleeping and
I'm always para when I haven't been sleeping. It isn't the drugs
that make me para, it's the lack of sleep that makes me para. The
drugs only make it hard for for me tae sleep, so they're only
indirectly responsible. If I could just get something to make me
fuckin sleep . . .

— This 'ah didnae ken ah hud a problem' shite, Penman
scoffs. — Wuv aw goat problems. Every cunt in this bar's goat
problems. He sweeps his arm around the seedy pub. It wasn't
easy to refute that proposition. — Every cunt in the world's goat
problems.

— This isnae the maist representative sample . . . I say, but he
picks up on this and cuts in.

— There ye go again: 'this isnae the maist representative
sample . . .' he mocks me, using a voice that sounds more like
Denise's than ma own. — Ah'm tellin ye mate, yir awright, but
yir too much ay a smart cunt. Point is, everybody laps up a smart
cunt at one time or another. The smart cunt makes a joke, every
fucker's chuffed tae bits. Then the smart cunt gits oan people's

tits. Then the smart cunt gits a burst mooth. That's the way it works.

I sit flabbergasted.

— Now ah'm no saying that you've like, croassed that line. Aw ah'm sayin is that some cunts kin git away wi it mair thin others.

— Whit dae ye mean?

— Take Denise fir instance. Every cunt kens what he's like. So he gits away wi things thit you or me couldnae. One day though, he'll go too far . . .

I was really para now. I'd never had Penman talk tae me like this before. — Any cunt said anything tae ye aboot ays?

— Look mate, aw ah'm sayin is thit yir startin tae gie oaf a vibe, he takes a sip of his coke and puts his arm around ma shoulder.

— Ah dinnae go aboot thinkin ah'm better thin any cunt else, I plead.

— Look mate, dinnae go taking it aw personally. Ah'm jist sayin watch. Right? He shakes his head for a while, then lets it fall into his hands. — Aw look, he gasps in exasperation, — forget whit ah sais, it's jist the acid.

— Naw bit, you look, whit's the score? Whae's been sayin things?

— Forget it.

— Naw come oan, ah want tae ken. What's the fuckin score?

— Ah sais forget it. Ah wis oot ay order, right?

There is a hardness in Penman's eyes, so I feel comfortable deferring to him. — This fuckin acid man . . . I observe.

— Aye, that's right . . . he agrees, but there is a meanness about him, an unsettling edge. I feel like bursting into tears and begging: PLEASE BE NICE TO ME.

Penman had fucked up ma heid. Penman and the acid. When I started to come down I went back tae ma auld man's place and up tae ma room. I lay on the bed taking stock of my life with a cruel, self-loathing brutality. No job, no qualifications except O Grade English and Art, no romantic attachment now that she's away and definitely not coming back, mates who only tolerated me. Prospects pretty fuckin grim all round. Yes, I did have a certain outgoing social vivaciousness but the self-belief that drove me on in face of all overwhelming evidence to the contrary was now evaporating rapidly. Penman wrote my epitaph: A Smart Cunt. Nobody likes a smart cunt; a smart cunt who is also an accessory to murder has got real problems.

It could be the drugs, it could be Blind Cunt, or I could be going mental, but things are not right. When I get on a bus or go into a pub, people stop talking when they see me. On the bus nobody sits beside me. I am the very last person anybody will sit beside. Do I smell? I think I do smell of something. I sniff at my clothes, armpits, crotch. I take a shower. Am I ugly? I look at myself in the mirror for ages. I am ugly. No worse, I'm totally unremarkable. A completely bland face; no character in it. I have to get out of here, so I go to Roxy's.

— This Blind Cunt thing's fuckin ma heid, man, I tell him. — How fucked is it?

— It's drugs that's fuckin you up, he scoffed, — leave them alane and stay cool ya daft cunt.

— Ah might go doon tae London for a bit. This place gies ays the fuckin creeps. There's some tapped people oan the streets, man. Yir walkin hame and any cunt could be cairryin a knife, jellied oot thir box. That could be your life over, jist like that. Some cunt who gets a result fae the AIDS clinic: You tested positive. What have they goat tae lose? They could just grab a car and mow ye doon.

— Bullshit.

— Look at Blind Cunt, though. It happened tae him! We did it tae him! It could happen tae us. It should happen tae us. Justice n that.

I was shaking and my teeth were chattering. There was a raw core of queasy fear in the centre of my body which was spreading toxic shivers through my limbs.

— That's shite. Awright, so it wis mibbe a bit ootay order whit we did tae Blind Cunt, but that brain thing could've happened anytime. That's a time-bomb, that sort ay thing. Disnae make us murderers or nowt like that. The cunt could've goat up one morning and hud a yawn tae hisel and bingo! Goodnight Vienna. Jist cause it happened tae happen by coincidence when ah panelled the cunt means fuck all. Ah read aw aboot this brain haemorrhage shite in the library. It's a shame fir Blind Cunt but it disnae mean tae say that we should fuck oor lives up. Tell ays thit us gittin the nick's gaunny bring Blind Cunt back, cause that's shite!

— Aye bit . . . I started.

— Listen the now, Bri, he interrupted, his head shaking belligerently. — Dinnae shed any tears fir Blind Cunt. Tell ays he wisnae an annoyin fuck. That cunt would've got his eventually, the wey ah see it.

— Blind Cunt might have saw it a wee bit differently, I replied, suddenly realising the ugly irony of what I'd said. The poor bastard. I felt awful. Roxy didn't spare me.

— Blind Cunt saw fuck all, that's how he wis called Blind Cunt, he said, contorting his face in a cruel sneer.

Once again I wanted to leave. I was surrounded by demons and monsters. We're all bad people. There's no hope for the world. I left and walked along the disused railway line and cried my eyes out at the futility of it all.

9

PLASTIC SURGERY

I'm sitting holding my face together in my hands; or that's how it seems. I'm aware of people around me, their outraged gasps indicating that it's bad. I know that. The blood falls through my fingers and hits the wooden pub floor in steady, even drops.

Hobo and I were close mates once, a few years ago now. He didn't like me pulling him around, begging him to get me sorted out.

— Git ootay ma fuckin face, Bri, ah'm warnin ye, man!

I was given plenty of warning. I never took Hobo seriously enough. I always thought he was bit of a poser, him hinging aboot wi they nutters. By keeping that company, though, you can become a nutter yirself. He's far more a man of substance than I thought. Being proved wrong hurts almost as much as my face. My cells, my fucking sick junk-deprived cells hurt the most. I hit the smack heavily this week. Things were getting a bit much; I needed to blot it all out. Everything.

It took one sweeping motion of the glass. One motion and I'm here holding my face together, and Hobo's shouting defensively about junkies fuckin hassling him, and extracting himself from the bar as the collective wrath develops:

— That wis ootay order . . .

— Boy wisnae bothering nae cunt . . .

Hobo slips away. I've no resentment, no thoughts of revenge. No yet anyway; I've bigger fish to fry. I need something to get this fevered ape off my back. Let Hobo think I'm obsessed with him, scheming revenge . . . it's all divine retribution for Blind Cunt, and if so, I've got off lightly. I deserve to suffer . . .

Why did she go.

She goed because of the same reason you got a glass in your face man different manifestations of the same reason namely that you are a

Somebody's dabbing at my face with a hanky. — Better get him to the hospital, that'll need stitching. A woman's voice. I can see out of at least one eye. Not like poor Bli . . . No

A gothic angel of mercy; black hair, black eyes, white face . . . it could be any old hound from the City Cafe . . .

I'm going down the road with her and some others, but I'm only aware of her, my sick body and the stinging air in my face. God, the wounds are fuckin sair now. — You got a weedjie accent? I ask this benign goth–dess.

I saw it on her lapel. The hammer and sickle badge of a Stalinist Goth. The one that kb'd me. The one that fag–hagged Denise oot.

— Ah'm fae Ayrshire, she said.

— What was it Burns said about Ayr: nae toon surpasses for honest men and bonnie lassies . . .

— I'm from Saltcoats, not Ayr.

— Saltcoats . . . the Metro. Good club. Apart fae that though, it's no really got a lot going for it, has it?

— Oh aye? And whair dae you come from then?

— Muirhouse.

— Huh! you're in no position tae talk.

— Listen, at ma auld man's hoose he's got panoramic views across the Forth over tae Fife. There's a golf course across the road, a nice beach a pleasant fifteen minutes' walk away. Additionally, there's a well-stocked library particulary strong on biographies of the famous . . .

More blood spurts out.

— Shh, she says, — you're stretching the wound.

It's getting sore. God, it's sair.

— Good! says the boy at the Infirmary. — That means it's not damaged any nerves. Quite a superficial cut, really. It only needs about eight stitches.

He sewed me up. Eight poxy stitches. I was right first time; Hobo was a namby-pamby blouse. Eight stitches. I laughed nervously, — Eight stitches.

I was brave when they put the stitches in. It looked quite good on my cheek; with any luck it wouldn't fade too much. My bland face needed a bit of character. The scar was a conversation piece. People would think I was a hard man. It's okay for Yul Brynner to say, in *The Magnificent Seven*: It's the guy that gave him the scars you have to worry about, he never drank in the Gunner, the shitein cunt.

The goth woman tells me she is called Olly. — As in Stan and Ollie? I ask.

— Oh, that's very good. Nobody's ever thought of that one before, she said, her tongue dripping sarcasm. — Actually, it's short for Olivia, she explained patiently. — The only famous Olivia is Olivia Newton-John and I hate her. So it's Olly.

I could understand that. It must be bad shite to be a goth and get compared with Ms Neutron-Bomb. — What about Olivia De Havilland? I asked.

— Who?

— She was a film star.

— Before my time, I'm sure.

— Mine as well. It's just that ma auld man had the hots for her. Used to say ma mother was her double.

I saw boredom etched onto her face. Why had she helped me? — Eh, thanks for helping me, I said.

— That bastard Hobo. I hate that crowd. Forrester and aw that bunch. You know that Forrester raped Liz Hamilton? He fuckin raped her! she hissed. Olly hated someone who was the friend of someone who assaulted me.

— Listen, dae ye ken anybody whae can get ays some jellies? I asked.

— Nup! Ah widnae touch them fir anything!

I needed some. — Can I use your phone?

We went back to hers and I lay on the couch, strung out. I tried to phone Ronnie but he'd vanished. His Ma had seen nothing of him for weeks and seemed completely unconcerned as to his whereabouts.

Olly eventually got a hold of a guy called Paul who came along and brought me some valium. I swallowed a few then smoked some blow. He left and Olly and I went to bed. I couldn't shag her though, I felt too sick. I had an erection but the idea of our bodies together was terrifying to me. I waited until she was asleep and I had a wank over her, shooting against her back.

The next day we had a good shag in the morning. It was barry having sex. She had a skinny body and it was therapeutic. It got the system going. In the afternoon we did it from the side, on the couch, so that I could watch the scores coming in on the videoprinter. I was happy.

5.40

PREM Manchester City 1 Nottingham Forest 0

D2 Bolton 3 Gillingham 1

— Oh this is lovely baby . . . really fuckin beautiful . . .

D1 Newcastle 4 Portsmouth 1

SC1 Cowdenbeath 0 Raith Rovers 4

D3 Barnet 2 Colchester 2

SPL Aberdeen 6 (Six)*

— Oh babes . . . I'm coming . . . I'm coming . . . I start to rant.

— Hud oan, hud oan . . . she twists and thrusts.

5.41

SPL Aberdeen 6 (Six) Heart of Midlothian 2

— Ya beauty! Yes! Jesus Christ, ah cannae keep gaun . . .

— OOOOOHHHH BRIAN I'M COMING . . . OH MY GOD!

D2 Oxford United 2 Bristol City 1

PREM Wimbledon 1 Tottenham Hotspur 1

PREM Chelsea 2 Everton 1

— Ah'm gaunny keep going babes, you're gaunny get there again . . .

— Oh God Brian, keep fucking me . . .

— Easy for Bri, doll, it's all too easy . . .

5.42

SC2 Arbroath 3 Stenhousemuir 0

D2 Southend United 0 York City 0

. . . for Bri, when ah get intae ma stride ah kin fuck all night . . .

SPL Hibernian 3*

. . . ooh ooh OOOHHH OOOHHHH

SPL Hibernian 3 St Johnstone 1

. . . AAGGHHHH!!! OH YA FUCKER!

God, the earth moved. How good was that. Glory glory to the Hi-bees.

We ate a Chinese takeaway and watched game-shows on the box that night. It was what I needed. Relaxation.

What I needed.

What did she need?

Olly had looked after me. Kindness was what I needed. What was in it for her? Perhaps some people are just basically good and kind. I thought of her and Denise. Of the time she knocked me back.

— Why did you knock me back that time?

— You were out of your face and totally obnoxious, she replied. — Just really-so-fuckin-boring . . .

I suppose it was a good enough reason.

She was not so happy when I mentioned Denise's name.

— I hate that sick little bastard. Fucking sick queer. He's been saying I went with him. Why would I go wi a poof? I'm no fuckin fag-hag. He's giein his mind a treat, the dirty wee prick. What does he think he's trying to prove by talkin shite like that?

I decided to drop the subject. My face was tight and numb. It was a sore numbness, not a comfortable numbness. It felt like it was made of badly sunburned tissue which had been crudely sellotaped together. It was worth it though. Yes, it definitely had a lot more character now and yes, it would be an interesting conversation piece. There was also the prospect of sympathy. On balance, it was for the best the way things had panned out.

10

YOUNG QUEENS

I've been trying to moderate my drink and drugs intake so I can get some kip in and feel less para. My old mate Donny Armstrong has come up to see my auld man. They've been arguing about politics. As a revolutionary, Donny tends to hunt out the single-issue punters in the community groups, like the auld man, and attempt to convert them to fully-fledged revolutionary politics.

— Some Mars Bar you've got yourself there, man, Donny says.

— You should see the other guy, I say, all cocky. It sounds good. The other guy, Hobo, has a face like a bairn's powdered arse and is about as concerned at the prospect of me looking for him (and I'm not looking too hard) as the continental big guns are at Hearts returning to European action.

The auld man exasperates him, though. Donny has to admit defeat here. Norma pops her head around the door and my father slyly slips away. Donny turns his attention to me, trying to recruit me into the 'party'. — You can't skate over the surface of social reality all your life, he says. This depresses me, it's revolutionary speak for: Ye cannae be a smart cunt aw yir life.

The answer, according to Donny, is to build the revolutionary party. This is done by militant political activity in the workplaces and communities at the point of oppression. I ask him how effective he feels this has been, and whether the collection of students, social workers, journalists and teachers that seem to make up the membership of his party constitutes a fair cross-section of the proletariat.

— Granted man, but it's the downturn, he says, as if that explains it.

— How is it, though, that Militant seem to be able to get ordinary punters while you lot get all those middle-class types?

— Look man, I'm not going to slag Militant, cause there's enough sectarianism on the left, but . . .

He launches into a long and bitter attack on the politics and personalities of Scottish Labour Militant. I'm thinking, what can I do, really do for the emancipation of working people in this country, shat on by the rich, tied into political inaction by servile reliance on a reactionary, moribund and yet still unelectable Labour Party? The answer is a resounding fuck all. Getting up early to sell a couple of papers in a shopping centre is not my idea of the best way to chill out after raving. When people like Penman, Denise, Veitchy and Roxy are ready to join the party, then I'll be ready. The problem is, there's too many, God rest his soul, Blind Cunt types in that sort of thing. I think I'll stick to drugs to get me through the long, dark night of late capitalism.

Donny goes, the both of us totally drained by our arguments. He does look healthy and happier than me though; he has a glow to him. The involvement in the process of political struggle may indeed be quite liberating in itself, irrespective of the results it yields, or rather doesnae yield. I'm still pondering it all an hour later when Ronnie shows up. I haven't seen him since that regrettable incident last weekend.

He touches my stitches lightly, and smiles with a weary compassion. Then he shuts his eyes and wiggles his finger in the air.

— Ron, man, ah'm really sorry about the other night . . . I start, but he puts his finger to his lips and shakes his head slowly. He staggers through the hallway, into the living-room. He's on the couch like an American heat-seeking missile onto a Baghdad orphanage. Nice one, Ronnie.

— Jellied, Ron?

He shakes his head slowly and blows out heavily through tightly-puckered lips. I put on a video and he dozes. I put on a second one and I fall asleep in the middle of it. I feel a tapping on the sole of my foot, and look up to see Ronnie going. He raises his thumb slowly, mumbles something and vanishes into the night.

Deek comes in. — Whair's Dad? he asks.

— No sure. He went oot wi Norma fi upstairs.

Deek rolls his eyes and leaves.

I stagger up to bed.

The next day I've arranged to met Denise in the Beau Brummel.

Denise is in a state of transformation from one queen stereotype into another. I suppose he's no a wee laddie any mair. None of us are. It comes home to me when he walks into the Beau Brummel with a pair of young queens who look exactly like Denise used to look. Denise, on the other hand, looks like a cruel scoutmaster in his flak jacket.

— Drink fir ma friend. A whisky, he snaps at one of the young queens. The wee buftie immediately springs up to the bar. I was going to say something because I don't really like whisky but Denise always loves to decide what will be the appropriate drink for his friends based on his view of how they look and I hate to spoil his sense of theatre. My need to have Denise exhibit that sense of theatre is stronger than my need to exercise freedom of choice in my drug-taking. Therein lies an illustration of the bigger problem.

— I saw your ma the other day, I tell him.

— My Ma! How is she!

— No bad.

— Whair wis this? The scheme?

— Naw, in toon.

— Ah'll huv tae arrange tae meet her in toon fir a cup ay tea. Ah cannae be bothered gaun tae the scheme. Too fuckin depressin. Ah fuckin hate that place.

Denise never really fitted in back there. Too camp; too much of a superiority complex. Most people hated that, but I loved him for it.

One of the bufties makes a terrible error of protocol and puts on Blondie's 'Denis', as in 'Denise Denee'. This upsets the fuck out of Denise.

— WHAE PIT THAT OAN!? WHAE?! he stands up and screams over at the juke box.

One of the young queens apologetically pouts, — Bit Din-e-e-e-esssse, you sais the other night thit is wis yir favourite song, mind the other night, at Chapps?

The other buftie boy looks on in malicious enjoyment at his friend's discomfort.

Denise clenches his fists then lets them fall by his side. — THE WHOLE POINT IS THIT IT'S MA FAVOURITE SONG! AH'M THE ONLY YIN THIT'S ALLOWED TAE PIT OAN THAT FUCKIN SONG! BATTER YIR FUCKIN CUNT IN, SON! He shakes his head angrily, — Dinnae bother ays, jist dinnae fuckin bother ays, son, he dismissively hisses. The disgraced young queen slopes off. Denise turns to me and says, — Young queens, ten a penny, the fuckin wee jessies.

The observation of such protocol is crucial with Denise. Everything has to be done just right. I remember several years ago he gave me a blank cassette tape to record this Fall record. — Remember, he told me, — dinnae write the track list doon oan the index caird. Write it doon oan a separate bit ay paper n ah'll copy it oantae the index caird. Ah've goat a special wey ay daein it. It's only me thit kin dae it.

I cannae really remember whether I genuinely forgot, or whether I did it deliberately to wind him up, but I biroed the track listings doon ontae the cassette card. Later, when I presented the tape tae him, he freaked. It was too mad. — WHIT'S THIS? AH FUCKIN TELT YE! AH FUCKIN TELT YE NO TAE WRITE THUM IN, he hissed. — IT'S SPOILED NOW! THE WHOLE THING'S NAE FUCKIN USE NOW!

He crushed the tape and case under the heel of his boot. — FUCKIN SPOILED EVERYTHING!

How uptight is the cunt?

We have a few drinks. I don't mention Olly to him. His queen patter with the young guys is mildly amusing for a while. Gay punters that hang around Chapps, The Blue Moon and The Duck hate Denise. His stereotypical queen stuff embarrasses most homosexuals. Denise loves to be hated. They detested his high-camp act back in the scheme. It was funny then, funny and brave, but now it starts tae grate and I make my excuses and depart, wondering, as I leave, what he's going to say about me behind my back.

11

LOVE AND SHAGGING

Olly's mate Tina was a friendly, nervy, high-adrenalin lassie who was always on the move; talking, chewing gum, checking out everything and everyone with sharp, hawk-like eyes. At the party at Sidney's, Olly said, in a mock-schoolie way: — She fancies yir mate. Ronnie.

— Fuck off, Tina hissed, either embarrassed or pretending to be. Ronnie was sitting on the floor watching the Christmas tree, mesmerised by it. He'd taken a few jellies. Sidney, somewhat surprisingly, was jellied as well. He explained to me that he'd been getting 'too uptight' about the flat getting trashed and had been giving the party 'negative vibes', so he had taken some jellies to 'mellow out'.

Olly then said to me, — If that sick poof Denise comes up, don't you talk tae him! No while ah'm around anyway!

I found this a bit irritating and offensive. Her feud with Denise had nothing to do with me. — Of course I have to talk to Denise, he's my friend. I practically fuckin grew up wi Denise. And stop aw this homophobic shite: it's a total drag.

She then said something which frosted me over. — No wonder people say you're a smart cunt, she hissed, storming away.

— What . . . who said . . . I moaned at the back of her head as she vanished into the kitchen. I was too mellow to get para; but her words rang around in ma head and the paranoia would eventually come, as sure as night follows day. I'd be sitting tomorrow at my old man's trying to pretend that I wasn't feeling sick and miserable and worthless, and her words would shudder

245

through my system like psychic spears and I'd agonise over their meaning, relentlessly torturing myself. I've a lot to look forward to.

I started talking to Spud Murphy, a mate of Raymie Airlie's. I like listening to Spud and Raymie. They've got a few years on me, they've been there, and they're still around. Survivors. You can't really learn anything from people like that, but their patter's okay. Spud's still lamenting getting ripped off by his best mate ages ago. It was a junk deal, and his mate absconded with the loot. — Best mates, likesay, man, best mates, ken? Then the cat goes n pills a stunt like that. Completely doss, likesay. Ken?

— Aye, ye cannae even trust mates these days, I said, the realisation bringing on my first substantial para attack of the day. I finger my scar. Thank fuck for Hobo; at least I've got a bit of concrete evidence for my paranoia.

— It's jist, likesay, drugs, man. It's horrible, likes, but whenever thir's collies involved friendships go oot the windae, ken?

We spraff on for a bit, then Tina comes over to us, a bit drunk, waving a Diamond White bottle in her hand. — Ah'm gaunny fire intae yir mate, she says, matter-of-factly, before going over and sitting beside Ronnie. The next time I look they're necking, or rather, Tina's eating Ronnie's face.

— Could dae wi somebody firin intae me like that, man, that would dae me barry, likesay, Spud said.

— Naw, ah'm disillusioned wi women. I'm useless in relationships, Spud. I'm a selfish fucker. Thing is, I never, ever pretend tae be anything other than a selfish fucker. Take Olly there, I ventured.

— That wee goth love-cat ye came wi, likesay? he asked.

— She played the saint. Took ays hame eftir ah'd been glessed by that Hobo cunt . . .

— That sounds a good woman, man. Ye want tae hud oan tae her, likes.

— Ah bit listen tae this: one decent act ay kindness and she thinks that gies her the right tae tell me how tae live ma life. It's: nae collies, get a job, go tae college, buy some clathes, dinnae speak tae people ah dinnae like, even if yuv kent them yir whole fuckin life . . . aw that typical burd shite, man. How bad is that?

— That's a bit seriously radge, catboy. No that ah kin really gie much advice, ken? Chicks n me, likes, sortay oil n water, ken? Ah'd love us tae mix mix mix a wee bit better, but somehow the gig jist nivir quite materialises, ken?

Olly came back over to us. She put her arms around me. — I want to go home, she whispered. She thought she was Joan of Arc. — I want to go home and fuck you.

I shuddered in fear at the thought. I'd had far too many drugs over the weekend. I couldn't be bothered shagging. It just seemed so pointless, a total waste of time. We didn't have strong feelings for each other, we were just playing out time waiting for the real thing tae come along. I dinnae like shagging just for the sake of it; I like to make love. That means with somebody I love. There are times, sure, when the bag just needs to be emptied, but no when you're full of drugs. It was like the other day when we were shagging; it was just like two skeletons rattling away the gither. I just thought: why the fuck are we doing this?

The thing that worried me even more than the shagging was staying round at Olly's for any length of time. I disliked her friends. They were hostile and offhand to me, which didn't really bother me, in fact I enjoyed it. What fucked me over though was the way they patronised her. They were all City Cafe types: waitresses, insurance salesmen, local government clerks, bar persons et cetera, who wanted to be musicians, actors, poets, dancers, novelists, painters, playwrights, film-makers, models and were obsessed with their alternative careers. They played their dull tapes, recited their crap poems, strutted around like peacocks and pontificated with endless dogmatism on the arts that they were excluded from. The thing was, Olly lent herself to this patronisation. Her friends wanted to be like somebody else; she only wanted to be like them. I thought I had low ambition, but she couldn't see what limited horizons she had. When I mentioned this I was dismissed as jealous and bitter.

We got into an argument and I ended up staying the night at Roxy's place. I told him about her friends and he said: — So you should be perfectly at home there, man.

He clocked my tense, hurt expression and said: — Fuck me, tell ays you're no nippy the day. Only joking man. But I knew he wasn't. Or maybe I was just being para. Or maybe not. I was still full of drugs and hadn't slept properly in donks.

Anyway, I gave Olly as wide a berth as I could until I got it together. I tried to chill at ma old man's which was difficult as the house was always full of his campaign mates, or Deek's pals. Deeks pals never seemed to drink or take drugs or go raving. They 'werenae intae that shite'. All they did was nothing, they just sat around and did nothing. Deek had passed his Civil Service Executive Officer exams, but showed no excitement about it, or any interest in a career. I admired his nihilism relating to work, that made sense to me, but he and his pals seemed to have no interest in anything at all. Everything was 'shite' to them: drugs, music, fitba, violence, work, shagging, money, fun. They seemed to be a bunch of completely isolated basket-cases.

Olly harassed me on the phone. She was rambling and expansive when she talked about what her friends had done or were doing, but when she focused on us she always became tense and confrontational. It would end up with her abusing me over the phone, then slamming it down as if she was the aggrieved party.

— Woman problems? my dad would laugh. — Never run for a bus or a woman, son. There's always another one coming around the corner.

A great strategy that one. That's why he's never had his hole in fourteen years since my Ma fucked off. That's why one day they'll probably find him dead through hypothermia at a bus-stop.

After a few days of living on tea, chocolate digestives, McCain's oven chips and Presto's pizzas, I feel strong enough to go into town. I've read David Niven and Maureen Lipman's biographies, both absolutely fucking dreadful. I take them back to the library and ask the librarian if he can keep the Viv Nicolson biography back for me. I don't want to take it into town, as I might end up wrecked and lose it. Besides, I hate carrying things about. He refuses, saying I'll have to take my chances. I board a bus and start to feel horny with the vibrations from the engine. I make a mental list of all the women I'd like to have sex with. I feel awkward and self-conscious getting off the bus with an erection. It subsides, however, as I stand at the West End at a bit of a loss as to what to do next. Shoplifting is a possibility, and I try to think of what I need, so I can go to the appropriate store rather than just go somewhere and chory for chorying's sake.

I see Tina. It's good to see someone by chance in town. — Tina! Where ye off tae?

— Gaunny git something fir Ronnie. It's his birthday oan Thursday.

Of course it is. I remember Ron's birthday. I get him fuck all, not even a card, but I always remember the date. — How's it gaun wi yous pair? I ask, raising my brows in what I hope is a light, playful gesture.

— It's awright, she says, chewing briskly and never looking at me as we walk side by side up Lothian Road, — but he's ey jellied aw the time. Ah mean, the other week, we goes tae the pictures. Ah peys tae git us in. *Damage*, that wis the film, likes. He jist sat there asleep fir the whole film, and ah couldnae git him awake once it finished. Ah jist fuckin well left um.

— That's wise, I reflected. I liked this lassie, I empathised with her. I was still feeling a bit strung out, but my load seemed lighter these last few days. I realised why: no Ronnie. Tina had taken a considerable burden off my shoulders.

— Another thing, ah took um up tae ma hoose the other day. He jist crashed oot oan the couch. Never even spoke tae ma Ma or ma Dad. Jist nodded at thum, then sortay dozed oaf.

— No the wey tae make a favourable impression, I ventured.

— Well, ma Dad never really bothers that much aboot people talkin, but if he thinks it's drugs, he'll go pure radge. Mibbe next

249

time you n Olly could come up wi ays, so that they can see that aw ma pals n Ronnie's urnae intae drugs.

It was the first time in my life that I'd ever been asked tae provide a character reference of this sort. While touched, I was a little wary and a bit doubtful of Tina's powers of observation. — Eh, ah'm no sure that ah'm the best person for a home visit. Did Olly no tell ye about how ah met her, how she took ays back that time?

— Aye, but that wisnae your fault. At least you can stey straight sometimes, she said.

We parted and I felt great for a bit. After reflecting why I felt great, I started to feel terrible. It seemed that drug-taking over the years had reduced me to the sum total of the negative and positive strokes I received from people; a big blank canvas others completed. Whenever I tried to find a broader sense of self the term: A SMART CUNT would come back to mind.

Ronnie was face-fucked when we all met up in the Gorgie-Dalry Oyster Bar. What's that cunt like. He was awake, but was lolling his tongue around his mouth and rolling his eyes like he was having some kind of stroke. I was a bit angry at being put in this position. Olly and I had shagged a lot that afternoon and my genitals felt very raw and sticky with our juices. I hadn't been into washing. I always felt disorientated after sex, always wanted to be alone. We'd smoked some hash, and that part was good, but now all these people were around me in this bar.

I said nothing in the bar, nor anything in the taxi up to Clermiston. Tina and Olly blethered away, ignoring me, while Ronnie stared out of the window. I heard him say: — Clermiston, mate, to the driver when we were already halfway there. The driver took no notice; nor did anyone else. Ronnie just kept whispering: — Clermiston, mate, and giggling under his breath. The cunt was getting on my fuckin tits.

— Try to be civil, Olly hissed at me, clocking my sour puss as Tina's ma let us in.

It was embarrassing. Ron just flopped down on the couch and twisted his head, taking in the room with one eye. I sat beside him, Olly sat next to me and Tina curled up at our feet. Her father sat in a chair facing the television and her mother put some drinks and snacks out on the table. She then settled down in another chair and lit a cigarette. The telly was still on and it took all Tina's dad's attention.

— Dig in, he mumbled, — we dinnae stand oan ceremony in this hoose.

I grabbed a somosa and a couple of sausage rolls. The blow I had smoked with Olly after our shagging session had given me the munchies really bad.

Ronnie started to snore, but Tina elbowed him and he shuddered awake. Her old man was very unimpressed. I should have sat back and enjoyed this, but I seemed to be all on edge.
— Backshift, I said stupidly, — that's the problem, eh Ron? The backshift. Yir like the livin dead comin oaf the backshift.

Ronnie looked perplexed; in fact he looked stupid and subnormal.

Tina's father snorted at her, — Ah thoat you sais he wisnae workin?

— He's been daein a wee bit wi me, no through the books or nowt like that, I cut in. — Fittin smoke alarms. Wi aw they tenement fires, everybody wants yin. We've been daein the Sheltered Housing schemes for the council, ken? Long shifts.

Her father nodded in apathetic acknowledgement. Tina, her mother and Olly blethered about the sales and the old man fell asleep. Ronnie was also soon back in the land of the nod. I just sat stuffing my face, bored and hash-greedy. It seemed like the worst evening I'd ever spent. I was elated when we got ready to leave.

After we taxied back to Dalry, Olly wanted to go home and fuck. I wanted to go to Ryrie's and get drunk. We argued and went our separate ways. In the pub I met Roxy and The PATH. The PATH was just on his way out to meet this woman in the Pelican. — Come doon, he suggested.

— Mibbe later, I said. I needed a drink. I needed several. He left us. Roxy and I got a good lash on, without once mentioning Blind Cunt.

After a bit we decided to go to the Pelican. A smarmy English middle–class student-type cunt was on the door and wasn't going to let us in, but fortunately Rab Addison was coming out and let on to us. He gave the wanker a steely look and the poor cunt almost shat himself. Roxy and I walked in like the Duke and Duchess of Westminster.

The place was mobbed out, and we couldn't see The PATH, although we could hear him.

— ROXY! BRI!

Looking in the direction of the sound I could only see this large, fat woman smiling at me. She was absolutely gross, and had a bloated red face, which was nonetheless very kind and pretty looking. The PATH's head poked out from the side of her. I realised that he was sitting on her knee.

— This is Lucia, he said, slurping on a pint.

— Hiya, Lucia, I said.

Lucia turned to The PATH. — Ye want ays tae suck yir mates oaf n aw? she said, in a high excited voice. I couldn't catch The PATH's reply.

Then she put her hand on Roxy's thigh. — What's it they call you?

— Loads ay things, doll, he smiled. She felt him up for a bit through his troosers, his cock n baws. He seemed amused, yet unaroused. I was quite turned on. My head was starting to swim with the thought of the three of us fucking this big cow at the same time. The PATH gave me a lecherous wink.

Lucia then pressed her face close to mine and put a tongue which tasted of sick into my mouth. I sat transfixed as she slurped around inside my mouth. She flicked her tongue in and out for a bit, then pulled slowly away. — See you n yir mate here? she nodded at Roxy, — ah could bring yous oaf in nae time at aw!

— You already have, I told her.

She liked that, letting out pneumatic-drill laughter which cut through the loud buzz of the surrounding conversations. Then her elbows thrashed at The PATH, who had his hands up her skirt from the back, right between those meaty, cellulite thighs.

We drank on. The PATH told a joke about a guy who had an arsehole transplant and we all laughed loudly. I laughed, even though I'd heard it before. Lucia laughed the loudest. She laughed so much she started gagging. She drank back some Guinness from her pint, then threw it up, back into her glass. She looked only momentarily upset, then she slung the mass of blackened vomit back down her gullet in a oner.

— That's ma doll, said The PATH, and they French-kissed languidly.

I was into fours up, no question about it. I nodded to Roxy, — Your place?

— Like fuck, he scoffed. — Tell ays you're no sick, by the way. Ah widnae touch that wi a fuckin bargepole. Nae wey eftir The PATH had been thair.

That was a consideration. I got some more drinks up, and got some speed from a guy called Silver who was alright. I whizzed around the bar, talking shite. I was talking shite anyway, but now I was talking it with more purpose and conviction.

We didn't see The PATH go, but when we came up Anderson's Close we could hear his and Lucia's voices. He was bouncing on top of her like a football on a spacehopper. He's screaming: TAKE THE FUCKIN LOAT YA BITCH! YE COULDNAE TAKE MA FUCKIN COCK! SPLIT YE IN TWO!

She's saying: THIR'S FUCKIN WELL NOWT THAIR! GEEZ IT WELL! IS THAT YOU STARTED HA HA HA.

We walked past them, then stopped to watch for a while. Lucia rolled the PATH over and got on top. Her wobbly flesh hung over him.

— MOVE THEN IF YIR GAUN OAN TOAP! MOVE, YA BASTARD! he roared.

She shook her flesh over him, then looked up at us, — Yis want tae help um oot boys?

— We'd nivir git in the wey ay true love, Lucia, Roxy smiled.

We walked up the close a bit and pished. Our two steaming rivulets joined together and sped towards them, around the PATH's head, neck and shoulders. They kept shagging. Two guys walked nervously past us.

— Depraved wee cunt, The PATH, Roxy shook his head.

— Yeah, real fuckin slag.

I was feeling horny, and I was tempted to go to Olly's. Roxy was into more beer. There was a way to kill two birds with one stone: Olly would probably be at this party a friend of her's was having, a trendy, posey cow named Lynne.

Roxy never let me down at the party; he detests that sort of scene. We installed ourselves in the kitchen and freeloaded as much drink as possible. When Olly arrived she was in the company of some cunts and cold-shouldered me. We'd been shagging during the day, now she treated me like I was a stranger. Yet it somehow made sense. Life was a weird gig.

I woke up on the floor the next morning, to the sound of people cleaning the flat. Roxy lay next to me.

— God, thir's some fuckin foul taste in ma mooth, he said.

— That's ma fault, I shrugged, — ah shouldnae huv given The PATH one up his shitter before ah goat you tae gam ays.

— So that's what happened. Well, that makes sense. There's fuck all memorable aboot gammin you.

Lynne was clearing up; throwing cans and emptying ashtrays into bin-liners, flashing us looks which said: LEAVE IMMEDIATELY.

A merchant-school voice pleads, — C'mon lads, get up and give us a hand with the tidying up.

— Suck ma fuckin cock, ya radge, Roxy snapped. The boy moved away, taking this as a sign that he was on his own with the tidying. — Tell ays that cunt wisnae wide. That's fuckin

Edinburgh, fill ay fuckin English bastards and snobby rugby cunts. Treat ye like a fuckin peasant in yir ain toon. Well, fuck them, lit them clean up oor shite, it's aw the cunt's are fuckin good fir! he boomed.

I got to my feet and found some bottles of beer. We staggered out of the flat, down the stair and into the street, drinking. — Whair is this? I wondered.

— Stockbridge, Roxy said, — ah mind gaun through the New Town last night.

— Naw naw. I remembered. It was Lynne's. The South Side. We emerged onto South Clerk Street.

Roxy's mouth opened.

— Aye, Stockbridge, right enough! I said. — What are ye like!

We decided to head for the Captain's Bar, which opened at seven o'clock, about three hours ago. My nerves were starting to fray and I just wanted a few beers inside me to take the edge off things.

I was shaken to the core by a blood-curdling scream: — BRIAN!

Mad Audrey stood propped up against a bus-shelter. She wore a long black imitation-leather trenchcoat with padded shoulders. Two greasy flaps of black hair hung on either side of her white pimply face. Her sharp, vicious features contorted as she slurped from a carton of milk, some of which trickled down her front.

— WHAIR'S THE FUCKIN PATH?!

— Eh, no sure Auds. We left him last night, at the Pelican.

— TELL UM HE'S GITTING FUCKIN STABBED WHEN AH SEE UM! HE WIS WI THAT FUCKIN FAT SLUT! TELL UM HE'S FUCKIN DEID! N HUR N AW! MIND, YOU'D BETTER FUCKIN TELL UM!

— Eh, aye, ah'll mention it tae him, likes, I tell her. We don't stick around. The Captain's Bar had been calling loudly; now it was screaming.

— MIND N TELL UM! she shouted after us. — N TELL

UM TAE COME DOON TAE THE MEADOW BAR AT SEVEN!

I waved back at her. Roxy said, — When The PATH dies, aw the repulsive hing-oots in toon should git the gither n build a monument tae the cunt.

— Aye, wi a vibrating prick they can impale themselves oan.

A few in the Captain's did the trick. I went back to Roxy's and had a good long kip on his couch. When he woke me I was fucked. — The PATH phoned, he told me. — He's meeting us doon the Meadow Bar at seven.

— The Meadow? What did ye say that fir . . . you, ya bastard, I laughed. This would be a good one.

— Ah telt um tae bring big Lucia along n aw. Audrey versus Lucia, some fuckin swedge that would be. A dog-fight in the Meadows. Who needs Hank Jansen? Cannae wait tae see The PATH's face. Tell ays he'll no be shitein his keks.

I missed out on it, simply because I couldn't move. I got an account from The PATH though. Audrey was more vicious, and scored Lucia's face heavily, but eventually the larger woman used her superior strength and power to subdue Auds and pound her into the turf. She was lucky it was a square-go and Audrey wasn't tooled. Apparently, while the swedge was going on, The PATH was rubbing his crotch discreetly. He went home with the winner.

12

CAREER OPPORTUNITIES
AND FANNY LICKING

Cliff from London got in touch and told me that Simmy had got put away. Cliff himself had moved into a new flat, over in Hanwell. There was a space for me, he said. My bags were packed and I was back down to the Smoke.

It was a good gaff. I was on the floor in the front room for a couple of weeks, but I picked up a temporary job in the offices of Ealing Council. It involved keying information on planning applications into a VDU. They had put in all this new technology, but needed dogsbodies to key in all the manual records. Myself and four middle-aged women were taken on. The work was not interesting.

A bloke called Graham moved out of the flat and I got his room. He was a bit of an alcoholic and his mattress smelled badly of pish, so I got a new one on the Sunday, and was looking forward to a good night's kip before work on Monday. I'd never been able to kip properly in the front room; too many people coming and going at all hours.

— Wakey, wakey! Cliff shouted to me, poking his head around my door. I'd had no drugs the night before, not even hash. I'd gone to bed early and it was like I had only slept for an hour.

— It's surely no yon time already, surely tae fuck, I whinged.

— Yeah, seven-fifteen. C'mon mate, rise n shine!

I rose, but didn't shine. It was brutally cold as I made my way to the bathroom in my t-shirt and pants. I had to get to work on time. Gleaves, the office manager, was watching me. However, I was going to May and Des's for tea tonight, god bless them, so

I decided to wash my cock, balls and armpits in lukewarm water. It wasn't a comfortable experience. I brushed my teeth, squeezed a couple of spots, pulled on my ripped jeans and my cashmere sweater. I laced up my Doc Martens and stuck on my Oxfam overcoat and my scarf and mittens. No breakfast; it's hi ho hi ho . . .

Work is a fuckin drag. Gleaves thinks I'm demotivated. That's how he describes me. Gleaves recruited me: rather than say I picked a duffer and couldn't pick my nose, he persists in this delusion that inputting into a VDU, stuffing papers in envelopes and photocopying will sort me out. I'd bought a guitar and was jamming with Cliff and Darren in the flat but this job was costing me valuable practice time. However, I need the money for that amp. Stardom is surely just around the corner.

When I get in May says softly to me, — Mister Gleaves wants to see you, love. As soon as you get in, he said.

Fuck me. What now? Is that cunt tapped or what.

Penny has a gleeful expression on her face. That cow has hated me since I was too out of it to fuck her at somebody's leaving party. Women hate these things. If they're going to lose control and go away with someone, they figure they might as well get a good shag out of it. If they go away with someone and the someone can't get it up, well that's a big fuck-up: the worst of all worlds.

Gleavsie, as I call him in a Chinese accent (the Slaint and Gleavsie), is a small, overweight man with glasses and a Russian-style beard. He has a small, stumpy cock, the kind that is practically all cherry, but which is hopefully more formidable when erect. (I stood next to him in the latrine in the staff toilets to check it out.)

— Mister Gleaves, I smile, taking a seat.

— I want to talk about your dress, Brian.

— Which one is that? The yellow chiffon one, or the blue print number, I ask rolling my eyes.

— I'm deadly serious, Gleaves sombrely informs me, sounding like a character in a middle-class soap opera. Big fuckin drama queen. — For God's sake Brian, the arse is hanging out of your trousers.

That was true. My purple pants were clearly visible. My bum was freezing. My cock and balls were shrivelling up. They'd invert to a fanny by the end of the month. Next pay cheque it's Carnaby Street. I shouldn't travel so light.

— Well, at least when I'm famous you can say with justification you knew me when the arse was hanging out of my trousers.

— I'm not sure you understand the gravity of the situation . . .

— Okay okay. It's healthy having this circulation of air. It keeps me ventilated.

— You're either deliberately missing the point or you've lost the sense God gave you. I'm going to have to spell it out for you. At Ealing Borough Council we try to maintain certain standards of dress and behaviour. The local citizen, after all, pays our wages and it entitled to . . .

— I'm a local citizen n aw. I pay my poll tax, I lied.

— Yes, but . . .

— Whose standards are we talking about here? Just who's setting themself up as the big fashion consultant here?

— We're talking about corporate standards! The standards we expect from all employees of this authority.

— Listen, man, ah cannae afford tae buy a tin flute. Ah choose tae dress functionally, tae dress in gear ah feel comfortable in, soas ah kin perform better in ma joab. Ah couldnae hack wearin a tie, man, that's a pure phallic symbol, a compensatory psychological device for men who feel insecure about their sexuality. I cannae get into that sortay arena. I cannae be made to conform to the mass psychological hang-ups of Ealing Borough Council's male employees. What are yis like?

Gleaves shook his head in exasperation. — Brian. Please be quiet for a second. Look. I understand how you feel. I know what you're about. You're an intelligent guy, so don't act the fool. It'll get you nowhere. You've got the potential to get on within this organisation, he tells me, his tone changing to one of encouragement.

That was a statement which would have been humorous had it not been so frightening. — To do what? I asked.

— To get a better job.

— Why? I mean, what for?

— Well, he began in tone of slightly smug self-justification, — the money's not bad when you get to my level. And it's a challenge being involved in the full range of council activities.

He stopped, sensing his growing ridiculousness in my eyes. — Listen, Brian, I know you think you're some kind of big radical and I'm some reactionary, fascist pig. Well I've got news for you: I'm a socialist, I'm a union man. I know you just see me as an establishment figure in a suit, but if the Tories had their way, we'd have kiddies down the mines. I'm every bit as anti-establishment as you, Brian. Yes, I own my own home. Yes, I live in a desirable area. Yes, I'm married with two children, I take two foreign holidays a year and drive an expensive car. But I'm as anti-establishment as you, Brian. I believe in public services, in putting people first. It's more than just a cliché for me. For me, being anti-establishment is not about dressing like a tramp, taking drugs and going to rave-ups or whatever they're called. That's the easy way out. That's what the people that control things want; people opting out, taking the easy route. For me it's about knocking on doors on cold evenings, attending meetings in school halls to get Labour back in and Major and his mob out.

— Yeah . . .

This guy makes the term arsehole redundant.

— Well, I've almost had it with you, Brian. Unless you buck up your ideas, your behaviour and your dress, you are on a disciplinary. Look at you. Worse than a tramp. I've seen better-dressed people in cardboard city.

— Listen. Are you talking to me as employer to employee, or as man to man? Cause if it's employer to employee I consider your behaviour insulting and harassing and I want my union representative in here to witness this victimisation. If you're talking to me man to man, then it's more straightforward. We can go outside and settle it. Ah'm no taking this shite, I said, rising. — If there's nothing else, I'd like to go and get some work done.

I left the shitein cunt red-faced behind his desk. He muttered something about last warnings. How many last warnings can you have? I swaggered back to my work station and plugged away for a bit at the NME crossword. I was entitled tae a brek, for fuck's sake.

At finishing time, May took me home to her and Des's. They were a lovely couple from Chester-Le-Street, Co. Durham, who had sort of adopted me. May would cook up a big scran, lamenting my thinness, while Des and I talked football over cans of Tetley Bitter. He was a great Newcastle United fan and he'd wax on about Jackie Milburn, Bobby Mitchell, Malcolm McDonald, Bobby Moncur and the like.

A normally very relaxed and laid-back couple, they used to fret a great deal over what I took to be their son. — Nae sign o the lad, Des would frown at the clock, — he's never normally as leet as this.

I knew they had four daughters between the ages of sixteen and twenty-two. The girls were always out, taking drugs, going to clubs, shagging guys, the things girls that age with any sense did. One of them went to the Ministry of Sound, which was sound. That was the one I fancied, the sort of New Age lassie, the youngest, I think. I fancied all of them really. However, Des and May didn't seem to bother about them, their chief concern was the welfare of the lad.

— There he is! Des exclaimed, as a noise came from the back door of the kitchen and a grumpy-looking selfish black cat meandered in through the flap. — C'mere lad, owah heah by the fyah! You moost be freezin! Tell us what you've been oop to then? Eeeh, you leetal boogah!

It is a good scoff and I get back to the flat a little bevvied. It's good to have a stomach full of stodgy food again. Best of all,

Monday was cracked. Granted Tuesday was a cunt, but it got better on Wednesday. We all went down the local pub on Wednesday nights, me, Cliff, Darren, Gerard, Avril and Sandra. It was good living in the same flat as lassies; they kept standards high, well, higher than they would have been otherwise. It was a barry flat and everyone got on or got on most of the time. I thought of Simmy languishing in the Scrubs for housebreaking and felt pretty good about it. I tried not to think of her, of Blind Cunt, of my mum, of Scotland. We all did drugs here, but it seemed less desperate, more of a recreational thing rather than a lifestyle. We'd sit in the pub on Wednesday and Thursday nights talking about what clubs, gigs and drugs we'd be into at the weekend.

After getting home from Des and May's, I went straight to my room. I put on a KLF tape and lay back on the bed feeling pretty pleased with myself. I thought of Des and May's daughters, then of Gleaves, and resolved to borrow a pair of strides from Cliff, to keep the tie-wearing penile-challenged toss-bag oaf ma case.

There was a knock on the door and Avril came in. I didn't really know her that well to talk to; she was far more self-contained than Sandra, though pleasant enough.

— Can I talk to you for a bit? she asked.

— Sure, sit down, I smiled. There was a basket-chair in the room. My spirits rose. It was fairly obvious that she nursed a passion for me and wanted to shag me. I should have picked up the vibes before. I expanded my smile and let a bit of soul seep into my watery eyes. This poor lassie's been besotted and I haven't even noticed.

— This is really difficult, she began, — but I just have to say it.

I felt for her. — Listen, Avril, you don't have to say anything.

— Darren . . . Gerald . . . they've told you? I told them not to tell you! I wanted to say this myself!

— No, no, they haven't . . . it's just . . .

— What? It's not you, is it?

This was confusing. — It's not me what?

She took a deep breath. — Listen, I think we're talking at cross-purposes here. This is very hard for me to say.

— Eh, but . . .

— Just listen. I want you to know I'm not accusing you of anything. Please understand that. I've spoken to Darren and Gerald. I've not had a chance to speak to Cliff yet, but I will. This is pretty embarrassing. It's just that some of my underwear's been taken from my drawer. I'm not accusing you, though. I want to talk to everyone. It's just that I don't like the idea of living with a pervert.

— I see, I said; hurt, disappointed but intrigued. — Well, I smiled, I'm certainly a pervert, but not that type.

That got a mild, brief laugh. — I'm only asking.

— Yeah, well it has to be somebody, I suppose. To you, it's as likely tae be me as anybody. I can't see Cliff or Darren, or even Gerard behaving in that sortay way. Well, Gerard would, but he widnae be sneaky aboot it. That's no his style. He'd go intae the pub wi yir knickers aroond his heid.

That thought didn't amuse her. — As I said, I only asked.

— You don't think it's me, do you?

— I don't know what to think, she said sourly.

— Well, that's fuckin' great. My boss thinks I'm a smelly tramp and someone I live with thinks I'm a pervert.

— We don't live together, she frostily corrected me, — we share a house.

— Well, I said, as she got up to leave, — if I see anyone behaving suspiciously, like not taking drugs, paying the rent on time, that sortay thing, I'll let you know.

She left, obviously unable to see the funny side. It made me wonder who was the pervert. I thought it had to be Sandra.

On Thursday I was back at May's for tea again. I stayed late because Lisanne, her youngest but one daughter was in. She was good to talk to and look at. Moreover, she didn't think I was a pervert, although, I suppose, she didn't really know me that well. Des was out, and May insisted on giving me a lift home.

This was unusual, but it was late. I thought nothing of it as I piled into the car. She was chatty, but nervously so, as we drove along the Uxbridge Road. Then she pulled off at a turning and stopped in a carpark at the back of some shops.

— Eh, what's up May? I asked. I thought something must be wrong with the car.

— Do you like Lisanne, then? she asked.

I felt a bit coy. — Eh, aye, she's a really nice lassie.

— Surprised you haven't got yourself a girlfriend.

— Well, ah'm no really intae getting too involved.

— The love em n leave em type are you?

— Well, ah widnae really say that . . .

I was more the love em and they leave me type.

She put her finger in one of the rips on my jeans and started stroking my bare thigh. Her hands were doughy, her fingers like stumps. — Mister Gleaves was right about you. You're going to have to invest in a new pair of jeans.

— Eh, ay, I replied. I was feeling uneasy. Not aroused, far from it, but gripped with a morbid curiosity as to what she was about.

I looked at her face and all I could see were teeth. She started making circles in my flesh with her fingers. — You've got baby-soft skin, haven't you?

There isn't really much you can say to that. I just laughed.

— You think I've got a good body? I'll bet you reckon I'm past it, don't you?

— Naw, naw, ah widnae say that, May.

I thought: by light years.

— Des is on these pills you see. He had a heart-attack a while back. It stops the blood coagulating by keeping it thin. Trouble is, he don't get hard. I love Des, see, but I'm still a young woman, love. I need a little bit of fun, a little bit of harmless fun, don't I? That's not so unreasonable, is it, love?

I looked harshly at her. — Do these seats fold down?

They did.

I went down on her and gave head; flicking my tongue deftly onto her clit, then lolling it around teasingly. I started thinking about Graeme Souness, because he had heart trouble. I wonder if he has a problem getting it up due to the pills? I started to think about his career, focusing on the 1982 World Cup in Spain which I remember watching with my dad. My mum had only been gone three years, and we'd come back from my Auntie Shirley's. She'd looked after us all that time, until Dad felt able to cope. He'd had some sort of breakdown. Never talks about it. Thing was, we had liked it at Shirley's in Moredun, and we didn't really want to go back to Muirhouse, or have 'the family all together' as he described it. As a sweetener, he let us watch all the 1982 World Cup games. A huge wallchart was stuck up in the front room above the fireplace. The tapemarks still show where the four corners were, although it's been painted over at least once to my knowledge. Cheap paint, I suppose. Anyway, the praise that was heaped on Souness then, but I thought that he just posed and preened his way through that tournament. I mean, the two-each draw with the Soviet Union, for fuck sake.

— Ohh, you're a naughty one and no mistake . . . ooh . . . ooh, she hissed excitedly, crushing my face against her cunt. I was going nowhere, struggling to take in air through nostrils which were filled with a pungent scent. There was no taste, only the smell which suggested it.

I have an image of Souness strutting arrogantly like a peacock in the middle of the park, but he's doing nothing with the ball, just holding it, and we need a win as the seconds tick by. Still, that was in the days when people actually gave a toss about the Scottish national football team.

— Give it to me . . . she whispered, — you've got me all juiced up, lovey, now give it to me . . .

I was too soft to go in, but she took it in her mouth for a bit and I firmed up. I got in and she was moaning so loud I got really self-conscious. I jutted out my jaw Souness-style and pumped away. After about half a dozen strokes she came power-fully, kneading my buttocks in her hands. — YOU DORTY

LITTLE BOOGAH! EEH, YOU DORTY LITTLE SHITE! LOOVLEY . . . she screamed.

The old tongue-job never fails. The only fuckin real use for the guid Scotch tongue. I thought about her daughter and blew my muck inside her.

I wondered if I'd get asked back for tea again.

13

MARRIAGE

May carried on as if nothing had happened, except that she gave me an occasional saucy smile and she'd also taken up goosing my arse by the photocopier. I was a bit bemused by the whole thing. How mad was that.

It was the next week after my liaison with May that the invitation came through the door. It read:

TOMMY AND SHEILA DEVENNEY

Invite you to join them at the wedding
of their daughter

Martina

to

Mr Ronald Dickson

on Saturday, 11 March 1994 at 3.00 p.m.
at Drum Brae Parish Church, Drum Brae,
Edinburgh and afterwards at the Capital
Hotel, Fox Covert Road.

I stuck it on my bedside table. It was next month. In one month's time Ronnie would be a married man, although the potential hurdles that stood in the way of that actually happening didn't bear examination.

A couple of days later I got a phone-call from Tina. I was tempted to offer congratulations, but I hedged my bets in case the gig was off. The whole thing wasn't really constructed on a very firm basis.

— Brian?

— Aye.

— It's Tina, ken?

— Tina! Barry! How's tricks? Ah goat the invite. Brilliant! How's Ron? There was a silence from the other end of the line. Then: — Ye mean he's no thair wi you now?

— Eh . . . naw. Ah huvnae heard fae him.

The pause was even longer this time around.

— Tina? I wondered whether she'd hung up.

— Sais he wis gaun doon tae see ye. Tae ask ye tae be best man. Wanted tae ask ye tae yir face, he sais.

— Fuck . . . dinnae worry aboot Ronnie though, Tina. Must've goat waylaid. Probably jist a bit emotional, wi the weddin n that, ken? He'll show.

— He fuckin well better, she snapped.

Three days later I had just got home from work and was eating a bacon sanny and watching the six o'clock news with Darren. We were ranting bitterly everytime someone we hated appeared on the box, which was every other feature. Avril was reading a magazine. She got up to answer the door.

— There's someone here for you, Brian, she said. — A Scots guy . . . he seems a bit out of it.

Ronnie slouched into the room behind her, obviously jellied. I didn't even attempt to ask him where he'd been. I took him upstairs and let him crash on my floor. Then I phoned Tina to tell her he'd shown up. After this I went downstairs and sat on the couch.

— A friend of yours? Avril asked.

— Yeah, it's this mate who's getting married. Wants me tae go best man. I think he's had a tiring journey.

— Look at that slimy cunt Lilley, Darren hissed at the image of this politician on the box, — I'd like to get that fucking arsehole and cut his bollocks off. Then I'd like to stuff them down his throat and sew his mouth up so he has to swallow them . . . fucking child-killing cunt!

— That's terrible, Darren, Avril tutted, — you're no better than he is if you think like that. She looked at me for support.

— No, Darren's perfectly correct. Sick, exploitative vermin ay that sort need tae be destroyed, I said and, recalling Malcom X, added, — by any means possible.

I had been reading the biographies of radical black Americans. X's was an interesting read but Bobby Seale's *Seize The Time* was far more enjoyable, as was Eldridge Cleaver's *Soul On Ice*. My favourite was *Soledad Brother* but I can't remember which of the Jackson brothers, Jonathan or George, actually wrote it. Perhaps it was Michael.

Darren shook a clenched fist at me. — That's the difference between me and those fucking wimpy arsehole socialists, I don't want the Tories out, I want them fucking dead. Just because I've got a bus-pass doesn't mean I'm part of the system. An anarchist with a bus-pass is still a fucking anarchist. All hate to the state!

— You're sick, Darren. Avril shook her head. — Violence achieves nothing.

— It is satisfying when you see a polisman with his heid burst open though, you have to admit it, I ventured.

— No it's not. There's nothing satisfying about it at all, she replied.

— Naw, c'moan Avril. You're no tryin tae tell me that you didnae feel good when you saw the pictures of those slimy deadsouls looking shit-scared in that pile of rubble after the Brighton bomb? Tebbit n that?

I remember that well. When it came on the telly, my old man said, — Aboot time somebody had a go at those fuckers. I remember being full of pride and admiration for him.

— I don't like to see any human being suffer.

— That's all very well as an abstract moral principle, Avril, a coffee-table theoretical construct, but there's no denying the sheer gratuitous pleasure to be derived from seeing members of the ruling class in pain and torment.

— I really hope that you two are winding me up, she said

pityingly, — I really hope so for your sake. If not, you're sick, brutalised people.

— Too right, said Darren, — but at least we're not brutalising anybody else in turn. We don't mug, rape, serial-kill or starve the innocent. We just fantasise about destroying the vermin that have been fucking us over for years. And another thing we don't do, he added snidely, — is steal people's underwear.

Avril told him to fuck off, and left us. It was at that point I strongly began to suspect that Darren was the guilty man, the undergarment thief.

Ronnie didnae really get to know anyone. He slept for two days, and on the odd occasion he joined us was almost comatose. Then it was time for him to return as his ticket had been booked. He took some downers before getting on the bus at Victoria Station. I didn't bother waving at him as the bus pulled away; he had fallen asleep as soon as he'd taken his seat. The only things I remember him saying during the time he was down were: Darren . . . I thought, naturally, that he was talking about Darren in the flat, but I realised he wasn't. — Darren Jackson, followed by an appreciative nod, and, — Best man . . . sound, with a wink and cock of his head. When Ronnie winked, the act involved the opening, rather than the closing, of one eye.

The month dragged. I was looking forward to getting back to Edinburgh but no so much tae the wedding. I got into town the night before the stag and took a taxi tae the auld man's.

When I got in, Norma Culbertson and her wee lassie were there. There was something different about the house.

— Hello, son, my dad said awkwardly, — Eh, sit doon. I suppose I should have told you this before, but eh, well, wi you bein in London n that. You know how things are . . .

— Aye, I replied, totally fuckin clueless as to how things were.

— Has Derek, eh, mentioned anything?

— Naw . . .

— Well, Derek's moved out. He's in a flat now, in Gorgie.

Stewart Terrace. No bad flat as well. Wi him getting that Civil Service promotion, he had to go for it. You know?

— Jeff . . . Norma urged.

— Oh, eh, aye. The thing is, son, Norma and I have decided to get married, he smiled weakly, apologetically.

Norma simpered and exposed an engagement ring for my examination. I felt a dull thud in my chest. Surely this was a wind-up. Norma was a young woman; not bad looking either. Deek once admitted to me he used to wank about her, though that was a while ago. She was too young for Dad; he was old enough to be her father. Mind you, Dino Zoff was still playing European club football at my auld man's age. But that was Dino Zoff. This was real life.

My Ma and him

My Ma this was too young for him anyway my Ma gone for years him getting married again his business, what's it to me?

— Many happy returns, I stammered, — eh, I mean, congratulations . . .

Norma started talking about how she wanted us to be friends and my auld man ranted on about my mother . . .

— I'm saying nothing against her, but she abandoned yous laddies. Abandoned yous and never wanted tae see yis. Surely a real mother would want tae see her sons . . . bit no her, no sae much as a letter . . .

I started to feel a bit sick and thankfully the door went, saving us all further embarrassment. It was Crazy Col Cassidy, an animal from the scheme with a fearsome reputation for violence against the person. — Yir auld man in? he growled.

Well, the chickens have come home to roost now, Daddy. This anti-drugs campaign is about to blow up in your face.

— Col! my dad shouts. — Come in mate, come in! Cassidy pushes past me. My auld man gives him a matey slap on the shoulder. — This is ma laddie, he says, — he's been in London.

Cassidy growls an incomprehensible greeting.

— Col's the secretary of Muirhouse Action on Drugs, he explained.

I might have guessed: the nutters will always take the side of the forces of reaction.

— We ken the dealers in this scheme, son. We're gaunny drive them out. The polis willnae dae it, so we will, my auld man says, seemingly unaware that he's talking in a low Clint Eastwood drawl.

— Good luck with your campaign, Dad, I said. I had no doubt that he, with Cassidy's assistance, would succeed; succeed in making every fucker's life a misery. I made to hit the town.

— Oh, son, remember that wee Karen's got your old room. You'll be down here on the couch now.

Welcome home: evicted from your room in favour of some cretinous brat. I left and bounced up the town. The stag started off good-naturedly enough. Ronnie was jellied, out of his face, when we met up. Things were happy but uneventful until we met Lucia and a couple of her mates who insisted on tagging along with us. She got drunk and had a heavy spraff with Denise about who should get tae suck Ronnie off.

We went on to a few pubs, a couple of silly arguments started and a fight broke out. I swung at Penman who'd been on my case all night. I was held by Big Ally Moncrief while Penman danced away from me gesticulating sharply and breathlessly: — Moan then, moan then . . . ootside . . . think yir a wide-o . . . cunt think's he's a wide-o . . . moan then, ootside . . .

Big Moncrief said that he hated to see mates fight, particularly on such an occasion. Denise said that we should kiss and make up. We didn't, but we did hug and make up. We did an ecky each and clung to each other like limpets to a rock for the rest of the evening. I'd never felt so close to anyone, well, not another man, as I did to Penman that night. It was a lovers-without-the-shagging type scene. Conversely, I've seldom felt so awkward as I did when we met up with Tina's crowd at the Citrus. Olly was there. Former lovers generally find these things a strain; too much ego, no too much id involved. Once you've been with each other in a primal, shagging state, it's hard to talk about the weather.

Olly called herself 'Livvy' now. She had been going through A Period Of Personal Growth and now seemed enough like her friends to want to be like someone else, someone they wanted to be like. She was painting now, she told me. It seemed to me that what she was actually doing was talking and drinking. She asked what I was doing. I told her and she said: — Same old Brian, in a condescending way, as if to make the point that I was a useless reprobate from a mildly embarrassing past she'd left behind; a figure of pity.

She then shook her head in contempt, though I was not her target. — I've tried to tell Tina that she's being stupid. She's too young and Ronnie . . . well, I don't think I can ever comment on him because I don't know him. I've never seen him straight; never had a conversation with him. What the hell does he get out of being like that?

I thought about it. — Ronnie's just always enjoyed the quiet life, I told her. She started to say something, then stopped, and made her excuses and left me. She looked good, the way that somebody who used to be but is no longer into you can do. I was glad she'd left though. People who are undergoing Periods Of Personal Growth are generally pains in the arse. Growth should be incremental and gradual. I hate these born-again wankers who try to completely reinvent themselves, and burn their past. I went over and held Penman in my arms for a long time. Over his shoulder I cringed as I caught Roxy's malevolent gaze and I thought of Blind Cunt for the first time in ages.

I could see the stag passing into the next week. I'd be drunk and stoned the whole time, and it would roll seamlessly into the wedding. I was wondering whether or not I'd bother going back to London, my room in that flat, my arrears and my crap job.

The day after the stag, when I had been in the Meadow Bar with The PATH and Sidney, I ran into Ted Malcolm, a guy from the parks. He was at me to put my name down for a Seasonal Park Officer job. — You wir ey well thought ay in the parks, ken? he told me in the confidential bullshit manner that people associated with the council used. The culture of civic corruption and innuendo permeated down from the shit-brains at councillor level to the ranks of the lowest official; Stalinism with a sweetie-wife's face, complete with headsquare.

— Aye, I said noncommitally.

— Garland always liked ye, he nodded.

Yes, in spite of it all, I'd maybe give Garland a bell. London had been starting to feel like Edinburgh had before I'd left it. Gleaves, May, even Darren, Avril, Cliff, Sandra and Gerard; they all constituted a set of expectations which snapped around me like a sprung trap. You can only be free for so long, then the chains start to bind you. The answer is to keep moving.

It was a nightmare getting Ronnie up and ready for the church. A total fuckin nightmare. His ma gave me a hand dressing him. She never seemed to show any concern at his state. — It must've been some night last night, eh? Well, ah suppose ye only git married the once.

I felt like saying, don't count on it, but I held my tongue. We bundled Ronnie into the car then into the church.

— Do you, Ronald Dickson, take Martina Devenney, to be your lawful wedded wife, to have and to hold, to love and to cherish, forsaking all others, so long as you both shall live?

Ron was jellied, but he managed tae gie the minister cunt the nod. It wasn't enough for this fucker though, he looked intently at him, trying tae elicit a more positive reaction. I nudged Ronnie harshly.

— Sound, he managed to mumble. It would have to do. The minister tutted under his breath, but left it.

— Do you, Martina Devenney, take Ronald Dickson to be your lawful wedded husband, to have and to hold, to love and to cherish, forsaking all others so long as you both shall live?

Tina looked a bit reluctant, as if it had at last dawned on her that this was serious shite she was getting intae. Eventually she managed to cough out, — I do.

Anyway, they were duly pronounced catatonic and wife.

We went to the Capital Hotel for the meal and Ronnie fell asleep during my speech. It wasn't a particularly inspired speech, but it scarcely deserved that sort of response.

At the reception I got a stance up at the bar with Raymie Airlie and Spud Murphy, two space cowboys of the highest order.

— Crimson style, bantam prince, Raymie observed, looking round the bar.

— You took the words right out of my mouth, Raymie, I smiled, then turning to Spud, — still skag-free, ma man?

— Eh, yeah . . . until there's free skag, ah'm skag-free, ken, catboy?

— Aye, me n aw. Ah went a wee bit radge the other week thair, but ah dinnae want tae git a habit, ken? Ah mean, how bad is that, right?

— Yeah, habits are nae fun, likesay. Sortay full-time occupation, catboy, ken? Sortay diverts the attention fae what's gaun oan.

— Mind you, it's the jellies that's fuckin every cunt now. Look at Ronnie. His ain fuckin wedding fir fuck's sake . . .

Raymie sighs and sings a chorus of Echo and The Bunnymen's 'The Cutter', then puts his tongue in my ear. I peck him on the cheek and pat his arse. — You're raw sex, Raymie, raw fuckin sex man, I tell him.

The PATH, Big Moncrief and Roxy come over to join us. I do some intros. — Awright boys, yous ken Spud n Raymie, eh?

Looks of suspicious acknowledgment are exchanged. My bevvy and druggy mates never really hit it off.

— Funny thing though, the marriage stakes n that, ken? Good if ye kin work it oot, likesay, Spud ventures, breaking an uneasy silence.

— The only thing that marriage is good for is sex oan tap, Moncrief says, with more than hint of belligerence.

Roxy puts on a Glasgow accent: — But ah like tae go oan the boatum sometimes.

We all laugh at this, except Moncrief. One thing about hard

cunts that I've never understood: why do they all have to be such big sensitive blouses? The Scottish Hardman ladders his tights so he rips open the face of a passer-by. The Scottish Hardman chips a nail, so he head-butts some poor fucker. Some other guy is wearing the same patterned dress as the Scottish Hardman, and gets a glass in his face for his troubles.

We move onto television. — Telly's fuckin shite, says Moncrief, — the only thing worth watchin oan the fuckin telly is they nature programmes. Ken wi that cunt, what's his name, that David Attenborough cunt.

— Aye, agrees Spud, — that cat's got the gig sussed, likesay. That's the kinday job that would be right up ma street, man, ken wi aw they animals, likesay. Freaky that would be, ken?

We spraff on all night, too drunk to dance with the wizened aunties and shaggable cousins. I drop some acid and note that Roxy's taken something. He's drunk, but he's taken something. Spud's given him one of those Supermarios. That's far too much for the Rox. He's an alcohol man. He's shaking his bowed head and babbling, — Ah kilt um! Ah fuckin kilt um, and he's close to tears.

I was struggling with the acid as well. It was not a good idea. These Supermarios; fuck me the whole world could be a hallucination the colours are clashing and reverberating and Tina's face is sick and vampire-like in that dress and Roxy's babbling and there's a polar bear running around on all fours . . .

— Spud, d'ye see the bear, man? I asked.

— It's no a bear, man, it's a sortay bear-dug likesay, sortay half-man half dug but wi a bit ay bear in it, ken?

— Raymie, you saw it, you ken it wis a bear?

— Yes, I personally thought it was a bear.

— Fuck me! Raymie! You've just said something straight, something sensible.

— It's just the acid, he tells me.

Roxy's still shaking his heid; — That perr boy . . . that fuckin blind boy . . . they took his eyes . . . ah took his life . . . fool's fuckin gold . . . ma soul's sick, made sick for fool's fuckin gold . . . tell ays that's no sick . . .

— This acid is mental shit . . . Spud says.

I see Moncrief, sitting beside this plant monster. Moncrief's face is changing colour and shape. I see that he's no a human being. Denise comes over: — Taken any ay they Supermarios?

— Aye . . . too much, man.

He buys one from Spud. Eight quid for this. My skin's been taken off. Eileen Eileen Eileen the Montparnasse Tower I had and lost love cause I was too young too stupid to identify and recognise it as such and it'll never come my way again not ever in a million fuckin years and I'll never make three score years and ten and anyway I don't want to without her what a mess that would be without Eileen who's at college in London I don't know what which one or at least was last year I hope you're happy now happy without your old smart cunt boyfriend who thought he was being entertaining but was just being an exasperating immature selfish prick not exactly a shortage of them never is and you were right to leave him as a decision purely rational . . .

— Whit's up wi Roxy, Denise asks.

— Too much acid. They Supermarios . . .

I grabbed Roxy's face in my hands. — Listen, Roxy, you're having a bad trip. We've got tae git ootay here. There's too many malignant spirits aroond here, Rox.

We were out of our faces, but we had to get out into the air. Olly gave me a disgusted look, but there was a little bit of pity in it. — Don't fuckin pity me, I shouted, but she couldn't hear me, or maybe she could but I got outside with Roxy, my legs rubber. The PATH tried to follow us but I told him it was okay, and he goes back inside to look for a shag.

It was a cold and crisp evening, or maybe it was just the Supermarios.

— AH KILT UM, AH FUCKIN KILT UM! Ah'm gaun tae the polis . . . Roxy was in torment. His face seemed to be folding in on itself . . .

I grabbed his shoulders. — Naw yir no! Think fuckin straight! Git a grip fir fuck's sake! Us gaun doon's no gaunny bring that cunt back, is it?

— Naw . . .

— Then thir's nae sense in it. It was a fuckin accident, right!

— Aye . . . He grows a little calmer.

— An accident, I repeat. — Yuv goat tae keep control ay yir tongue. It's that acid. Jist dinnae fuckin touch it again, it disnae agree wi ye. Stick tae the bevvy. Ye'll be awright whin ye come doon. Ye cannae go spraffin shite like that aroond. Yill git us fuckin jailed man. Thir's nae such thing as truth, Roxy, no wi these cunts. The polis willnae bother a fuck. It's jist another couple ay bodies fir thaim. Makes thaim look better, thaim n aw they slimy politician cunts, whae can say that the polis are winnin the war against crime; how sick is that? Blind Cunt's death wis fuckin tragic, let's no make it even mair tragic by giein they cunts what they want. Wise up! It wis a fuckin accident!

He looks at me with fear in his eyes, as if he's realised for the first time what he's actually been saying: — Fuckin hell, yir right man. What wis ah fuckin thinkin aboot spraffin away like that . . . nae cunt heard ays, did they, Bri? NAE CUNT HEARD AYS, BRI?

— Naw, jist me. No this time. But leave the fuckin acid alane. Right?

— Aye . . . this is mad. Ah took acid before, Bri, yonks ago. It was fuck all like this bit, this is fuckin mad. How fuckin mad is this, Bri?

— It's awright. Will go back tae your place and come down. Any bevvy in the hoose?

— Aye, loads ay cans. Whisky n aw.

It's strong acid, real head-fucking gear, but when we get to Roxy's we start drinking like there's no tomorrow. It's all you can do on acid, just thrash it out your system with alcohol. Pish is a depressant; it bring you down. You start to get control back.

It was imperative that Roxy didn't speak. I hadn't booted snow in Blind Cunt's face that night. I'd booted *him* in the face.

278

The decisive blow was as likely to have been mine as it was Roxy's. It was wrong; just horrible, stupid, cowardly and reckless. I can't wreck my life for that one stupid mistake in the heat of the moment. No way. I just won't fuckin well do that. The Blind Cunt and the Smart Cunt; a tale of two cunts. Well that's that tale finished, I hope. Finished for good.

14

INTERVIEW

Fuckin hell, it's yon time again. I got a hell of a shock when Garland's signature appeared under the Edinburgh District Council logoed notepaper, inviting me along for an interview.

I had gone back down to London, but after the job at Ealing folded I did the Euro-Rail with Darren and Cliff. Darren and I ended up in Rimini. He's still there, doing barwork, security work, raving and shagging all the time. It was sound, but I had to come back for another wedding, my auld man's this time. They moved out of the scheme, into a Barratt box across the road in Pilton. It would be a slum within five years. The government wanted home-ownership to regenerate the area. It makes no real difference whether you pay rent to the council for a shit-house or mortgage payments to a building society for one. Stop paying the mortgage and you see exactly where the ownership lies. I had planned to head back to Rimini but got a chilly note from Darren saying that he had got into a big heavy lovey-shag scene with this woman and while I was welcome to stay in the gaff for a while . . . blah blah blah. So I moved in with Roxy and put my name down for the parks.

— Hello, Brian, Garland extended his hand and I shook it.

— Mister Garland.

— Let me say, he began, — that the regrettable incident last year, I feel, on mature reflection, was a little out of character with you. I'm assuming that you've overcome all your, eh, depression problems?

— Yes, I feel on top of things now, Mister Garland. Health-wise, that is.

— That's good. You see, Brian, you were a model SPO until that little problem with Bert Rutherford. Now Bert is the salt of the earth, but I'm prepared to admit that he can be a zealot. The patrol needs Bert Rutherfords, otherwise the service would collapse into apathy and disarray. You've been at the coal-face, Brian; you know what a dull job it can be. You realise that the parks tend to attract disaffected groups of youths, who are not there to use it as a place of recreation, but for more sinister purposes . . .

— I believe that to be the case, yes.

— That's why I want you back on the patrol, Brian. I need people this summer who know the ropes. Above all, I like you because you're a reader, Brian. A reader will never be bored. What are you reading these days?

— I've just completed Peter O'Toole's biography. I never realised he was from Leeds.

— Was he indeed?

— Yes.

— Good. So have you started on anything else?

— Yeah, I'm reading Jean-Paul Sartre's biography.

— Good. Biographies are good, Brian. Some seasonals read all those heavy philosophic and political works, books that by their very nature encourage discontent with one's lot, he said sadly. — After all, a beautiful day in a park. Life could be worse, eh!

— That's true, Mister Garland.

I was back on the parks. How weird was that?

15

PISH

I found myself in the City Cafe. I hated the place, but that's how it goes. The main reason I was here was that it was full of fanny and I hadn't had a shag in five months. That is far too long for someone my age; it's far too long for someone of any age. I always ended up here when I was feeling shite and wanting to feel better. That's probably why I hated it.

I'd been in there for about twenty minutes, drinking a coffee, when I felt someone sit beside me. I didn't turn around to see who it was until I heard the words: — No speakin?

It was Tina. I'd heard that she and Ronnie had split up recently.

— Awright, Tina?

— Aye, no bad. Yirsel?

— Sound, eh, sorry tae hear aboot you n Ron, but.

She shrugged and told me: — He goat really borin. It started when he goat that Nintendo system. Ah preferred it when he wis jellied; ye goat mair ootay um then.

I knew that Ronnie had taken to that Nintendo game system like a duck to water. I thought that it was a positive step though, that it would give him an interest other than just being jellied all the time. — Did it no gie him an interest ootside ay drugs?

She looked at me with an ugly bitterness. — What aboot me? Ah should've been an interest! Him sittin thair plugged intae that telly, aw day n night, shakin like a leaf when ah came in fae work in case ah wanted tae watch somethin other thin his silly fuckin games! Me workin aw day, then huvin tae watch him playin games aw night!

— What's he fuckin like? Ah might go roond n see um, Tina. Try to talk some sense intae his heid.

She shook her head knowingly, recognising the impossibility of the task, yet warming to me for offering support. — Come n sit wi us, she suggested, pointing through the back.

— Is Olly thair?

— Aye, but it's cool, likes.

— Any of her friends around?

Tina raised her eyebrows in disdainful acknowledgement.

— Dunno, ah wis thinkin ay gaun doon tae the Pelican tae see Sidney n The PATH.

I had no intention of going to the Pelican, but then I heard a voice coming from Olly's table. It was loud, overbearing, posh and grating: — AND SHE'S A FREELANCE JOURNALIST WHO'S BEEN DOING A FEW BITS AND PIECES FOR *THE LIST*. SHE'S ONLY BEEN SEEING TONY FOR A COUPLE OF MONTHS BUT SHE WAS HAVING INCREDIBLE HASSLES WITH THIS FLAT SHE MOVED INTO, SO THE NATURAL THING SEEMED TO BE . . .

I had every intention of going to the Pelican. Tina did as well. When we got down The PATH was there with this lassie who looked a bit radge; radge in the sense of not being all there. The PATH freely admits that the Government's Community Care policies have been the best thing that ever happened to his sex life. Sidney was chatting with these women who looked disinterested to the point of boredom. — Awright, boys? Nae Roxy the night?

He was there though, holding up the bar, spraffin wi some wee guy.

We just sat around, drinking and blethering. Sidney and Tina seemed to be getting on. By chucking-out time they were feasting on each other's faces. The PATH and his troubled accomplice vanished into the night, while I left with Roxy.

— Ah'm gaunny take ye somewhair, he said. — Secret destination.

We piled into a taxi. It headed down to Leith, but then we

continued, heading out to Portobello. We stopped in Seafield Road and got out: the middle of fuckin naewhair.

— Whair the fuck's this? Eh? I asked.

— Follow me.

I did. We went around the back of Seafield Crematorium and climbed over a wall. It was a long drop down into the darkness on the other side, and I twisted my ankle badly in the fall. I was too drunk to feel much pain, but I'd feel it tomorrow alright, nothing was surer.

— What the fuck's this? I asked as he took me around some of the graves. Some of the headstones were recent. — How's it they bury people here? Ah thoat it wis supposed tae be a crematorium.

— Naw, thir's some plots ay land. Fir faimlies, likes. Recognise this yin?

CRAIG GIFFORD

— Naw . . .

— Look at the date.

BORN 17.5.1964
DIED 21.12.1993

— It's . . . the boy . . . I couldn't bring myself to say it.

— Blind Cunt, said Roxy. — That's the cunt's grave. It's time tae exorcise the cunt's memory at long last . . .

He had his cock out and was pishing. On Bli . . . on Craig's grave.

BELOVED SON OF ALEXANDER AND
JOYCE GIFFORD
WE WILL NEVER FORGET YOU

— CUNT! I shouted. I punched the side of his head.

He grabbed me, but I tore free from his grip and booted and punched him. This was not a good idea. He took off his glasses and fairly wired into me. Every blow I dispensed seemed puny, while every one he hit me with threatened to break me into pieces. My nose burst open, but thankfully the sight of my blood seemed to make him stop.

— Sorry, Bri, he said. — Nae cunt punches me though, Bri, understand. Nae cunt.

I stemmed the blood with one hand while holding him off in acknowledgment with the other. Roxy is a big cunt, but I'd always thought of him as a gentle giant. Huge cunts always seem that way, until one of them panels you. Still, at least I was pished. I realised then a sick and horrible truth: getting a kicking from some cunt is worse than killing some other cunt. The ugly fact of the matter is that this has become a governing principle for too many people. If I'd had a blade on me I would have used it on Roxy. I might have only felt that way for a few seconds, but that's all it would take. What a fuckin thought. How sick a species are we?

Craig Gifford.

If only Roxy knew.

If Roxy knew, I'd be the one who went down. He'd probably be pointing his finger at this dangerous psycho.

— It's no that bad. Sorry, Bri. Ye shouldnae huv punched ays though, Bri. Ma eye's gaunny be oot in the mornin. Ma shin as well, Bri, ye caught ays a beauty thair. Me n you swedgin though bit, Bri, tell ays that's no too mad.

The daft cunt's trying to make me feel better by cataloguing the damage I've inflicted on him. There's no victors in this type of gig; only those who lose the least. Roxy's lost the least, in terms of both physical injury and macho self-esteem. We both know it, but I appreciate him trying to make me feel better.

I leave him, fuck knows how I get out of the cemetery, and head for the auld man's. I throw up down my front on the way. Confused, I go back to the old place in Muirhouse. The hoose was still a void property, it hadn't been let. I tried to kick the door down and I would've, had auld Mrs Sinclair next door not reminded me that my dad had moved.

I staggered off and threw up again. My front was a mess of

sick and blood. A couple of boys came up to me at the shopping centre. — That cunt's ootay his face, one observed.

— Ah ken that cunt. You hing aboot wi that poof, eh mate?

— Eh . . . I tried to articulate a reply but I couldn't. I was aware enough, it just wouldnae come oot.

— If ye hing aboot wi poofs, that makes you a poof, that's the wey ah see it. What dae ye say tae that then, mate?

I look at the guy, and manage to ask, — Any chance ay a gam?

They look at me incredulously for a few seconds, then one says, — Smart cunt!

— That's ma name, boys, I concede. I feel a numb blow and crash to the ground. I take a kicking I can't feel. It seems to last quite a while, and that worries me, because you can usually judge the severity of a kicking by its duration. However, I take it with the passive, sick calm of an alienated worker putting in his shift and when I'm convinced it's over I stagger to my feet. Perhaps it's no too bad; I can walk easily. In fact, it seems to have cleared the mind a bit. Thanks, boys.

I cross the dual-carriageway, leaving posh Muirhoose, and get over to scruffy Pilton. That might no be how people see things now, but that's how it's always been tae me. Muirhoose is the newer hooses. Pilton's for the scruffs. It disnae matter what problems Muirhoose's got now and how much they tart up Pilton. Pilton's Pilton and Muirhoose is Muirhoose, always fuckin well will be. Fuckin scruffy Pilton cunts. These cunts that gave me the kicking were fae Pilton; that's these cunts' mentality. I've probably got fuckin lice jist through being in the vicinity of the dirty Pilton scruffy fuckin cunts.

I find the hoose and I don't know who lets me in.

The next morning I pretend to be asleep until they all leave for some twee little family outing: Dad, Norma and her loud, excitable daughter. I feel fucking shattered. When I try to get up I can barely walk. I'm covered in cuts and bruises and I piss blood, which shits me up. I have a bath and things start to feel a bit better, so I decide to have a sniff around. There's still a lot of stuff in packing cases. They are decorating this tawdry little egg-box of a home. I come across this small leather case which I haven't seen before, and I assume it's Norma's. It's not, however.

The case was full of photographs. Of me and Deek as bairns, of him, of my Ma. Photos I'd never seen before. I looked at her, with him. I tried to imagine I could see the hurt in her, see the discontent, but I couldn't. Not at first. Then I got to some photos which I knew were later ones, cause Deek and me were a bit bigger. In those pictures I could read it; with the benefit of retrospect it was all too easy; her eyes screamed pain and disillusionment. My tears spilled onto the tacky photographs. There was a lot worse in this leather case, however.

I read all the letters, every one. They were all really similar in content, only the dates differed. They ranged from a few months after she left right through to 1989. She'd been writing to him for eight years from Australia. All the letters had the same basic propositions repeated ritually:

I want to get in touch with the boys.

I want to have them over to stay.

Please let them write to me.

I love them, I want my children.

Please write to me, Jeff, please get in touch. I know you're getting my letters.

What happened in 1989, I don't know, but she never wrote back after that.

I copy down the address and phone number in Melbourne onto a piece of scrap paper. This is total shite. This is another load of shite to get through. There's always more, always more of this fuckin shite to get through. It never ends. They say it gets easier to handle the older you get. I hope so. I hope tae fuck.

It takes a while tae get through on the international direct-dialling. I want to talk to my Ma, a long talk, get her side of the story, at his expense as well. A guy answers the phone. I got him out of bed; the time difference; I forgot. He asks me who I am, and I tell him.

The guy was really upset. He sounded okay, I have to say that, the boy sounded okay. He told me that there was an electrical fire in their home. It was bad. My Mum died in it, back in 1989. She managed to get their daughter out, but she died of smoke inhalation. The guy was breaking down on the line.

I put the phone down. As soon as I put it down it started ringing again.

I let it ring.